ROYALS

Claimed by the Prince

ROYALS

COLLECTION

ROYALS
Claimed by the Prince

December 2017

ROYALS
A Dutiful Princess

January 2018

ROYALS
Wed to the Prince

February 2018

ROYALS
For Their Royal Heir

March 2018

ROYALS
Chosen by the Prince

April 2018

ROYALS
His Hidden Secret

May 2018

ROYALS
Claimed by the Prince

Kim
LAWRENCE

Penny
JORDAN

Lucy
MONROE

MILLS
BOON

Published in Great Britain 2017
By Mills & Boon, an imprint of HarperCollins*Publishers*
1 London Bridge Street, London, SE1 9GF

ROYALS: CLAIMED BY THE PRINCE
© 2017 Harlequin Books S.A.

The Heartbreaker Prince © 2014 Kim Lawrence
Passion and the Prince © 2011 Penny Jordan
Prince of Secrets © 2013 Lucy Monroe

ISBN: 978-0-263-93137-2

09-1217

Our policy is to use papers that are natural, renewable and recyclable products and made from wood grown in sustainable forests.
The logging and manufacturing processes conform to the legal environmental regulations of the country of origin.

Printed and bound in Spain
by CPI, Barcelona

THE HEARTBREAKER PRINCE

KIM LAWRENCE

For Barbara, thanks for all your support.

Kim Lawrence lives on a farm in Anglesey with her university lecturer husband, assorted pets who arrived as strays and never left, and sometimes one or both of her boomerang sons. When she's not writing she loves to be outdoors gardening or walking on one of the beaches for which the island is famous – along with being the place where Prince William and Catherine made their first home!

CHAPTER ONE

HANNAH WAS NOT sleeping when the key turned in the lock. Apart from a few snatched moments she had not slept for forty-eight hours straight but she was lying down, her eyes closed against the fluorescent light above her head, when the sound made her sit bolt upright and swing her legs over the side of the narrow metal bed.

She made a few frantic attempts to smooth her tousled hair back from her face and clasped her shaking hands on her lap. She was able to mould her expression into a mask of composure, but recognised that it was no longer a matter of *whether* she lost it and cracked wide open, but *when*. For now at least she cared about maintaining an illusion of dignity.

She blinked against the threat of tears that stung like hot gravel pricking the backs of her eyes. Gouging her teeth into her plump lower lip, she found the pain helped her focus as she lifted her chin and pulled her shoulders back, drawing her narrow back ramrod straight. For the moment at least she was determined she wouldn't give the bastards the satisfaction of seeing her cry.

This was what happened when you tried to prove...

prove…what? And to whom? The tabloids? Your father? Yourself…?

She took a deep breath. Focus on the facts, Hannah. The fact is you messed up big time! You should have accepted what everyone else thinks: you are not meant for serious thoughts or fieldwork. Stick to your safe desk job, and your perfect nails… She curled her fingers to reveal a row of nails bitten below the quick and swallowed a bubble of hysteria.

'Stiff upper lip, Hannah.'

She had always thought that was an absurd phrase.

About as absurd as thinking working a desk job for a charity qualified you for working in the field in any capacity!

'I won't let you down.'

Only she had.

She lowered her eyelids like a shield and tensed in every nerve fibre of her body just before the door swung in. Focusing on the wall, she uttered the words that had become almost a mantra.

'I'm not hungry, but I require a toothbrush and toothpaste. When can I see the British consul?'

She wasn't expecting a straight answer. She hadn't had one to this, or any of the other questions she had asked, since she had been arrested on the wrong side of the border. Geography never had been her strong point. No answers, but there had been questions, many questions, the same questions over and over again. Questions and unbelieving silences.

Humanitarian aid did not translate into Quagani military speak. She told them she was not a spy and she had never belonged to a political party, and when they tried to refute her claim with a picture of her waving a banner at a protest to stop the closure of a local village infant school, she laughed—perhaps ill-advisedly.

When they weren't calling her a spy they were accusing her of being a drug runner. The evidence they used to illustrate this was boxes of precious vaccines that were now useless because they had clearly not been kept refrigerated.

For the first day she had clung to her belief that she had nothing to worry about if she told the truth. But now she couldn't believe she had ever been so naïve.

Thirty-six hours had passed, the news hadn't even made the headlines, and the diplomatic cogs had not even thought about turning when the King of Surana picked up his phone and dialled his counterpart in a neighbouring country, Sheikh Malek Sa'idi.

Two very different men stood awaiting the outcome of that conversation, and both had a vested interest.

The older was in his early sixties, of moderate height with a straggly beard and shaggy salt-and-pepper hair that curled on his collar and stuck up in tufts around his face. With his tweed jacket and comically mismatched socks, he had the look of a distracted professor.

But his horn-rimmed glasses hid eyes that were sharp and hard, and his unkempt hair covered a brain that, combined with risk-taking inclinations and a liberal measure of ruthlessness, had enabled him to make and lose two fortunes by the time he was fifty.

Right now he stood once more on the brink of either major success or financial ruin, but his mind was not focused on his financial situation. There was one thing in the world that meant more to Charles Latimer and that was his only child. In this room, behind closed doors, his poker face had gone, leaving only a pale and terrified parent.

The other man wore his raven-black hair close cropped, and his olive-toned skin looked gold in the light that flooded the room through massive windows that looked out over a courtyard. He was several inches over six feet tall, with long legs and broad shoulders that had made him a natural for the rowing teams at school and university. Rowing was not a career in his uncle's eyes, so his first Olympics had been his last. He had gold to show for it, even if the medal lay forgotten in a drawer somewhere. He liked to push himself, he liked winning, but he did not value prizes.

Charles Latimer's restless, hand-wringing pacing contrasted with this younger man's immobility—although he was motionless apart from the spasmodic clenching of a muscle in the hollow of one lean cheek, there was an edgy, explosive quality about him.

This man was of a different generation from the anguished parent—it was actually his thirtieth birthday that day. This was not the way he had planned to celebrate, though nothing in his manner hinted at this frustration. He accepted that his feelings were secondary to duty, and duty was bred into his every bone and sinew.

He got up suddenly, his actions betraying a tension that his expression concealed. Tall and innately elegant, he walked to the full-length window, his feet silent on the centuries-old intricate ceramic tiles. Fighting a feeling of claustrophobia, he flung open the window, allowing the sound of the falling water in the courtyard below to muffle his uncle's voice. The air was humid, heavy with the scent of jasmine, but there was no sign of the dust storm that had blown up after he had landed.

It was a good twenty degrees hotter than it would have been in Antibes. Through half-closed eyes he saw Charlotte Denning, her lithe, tanned body arranged on a sun lounger by the infinity pool, a bottle of champagne on ice, ready to fulfil her promise of a special birthday treat.

Recently divorced and enjoying her freedom, she was making up for a year spent married to a man who did not share her sexual appetites.

In short she was pretty much his ideal woman.

She would be angry at his no-show and later, when she found out the reason, she would be even angrier— not that marriage would put him out of bounds. Knowing Charlotte, he thought it might even add an extra illicit thrill.

There would be no thrills for him. Marriage would put the Charlottes of this world off-limits. He had his memories to keep him warm. The ironic curve of his lips that accompanied the thought flattened into a hard line of resolve. He would marry because it was his duty. For a lucky few duty and desire were one and the same... Once he had considered himself one of the lucky ones.

He took a deep breath of fragrant air, and closed the window, refusing to allow the insidious tendrils of resentment and self-pity to take hold. If he ever thought he'd got a bad deal he simply reminded himself that he was alive. Unlike his little niece, Leila, the baby who might have become his, had things been different. She died when the plane that was carrying her and her parents crashed into the side of a mountain, killing all on board, starting an avalanche of speculation and changing his future for ever.

He *had* a future, one he had inherited from Leila's father. Since becoming the heir and not the spare he had not thought about marriage except as something that would happen and sooner rather than later. With limited time he had set about enjoying what there was of it and in his determined pursuit of this ambition he had gained a reputation. At some point someone had called him the Heartbreaker Prince, and the title had stuck.

And now a freak set of circumstances had conspired to provide him with a ready-made bride who had a reputation to match his own. There would be no twelve-month marriage for him; it was a life sentence to Heartless Hannah. Those tabloids did so love their alliteration.

'It is done.'

Kamel turned back and nodded calmly. 'I'll set things in motion.'

As the King put the phone back down on its cradle Charles Latimer shocked himself and the others present by bursting into tears.

It took Kamel slightly less than an hour to put arrangements in place and then he returned to give the two older men a run-through of the way he saw it happening. As a courtesy he got the plan signed off by his uncle, who nodded and turned to his old college friend and business partner.

'So we should have her with you by tonight, Charlie.'

Kamel could have pointed out that more factually she would be with *him*, but he refrained. It was all about priorities: get the girl out, then deal with the consequences.

Kamel felt obliged to point out the possibility he

had not been able to factor in. Not that this was a deal-breaker—in life sometimes you just had to wing it and he was confident of his ability to do so in most situations. 'Of course, if she's hysterical or—'

'Don't worry, Hannah is tough and smart. She catches on quick. She'll walk out of there under her own steam.'

And now he was within moments of discovering if the parental confidence had been justified.

He doubted it.

Kamel thought it much more likely the man had not allowed himself to believe anything else. Clearly he had indulged the girl all her life. The chances of a spoilt English society brat lasting half a day in a prison cell before she fell apart were slender at best.

So having been fully prepared for the worst, he should have been relieved to find the object of his rescue mission wasn't the anticipated hysterical wreck. For some reason the sight of this slim, stunningly beautiful woman—sitting there on the narrow iron cot with its bare mattress, hands folded in her lap, head tilted at a confident angle, wearing a creased, shapeless prison gown with the confidence and poise of someone wearing a designer outfit—did not fill him with relief, and definitely not admiration, but a blast of anger.

Unbelievable! On her behalf people were moving heaven and earth and she was sitting there acting as though the bloody butler had entered the room! A butler she hadn't even deigned to notice. Was she simply too stupid to understand the danger of her position or was she so used to Daddy rescuing her from unpleasant situations that she thought she was invulnerable?

Then she turned her head, the dark lashes lifting

from the curve of her smooth cheek, and Kamel realised that under the cool blonde Hitchcock heroine
attitude she was scared witless. He took a step closer
and could almost smell the tension that was visible in
the taut muscles around her delicate jaw, and the fine
mist of sweat on her pale skin.

He frowned. He'd save his sympathy for those who
deserved it. Scared or not, Hannah Latimer did not
come into that category. This was a mess of her own
making.

It was easy to see how men went after her, though,
despite the fact she was obviously poison. He even experienced a slug of attraction himself—but then luckily
she opened her mouth. Her voice was as cut glass as her
profile, her attitude a mixture of disdain and superiority,
which could not have won her any friends around here.

'I must demand to see the—' She stopped, her
violet-blue eyes flying wide as she released an involuntary gasp. The man standing there was not holding
a tray with a plate of inedible slop on it.

There had been several interrogators but always the
same two guards, neither of whom spoke. One was short
and squat, and the other was tall and had a problem with
body odour—after he had gone the room was filled with
a sour smell for ages.

This man was tall too, very tall. She found herself
tilting her head to frame all of him; beyond height there
was no similarity whatsoever to her round-shouldered,
sour-smelling jailors. He wasn't wearing the drab utilitarian khaki of the guards or the showy uniform with
gold epaulettes of the man who sat in on all the inter-
rogations.

This man was clean-shaven and he was wearing

snowy white ceremonial desert robes. The fabric carried a scent of fresh air and clean male into the enclosed space. Rather bizarrely he carried a swathe of blue silk over one arm. Her round-eyed, fearful stare shifted from the incongruous item to his face.

If it hadn't been for the slight scar that stood out white on his golden skin, and the slight off-centre kink in his nose, he might have been classed as pretty. Instead he was simply beautiful... She stared at his wide, sensual mouth and looked away a moment before he said in a voice that had no discernible accent and even less warmth, 'I need you to put this on, Miss Latimer.'

The soft, sinister demand made her guts clench in fear. Before she clamped her trembling lips together a whisper slipped through. 'No!'

This man represented the nightmare she had kept at bay and up to this point her treatment had been civilised, if not gentle. She had deliberately not dwelt on her vulnerability; she hadn't seen another woman since her arrest, and she was at the mercy of men who sometimes looked at her... The close-set eyes of the man who sat in on the interviews flashed into her head and a quiver of disgust slid through her body.

People in her situation simply vanished.

Staring at the blue fabric and the hand that held it as if it were a striking snake, she surged to her feet—too fast. The room began to swirl as she struggled to focus on the silk square, bright against the clinical white of the walls and tiled floor...blue, white, blue, white...

'Breathe.' Her legs folded as he pressed her down onto the bed and pushed her head towards her knees.

The habit of a lifetime kicked in and she took refuge behind an air of cool disdain.

'I don't need a change of clothing. I'm fine with this.'
She clutched the fabric of the baggy shift that reached
mid-calf with both hands and aimed her gaze at the
middle of his chest.

Two large hands came to rest on her shoulders, stopping the rhythmic swaying motion she had been unaware of, but not the spasms of fear that were rippling
through her body.

Kamel was controlling his anger and resentment: he
didn't want to be here; he didn't want to be doing this,
and he didn't want to feel any empathy for the person
who was totally responsible for the situation, a spoilt
English brat who had a well-documented history of bolt-
ing at the final hurdle.

Had she felt any sort of remorse for the wave of emotional destruction she'd left in her wake? Had her own
emotions ever been involved? he wondered.

Still, she hadn't got off scot-free. Some enterprising
journalist had linked the car smash of her first victim
with the aborted wedding.

Driven over the Edge, the headline had screamed,
and the media had crucified Heartless Hannah. Perhaps
if she had shown even a scrap of emotion they might
have softened when it turned out that the guy had been
over the drink-drive limit when he drove his car off a
bridge, but she had looked down her aristocratic little
nose and ignored the flashing cameras.

In London at the time, he had followed the story
partly because he knew her father and partly because,
like the man who had written off his car, Kamel knew
what it felt like to lose the love you planned to spend
your life with. Not that Amira had dumped him—if
he hadn't released her she would have married him

rather than cause him pain. She had been everything this woman was not.

And yet it was hard not to look into that grubby flower-like face, perfect in every detail, and feel a flicker of something that came perilously close to pity. He sternly squashed it.

She deserved everything that was going to happen to her. If there was any victim in this it was him. Luckily he had no romantic illusions about marriage, or at least his. It was never going to be a love match—he'd loved and lost and disbelieved the popular idea that this was better than not to have loved at all. Still, it was a mistake he would not make in the future. Only an imbecile would want to lay himself open to that sort of pain again. A marriage of practicality suited him.

Though Kamel had imagined his bride would be someone whom he could respect.

Why couldn't the brainless little bimbo have found meaning in her life by buying some shoes? Even facing financial collapse, Kamel was sure Daddy dear would have bought her the whole shop. Instead she decided to become an angel of mercy. While he could see the selfish delusion that had led her to do this, he couldn't understand why any legitimate medical charity would have taken her on, even on a voluntary basis.

'I asked you to put this on, not take anything off.' Kamel let out a hissing sound of irritation as she sat there looking up at him like some sort of sacrificial virgin...though there was nothing even vaguely virginal about Miss Hannah Latimer, and that quality was about the only one he didn't have a problem with in his future bride!

Digging deep into reserves she didn't know she had, Hannah got to her feet.

'If you touch me I will report you and when I get out of here—' Don't you mean *if*, Hannah? '—I'm going to be sick.'

'No, you are not,' Kamel said. 'If you want to get out of here do as I say so put the damned thing on.'

Breathing hard, staring at him with wide eyes, she backed away, holding her hands out in a warning gesture. 'If you touch me in an inappropriate way…' You'll what, Hannah? Scream? And then who will come running?

'I promise you, angel, that sex is the last thing on my mind and if it was…' His heavy-lidded eyes moved in a contemptuous sweep from her feet to her face before he added, 'I'm not asking you to strip.' He enunciated each scathing word slowly, the words very clear despite the fact he had not raised his voice above a low menacing purr since he'd come in. 'I'm asking you to cover up.'

Hannah barely heard him. The nightmare images she had so far kept at bay were crowding in.

Kamel had had a varied life, but having a woman look at him as though he were all her nightmares come true was a first. Conquering a natural impulse to shake her rather than comfort her, he struggled to inject some soothing quality into his voice as he leaned in closer. 'Your father says to tell you that…' He stopped and closed his eyes. What was the name of the damned dog? His eyes opened again as it came to him. 'Olive had five puppies.'

It had been a last thought: I need a detail, something that a stranger wouldn't know. Something that will tell her I'm one of the good guys.

Hannah froze, her wild eyes returning to his face at the specific reference to the rescue dog she had adopted.

'Yes, I'm the cavalry—' he watched as she took a shuddering sigh and closed her eyes '—so just do as you're told and cover up.' His glance moved to the honey-blonde tresses that were tangled and limp. 'And be grateful you're having a bad-hair day.'

Hannah didn't register his words past cavalry; her thoughts were whirling. 'My father sent you?'

She gave a watery smile. Her father had come through! She exhaled and sent up a silent thank you to her absent parent.

She took the fabric and looked at it. What did he expect her to do with it? 'Who are you?'

Possibilities buzzed like a restless bee through her head. An actor? Some sort of mercenary ? A corrupt official? Someone willing to do anything for money or the adrenalin buzz?

'Your ticket out of here.'

Hannah tilted her head in acknowledgement. The important thing was he had successfully blagged or bribed his way in here and represented a shot at freedom.

Her jaw firmed. Suddenly she felt the optimism she had not allowed herself to feel during her incarceration. It had been an hour to hour—hard to believe there had only been forty-eight, but then, in a room illuminated twenty-four-seven by the harsh fluorescent light, it was hard to judge time.

'Is Dad…?'

He responded to the quiver of hope in her voice with a stern, 'Forget your father and focus. Do not allow yourself to become distracted.'

The tone enabled her to retain her grip on her unravelling control. He had the shoulders but he clearly had no intention of offering them up for tears, which was fine by her. If a girl didn't learn after two failed engagements that the only person she could rely on was herself, she deserved everything she got!

'Yes...of course.'

Her fingers shook as she took the shimmering blue fabric. It fell in a tangled skein on the floor, the fabric unravelling... Just like me, she thought.

She took a deep breath and released it, slowly able to lift her chin and meet his gaze with something approaching composure as she asked, 'What do you want me to do?'

Kamel felt an unwilling stab of admiration.

'I want you to keep your mouth closed, your head covered, and follow my lead.'

He bent forward and took the fold of fabric from her fingers. The fabric billowed out of his hands and she was suddenly swathed in the stuff, covering her head and most of the ugly shift.

He stood back to see the effect, then nodded and threw the remaining fabric over her shoulder. His hand stayed there, heavy, the contact more reassuring than his stern stare.

'Can you do that?'

'Yes,' she said, hoping it was true.

'Right. You are going to leave here and you are going to do so with your head held high. Just channel all your...just be yourself.'

She blinked up into his dark eyes, noticing the little silver flecks, and struggled to swallow a giggle—she knew that once she gave in to hysteria that was it.

'And they are just going to let us out?' His confidence

bordered the insane but maybe that was a good thing for someone in charge of a jail break.

'Yes.'

'I don't know why they let you just walk in here but—'

'They let me just walk in here because to refuse me access would have caused offence and they have a lot of ground to make up.' They could arrest, interrogate and imprison a foreign national on charges that carried the death penalty, but not the bride-to-be of the heir to the Suranian throne.

Maybe if she had chosen another moment to stray across the border his uncle's influence alone would have been enough to gain her freedom, but with impeccable timing Hannah Latimer had wandered into an armed border patrol at a time when the ruling family of Quagani was politically vulnerable. Accused by rival factions of being unable to protect the country's interests against foreign exploitation, the royals had responded by instigating a draconian zero-tolerance policy: no second chances, no leniency, no special cases...*almost.*

His uncle had not ordered, he had not played the duty card—instead he had spoken of a debt he owed Charles Latimer and asked with uncharacteristic humility if Kamel would be willing to marry Hannah Latimer.

'She is not ideal,' the King admitted, 'and not the person I would have wanted for you, but I'm sure with guidance... She was a lovely child, as I recall. Very like her mother, poor Emily.' He sighed.

'She grew up.'

'It is your decision, Kamel.'

This was the first thing ever asked of him by his uncle—who was not just his King but also the man who had stepped in after his father's death and treated him as his own son. Kamel's response had never been in doubt.

Hannah heard the irony in her rescuer's voice but didn't have a clue what it meant. 'I don't understand a word you're saying.' Though he said it in a voice that had a tactile shiver-down-your-spine quality.

'You will.' Despite the smile that went with the words, she sensed an underlying threat that was echoed in the bleakness of his stare.

'Look, no one is about to ask you anything, but if they do, don't say anything. Burst into tears or something.'

That would not require much effort. The walking might, though—her knees felt like cotton wool.

'Just pretend you're running away from some sucker at the altar.'

Her shocked violet eyes widened to their fullest extent. The reputation she pretended not to care about had followed her to a jail halfway around the world. Ironically she had come here in the hope of rebuilding her reputation, or at least escaping the cameras.

'I believe you've had some practice,' he murmured before seamlessly raising his voice from the soft, for-her-ears-only undertone, to an authoritative command to the prison guards.

The words were unintelligible to her but the effect was magic. The guards she recognised stood either side of the open door, their heads bowed. Along the corridor there were uniformed figures standing to attention.

The man beside her spoke and the guards bowed lower. Hannah stared, astonished—it wasn't just their reaction; it was the man himself. He seemed to have as-

sumed a totally new persona, and it fitted him as well
as the flowing robes. He was clearly immersing himself
in his role; even his body language had changed. The
arrogance was still there but it was combined with an
air of haughty authority as he strode along, shortening
his step so that she could keep pace.

What the hell was happening?

She had expected to be smuggled out of some back
entrance, not to receive the red-carpet treatment.

Like a sleepwalker, Hannah allowed her tall escort to
guide her down the corridor. Nobody looked directly at
her or her companion as they walked past. The silence
was so intense she could feel it.

Outside, the heat hit her—it was like walking into
a shimmering wall, but the sun was infinitely preferable to the ten-foot-square, white-walled cell. It was the
thought of being discovered and ending up back there
and not the temperature that brought Hannah out in a
cold sweat.

A leashed guard dog began to bark, straining at the
lead as they walked on. Could dogs really smell fear?
As his handler fought to control the animal the man
beside her turned, clicked his fingers and looked at the
dog, who immediately dropped down on his belly and
whimpered.

Neat trick, Hannah thought, momentarily losing her
balance as a jet flew low overhead. She had heard the
sound before many times over the last days but it was
a lot quieter in her cell.

'I'm fine,' she mumbled as the hand on her elbow
slid to her waist. In that moment of contact she registered the fact that his body had no give—it was all hard

muscle. For a moment she enjoyed an illusion of safety before she was released.

Hannah, who had been totally disorientated when she had arrived in darkness, realised for the first time that she had been incarcerated on a military base.

Almost as if some of his strength had seeped into her, she felt more confident, enabling her to adopt a fatalistic attitude when they were approached by a mean-looking man with shoulders the size of a hangar, dressed similarly to the man she struggled to keep pace with.

Hannah wanted to run, every survival instinct she had was screaming at her to do so, but the hand that reached down and took her own had other ideas. Her escort had stopped when he saw the other man and waited. Under her blue silk and grubby shift Hannah sucked in a shaky breath and began to sweat—but the hand that held her own was cool and dry.

'This is Rafiq.'

So clearly friend, not foe. She managed a shaky half-smile when the big man acknowledged her presence with a respectful tip of his covered head. He responded with calm, one-word replies to the questions her escort threw at him, even earning a tight smile that might have been approval.

Hannah, who hadn't been able to follow a word, was unable to restrain herself. 'Is everything all right?'

'You mean are you about to escape justice?'

'I'm innocent!'

Her protest drew a sardonic smile from her rescuer. She had the impression he wasn't her greatest fan, but she didn't mind so long as he got her out of here.

'We are all guilty of something, angel. As the man

said, there's no such thing as a free meal, but, yes, your taxi awaits.'

Hannah spun to face the direction in which he had nodded and saw a jet with a crest on the side that seemed vaguely familiar.

CHAPTER TWO

AT THE SIGHT of the private jet Hannah felt her heart race. Her anticipation of imminent escape and the possibility that her father was inside waiting were mingled with the equally powerful conviction that any minute someone would catch on. To be caught when freedom was literally within sight, touch and smell would be so much harder than if she had never hoped.

'Keep it together.'

She turned her head sharply, the action causing the silk to fall away from her cheek. She could not believe he could look so relaxed. Did the man have ice in his veins? No—she remained conscious of the warmth of his guiding hand on her elbow.

Hannah twitched the silk back into place and in doing so caught sight of someone who was approaching across the tarmac. Her eyes widened to large pools of blue terror in a face that had become dramatically pale.

'Do not run.'

Fear clutched her belly. 'He...'

Kamel watched as she licked her dry lips. Her eyes were darting from side to side like a cornered animal seeking an avenue of escape, but they kept moving back to the army colonel who carried a cane and an air of self-importance as he approached them, flanked by a small armed guard.

It didn't take a second for Kamel to experience a flash of vengeful rage that reminded him strongly of a time in his youth when, after escaping the security that he hated, he had encountered three much older boys in a narrow side street. He had not known at first what was lying on the ground there, but he had seen one boy aim a kick at it, and they had all laughed. It was the laughter he had reacted to with sheer, blinding, red-mist rage.

He had arrived back at the palace later, looking worse than the poor stray dog the trio had been systematically kicking the hell out of. He had freed the dog in the end, not by physical means but by offering them the ring he wore.

His father, the antithesis of a tyrannical parent, had been more bemused than angry when he'd discovered the ring was gone.

'You gave a priceless heirloom for this flea-ridden thing?' He had then progressed to remind Kamel how important breeding was.

It was an important lesson, not in breeding but in negotiation. In a tight situation, it was often a clear head rather than physical force that turned the tide. He controlled his instinctive rage now. Summing up the man in a glance, he knew he had come across the kind before many times: a bully who took pleasure from intimidating those he controlled.

'Did he interrogate you?'

Hannah shivered, not from the ice in Kamel's voice, but the memory.

'He watched.' And tapped a cane on the floor, she thought, shivering again as she remembered the sound.

The man's silence had seemed more threatening to her than the men who asked the questions. That and the look in his eyes.

Kamel's jaw was taut, and his voice flat. 'Lift your head up. He can't do a thing to you.'

'Highness, I am here to offer our sincere apologies for any misunderstanding. I hope it has not given Miss Latimer a dislike of our beautiful country.'

And now it was his turn.

His turn to smile and lie through his teeth. It was a talent that he had worked on to the point where his diplomacy looked effortless even though it frequently veiled less civilised instincts.

He uncurled his clenched fingers, unmaking the fists they had instinctively balled into, but he was spared having to produce the words that stuck in his throat by sudden activity around the waiting jet.

As something came screaming down towards them, one man raised a pistol. Kamel, who had the advantage of faster reflexes, reached casually out and chopped the man's arm, causing him to drop the gun to the ground. It went off, sending a bullet into a distant brick wall.

'Relax, it's just…'

He stopped as the hawk that had been flying above their heads dropped down, claws extended, straight onto the head of the uniformed colonel. His hat went flying and he covered his head protectively as the hooded hawk swooped again—this time escaping with what looked like a dead animal in his talons.

The colonel stood there, his hands on his bald head. Releasing a hissing signal from between his teeth,

Kamel extended his arm. The hawk responded to the sound and landed on his wrist.

'You are quite safe now, Colonel.' Kamel took the toupee from the bird and, holding it on one finger, extended it to the man who had curled into a foetal crouch, his head between his hands.

Red-faced, the older man rose to his feet, his dignity less intact than his face, which had only suffered a couple of superficial scratches, oozing blood onto the ground.

He took the hairpiece and crammed it on his head, drawing a smothered laugh from one of his escorts. When he spun around the men stared ahead stonily.

'That thing should be destroyed. It nearly blinded me.'

Kamel touched the jewel attached to that bird's hood. 'My apologies, Colonel. No matter how many jewels you put on a bird of prey, she remains at heart a creature of impulse. But then that is the attraction of wild things, don't you think?'

The other man opened his mouth and a grunt emerged through his clenched teeth as he bowed.

Kamel smiled. He handed back the pistol to the man who had tried to shoot it, having first emptied the barrel with a mild reproach of, 'Unwise.' He then turned to Rafiq and issued a soft-voiced command in French that Hannah struggled to make sense of.

The big man bowed his head, murmured, 'Highness,' and took Hannah's elbow.

Hannah, who had remained glued to the spot while the drama had played out around her, did not respond to the pressure.

Kamel, his dark eyes flashing warning, touched her cheek.

Like someone waking from a deep sleep, she started and lifted her blue eyes to his face. 'Go with Rafiq. I will be with you presently, my little dove.' Without waiting to see if she responded, he turned to the bleeding and humiliated colonel. 'Please forgive Emerald. She is very protective and responds when she senses danger. She is…unpredictable. But as you see—' he ran a finger down the bird's neck '—quite docile.'

Kamel could feel the effort it cost the man to smile. 'You have an unusual pet, Prince Kamel.'

Kamel produced a smile that was equally insincere. 'She is not a pet, Colonel.'

He could feel the man's eyes in his back as he walked away. Still, a poisonous stare was less painful than the bullet he would no doubt have preferred to deliver.

'No.' Hannah shook her head and refused to take the seat that she was guided to. 'Where is he?' she asked the monolith of a man who didn't react to her question. 'My father! Where is he?'

As the door closed behind him the hawk flew off Kamel's hand and onto her perch, the tinkle of bells making Hannah turn her head. 'Where is my father? I want my—'

He cut across her, his tone as bleak as winter, but not as cold and derisive as his eyes. 'You should know I have no taste for hysteria.'

'And you should know I don't give a damn.'

Kamel, who had anticipated her reaction to be of the standard 'poor little me' variety, was actually pleasantly surprised by her anger. If nothing else the girl was resilient. Just as well—as it was a quality she was going to need.

'I suppose it was too much to hope that you have learnt anything from your experience.' He arched a sardonic ebony brow. 'Like humility.'

Now wasn't that the ultimate in irony? She was being lectured on humility by a man who had just produced a master class in arrogance.

She hadn't expected to be told she'd done brilliantly or receive a pat on the back…but a lecture?

'You got me out of there, so thanks. But I'm damned if I'm going to be lectured by the hired help!' It came out all wrong. But what did it matter if he thought she was a snob? She needed to know what the hell was happening and he wouldn't even give her a straight answer.

At last she was now living down to his expectations. He peeled off his head gear, revealing a head of close-cropped raven-black hair. The austere style emphasised the classical strength of his strongly sculpted features. 'I suggest that we postpone this discussion until we are actually in the air.'

It wasn't a suggestion so much as an order, and his back was already to her. She had just spent two days in a cell experiencing a total lack of control—this man was going to give her answers!

'Don't walk away from me like that!'

Dragging a hand back and forth over his hair, causing it to stand up in spikes, he paused and turned his head towards her without immediately responding. Instead in a low aside he spoke to his massive stone-faced sidekick, who bowed his head respectfully before he whisked away—moving surprisingly quickly for such a large man.

His attentions switched back to Hannah. 'It's called prioritising, my little dove.'

Hannah felt her stomach muscles tighten at the reminder that the last hurdle was still to be negotiated. At least most of the quivering was associated with fear. Some of it...well, it wasn't as if she were struck dumb with lust, but a little dry-mouthed maybe? Previously her fear levels had given her some protection from the aura of raw sexuality this man exuded, but she felt it even more strongly when he hooked a finger under her chin and looked down into her face for a moment before letting his hand drop away.

The contact and the deep dark stare had been uncomfortable, but now it was gone she wasn't sure what she felt. She gave her head a tiny shake to clear the low-level buzz—or was that the jet engines? She was clearly suffering the effects of an adrenalin dip; the chemical circulating in her blood had got her this far, but now she was shaking.

'Sit down, belt up and switch off your phone,' he drawled, wondering if he hadn't been a bit too tough on her. But she acted tough, and looked... His eyes slid over the soft contours of her fine-boned face. She was possibly one of the few women on the planet who could look beautiful after two days in a ten-foot-square prison cell.

She sat down with a bump because it was preferable to falling. Had she thanked him yet?

'Thank you.' Hannah had been brought up to be polite, after all, and he had just rescued her.

She closed her eyes and missed the look of shock on his face. As the jet took off she released a long, slow sigh and didn't open her eyes again, even when she felt the light brush of hands on her shoulder and midriff as a belt was snapped shut.

Was it possible that she had jumped from the proverbial frying pan straight into...what? And with whom? It was only the knowledge that he carried the personal message from her father that had stopped her tipping over into panic as her imagination threatened to go wild on her.

'If you would like anything, just ask Rafiq. I have some work to do.'

She opened her eyes in time to see her rescuer shrug off his imposing desert robes to reveal a pale coffee-coloured tee shirt and black jeans. The resulting relaxed image should have been less imposing, but actually wasn't—even though he appeared to have shrugged off the icy-eyed hauteur that had reduced the aggressive colonel to red-faced docility.

He might be dressed casually, his attitude might be relaxed when he glanced her way, but this didn't change the fact that he exuded a level of sexuality that was unlike anything she had ever encountered.

He took a couple of steps, then turned back, his dark, dispassionate stare moving across her face. So many questions—Hannah asked the one that she felt took priority. 'Who are you?'

His mouth lifted at one corner but the dark silver-flecked eyes stayed coolly dispassionate as he responded, 'Your future husband.'

Then he was gone.

CHAPTER THREE

'IS THERE ANYTHING I can get for you?'

The words roused Hannah from her semi catatonic state. She surged to her feet and flung the man mountain before her a look of profound scorn before pushing past him into the adjoining cabin, which contained a seating area and a bed on which her tall, rude rescuer was stretched out, one booted foot crossed over the other, his forearm pressed across his eyes.

'I thought you were working.'

'This is a power nap. I want to look good in the wedding photos.'

Breathing hard, she stood there, hands on her hips, glaring at his concealed face—noticing as she did the small bloody indentations on the sides of his wrist, presumably from where the hawk had landed on his bare skin.

'Can you be serious for one moment, please?'

He lifted a dark brow and with a long-suffering sigh dropped his arm. Then, in one sinuous motion, he pulled himself up into a sitting position and lowered his feet to the ground.

He planted his hands on his thighs and leaned forward. 'I'm all yours. Shoot.'

Hannah heard *shoot* and shuddered, recalling the
scene on the tarmac where but for his lightning reflexes there might have been more than one bullet dis-
charged—a disaster narrowly averted.

'You should put some antiseptic on those.'

His dark brows twitched into a puzzled line.

She pointed to his arm. 'The bird.' She angled a wary
glance at the big bird. 'You're bleeding.'

He turned his wrist and shrugged in an irritatingly
tough fashion. 'I'll live.'

'I, on the other hand, am feeling a little insecure
about being on a plane with a total stranger going...'
she gave an expressive shrug '...God knows where. So
do you mind filling in a few blanks?'

He nodded. She didn't sound insecure. She sounded
and looked confident and sexy and in control. What
would it take to make her lose it? It could be he was
about to find out.

'My father sent you?'

He tipped his head in acknowledgement and she gave
a gusty sigh of relief. 'He sends his love.'

'I'm sure Dad appreciates your sense of humour,
but I'm a bit...'

'Uptight? Humourless?'

Her blue eyes narrowed to slits. She had very little
energy left, and being angry with him was using it all
up. She took a deep breath and thought, Rise above it,
Hannah. People had said a lot worse about her and she'd
maintained her dignity.

It was a power thing. If *they* saw it got to her *they*
had the power and she lost it. It didn't matter who *they*
were—school bullies, journalists—the same rule ap-

plied. If you showed weakness they reacted like pack animals scenting blood.

'I'd prefer to know what's happening, so if you could just fill me in…? Tell me where the plane is headed and then I'll let you sleep in peace.'

'Surana.'

The mention of the oil-rich desert state fired a memory. That was where she'd seen the crest on the plane before, and it fitted: her father had called in some favours. She knew he counted the King of Surana as a personal friend; the two men had met forty years earlier at the public school they had attended as boys. The friendship had survived the years—apparently the King had once dandled her on his knee but Hannah had no recollection of the event.

'So Dad will be there to meet us?'

'No, he'll be waiting at the chapel.'

Hannah fought for composure. Was this man on something? 'Hilarious.' She tried to laugh but laughing in the face of the ruthless resolve stamped on his hard-boned face was difficult. She hefted a weary sigh and reminded herself she was free. It was all up from here, once she got a straight answer from this man. 'This is not a joke that has the legs to run and run.'

His broad shoulders lifted in a shrug that suggested he didn't care. 'Look, I wish it were a joke. I have no more wish to marry you than you have me, but before you start bleating for Daddy ask yourself what you would have preferred if I'd offered you the option back there: marrying me, or spending twenty years in a boiling-hot jail where luxury is considered a tap shared by several hundred. Or even worse—'

'How does it get worse?'

'How about the death penalty?'

'That was never a possibility.' Her scorn faltered and her stomach clenched with terror. Had she really been that close? 'Was it?'

He arched a sardonic brow.

'So if I'd signed the confession...?' Her voice trailed away as she spoke until 'confession' emerged from her white lips as a husky whisper.

'You didn't.' Kamel fought the irrational feeling of guilt. He was only spelling out the ugly facts; he was not responsible. Still, it gave him no pleasure to see the shadow of terror in her wide eyes. 'So don't think about it.'

The advice brought her chin up with a snap. 'I wouldn't be thinking about it at all if you hadn't told me.'

'Maybe it's about time you faced unpleasant facts and accepted that there are some things we cannot run away from.'

Not several thousand feet off the ground, but once they landed Hannah intended to run very fast indeed from this man. 'I'm grateful to be free, obviously, but I didn't do anything wrong.'

'You entered a sovereign state illegally, carrying drugs.'

Hannah's clenched teeth ached. His righteous attitude was really getting under her skin.

'I got lost and I was carrying medicine. Vaccines and antibiotics.'

'Morphine?'

Feeling defensive, Hannah rubbed her damp palms against her thighs. With his steely eyes and relentless delivery he was a much more effective interrogator than her captors had been. 'Yes.'

'And a camera.'

'No!'

'Isn't there a camera on your phone?'

He would have thought better of her if she had the guts to hold up her hands and take responsibility for her own actions, but that obviously wasn't her style.

'Weren't you told to stay with the vehicle if it broke down?'

How did he know? 'It was an emergency.' And that was the only reason she had been entrusted the responsibility. There simply had been no one else available.

'And you were the one on the ground and you made a tough call...fine. But now you have to take the consequences for that decision.'

Struggling to keep pace with the relentless pace of his reasoning, she shook her head. 'So I have to marry you because you rescued me? Sure, *obvious*. I should have realised.'

The bored façade and the last shades of cynical amusement in his manner fell away as he vaulted to his feet.

He towered over her, eyes blazing with contempt. She could feel the anger spilling out of him and presumably so could the bird sitting on its perch—it began to squawk and Hannah lifted her hands to her head to protect herself.

The act of soothing the spooked creature seemed to help Kamel regain some semblance of control. 'She won't hurt you.'

Hannah dropped her hands, cast a quick sideways glance at the fascinating wild creature, and then returned her attention to the man. 'I wasn't worried about the *bird*.'

His jaw tightened in response to the pointed comment, and he stared at the mouth that delivered it...her wide, full, sexy lower lip. Hers was a mouth actually made for kissing.

'I wouldn't marry you even if you *were* sane!'

She might have a point. Wasn't it insane to be checking out her impossibly long legs? Wasn't it even more insane to actually like the fact she didn't back away from him, that her pride made her give as good as she got?

'And came gift-wrapped!' Hannah caught herself wondering how many women would have liked to unwrap him, and felt a lick of fear before she told herself that she was not one of them.

'You want facts? Fine. When we land in Surana in—' He turned his wrist and glanced at the watch that glinted against his dark skin.

'Thirty minutes. There will be a red carpet and reception committee for Your Royal Highness,' she finished his sentence for him, and, keeping her eyes on his face, she performed a graceful bow.

He took her sarcasm at face value.

'There will be no official reception under the circumstances. Things will be low-key. We will go straight to the palace where my uncle, the King—'

Her eyes flew wide. '*King?* You're asking me to believe you're really a prince?'

He stared at her hard. 'Who did you think I was?'

'Someone my father paid to get me out of jail. I thought you were pretending to—'

'I can't decide if you're just plain stupid or incredibly naïve.' He shook his head from side to side in an attitude of weary incredulity. 'You thought all I had to do was walk in, claim to be of royal blood and all the doors would open to release you?' What alternative universe did this woman live in?

Her eyes narrowed with dislike as he threw back his head and laughed.

'What was I meant to think?'

'That you were extremely lucky you have a father who cares so much about you, a father who is waiting with my uncle and Sheikh Sa'idi of Quagani. The only reason you are not now facing the consequences of your actions is because the Sheikh has been told that you are my fiancée.'

'And he believed that?'

'I think the wedding invite swung it.'

'Well, I'm out, so job done. You can tell him the wedding's off.'

'I can see that that is the way things work in your world.' A world with no honour.

'What is that meant to mean?'

The plane hit a pocket and he braced himself as it sank and rose while she staggered and grabbed the back of a chair. 'That you step away from commitment when it suits you.'

Hannah was waiting for her stomach to find its level but this not so veiled reference to her engagements brought an angry flush to her cheeks. 'I'm fine, thanks for asking,' she murmured, rubbing the area where her wrist had banged against the chair.

He continued as though she had not spoken. 'But that is not the way it works here. My uncle feels indebted to your father and he has given his word.'

'I didn't give my word.'

'*Your word!*' he echoed with acid scorn.

She felt the burn of tears in her eyes and furiously blinked to clear them. 'I won't be lectured by you!'

'Your word means...' he clicked his fingers '...nothing. It is otherwise with my uncle. He is a man of integrity, honour. I suppose I'm speaking a foreign language to you?'

'So your uncle would be embarrassed. I'm sorry about that—'

'But not sorry enough to accept the consequences of your actions?'

Consequences...consequences... Hannah fought the urge to cover her ears. 'This is stupid. What terrible thing is going to happen if we don't get married?' Hannah hoped the question didn't give him the false impression that she would even consider this.

'I'm glad you asked that.'

He opened the laptop that lay on a table and spun it around, stabbing it with his finger. 'We are a small country but oil rich, and we have enjoyed relative political stability. Since the discovery last year of these new reserves, we are set to be even more rich.'

She pursed her lips at his lecturing tone and stuck out her chin. 'I do read an occasional newspaper.'

'Don't boast about your IQ, angel, because,' he drawled, 'stupidity is the only possible excuse for your little escapade.'

An angry hissing sound escaped her clenched teeth. 'I know the country is a shining light of political stability and religious tolerance. What I didn't know was that the ruling family had a history of insanity—but that's what happens when you marry cousins.'

'Well, you will be a new injection of blood, won't you, angel? This will happen, you know. The sooner you accept it, the easier it will be.'

Hannah bit her lip. Even her interrogators had never looked at her with such open contempt and, though she refused to admit it even to herself, it hurt. As had the headlines and the inches of gossip all vilifying her.

'Shall I tell you why?'

He waited a moment, then tipped his head, acknowledging her silence.

'We have a problem. We are landlocked and the oil needs to get to the sea.' He flicked his finger across the screen and traced a line. 'Which means we rely on the cooperation of others. The new pipeline is at present being constructed in Quagani, and it crosses three separate countries. Did you know your father is building the pipeline?'

Hannah didn't but she would have died before admitting it. 'I'm surprised they haven't already married you off to some Quagani princess to seal the deal.'

'They were going to, but she met my cousin.' Kamel had fallen in love with Amira slowly. It had been a gradual process and he'd thought it had been the same for her. Had he not seen it with his own eyes, Kamel would have laughed at the idea of love at first sight. He had tried very hard not to see it. 'When she found him... preferable, her family were fine with it because he was the heir and I was, as they say, the spare.'

'Then where is the problem? If your families are linked they're not going to fall out.'

'He died...she died...their baby died.' The only thing that linked the rulers now was shared grief and a need to blame someone.

Like a sandcastle hit by a wave, Hannah's snooty attitude dissolved. Despite some throat-clearing her voice was husky as she said softly, 'I'm so sorry. But my father wouldn't force me to marry for any amount of money.'

He looked at the woman who sat there with spoilt brat written all over her pretty face.

'Has it occurred to you that your father, being human, might jump at the chance to get you off his hands? And if he did I don't think there are many who would blame him.'

'My father doesn't think of me as a piece of property.'

He might, however, think of her as a lead weight around his neck.

'Do you care for your father as much as he does you?'

'What does that mean?'

'It means if Quagani closes the new pipeline it won't just be the school programme in our country that suffers. Your father has a stake in the new refinery too.'

It was the mention of a school programme that brought a worried furrow to her brow. In her job she knew what a difference education could make. 'My father has a stake in many things.'

'My uncle let your father in on this deal as a favour. He knew of his situation.'

She tensed and then relaxed.

'What situation? Are you trying to tell me my father has lost all of his money again?'

Over the years her father's reckless, impulsive approach to business had led to dramatic fluctuations in fortune, but that was in the past. After the heart attack he had actually listened to the doctors' warnings about

the danger of stress. He had *promised* her faithfully that
the risky deals were a thing of the past.

'Not all of it.'

Hannah met his dark, implacable stare and felt the
walls of the cabin close in. Even as she was shaking her
head in denial she knew deep down that he was telling her the truth.

Kamel watched, arms folded across his chest, as the
comment sank in. The prospect of being the daughter of
a poor man seemed to affect her more than anything he
had said so far. The idea of slumming it or being forced
to make her own way in the world without the cushion
of Daddy's money had driven what little colour she had
out of her face.

'He has made a number of unfortunate ventures, and
if the pipeline deal fails your father faces bankruptcy.'

Hannah's heart started to thud faster and her heart
was healthy. *Stress*...what could be more stressful than
bankruptcy? Unless it was the humiliation of telling a
cathedral full of people that your daughter's wedding
was off.

She had accepted her share of responsibility for the
heart attack that very few people knew about. At the
time her father had sworn Hannah to secrecy, saying
the markets would react badly to the news. Hannah
didn't give a damn about the markets, but she cared a
lot about her father. He was not as young as he liked to
think. With his medical history, having to rebuild his
company from scratch—what would that do to a man
with a cardiac problem?

Struggling desperately to hide her concern behind a
composed mask, she turned her clear, critical stare on
her prospective husband and discovered as she stared

at his lean, bronzed, beautiful face that she hadn't, as she had thought, relinquished all her childish romantic fantasies, even after her two engagements had ended so disastrously.

'So you have made a case for me doing this,' she admitted, trying to sound calm. 'But why *would you*? Why would you marry someone you can't stand the sight of? Are you really willing to marry a total stranger just because your uncle tells you to?'

'I could talk about duty and service,' he flung back, 'but I would be wasting my breath. They are concepts that you have no grasp of. And my motivation is not the issue here. I had a choice and I made it. Now it is your turn.'

She sank onto a day bed, her head bent forward and her hands clenched in her lap. After a few moments she lifted her head. She'd made her decision, but she wasn't ready to admit it.

'What will happen? If we get married…after…?' She lifted a hank of heavy hair from her eyes and caught sight of her reflection in the shiny surface of a metallic lamp on the wall beside her. There had been no mirrors in her cell and her appearance had not occupied her thoughts so it took her a few seconds before she realised the wild hair attached to a haggard face was her own. With a grimace she looked away.

'You would have a title, so not only could you act like a little princess, you could actually be one, which has some limited value when it comes to getting a dinner table or theatre ticket.'

'Princess…?' Could this get any more surreal?

The ingenuous, wide-eyed act irritated Kamel. 'Oh,

don't get too excited. In our family,' he drawled, 'a title is almost obligatory. It means little.'

As his had, but all that had changed the day that his cousin's plane had gone down and he had become the Crown prince.

That was two years ago now, and there remained those conspiracy theorists who still insisted there had been a cover-up—that the royal heir and his family had been the victims of a terrorist bomb, rather than a mechanical malfunction.

There was a more sinister school of thought that had gone farther, so at a time when Kamel had been struggling with the intense grief and anger he felt for the senseless deaths—his cousin was a man he had admired and loved—Kamel had also had to deal with the fact that some believed he had orchestrated the tragedy that wiped out the heirs standing between him and the crown.

He had inherited a position he'd never wanted, and a future that, when he allowed himself to think about it, filled him with dread. He'd also inherited a reputation for bumping off anyone who got in his way.

And now he had a lovely bride—what more could a man want?

'My official residence is inside the palace. I have an apartment in Paris, and also a place outside London, and a villa in Antibes.' Would the lovely Charlotte still be there waiting? No, not likely. Charlotte was not the waiting kind. 'I imagine, should we wish it, we could go a whole year without bumping into one another.'

'So I could carry on with my life—nothing would change?'

'You like the life you have so much?'

His voice held zero inflection but she could feel his contempt. She struggled to read the expression in his eyes, but the dark silver-flecked depths were like the mirrored surface of a lake, deep and inscrutable yet strangely hypnotic.

She pushed away a mental image of sinking into a lake, feeling the cool water embrace her, close over her head. She lowered her gaze, running her tongue across her lips to moisten them.

When she lifted her head she'd fixed a cool smile in place...though it was hard to channel cool when you knew you looked like a victim of a natural disaster. But her disaster was of her own making.

Her delicate jaw clenched at the insight that had only made her imprisonment worse. The knowledge that she was the author of her own disaster movie, that she had ignored the advice to wait until a driver was available, and then she had chosen not to stay with the vehicle as had been drilled into them.

'I like my freedom.' It had not escaped his notice that she had sidestepped his question.

'At last we have something in common.'

'So you...we...?' This was the world's craziest conversation. 'Is there any chance of a drink?' With a heavy sigh she let her head fall back, her eyes closed.

Exhausted but not relaxed, he decided. His glance moved from her lashes—fanning out across the marble-pale curve of her smooth cheeks and hiding the dark shadows beneath her eyes—to her slim, shapely hands with the bitten untidy nails. Presumably her manicure had been a victim of her incarceration.

She had some way to go before she could collapse. Would she make it? It appeared to him that she was running on a combination of adrenalin and sheer bloody-minded obstinacy. His expression clinical, he scrutinised the visible, blue-veined pulse hammering away in the hollow at the base of her throat. There was something vulnerable about it... His mouth twisted as he reminded himself that the last two dumb guys she'd left high and dry at the altar had probably thought the same thing.

'I'm not sure alcohol would be a good idea.'

Her blue eyes flew open. 'I was thinking more along the lines of tea.'

'I can do that.' He spoke to Rafiq, who had a habit of silently materialising, before turning his attention back to Hannah. 'Well, at least our marriage will put an end to your heartbreaking activities.'

'I didn't break anyone's—' She stopped, biting back the retort. She'd promised Craig—who had loved her but, it turned out, not in 'that' way—that she'd take responsibility.

'You're more like a sister to me,' Craig had told her. 'Well, actually, not like a sister because you know Sal and she's a total...no, more like a best friend.'

'Sal is my best friend,' Hannah had replied. And Sal had been, before she'd slept with treacherous Rob.

'That's why I'm asking you not to tell her I called it off. When we got engaged she got really weird, and told me she'd never ever forgive me if I hurt you. But I haven't hurt you, have I...? We were both on the rebound—me after Natalie and you after Rob.' He had patted her shoulder. 'I think you still love him.'

Somehow Hannah had loved the man who had slept his way through her friends while they were together.

She had only known about Sal when she had given him back his ring after he stopped denying it.

She hated Rob now but he had taught her about trust. Mainly that it wasn't possible. Craig, who she had known all her life, was different. He was totally predictable; he would never hurt her. But she had forgotten one thing—Craig was a man.

'You know me so well, Craig.'

'So, are you all right with this?'

'I'm fine.'

'So what happens now?'

People who had never met you felt qualified to spend time and a lot of effort ripping you to shreds. 'I don't know,' she lied.

Her lips twitched as she recalled her ex-fiancé's response. Craig never had been known for his tact.

'Well, what happened last time?'

Hannah had shrugged guiltily. The last time her dad had done everything. Even though pride had stopped her revealing that her fiancé had slept with all her friends— pride and the fact that her father would have blamed himself, as Charles Latimer had introduced her to Rob and had encouraged the relationship.

The second time he'd run out of understanding. He'd been furious and dumped the whole nightmare mess in her lap. Her glance flickered to the tall, imposing figure of her future husband and she struggled to see a way through the nightmare he represented.

CHAPTER FOUR

THIS TIME HANNAH was aware of the man mountain before he appeared—just as they hit another air pocket, he entered apologising for the tea he had slopped over the tray he was carrying.

'I will get a fresh tray.'

'It'll be fine,' Kamel responded impatiently. 'We need not stand on ceremony with Miss Latimer. She is one of the family now. Considering the nature of my trip I kept staffing down to a minimum.' He murmured something in what she assumed was Arabic to the other man, who left the compartment. 'Rafiq can turn his hand to most things but his culinary skills are limited.' He lifted the domed lid on the plate to reveal a pile of thickly cut sandwiches. 'I hope you like chicken.'

'I'm not hungry,' she said dully.

'I don't recall asking you if you were hungry, Hannah,' he returned in a bored drawl as he piled an extra sandwich onto a plate and pushed it her way.

She slung him an angry look. 'How am I meant to think about food when I'm being asked to sacrifice my freedom?' That had been her comfort after the battering her self-esteem had taken after being basically told she was not physically attractive by two men who had claimed to love her. At the very least she still had her freedom.

He smiled, with contempt glittering in his deep-set eyes.

'You will eat because you have a long day ahead of you.'

The thought of the long day ahead and what it involved drew a weak whimper from Hannah's throat. Ashamed of the weakness, she shook her head. 'This *can't* have been Dad's idea.'

She looked and sounded so distraught, so young and bewildered that Kamel struggled not to react to the wave of protective tenderness that rose up in him, defying logic and good sense.

'It was something of a committee decision and if there is an innocent victim in this it is me.'

This analysis made her jaw drop. Innocent and victim were two terms she could not imagine anyone using about this man.

'However, if I am prepared to put a brave face on it I don't see what your problem is.'

'My problem is I don't love you. I don't even know you.'

I am Kamel Al Safar, and now you have all the time in the world to get to know me.'

Her eyes narrowed. He had a smart answer for everything. 'I can hardly wait.'

'I think you're being unnecessarily dramatic. It's not as if we'd be the first two people to marry for reasons other than *love*.'

'So you're all right with someone telling you who to marry.' Sure that his ego would not be able to take such a suggestion, she was disappointed when he gave a negligent shrug.

'If I weren't, you'd still be languishing in a jail cell.'

She opened her mouth, heard the tap, tap of the uniformed officer's stick on the floor and closed it again. 'Don't think I'm not grateful.'

He arched a brow. 'Is that so? Strange, I'm not feeling the love,' he drawled.

Her face went blank. 'There isn't any love.'

'True, but then basing a marriage on something as transitory as *love*—' again he said the word as though it left a bad taste in his mouth '—makes about as much sense as building a house on sand.'

Was this a man trying to put a positive spin on it or was he genuinely that cynical?

'Have you ever been in love?' It was a weird thing to ask a total stranger, but then this was a very weird situation.

And just as weird was the expression she glimpsed on the tall prince's face. But even as she registered the bleakness in his eyes his heavy lids half closed. When he turned to look directly at her there was only cynicism shining in the dark depths.

'I defer to you as an expert on that subject. Two engagements is impressive. Do you get engaged to every man you sleep with?'

'I'm twenty-three,' she tossed back.

He tipped his dark head. 'My apologies,' he intoned with smiling contempt. 'That was a stupid question.'

Hannah didn't give a damn if he thought she had casual sex with every man she met. What made her want to slap the look of smug superiority off his face were the double standards his attitude betrayed.

How dared a man who had probably had more notches in his bedpost than she'd had pedicures look down his nose at her?

'And this is all about money and power. You have it and you're prepared to do anything to keep it. You carry on calling it duty if it makes you feel any better about yourself, but I call it greed!'

Kamel struggled to contain the flash of rage he felt at the insult. 'Only a woman who has always had access to her rich daddy's wallet and has never had to work for anything in her life could be so scornful about money. Or maybe you're just stupid.'

Stupid! The word throbbed like an infected wound in her brain. 'I do work.' If only to prove to all those people who called her stupid that people with dyslexia could do as well as anyone else if they had the help they needed.

'I think you might find your role is no longer available.'

'You couldn't say or think anything about me that hasn't been said,' she told him in a voice that shook with all the emotion she normally cloaked behind a cold mask. 'Thought or written. But enough about me. What's your contribution to society? I forget,' she drawled, adopting a dumb expression. 'What qualifications do you need to be a future King? Oh, that's right, an accident of birth.' She stopped and released a long fractured sigh. 'That's not what I wanted to say.'

He stared at her through narrowed eyes, resisting the possibility that a woman with feelings, that a woman who could be hurt, lurked behind the icy disdain.

'Well, what did you want to say?'

Relief rippled through her. This was not the response she had anticipated to her outburst.

'Would this marriage be a...paper one?'

'*Will*...get the tense right,' he chided. 'There will be official duties, occasions when we would be expected to be seen together.' He studied her face. 'But that isn't what you're talking about, is it?'

She gnawed on her lower lip and shook her head.

'It will be expected that we produce an heir.'

Shaken by the image that popped into her head, she looked away but not before her mind had stripped him naked. The image refused to budge, as did the uncomfortable feeling low in her belly.

'You might find it educational.'

The drawled comment made her expression freeze over; it hid her panic. 'The offer of lessons in sex is not a big selling point!' My God, he was really in for a disappointment.

His laugh cut over her words. 'I wasn't referring to your carnal education, though if you want to teach me a thing or two I have no problem.'

The riposte he had anticipated didn't come. Instead, astonishingly, she blushed. Kamel was not often disconcerted, but he was by her response.

Hannah, who had conquered many things but not her infuriating habit of blushing, hated feeling gauche and immature. From somewhere she dredged up some cool. 'So what were you referring to?'

'I'm assuming that your average lover is besotted. I'm not.'

'What, besotted or average?' Stupid question, she thought as her eyes slid down his long, lean, powerful frame—average was not a word anyone would use when referring to this man. 'I can't just jump into bed with you. I don't know you!'

'We have time.' He produced a thin-lipped smile. 'A lot of it. But relax, I don't expect our union to be consummated any time soon, if you can cope with that?'

'With what?'

'No sex.'

Her lashes came down in a concealing curtain. 'I'll manage.'

'Because your little adventures will be over. There can be no questioning the legitimacy of the heir to the throne,' he warned.

'And does the same rule apply to you?' Without waiting for him to reply she gave a snort of disgust. 'Don't answer that. But perhaps you could answer me this...'

He turned and she dropped the hand she self-consciously had extended to him. 'Do you know...' he seemed to know everything else with a few exceptions '...did they get the vaccinations to the village in time?'

The anxiety in her blue eyes was too genuine to be feigned. Perhaps the woman did have a conscience, but not one that stopped her doing exactly what she wanted, Kamel reminded himself.

'It is a pity you didn't think about the village when you decided to cross a border without papers or—'

'My Jeep broke down. I got lost.' Hating the whining note of self-justification, she bit her lip. 'Do you know? Could you find out?' The report that had reached the storage facility where she had been organising local distribution had said the infection was spreading rapidly; the death toll would be horrific if it wasn't contained.

'I have no idea.'

She watched as he moved away, not just in the physical sense to the other end of the cabin, but in every way. He tuned her out totally, appearing to be immersed in whatever was on the laptop he scrolled through.

Studying the back of his neck, she had to crane her own to see more than the top of his dark head. Hannah envied him and wished she could forget he existed. Was this a foretaste of the rest of her life? Occupying the same space when forced to, but not interacting? She had given up on romance but the thought of such a clinical union lay like an icy fist in her stomach.

He didn't even glance at her when the plane landed; he just left his seat, leaving her sitting there. It was the massive bodyguard who indicated she should follow Kamel down the aisle to the exit with one of his trade-mark tilts of the head.

She was between the two men as they disembarked. Hannah blinked in the bright sun—the blinds had been down in the cabin and for some reason she had expected it to be dark. She had lost all sense of time. She glanced down at her wrist and felt a pang when she remembered they had taken her watch. It was one of the few things she had that had been her mother's. When she was ar-rested they'd taken everything she had, including her sunglasses, and she would have given a lot for dark lenses to hide behind.

Her eyes flew wide with alarm.

'I don't have my passport!'

At the bottom of the steps he paused and looked up at her, his cold eyes moving across her face in a zero-tolerance sweep. 'You will not need your passport.'

'One of the perks of being royal?' Like the daunting armed presence and salutes, she thought, watching the suited figure who was bowing deferentially in response to what Kamel was saying.

Glad to be off his radar, she ran her tongue across her dry lips, frightened by how close to total panic she had come in that moment she'd thought that without a passport she would be denied entry. The thought of the cell she had escaped made her knees shake as she negotiated the rest of the steps and stood on terra firma.

There were three massive limos with darkened glass parked a few feet away on the concrete, waiting to whisk them away. One each? Unable to smile at her own joke in the presence of such an overt armed presence, she took a hurried step towards Kamel, who was striding across to the farthest car, only to be restrained by a heavy hand on her shoulder.

She angled a questioning look up and the massive bodyguard shook his head slowly from side to side.

She pulled herself back from another panic precipice and called after Kamel. 'You're leaving?'

She was literally sweating with her effort to project calm but she could still hear the sharp anxiety in her voice.

He turned his head and paused, his dark eyes sweeping her face. 'You'll be looked after.'

Hannah lifted her chin, ignoring the tight knot of loneliness in her chest. She hated the feeling; she hated him. She would not cry—she would not let that damned man make her cry.

Kamel ruthlessly quashed a pang of empathy, but remained conscious of her standing there looking like some sort of sacrificial virgin as he got into the car. He resented the way her accusing blue eyes followed him, making him feel like an exploitative monster. It was illogical—he'd saved her. He hadn't expected to be hailed as a hero but he hadn't counted on becoming the villain of the piece. It was a tough situation, but life required sacrifice and compromise—a fact that she refused to recognise.

He pressed a button and the dark tinted window slid up. She could no longer see him but he could see her.

'What's happening to me?' She managed to wrench the question from her aching throat as she watched the sleek car draw away.

She had not directed the question at anyone in particular so she started when Rafiq, the man of few words, responded.

'My instructions are to take you to Dr Raini's home.'

He tipped his head in the direction of the open car door, clearly expecting her to get in. It hadn't even crossed his mind that she wouldn't.

Hannah felt a tiny bubble of rebellion. She'd had her independence taken away from her during the past few days, and she would not allow it to happen again. She would not become some decorative, docile wife producing stage-managed performances to enhance her husband's standing, only to become invisible when she was not needed.

Then show a bit of backbone, Hannah.

She lifted her chin and didn't move towards the open car door. 'I don't need a doctor.'

The big man, who looked thrown by her response, took his time before responding. 'No, you misunderstand. She is not that sort of doctor. She is a professor of philosophy at the university. She will help you dress for the ceremony, and will act as your maid of honour.'

He stood by the door but Hannah stayed where she was.

'What about my father?'

'I believe your father is to meet you at the royal chapel.'

The mention of a chapel drew her delicate brows into a bemused frown. She recalled the rest of the article in the Sunday supplement where she had garnered most of her knowledge about Surana—as well as being a peaceful melting pot of religions, the country was known for its royal family being Christian, which made them a rarity in the region.

After the car left the airport it turned onto a wide, palm-fringed boulevard where the sun glinted off the glass on the tall modern buildings that lined it. From there they entered what was clearly an older part of the city, where the roads were narrow and the design less geometric.

The screen between the front and back seat came down.

'We are nearly there, miss.'

Hannah nodded her thanks to Rafiq and realised they had entered what appeared to be a prosperous suburb. Almost immediately she had registered the air of affluence, and their car turned sharply through an open pair of high ornate gates and into a small cobbled courtyard hidden from the street by a high wall.

The driver spoke into his earpiece as the gates closed behind them and a suited figure appeared. The big bodyguard spoke to the man and then, with the manner of someone who habitually expected to find danger lurking behind every bush, he scanned the area before opening the door for her.

Hannah's feet hit the cobbles when the wide wooden door of the three-storey whitewashed house was flung open.

'Welcome. I'm Raini, Kamel's cousin.'

The professor turned out to be an attractive woman in her mid-thirties. Tall and slim, she wore her dark hair in a short twenties bob, and her smile was warm as she held out her hands to Hannah.

'I'd ask what sort of journey you had but I can see—'

The kindness and genuine warmth cut through all Hannah's defences and the tears started oozing out of her eyes. Embarrassed, she took the tissue that was pushed into her hand and blew her nose. 'I'm so sorry, I don't normally, it's just…I know I look like a nightmare.'

The woman gave her a hug and ushered her into the house, throwing a comment over her shoulder to the bodyguard as she closed the door very firmly behind them.

Hannah half expected the door to be knocked down; her respect for the woman went up when it wasn't.

'No need to apologise. If I'd been through what you have I'd be a basket case.'

'I am.' Hannah blinked. Inside the house was nothing like the exterior suggested: the décor was minimalist and the ground floor appeared to be totally open-plan.

'Of course you are.' She laid a comforting hand on Hannah's arm. 'This way,' she added, and opened a door that led into a long corridor. Several of the doors lining it were open, and it appeared to be a bedroom wing.

The older woman caught Hannah's bewildered expression. 'I know, it's bigger than it looks.' She smiled sympathetically. 'I'd love to give you the guided tour and I know you must be dead on your feet but we're on the clock, I'm afraid. Just in here.' She pushed open a door and waited for Hannah to enter ahead of her.

It was a big square room with tiled floors. One wall had French doors and another a row of fitted wardrobes. The large low platform bed was the only piece of furniture in the room.

'I know, bleak. I love clutter, not to mention a bit of glitz, but Steve is a minimalist with borderline OCD.' The thought of Steve, presumably her husband, brought a fond smile to her face.

The look reminded Hannah of what she wouldn't have, what she had refused to acknowledge she still wanted. She looked away, conscious of a pain in her chest, and sank down onto the bed. It was a long way down but she barely noticed the soft impact as she landed on the deep duvet. She lifted her hands to her face and shook her head.

'None of this should be happening.'

Watching her, the other woman gave a sympathetic grimace. 'I know this isn't how you envisioned your wedding day,' she said gently, 'but really it's not the wedding that counts. Everything that could go wrong did at mine. It's the person you're going to spend the rest of your life with that matters. How did you and Kamel meet?'

Hannah lifted her head. 'Sorry?'

The other woman misinterpreted her blank look. 'Don't worry, it's a story for another day, I'm just so glad he's found someone. All that playboy stuff, it was so *not* like him, but he isn't as bad as those awful tabloids painted him, you know.'

'I never read the tabloids,' Hannah responded honestly.

The other woman patted her hand and Hannah, who was more confused by these tantalising snippets of information than she had been before, realised two things: that his cousin thought the marriage was for real, and that she would be married to a man who, even his very fond cousin had to admit, had a horrific reputation.

'I prayed he'd recover from Amira one day, but when you lose someone that way...' She gave an expressive shrug. 'I ask myself sometimes, could I have been as noble if I knew that Steve had fallen for someone?'

For a moment a frustrated Hannah thought the flow of confidences had ended, but then Raini's voice dropped to a confidential whisper.

'Amira told me that Kamel said she'd make a beautiful queen, and that all he wanted was for her to be happy. He and Hakim were like brothers—talk about triangles.'

Hannah gave a non-committal grunt, struggling to put the people and places mentioned in context, and then she remembered what he had said: '*She found him... preferable.*' This love that Hannah was meant to be replacing was the woman who had married Kamel's cousin, only to lose her life in the plane crash that had moved Kamel up the line of succession. He had acted as though he didn't care but if his cousin had it right...? She shook her head, struggling to see the man who had showed her zero empathy caring for anyone. It was almost as strange an idea as him being rejected. Whether he wore a crown or not, Kamel was not the sort of man women ran away from.

'She would have, too.'

Hannah wrenched her wandering thoughts back to the present and shook her head, mumbling, 'Sorry?'

'She would have made a beautiful queen. But she never got the chance...' Raini breathed a deep sigh. 'So sad.' Then, visibly pulling herself together, she produced a warm smile. 'But this is not a day for tears. *You will* make a beautiful queen, and you're marrying a man in a million.'

Hannah knew she was meant to respond. 'I would still be in the jail cell if it hadn't been for him.'

The other woman looked mistily emotional as she nodded. 'He's the man you need in an emergency. When Steve was kidnapped...' She gave her head a tiny shake and pulled open the wardrobe door. 'Like I said, Kamel is a guy in a million but patience is not one of his virtues, and my instructions are to have you on the road in thirty minutes.

'Take your pick of the dresses, Hannah.' She indicated a row of white gowns. 'They delivered a few.'

Hannah blinked at the understatement, and Raini continued to deliver the information at the same shotgun speed.

'Your father wasn't sure of your size so I got them to send them all in three sizes, but...' Her bright eyes moved in an assessing sweep up and down Hannah. 'You're an eight?'

Hannah nodded.

'Shower that way.' Her efficient mother hen nodded at a door. 'You'll find toiletries and make-up by the mirror—anything you want just yell. I'll just go and get changed into something much less comfortable.'

The shower was bliss. All the gowns were beautiful but she selected the simplest: a column with the hem and high neck heavily encrusted with beads and crystals. It fitted like a silken glove. Smooth and butter-soft, in dramatic contrast to the emotional rawness of her emotions. She took a deep breath and pulled the shattered threads of her protective composure tight about her shoulders, refusing to acknowledge the fear in her belly.

When Raini returned, looking elegant in a tailored silk trouser suit, Hannah was struggling with her hair. Freshly washed, it was evading her efforts to secure it in an elegant chignon.

'You look beautiful,' the older woman said, standing back to view her. 'I thought you might like this.'

Hannah's eyes travelled from the mist of emotional tears in the other woman's eyes to the lace veil she held out and her armour of cool detachment crumbled.

'It's beautiful,' she said, hating the fact she couldn't tell this woman who was so genuine the truth—that this marriage was all an awful sham.

'It was my grandmother's. I wore it when I was married. I thought you might like it.'

Hannah backed away, feeling even more wretched that she was playing the loving bride for this woman. 'I couldn't—it looks so delicate.'

'I insist. Besides, it will go perfectly with this.' She presented what Hannah had assumed was a clutch bag, but turned out to be a large rectangular wooden box.

'What beautiful work.' Hannah ran a finger along the intricate engraving work that covered the rosewood lid.

'Not nearly as beautiful as this.' With a magician's

flourish Raini flicked the lid open. Her eyes were not on the contents, but on Hannah's face. She gave a smile as Hannah's jaw dropped.

'No, you're really kind, but I *really* couldn't wear that. It's far too precious. This is lovely,' she said, draping the lace veil over her head, 'but really, no.' She stepped back, waving her hands in a fluttering gesture of refusal.

'It's not mine...I wish.' Raini laughed, removing the tiara from its silken bed. The diamonds in the delicately wrought gold circlet glittered as she held it up. 'Kamel had it couriered over. He wants you to wear it. Let me...' Her face a mask of serious concentration, she placed the tiara carefully on top of the lace. *'Dieu,'* she breathed reverently. 'You look like something out of a book of fairy tales. You really are a princess.'

Hannah lifted her hands to remove it. 'I haven't put my hair up yet.'

'If I were you I'd leave it loose. It's very beautiful.'

Hannah shrugged. Her hairstyle was the least of her worries.

CHAPTER FIVE

HANNAH'S FIRST GLIMPSE of her future home drew a pained gasp from her lips.

'I know.' Raini was all amused sympathy. 'I'd like to tell you it's not as awe-inspiring as it looks, but actually,' she admitted, directing her critical stare at the multitude of minarets, 'it is. Even Hollywood couldn't build a set like this. The family, as you'll learn, has never been into less is more. When I lived here—'

'You lived here?' How did anyone ever relax in a setting this ostentatiously grand?

Raini gave a warm chuckle. 'Oh, my parents occupied a small attic,' she joked. 'Until Dad got posted. He's a diplomat,' she explained. 'By the time I was eighteen I'd lived in a dozen cities.' They drove under a gilded archway into a courtyard the size of a football pitch, filled with fountains. 'But nothing ever came close to this.'

Hannah believed her.

Rafiq escorted them into the building through a small antechamber that had seemed large until they stepped through the next door and entered a massive hall. The wall sconces in there were all lit, creating swirling patterns on the mosaic floor.

The awful sense of impending doom that lay like a cold stone in Hannah's chest became heavier as they followed the tall, gowned figure down a maze of marble-floored empty corridors. By the time she saw a familiar figure, she was struggling to breathe past the oppressive weight.

'Dad!'

'Hello, Hannah! You look very beautiful, child.'

Hannah struggled to hide her shock at her father's appearance. She had never seen him look so pale and haggard. Not even when he'd lain in a hospital bed attached to bleeping machines had he looked this frail. He seemed to have aged ten years since she last saw him.

Any lingering mental image of her walking into his arms and asking him to make everything right vanished as the tears began to slide down his cheeks. She had never seen her ebullient parent cry except on the anniversary of her mother's death—her birthday. On that day he always vanished to be alone with his grief, and the sight of tears now was as painful to her as a knife thrust.

Intentionally or not, it always felt as if she was the cause of his tears. If she hadn't been born the woman he loved would not have died and now this was her fault. About that much Kamel was right.

She had been doing a job that she was ill qualified to do and she'd messed up. But the consequences had not been just hers. Other people had suffered. She lifted her chin. Well, that was going to stop. She'd made the mistake and she'd take the nasty-tasting medicine, though in this instance it came in the shape of the dark and impossibly handsome and arrogant Prince of Surana.

'I thought I'd lost you,' her father cried. 'They have

the death penalty in Quagani, Hannah. It was the only way we could get you out. They wanted to make an example of you, and without the King's personal intervention they would have. Kamel is a good man.'

It seemed to be a universally held opinion. Hannah didn't believe it. Nonetheless, it was clear that he had not just freed her, he had saved her life.

'I know, Dad. I'm fine about this,' she lied.

'*Really?*'

She nodded. 'It's about time I finally made it down the aisle, don't you think?'

'He'll take care of you.' He squeezed her hand. 'You'll take care of each other. You know your mother was the love of my life…'

Hannah felt a heart-squeezing clutch of sadness. 'Yes, Dad.'

'She didn't love me when we got married. She was pregnant, and I persuaded her… What I'm trying to say is that it's possible to grow to love someone. She did.'

Incredibly moved by his confidences, she nodded, her throat aching with unshed tears. There was no point telling him the cases were totally dissimilar. Her father had loved the woman he had married, whereas Hannah was marrying a man who despised her.

A man who had saved her life.

Any moment she would wake up.

But it wasn't a dream. However surreal it felt, she really was standing there with her hand on her father's arm, about to walk down the aisle to be married to a stranger.

'Ready?' her father asked.

She struggled to relearn the forgotten skill of smiling for his benefit and nodded. Ahead of her the elegant

Raini spoke to someone outside Hannah's line of vision
and the big doors swung open.

Hannah had anticipated more of the same magnifi-
cence she had encountered so far, but she had the impression of a space that was relatively small, almost
intimate…peaceful. The tranquillity was a dramatic
contrast to the emotional storm that raged just below
her calm surface.

If you discounted the priest and choir there were only
four people present: two robed rulers in the pews, and
the two men who stood waiting, one tall and fair, the
other…the other tall and very dark. She closed her eyes
and willed herself to relax, to breathe, to do this… She
opened them again and smiled at her father. He felt bad
enough about this without her falling apart.

'Nervous?'

Kamel glanced at his best man. 'No.' Resigned would
be a more accurate description of his mindset. There
had only ever been one woman he had imagined walking down the aisle towards him and he had watched her
make that walk to someone else. He would never forget
the expression on her face—she had been incandescent
with joy. Yet now when he did think of it he found another face superimposing itself over Amira's. A face
framed by blonde hair.

'I suppose you could call this a version of a shotgun
wedding,' the other man mused, glancing at the two
royal personages who occupied the empty front pews.
'She's not…?'

He tried to imagine those blue eyes soft as she held
a child. 'No, she is not.'

'There's going to be a hell of a lot of pressure for you

to change that. I hope she knows what she's letting herself in for.'

'Did you?' Kamel countered, genuinely curious.

'No, but then I didn't marry the heir apparent…which
is maybe just as well. Raini and I have decided not to go
for another round of IVF. It's been eight years now and
there has to be a cut-off point. There is a limit to how
many times she can put herself through this.'

Kamel clasped the other man's shoulder. 'Sorry.'

The word had never sounded less adequate. Kamel
never lost sight of the fact that life was unfair, but if he
had this would have reminded him. The world was filled
with children who were unloved and unwanted and here
were two people who had all the love in the world to
give a child and it wasn't going to happen for them.

One of life's cruelties.

'Thanks.' Steven looked towards a security guy who
nodded and spoke into his earpiece. 'Looks like she's
arrived on time. You're a lucky man.'

Kamel glanced at Steven and followed the direction
of his gaze. The breath caught in his throat. Bedraggled,
she had been a beautiful woman, but this tall, slender
creature was a dream vision in white—hair falling like
a golden cloud down her back, the diamonds glittering on her lacy veil fading beside the brilliance of her
wide blue eyes.

'That remains to be seen.'

Kamel's murmured comment drew a quizzical look
from his best man but no response that could be heard
above the strains of 'Ave Maria' sung by the choir as
the bride on her father's arm, preceded by her matron
of honour, began her progression.

A weird sense of calm settled on Hannah as she stood

facing her bridegroom. It did not cross her mind until afterwards that the whole thing resembled an out-of-body experience: she was floating somewhere above the heads of the people gathered to witness this parody, watching herself give her responses in a voice that didn't even hold a tremor.

The tremor came at the end when they were pronounced man and wife and Kamel looked directly at her for the first time. His dark eyes held hers as he brushed a fold of gossamer lace from her cheek and stared down at her with a soul-stripping intensity.

In her emotionally heightened state she had no idea who leaned in to whom; Hannah just knew she experienced the weirdest sensation, as though she were being pulled by an invisible thread towards him.

Her eyes were wide open as he covered her lips with his, then as the warm pressure deepened her eyelids lowered and her lips parted without any coercion and she kissed him back.

It was Kamel who broke the contact. Without it, her head was no longer filled with the taste, the texture and the smell of him, and reality came flooding back with a vengeance. She'd just kissed her husband and she'd enjoyed it—more than a little. That was wrong, so *very* wrong on every level. It was as if he had flicked a switch she didn't know she had. She shivered, unable to control the fresh wave of heat that washed over her skin.

He took her hand and raised it to his lips, watching the rapt glow of sensual invitation in her velvet eyes be replaced by something close to panic. He was not shocked but he was surprised by the strength of the physical response she had shown.

'Smile. You're the radiant bride, *ma belle*,' he warned.

Hannah smiled until her jaw ached. She smiled all the way through the formality of signatures, and all she could think about was that kiss. The memory felt like a hot prickle under her skin. For the first time in her life she understood the power of sex and how a person could forget who they were under the influence of that particular drug.

She was kissed on both cheeks by the leaders of two countries, and then rather more robustly by her father, who held her hand tightly.

'You know that I am always there for you, Hannah.'

'I know, Dad. I'm fine.' She blinked away emotional tears but couldn't dislodge the massive lump in her throat.

'I will take care of her, Charles.'

His sincerity made her teeth ache. You couldn't trust a man who could lie so well, not that Hannah had any intention of trusting him. Aware that her father was watching, she let it lie when Kamel took her hand in his, not snatching it away until they were out of sight.

His only reaction was a sardonic smirk.

It took ten minutes after the farewells for them to walk back to his private apartments. His bride didn't say a word the whole time.

It was hard not to contrast the brittle ice queen beside him with the woman whose soft warm lips he had tasted. That small taste, the heat that had flared between them, shocking with its intensity and urgency, had left him curious, and eager to repeat the experience.

He was lusting after his bride. Well, life was full of surprises and not all of them were bad. The situation suited a man who had a very pragmatic approach to sex.

The room they stood in was on the same grand scale
as all the others. This one apparently connected two
bedrooms, if she had understood him correctly. Her exhausted brain was filled with a low-level hum of confusion, and two images from the wedding kept flitting
through her head—her father's tired, ill face and the
predatory heat in Kamel's eyes when he claimed his
kiss.

'Has it occurred to you that this marriage might not
be something to be endured...but enjoyed?'

Hannah's fingers slipped off the door handle. She
turned around, her back against the wooden panels. He
was standing too close...much too close. She struggled
to draw in air as her body stirred, responding to the
slumberous, sensual provocation shining in his dark
eyes.

'The only thing I want to enjoy tonight is some privacy.'

'That is not what you would enjoy.'

She threw up her hands in a gesture of exasperated
defeat. 'Fine! So I find you attractive. Is that what you
want to hear?' She angled a scornful glance up at his
lean dark face. 'I find any number of men attractive,
but I don't sleep with them all.'

Make that none.

'You're discerning. I like that in you.'

'You may be good to look at but your ego is a massive turn-off.'

'I could work on it. You would teach me.'

Big, predatory, and sinfully sexy—she was willing
to bet that that were quite a few things he could teach
her! Her stomach tightened in self-disgust. Shocked
by the thought that had insinuated itself into her head,

she tilted her chin, channelling all the ice princess she could muster, and retorted haughtily, 'I'm not into casual sex or tutoring.'

'We're married, *ma belle*. That is not *casual*…and I do not need instruction.'

Hannah's eyes went to the ring on her finger. It felt heavy. She felt…*consumed*. She frowned at the word that formed in her head. Consumed by feelings, a need. She gave her head a tiny shake. It was dangerous to imagine something that was not there. She blamed the bottle of champagne that Raini had cracked open in the limo. Had she had one or two glasses? Regardless of her alcohol consumption, the only thing she needed was sleep.

He laid a hand on the door beside her head and leaned into her. 'Well, if you change your mind you know where I am.' His eyes not leaving hers, he tipped his head at the door next to her own. 'And for the record I'm fine with…just sex. I will not feel used or cheap in the morning.'

His throaty, mocking laugh was the last straw.

Her blue eyes narrowed and her chin lifted to a combative angle. She could actually feel something inside her snapping as she reached up and pulled his face down until she could reach his lips. In the instant before she covered his mouth with hers she saw his expression change—saw the mockery vanish and the dark, dangerous glow slide into his heavy-lidded eyes.

In the tiny corner of her mind that was still sane Hannah knew she was doing something incredibly stupid, but it was too late to pull back, and then he was kissing her back with a sensual skill that made her sleep-deprived brain shut down—she just clung on for the ride.

Kamel was a man who was rarely surprised—but Hannah had surprised him twice already. First when she kissed him, and second when lust slammed through his body.

Had he ever wanted a woman this badly?

Then he identified the flavour of her kiss. As he pulled away she clung like a limpet, a very soft, warm, inviting limpet, but he gritted his teeth. He knew that if he let it go on a moment longer he wouldn't be able to stop. And when he made love to his wife he wanted her not just willing but awake and sober!

He studied her flushed face, the bright, almost febrile glitter in her eyes. He had seen the same look in the eyes of a friend who, after pulling three consecutive all-nighters before an exam, had fallen asleep halfway through the actual exam. Hannah was seriously sleep deprived, and more than a bit tipsy.

As a rule he thought it was nice if the person you were making love to stayed conscious. He gave a self-mocking smile. Being noble was really overrated—no wonder it had fallen out of fashion.

'You've been drinking.'

She blinked at the accusation, then insisted loudly, 'I'm not drunk!'

The pout she gave him almost broke his resolve. 'We won't argue the point,' he said wearily. 'I think we should sleep on this. Goodnight, Hannah.'

And he walked away and left her standing there feeling like…like…like a woman who'd just made a pass at her own husband and got knocked back. So not only did she now feel cheap, she felt unattractive.

Rejected by two fiancés, and now a husband, but she couldn't summon the energy to care as, with a sigh, she fell backwards fully clothed onto the bed, closed her eyes and was immediately asleep.

CHAPTER SIX

TOO PROUD TO ask for help, Hannah was lost. She finally located Kamel in the fourth room she tried—one that opened off a square, windowless hallway that might have been dark but for the daylight that filtered through the blue glass of the dome high above.

Like the ones before it, this room was massive and imposing, and also came complete with a built-in echo, and her heels were particularly noisy on the inlaid floor. But Kamel didn't look up. The hawk on its perch followed her with its dark eyes while her master continued to stare at the screen of his mobile phone with a frown of concentration that drew his dark brows into a straight line above his aquiline nose.

Choosing not to acknowledge the strange achy feeling in the pit of her stomach, she walked up to the desk and cleared her throat.

When his dark head didn't lift she felt her temper fizz and embraced the feeling. If he wanted to be awkward, fine. She could do awkward. She felt damned awkward after last night.

'Is this your doing?' Realising that her posture, with her arms folded tightly across her stomach, might be construed as protective, she dropped them to her sides.

Kamel stopped scrolling through his emails, looked up from his phone and smiled. 'Good morning, dear wife.'

Kamel did not feel it was a particularly good morning and it had been a very bad night. He felt tired, and more frustrated than any man should be after his wedding night. A cold shower, a long run and he had regained a little perspective this morning. But then she walked in the room and just the scent of her perfume… He wanted her here and now. *The difference between want and need* was important to Kamel. He had not allowed himself to *need* a woman since Amira.

He *needed* sex, not Hannah. And the sex would be good—his icy bride turned out to have more fire in her than any woman he had ever met. But afterwards he would feel as he always did—the escape from the tight knot of brutal loneliness in his chest was only ever temporary.

Hannah's lips tightened at the mockery but she did not react to it; instead she simply arched a feathery brow. *'Well?'*

'I feel as though I am walking into this conversation midway through. Coffee?' He lifted the pot on the desk beside him and topped up his half-filled cup and allowed his gaze to drift over her face. 'Hangover?'

'No,' she lied. The delicious aroma drifted her way, making her mouth water. She felt shivery as she struggled to tear her eyes off his long brown fingers. 'I don't want coffee.'

'So can I help you with something?'

She emitted a soft hissing sound of annoyance. Without looking back, she pointed to the open doorway where a suited figure stood, complete with enigmatic expression and concealed weapon. 'Did you arrange for him to follow me?'

Kamel stood up from the desk and walked past her towards the open door. Nodding to the man standing outside, he closed it with a soft thud and turned back to Hannah, though his attention appeared to be on the lie of his narrow silk tie that lay in a flash of subdued colour against his white shirt. The jacket that matched the dove-grey trousers was draped across the back of the chair.

'For heaven's sake, you look ridiculously perfect.'

Her delivery lacked the scornful punch she had intended, possibly because the comment was no exaggeration. The pale grey trousers that matched the jacket were clearly bespoke and could have been cut to disguise a multitude of sins if he'd had any, but there was no escaping the fact that physically at least he was flawless.

He raised his brows and she felt her cheeks colour. 'I despise men who spend more time looking in the mirror than I do.'

'Rather a sexist thing to say,' he remarked, his tone mildly amused and his eyes uncomfortably observant. 'But each to his own. I'm sorry I don't measure up to your unwashed grunge ideal.'

Having dug herself a hole, she let the subject drop. He could never fail to live up to any woman's ideal, on a purely eye-candy level, of course. 'I do not require a bodyguard.'

'No, obviously not.'

Her pleased smile at a battle so easily won had barely formed when his next words made it vanish.

'You will require a team of them.'

'That's ludicrous!' she contended furiously.

The amusement in his manner vanished as he countered, 'It's necessary, so I suggest you stop acting like a diva and accept it.'

'I refuse.'

His glance slid from her flashing eyes to her heaving bosom, lingering there long enough to bring her hand to her throat. 'Refuse all you like, it won't alter anything. I appreciate this is an adjustment and I'll make allowances.'

That was big of him. 'Allowances! This is a palace! How do I adjust to that?'

'I have been to Brent Hall and it is hardly a council flat,' he retorted, thinking of the portrait that hung above the fireplace in the drawing room. Had Hannah Latimer ever possessed the dreamy innocence that shone in the eyes of her portrait, or had the artist been keen to flatter the man who was paying him?

She opened her mouth to retort and then his comment sank in. 'You've been to my home?'

He tipped his head. 'I stood in for my uncle on one social occasion, actually two. I predict you will adjust to your change in status. After all, you have played the pampered princess all your life. The only difference now is you have an actual title, and, of course, me.'

'I'm trying to forget.'

'Not the best idea.'

Despite the monotone delivery, she heard the warning and she didn't like it, or him.

Kamel gave a tolerant nod and picked up a pen from the desk. 'It is a fact of life. You will not leave this building without a security presence.'

'I wasn't outside the building. He was waiting outside my bedroom. What harm was I likely to come to there?'

'Oh, so your concern is for your privacy.'

'Well, yes. Obviously.' The idea of living like a bird in a golden cage did not hold any appeal. She'd given up her freedom but there had to be boundaries. Where were your boundaries last night, Hannah?

'We will be private enough, I promise you.'

The seductive promise in his voice sent a beat of white-hot excitement whipping through her body. As it ebbed she was consumed by hot-cheeked embarrassment.

'You blush very easily.'

She slung him a belligerent glare. 'I'm not used to the heat.' The desert heat she might grow accustomed to, but being around a man who could make her feel… feel…she gave a tiny gusty sigh as she sought for a word to describe how he made her feel, and it came— *hungry*! That was something she would never get used to. She just hoped it would pass quickly like a twenty-four-hour bug.

'So this is an example of how my life will not change?' she charged shrilly. 'I left one cell with a guard outside for another.'

'But the facilities and décor are much better,' he came back smoothly.

The languid smile that tugged the corner of his mouth upwards did not improve her mood. Neither did looking at his mouth. It was a struggle not to lift a hand to her own tingling lips. So far he hadn't mentioned the kiss. Had he forgotten?

She wished she had, but her memory loss only lasted until she had stood under a shower and then the whole mortifying scene came rushing back.

'This isn't a joke.'

The shriller she got, the calmer he became. 'Neither is it a subject for screaming and shouting and stamping your little foot.'

He glanced down at the part of her under discussion. She had very nice ankles but she had even nicer calves. He found his eyes drawn to the silky smooth contours and higher… The skirt of the dress she wore, a silky blue thing, sleeveless and cinched in at the waist with a narrow plaited tan belt, ended just above the knee. The entire image was cool, perfectly groomed…regal.

He refused to allow the image of his hands sliding under the fabric up and over the smooth curves—but the suggestion had been enough to send a streak of heat through his body where it coalesced into a heavy ache in his groin. He could have woken up this morning in her arms. Even while he had called himself a fool during the long wakeful night, he had known it was the right decision.

'I did not stamp my foot,' Hannah retorted and immediately wanted to do just that.

'But you have a tendency to turn everything into a drama, angel.'

Her brows hit her smooth hairline exposed by the severe hairstyle she had adopted that morning. The woman who had looked back at her from the mirror after she had speared the last hair grip into the smooth coil did not even look like a distant relative of the woman with the flushed face, feverishly bright eyes and swollen lips she had glimpsed in the mirror last night before she had fallen onto the bed fully dressed.

'If *this* isn't a drama, what is?'

'I appreciate this is not easy, but we are *both* living with the consequences of your actions.'

She threw up her hands and didn't even register the discomfort as one of the pearl studs she wore went flying across the room. She sighed heavily and asked, 'How many times a day are you going to remind me it's all my fault?'

'It depends on how many times you irritate me.' Kamel left his desk and walked to the spot where the pearl had landed beside the window.

'My breathing irritates you,' she said.

He elevated a dark brow. 'Not if you do it quietly.' He half closed his eyes, imagining hearing her breath quicken as he moved in and out of her body.

Hannah was not breathing quietly now. The closer he got, the louder her breathing became, then she stopped altogether. 'You are…' The trapped air left her lungs in one soft, sibilant sigh as he stopped just in front of her, close enough for her to feel the heat from his body.

'Have you ever heard of personal space?' she asked, tilting back her head to meet his challenging dark stare as she fought an increasingly strong impulse to step back. Her cool vanished into shrill panic as he leaned in towards her. 'What are you doing?'

More to the point, what was she doing?

She had tried so hard *not* to look at his mouth, *not* to think of that kiss, it became inevitable that she was now staring and not in a casual way at his mouth and the only thing she could think about was that kiss—the firm texture of his lips, the heat of his mouth, the moist…

'You lost this.'

It took a few seconds to bring into focus the stud he held between his thumb and forefinger. When she realised what he was holding her hand went jerkily to her ear…the wrong one.

'No, this one.' He touched her ear lobe, catching it for a moment between his thumb and forefinger before letting it drop away. 'Pretty.' Her head jerked to one side, causing a fresh stab of pain to slide like a knife through her skull. How long before the headache tablets she had swallowed kicked in?

The strength of her physical response to the light contact sent a stab of alarm through Hannah. She swayed slightly and shifted her position, taking a step back. It no longer seemed so important to stand her ground. Live to fight another day—wasn't that what they said about those who ran away?

'Thank you,' she breathed, holding out her hand as she focused on his left shoulder.

He ignored the hand and leaned in closer. *Help,* she thought, her smile little more now than a scared fixed grimace painted on. Her nostrils quivered in reaction to the warm scent of his body, his nearness. She could feel the heat of his body through his clothes and hers... imagine how hot his skin would feel without...

And she did imagine; her core temperature immediately jumped by several painful degrees as she stood there in an agony of shame and arousal while he placed a thumb under her chin to angle her face up to him.

She'd decided that the only plus point in being married to a man she loathed was that she would never again suffer the pain and humiliation of rejection. She wouldn't care. A lovely theory, but hard to cling to when every cell in her body craved his touch. She had never felt this way before.

She bit her lip, fearing that if she set free the ironic laugh locked in her throat there would be a chain reaction—she would lose it and she couldn't do that. Pretty much all she had left was her pride.

Listen to yourself, Hannah, mocked the voice in her head. Your pride is all you have left? Go down that road of self-pity and you'd pretty much end up being the spoilt shallow bitch your husband thinks you are.

Husband.

I'm married.

Third time lucky. Or as it happened, *unlucky.* She knew there were many women who would have envied her *unlucky* fate just as there had been girls at school who had envied her.

The influential clique who had decided to make the new girl's life a misery even before they'd discovered she was stupid. She'd thought so too until she'd been diagnosed as dyslexic at fourteen.

For a long time Hannah had wondered why—what had she done or said?—and then she'd had the opportunity to ask when she'd found herself sitting in a train compartment with one of her former tormentors, all grown up now.

Hannah had immediately got up to leave but had paused by the door when the other woman had spoken.

'I'm sorry.'

And Hannah had asked the question that she had always wanted to ask.

'Why?'

The answer had been the same one her father had given her when she had sobbed, 'What have I done? What's wrong with me?'

'It's got nothing to do with you, Hannah. They do it because they can. I could move you to another school, sweetheart, but what happens if the same thing happens there? You can't carry on running away. The way to cope with bullies is not to react. Don't let them see they get to you.'

The strategy had worked perhaps too well because, not only had her cool mask put off the bullies, but potential friends too, except for Sal.

What would Sal say? She closed off that line of thought, but not before she experienced a wave of deep sadness. She didn't share secrets with Sal any more; she had lost her best friend the day she had found her in bed with her fiancé. It was to have been her wedding day.

And now here she was, a married woman. Kamel's touch was deft, almost clinical, but there was nothing clinical about the shimmies of sensation that zigzagged through her body as his fingers brushed her ear lobe.

Hannah breathed again when he straightened up, keeping her expression as neutral as his.

'Thank you,' she murmured distantly. 'Could you tell me where the kitchen is?'

He looked surprised by the question. 'I haven't the faintest idea.'

'You don't know where your own kitchen is?'

Kamel, who still looked bemused, ignored her question. 'Why were you going to the kitchen?' he persisted. 'If you want a tour of the place the housekeeper will…'

'I didn't want a tour. I wanted breakfast.' She had eaten nothing the previous evening. Unfortunately she had not shown similar restraint when it came to the champagne.

'Why didn't you ring for something?'

'Do you really not know where your kitchen is?'

He arched a sardonic brow. 'And am I meant to believe you do? That you are a regular visitor to the kitchens at Brent Hall?' It was not an area he had seen on the occasion he had been a guest at Charles Latimer's country estate, a vast Elizabethan manor with a full complement of staff. The daughter of the house had not been home at the time but her presence had been very much felt.

There was barely a polished surface in the place that did not have a framed photo of her and her accomplishments through the years—playing the violin, riding a horse, looking athletic with a tennis racket, looking academic in a gown and mortar board.

And looking beautiful in the portrait in the drawing room over the fireplace.

'He really caught her,' the proud father had said when he'd found Kamel looking at it.

His sarcastic drawl set her teeth on edge. 'I left home at eighteen.'

And by then Hannah had been a very good cook, thanks to her father's chef at Brent Hall. Sarah Curtis had an impressive professional pedigree, she had worked in top kitchens around Europe and she had a daughter who had no interest in food or cooking. When she'd realised that Hannah did, she'd encouraged that interest.

For Hannah the kitchen was a happy place, the place her father came and sat in the evenings, where he shed his jacket and his formality. She had not realised then why...now she did.

'Yes, I can imagine the hardship of picking out an outfit and booking a table every night must have been difficult. What taxing subject did you study?'

'Classics,' she snapped.

'So you spent a happy three years learning something incredibly useful.'

'Four actually. I needed extra time because I'm dyslexic.'

'You have dyslexia?'

'Which doesn't mean I'm stupid.'

It was a taunt she had obviously heard before, and taunts left scars. Kamel experienced a swift surge of anger as he thought of the people responsible for creating this defensive reflex. In his opinion it was them, not Hannah, who could be accused of stupidity…ignorance…cruelty.

Kamel was looking at her oddly. The silence stretched. Was he worried their child might inherit her condition? He might be right, but at least she'd know what signs to look for—he or she wouldn't have to wait until they were a teenager before they had a diagnosis.

'You have dyslexia and you got a degree in Classics?' Now that was something that required serious determination.

'Not a first, but I can make a cup of tea and toast a slice of bread, and at least I don't judge people I don't know…' She stopped and thought, Why am I playing it down? 'I got an upper second and actually I'm a good cook—*very* good.' She'd be even better if she had accepted the internship at the restaurant that Sarah had wangled for her: awful hours, menial repetitive tasks and the chance to work under a three-star Michelin chef.

For once she hadn't been able to coax her father around to her way of thinking—he had exploded when he'd learnt of the plan. It hadn't just been to please him that instead she had accepted the prestigious university place she had been offered; it had been because she had realised that the contentious issue of her career had become a major issue between her father and his cook.

His mistress.

The smile that hitched one corner of Kamel's mouth upwards did not touch his eyes; they remained thoughtful, almost wary. 'I have married a clever woman and a domestic goddess. Lucky me.'

Her jaw tightened at what she perceived as sarcasm.

'Lucky me,' he repeated, seeing her in the wedding dress, her face clustered with damp curls, her lips looking pink and bruised, her passion-glazed eyes heavy and deep blue, not cold, but hot. He rubbed his thumb absently against his palm, mimicking the action when he had stroked her cheek, feeling the invisible fuzz of invisible downy hair on the soft surface.

The contrast with the cold, classy woman before him could not have been more dramatic; they were both beautiful but the woman last night had been sexy, sinfully hot, available—but married. He didn't sleep with drunk women; the choice was normally an end-of-story shrug, not hours of seething frustration while he wrestled his passion into submission, cursing his black and white sense of honour.

The same honour that had made him push Amira into Hakim's arms.

He was either a saint or an idiot!

Hannah gave a mental shrug and turned a slender shoulder, telling herself that it didn't matter what he thought of her...she still wanted to hit him.

Or kiss him.

Dusting an invisible speck off her silk dress, she gave a faint smile and thought about slapping that expression of smug superiority off his hateful face.

'Relax, we leave at twelve-thirty.'

Relax, no. But this was the best news she had had in several nightmare days.

'Where are you off to?' She didn't care but it seemed polite to ask.

'We.'

Her expression froze. 'We? What are you talking about? There is no we!'

'Please do not treat me to another bout of your histrionics. Behind closed doors there is no we.' Lips twisted into a sardonic smile, he sat on the edge of the desk. 'But in public we are a loving couple and you will show me respect.'

'When you stop lying to me. You said we would not have to live together.'

'You didn't really believe that. I said what you wanted to hear. It seemed the kindest thing at the time.'

She let out a snort of sheer disbelief—was this man for real? 'Perhaps I should thank you for kindly lying through your teeth.'

He glanced at the watch on his wrist, exposing the fine dark hairs on his arm as he flicked his cuff. 'Quite clearly we have things to discuss,' he conceded.

Hannah, who was breathing hard, flashed a bitter smile. 'Discuss' implied reasonable and flexible. It implied listening. *'You think?'*

He refused to recognise the irony in her voice. 'Yes, I do think.'

'You are giving me a time slot?' She was married to a man she was expected to make an appointment to talk to? Now that really brought home how awful this entire situation was. She had walked into it with her eyes wide open and her brain in denial. The fact was that deep down she had never stopped being a person who believed in happy ever after, who believed that everything happened for a reason.

A spasm of irritation crossed his lean, hard features.

She shook her head and gave a laugh of sheer disbelief. 'Or should that be granting me an audience?' she wondered, letting her head tip forward as she performed a mocking curtsey.

The childish reaction made his jaw clench.

'You're used to people dropping everything when you require attention. But I've got a newsflash...' He let the sentence hang, but the languid contempt in his voice made it easy to fill in the blanks as he glanced down at the stack of papers spread out on the inlaid table.

It wasn't that she wanted to be important to him, but a little empathy—she'd have settled for civility—would have made him human. Instead he intended to map out just how insignificant she was in the scheme of things from the outset. Did he really think she didn't know she was on the bottom rung of his priorities?

Hannah could feel the defensive ice forming on her features. 'Sorry,' she said coldly. 'I'm still living in a world where people have marriages based on mutual respect, not mutual contempt! It was unrealistic of me, and it won't happen again,' she promised. 'I won't disturb you any longer. Have your people talk to my people and...' The ice chips left her voice as it quivered... My people. I have no people. The total isolation of her position hit home for the first time.

She squeezed her eyes shut.

'I need an hour.'

She opened her eyes and found he was looking right at her. Her stomach immediately went into a dive.

'I could postpone this but I assumed you would prefer to arrive early at Brent.'

Her eyes flew wide. 'Brent!' She gave a shaky smile. 'You're taking me home?'

'This is your home.'

Swallowing the hurt and annoyed with herself for leaping to conclusions, she lifted her chin and stared at him coldly. 'This will never be my home.'

'That, *ma belle*, is up to you. But your father wanted to hold a wedding party for us, and for your friends. I think it would only be polite for us to be there. I will have some breakfast sent up to your room.'

Jaw clenched at the dismissal, Hannah left the room with her head held high.

CHAPTER SEVEN

HER FATHER WAS there to greet them at the private air-strip where they landed, and Hannah was relieved he looked better than the previous day, almost his old self. She was sandwiched between the two men in the back seat of the limo and by the time they arrived at Brent Hall the effort of maintaining a reassuring pretence for her father's sake had taken its toll, her persistent nagging headache showing signs of becoming a full-blown migraine.

'I think I might go to my room, unless you want me to help.' There was evidence of the preparations for to-night everywhere.

'No, you have a rest. Good idea. Tonight is all under control. I got a new firm in and they seem excellent—they're doing the lot. I have a few ideas I want to run past your husband.' He glanced towards Kamel and joked, 'Not much point having a financial genius in the family if you don't make use of him, is there? I'm sure he'll even write your thank-you letters.'

Hannah laughed and her father winked conspirato-rially at her. 'A family joke.'

And one that was at his daughter's expense, thought Kamel, who had seen the flinch before the smile. How many times, he wondered, had she been on the receiving end of such jokes? For a man who cared deeply for his daughter, Charles Latimer seemed remarkably blind to her sensitivity.

'I am aware of Hannah's dyslexia. Is that the family joke?'

'She told you?' Hannah's father looked startled.

'She did. But even if she hadn't I would have noticed how uncomfortable the family *joke* made her.'

Hannah's father looked horrified by the suggestion. 'It's just that some of her mistakes have been so…' His stammering explanation ground to a halt in the face of his new son-in-law's fixed, unsmiling stare. 'Hannah has a great sense of humour.'

'I don't.'

Instead of heading for her room, Hannah made her way down to the kitchens. But finding the place had been taken over by outside caterers, she made her way to Sarah's private flat.

The cook was delighted to see her. So was Olive, the dog sitting in her basket, surrounded by her puppies, who licked Hannah's hand and wagged her stumpy little tail.

Without being asked, Sarah produced some painkillers along with the coffee and cakes. 'Now, tell me all about it.'

Hannah did—or at least the approved version. She stayed half an hour before she got up to leave.

'Where are you going?' Sarah called after her.

'To my room. I need to get ready.' She pulled a face.

'Not that way, Hannah.' Sarah laughed. 'You can't sleep in your old bedroom. You're a married woman now.'

'Oh, God, I forgot!' Hannah groaned.

If the cook thought this was an odd thing to say she didn't let on. Instead she enthused about the complete refurbishment of the guest suite that Hannah was to stay in. 'Mind you, if you're used to palaces...'

'I'm not used to palaces. I'll never be used to palaces. I hate them and I hate him!' Then it all came tumbling out—the whole story.

'I knew something was wrong,' Sarah said as she piled sugar in a cup of tea and made Hannah drink it. 'I don't know what to say, Hannah. I really don't.'

'There's nothing to say. I'm sorry I dumped on you like this.'

'Heavens, girl, that's what I'm here for. You know I've always thought of you as my second daughter.'

'I wish I was,' Hannah replied fiercely, envying Eve her mother. 'Dad thinks I'm all right with it. You won't tell him, will you? I worry so much that the stress will...' She didn't have to explain her worries to Sarah, who knew about the heart attack. She'd been with Hannah when she'd got the call and had travelled with her to the hospital.

Having extracted a firm promise that Sarah would not reveal how unhappy she was, Hannah made her way to the guest room and discovered that Sarah had not exaggerated about the makeover.

She explored the luxurious bedroom. An opulent silk curtained four-poster bed occupied one end of the room. She quickly looked away, but not before several illicit images slipped through her mental block. Her stomach was still flipping lazily as she focused on the opposite end of the room where a bathtub deep enough to swim in sat on a raised dais.

Behind it there were two doors. One opened, she discovered, into a massive wet room—she pressed one of the buttons on a glass control panel that would have looked at home in a space station and the room was filled with the sounds of the ocean. Unable to locate a button that turned it off, she closed the door and pushed open the other door. The lights inside automatically lit up, revealing a space that was the size of her entire flat, lined with hanging space, mirrors and shelves.

It was not a full wardrobe, but neither was it empty. The selection of clothes and shoes that were hung and neatly folded were her own. Shoes, bags, under-clothes—there was something for every occasion, including an obvious choice for this evening where all eyes would be on her. She pushed away the thought of the evening ahead and lifted a silk shirt to her face. Feeling the sharp prick of tears behind her eyelids, she blinked them back.

After the last few days Hannah had imagined that nothing could shock her ever again. But when she opened the large velvet box on the dressing table and looked at the contents displayed on the silk lining, she knew that she had been wrong!

Kamel glanced at the closed door, then at his watch. He was expecting her to be late and he was expecting her to be hostile; she was neither. At seven on the dot the door opened and his wife stepped into the room.

Kamel struggled to contain his gasp. He had seen her at her worst and that had been beautiful. At her best she was simply breathtaking. The satin gown she wore with such queenly confidence left one shoulder bare, Grecian style. The bodice cut snugly across her breasts, continued in a body-hugging column to the knee where it flared out, sweeping the ground. Her skin against the black glowed with a pearly opalescence.

The silence stretched and Hannah fought the absurd urge to curtsey. What was she meant to do—ask for marks out of ten?

Anxiety gnawed her stomach lining and tension tied the muscles in her shoulders but her expression was serene as she took a step towards him and fought the ridiculous urge to ask for his approval. 'Am I late?'

'You are not wearing the diamonds,' he said, noticing the absence of the jewels he had had removed from the vault that morning.

'I'm a "less is more" kind of girl.' She could not explain even to herself her reluctance to wear the jewels.

He arched a sardonic brow. 'And I'm an "if you have it flaunt it" sort of guy.'

'All right, I'll put them on,' she agreed without good grace before sweeping from the room. 'Satisfied now?' she asked when she returned a short while later wearing the jewellery. On the plus side, nobody would be looking at her now—they'd be staring at the king's ransom she wore.

Hannah watched the lift doors opening and felt her stomach go into a steep dive. She did not question the instinct that warned her not to be in an enclosed space with this man. She picked up her skirt in one hand. 'I'm fine with the stairs.'

'I'm not.'

Not anticipating the hand against the small of her back that propelled her forward, she tensed before retreating into a corner and standing there trying not to meet her own eyes in the mirrors that covered four walls of the lift.

She exited the lift a step ahead of him, almost falling out in the process.

'Relax.'

The advice drew a disbelieving laugh from the resentful recipient, who turned her head sharply and was reminded of the chandelier earrings she wore as they brushed her skin. '*Seriously?*'

The man had spent most of their flight giving her a last-minute crash course in how princesses were meant to behave. The consequences of her failing had not been spelt out, but had left her with the impression the political stability of a nation—or possibly even a continent— could be jeopardised by her saying the wrong word to the wrong person or using the wrong fork.

So no pressure, then!

'If I'd been listening to a word you said I'd be a gibbering wreck, but happily I've started as I mean to go on. I tuned you out.' She smiled at his expression, catching the flicker of shock in his eyes, and chalked a mental point in the air. Then, producing a brilliant smile, she laid a hand on his arm as they reached the double doors of the ballroom.

'I do know how to work a room, you know.'

Despite the assurance, she was actually glad to enter the room beside a figure who oozed authority. She'd been acting as a hostess for her father for years, but it was a shock to find few faces she recognised in the room.

Despite her initial misgivings, a glass of champagne later she was circulating, accepting congratulations, smiling and doing a pretty good job of lying through her clenched teeth. Until she saw a familiar figure. She went to wave, and then the man he was speaking to turned his head.

She knew, of course, that her father and Rob Preston still saw one another on a personal and professional level, but her ex-fiancé had never been invited to any event when she was present previously.

Hannah moved across the room to where her father stood chatting.

'Excuse me, can I borrow my father for one minute?'

'What's wrong, Hannah?'

'Rob is here!'

'He is one of my oldest friends. You're married now, and I think it's time we drew a line under what happened, if Rob is willing to forgive and forget.'

'I should too.' She took a deep breath. This was what happened when you put your pride before the truth. 'You're right, Dad. Fine,' she said, thinking that it was so not fine.

As the party progressed a few people began to drift outside into the courtyard, and Hannah joined them, having spent the evening avoiding Rob, who to her relief had shown no inclination to speak to her.

With the tree branches filled with white lights and the sound of laughter and music from inside drifting out through the open doors, it was a magical scene. Most people had sensibly avoided the damp grass and remained on the paved area around the pool, laughing and talking, all except a middle-aged couple who reappeared from amongst the trees. The woman's hair was mussed and her shoes were in her hand.

Hannah looked down at her own feet—they ached in the high heels that matched her gown. She wriggled her cramped toes, forcing blood back into the cramped extremities and wincing at the painful burn. What page on the princess handbook said you weren't allowed to take off your shoes and walk on the grass? It would be there along with anything else spontaneous and fun. The wistful ache in her throat grew heavier as she watched the man…maybe her husband…slide a shoe back onto the pretty woman's foot while she balanced precariously on the other. The woman tottered and her partner caught her. There was a lot of soft laughter and a brief kiss before they went back indoors.

Hannah was taking a last deep breath of fresh air and painting on a smile just as a figure emerged, his eyes scanning as if he was searching for something or someone. Her bodyguard stood out like a sore thumb, albeit one in black tie.

Hannah found herself moving backwards into the shadow of a tree. She realised she was holding her breath and closing her eyes like a child who wanted to disappear. She looked down at her hands clenched into tight fists and slowly unfurled them. The sight of the deep grooves her nails had cut into the flesh of her palm drew a fleeting frown of acknowledgement but didn't lessen her defiance.

The buzz lasted a few moments, but as the exhilaration of her small rebellion faded away she stared at her shoes sinking into the damp ground. Was this going to be her life in future? Ignoring 'don't walk on the grass' signs just to feel alive?

As rebellions went it was pathetic.

She was pathetic.

She took a deep breath and, taking her shoes off and holding them in one hand, she used the other to lift her skirt free of the damp grass as she straightened her slender shoulder. 'Man up, Hannah,' she muttered to herself as she moved towards the lights that filtered through the bank of trees.

'Hello, Hannah. I knew you wanted me to follow you.'

Hannah let out a soft yelp of shock and dropped both her shoes and skirt. The fabric trailed on the wet ground as she turned around.

The comment came from a man with a massive ego, a man who thought everything was about him.

The acknowledgement shocked Hannah more than the fact Rob had followed her. Even after she had discovered his infidelities there had been a small, irrational corner of her brain that had made excuses for him.

There were no excuses, not for him and not for her either for being so damned gullible—for not seeing past the perfect manners, the practised smile and the thoughtful gifts. She'd seen little flashes of the real Rob and she'd chosen to ignore them and the growing unease she had felt. If she hadn't walked into Sal's room and found them...

She closed her eyes to blot out the mental image, and lifted her chin. She had been dreading this moment but now that it was here...how bad could it be? She'd spent two days in a prison cell. She could definitely cope with an awkward situation.

'Hello, Rob.' He'd been drinking heavily. She could smell it even before he stepped into the patch of moonlight and she was able to see his high colour and glazed eyes. Seeing Rob when she had thought he was the love of her life had always made her stomach quiver, but now it quivered with distaste.

'No, I didn't want you to follow me. I *really* didn't.'

He looked taken aback by her reaction. Clearly I'm not following the script he wrote, she thought. Drunk or not drunk, he was still a very handsome man, the premature silvered wings of hair giving him a distinguished look, along with the horn-rimmed glasses that she had been amazed to discover were plain glass, though they gave a superficial impression of intellect and sensitivity.

But then Rob always had been more about style than substance. Deep down Hannah had always known that, she had just chosen not to think about it. But for the first time now she was struck by a softness about him. Not just the thickness around the middle that regular sessions with a personal trainer could never quite eliminate, but in his features… Had he always looked that way or was it just the contrast? She had spent the last two days in the company of a man who made granite look soft.

An image of Kamel floated into her mind: his strong-boned aristocratic features, his mobile, sensual mouth.

'Just like old times. Remember the time we brought a bottle of champagne out here and—?'

Hannah stiffened and matched his hot stare with one of cold contempt. 'That wasn't me.'

He stopped, his eyes falling as his lips compressed in a petulant line. 'Oh! She never meant anything—'

Did he even remember who *she* was? The anger and bitterness was still there, and most of all the knowledge that she had been a total fool. But now she could see the black humour in it…in him.

He was a joke.

'And now you mean nothing to me.'

As he sensed her shift of attitude, sensed he had lost his power, his expression darkened. 'That's not true and we both know it.'

'Look, Rob, Dad wanted you to be here and that's fine. But you and I are never going to be friends. Let's settle for civil…?' She gave a sigh and felt relief. This was the moment she had been dreading—coming face to face with the man she had considered the love of her life only to discover he meant nothing.

Her relieved sigh became a sharp intake of alarm as Rob lumbered drunkenly towards her, forcing Hannah to retreat until her back hit the tree trunk. She winced as the bark grazed her back through the thin fabric of her gown.

'You were meant to be with me. We are soul mates… What went wrong, Hannah?'

A contemptuous laugh came from Hannah's lips. She was too angry at being manhandled to be afraid. 'Maybe all my friends—the ones you bedded after we were engaged?' She made the sarcastic suggestion without particular rancour. Rob was pathetic.

'I told you, they meant nothing. They were just cheap…' His lips curled. 'Not like you—you're pure and perfect. I was willing to wait for you. It would have been different after we were married. I would have given you everything.' He clasped a hand to his heart.

The dramatic gesture caused Hannah's discomfort to tip over into amusement. He looked so ridiculous.

His eyes narrowed at her laugh, then slid to the jewels that gleamed against the skin of her throat. 'But I wasn't enough for you, was I?'

She swallowed; the laugh had been a bad idea. 'I think I'd better go.'

'A love match, is it? Or should that be an oil deal?' He saw her look of shock and smiled. 'People talk, and I know a lot of people.'

On the receiving end of his fixed lascivious stare, she felt sick. 'Well, I'm not pure or perfect but I am extremely pis—'

Rob, in full florid flow, cut across her. 'A work of art,' he raved. 'Sheer perfection, my perfect queen, not his—he doesn't appreciate you like I would have. I'd have looked after you…the other women, they meant nothing to me,' he slurred. 'You must know that—you are the only woman I have ever loved.'

How did I ever think he was the man of my dreams? she wondered, feeling queasy as he planted a hand on the tree trunk beside her head and leaned in closer.

Struggling not to breathe in the fumes, she countered acidly, 'Well, you know, you can't miss what you've never had.'

Having followed the spiky imprints of her heels across the wet grass, Kamel took only a few minutes to locate the couple in the tree. He didn't pause. Unable to see them, he heard their voices as with a face like thunder he charged straight through a shrub.

This wasn't a moment to stop and consider, not a moment for subtlety. He'd bent over backwards to be reasonable but she wasn't a woman who responded to reasonable. Was she pushing boundaries, checking just how far she could push him? Or maybe she simply lacked any normal sense of propriety? This wasn't about jealousy. It was one thing to have a pragmatic approach to marriage, but she had not just crossed the line, she had obliterated it!

The couple came into his line of vision about the

same moment that he mentally processed the interchange he had just heard. It was astonishing enough to stop him in his tracks.

'Well, he's welcome to you!'

Hannah struggled and failed to swallow a caustic retort to this petulant response. 'Well, the idea that I was your soul mate didn't last long, did it?'

'Bitch!' Rob snarled. 'You think you've landed on your feet now, but we all know what happens to people when they get in your husband's way…'

Hannah was shaken by the malice and ugly jealousy in his face. *Jealousy…!* She shook her head in disbelief. Perhaps he'd been acting the injured party so long he actually believed it.

The full realisation of just how lucky she had been hit home. She could have been married to him.

Her stomach gave a fresh shudder of disgust as she pulled in a breath, trying to surreptitiously ease away from him. As nice as it would have been to drop the icy dignity that had got her through that awful day, this wasn't the time and definitely not the place, she thought, to have the last word.

This could get ugly.

'They have a habit of disappearing.' He mimed a slashing action across his throat. 'So watch yourself.'

The sinister comment drew a startled laugh from her. It was clearly not the reaction Rob had wanted, as his face darkened and he grabbed for her. Things happened with dizzying speed so that later when she thought about it Hannah couldn't recall the exact sequence of events.

Kamel surged forward but Hannah was quicker. Unable to escape, she ducked and her attacker's head hit the tree trunk with a dull thud.

Her attempt to slip under his arm was less successful, and by the time Kamel reached her the man, with blood streaming from a superficial head wound, had caught her arm and swung her back.

'Bitch!'

Hannah hit out blindly with her free hand and then quite suddenly she was free. Off balance, she fell and landed on her bottom on the wet grass. When she looked up Rob was standing with one hand twisted behind his back with Kamel whispering what she doubted were sweet nothings into the older man's ear, if the white-lipped fury stamped on his face was any indication.

Rob, who had blood seeping from a gash on his head, seemed to shrink before her eyes and started muttering excuses in full self-preservation mode.

'If I ever see you in the same postcode as my wife... if you so much as *look* in her direction...' Kamel leaned in closer, his nostrils flaring in distaste at the smell of booze and fear that enveloped the man like a cloud, and told him what would happen to him, sparing little detail.

Hannah struggled to her feet imagining the headlines. 'Don't hurt him!'

The plea caused Kamel's attention to swivel from the man he held to Hannah.

'Please?'

A muscle along his jaw clenched as he stared at her. Then, with a nod that caused two invisible figures to emerge from the trees, he stood aside and the trio walked away.

'Sure you don't want to go and hold his hand?'

'I wasn't protecting him. I was protecting you.' Why

are you explaining yourself to him? she wondered. It's not as if he's going to believe you and it's not like you care what he thinks.

A look of scowling incredulity spread across his face. '*Me?* You are protecting *me*?' He had no idea why her caring about someone who was clearly an abusive loser bothered him so much, but it did.

Her eyes moved slowly up the long, lean length of his muscle-packed body. It was hard to imagine anyone who looked less like he needed looking after.

'The press could dub you something worse than The Heartbreaker Prince.' She paused and saw him absorb her comment. His anger still permeated the air around them but it simmered now where it had boiled before. 'Rob likes to play the victim. I can just see the headlines now...'

'I wasn't going to hit him, but if I had he wouldn't have been running to any scandal sheet,' he retorted, managing to sound every bit as sinister as Rob had implied he was. While Hannah believed Rob's comments were motivated by malice, there was no escaping the fact that she knew very little about the man she had married and what he was capable of.

Unwilling to release his image of her as a cold-hearted, unapproachable ice bitch, he asked, 'What the hell were you thinking of meeting him out here?'

What the hell had she been thinking about getting involved with him to begin with? The man had been mentally filed in his head as a victim. Stupid, but a victim, and now he turned out to be a... His fists clenched as he found himself wishing he had not shown restraint.

Temper fizzed through her body, sparking wrathful

blue flames in her eyes. 'Are you implying that I arranged this? Rob followed me!'

'And I followed him.' It was an impulse that he had not checked even though it was a situation that had not required his personal intervention. In fact his abrupt departure had probably caused more speculation than Hannah's.

'Why? I thought you delegated all that sort of thing.'

'There are some things that a husband cannot delegate.' She might not be wife material but she was definitely mistress material. She might be the sort of woman he would normally cross the road to avoid, but there was no denying that physically she was perfect.

'So you thought it was your duty to rescue me.' She had about as much luck injecting amusement into her voice as she had escaping his dark, relentless stare. It was becoming harder to rationalise her response to his strong personal magnetism, or control the pulse-racing mixture of dread and excitement whenever he was close by.

'Little did I know you had it all under control.'

Her clenched teeth ached at the sarcasm. 'My hero riding to the rescue yet again.'

'I thought I was rescuing your...'

'Victim?'

He dragged his smouldering glance free of her cushiony soft lips and found himself staring at her heaving bosom. 'The man is...' He said a word that she didn't understand but it was not hard to get the drift. 'What is your ex doing at our wedding party?'

The accusation made her blink. 'The word party suggests celebration. Tonight has felt more like a punishment. And yes, we all know this is my fault, though

I have to tell you that line is getting a bit boring. I'm willing to take my medicine and make nice and pretend you're almost as marvellous as you think you are, but if this marriage is going to last, and I'm talking beyond the next few seconds, it won't be on a speak-when-you're-spoken-to, walk-two-steps-behind-me way. I am *not* willing to be a doormat!'

She released a shuddering sigh and warmed to her theme. 'So from now on I expect to be treated with some damned respect, and not just in public!' Oh, God! Overwhelmed with a mixture of horror and exhilaration, she could not recall losing control of herself quite so completely in her life. Hannah brought her lashes down in a protective veil as she gulped in several shallow breaths while her heart rate continued to race.

The ice queen is dead! Long live the princess of passion! His mental headline tugged the corners of his mouth upwards, but the curve flattened out as he felt his body stir lustfully. It wasn't the physical response that bothered him; it was the strength of it and the fact it kept intruding.

Mentally and physically, discipline and order were important to Kamel. He had never made a conscious decision to compartmentalise the disparate aspects of his life, but he took the ability for granted and it enabled him to combine the role he had unexpectedly inherited and any sort of personal life.

It had not crossed his mind that being married would lead to any overlap. Tonight came under the heading of duty, with a capital D. Such occasions were more than useful, they were essential, and he *definitely* shouldn't be thinking about how she'd look naked, and how soft and inviting her mouth was. Had she just said what he thought she had? He clenched his teeth and struggled to regroup his thoughts. Focus, Kamel—but not on her mouth.

'Would I be right in thinking that was an…' he spoke slowly, winged brows drawn into a straight line, and shaking his head slightly as though the concept he was about to voice was just so off the planet as to be unreal '…*ultimatum?*'

Hannah didn't pause to analyse the weirdness in his voice. If he wanted to call it that it was fine by her! Like an angry curtain, the protective veil of her lashes lifted, but her militant response was delayed as their glances connected and the subsequent sensual jolt caused her brain to stall.

'I if…I…?'

The nerve endings in her brain might have stopped sending messages, but during that long, nerve-shredding pause those elsewhere had stepped up to fill the vacuum. She could almost feel the blood racing through her veins—it felt dark and hot like the ache low in her pelvis. She snatched a breath, let it out in a quivering sigh, and lifted her chin.

'Yes, it is, and,' she added, wagging her finger as she took a squelchy step towards him, 'if you want to know about the damned guest list why ask me? Ask Dad. I probably know half a dozen people here by first name. You're the one in the loop. I'm here to smile and take one for the team.'

'Take one for the team?'

'What else would you call it?' His outrage struck her as the height of hypocrisy. 'Apologies to your ego, but don't expect me to pretend I like the situation when we're alone!'

'No. You'll just pretend you haven't thought about what it will be like.'

'What *what* would be like?'

His slow predatory smile sent a pulse of sexual heat through her body.

'Oh, that.' She faked amusement to cover her embarrassment. 'Now? Here?' She laughed a high-pitched laugh. 'Has anyone ever mentioned your awful timing?'

'Actually, no.'

She swallowed hard, thinking, That I can believe. 'Silly me! Of course, even if you were lousy in bed they'd still tell you how marvellous you were because you're—' She broke off and finished lamely, 'You're… a prince.'

'You're a princess.'

'What?'

'You're a princess.'

As in dignified, serene, gracious, aloof…qualities that when she'd been plain old Hannah Latimer she'd had in abundance. Now she was the real deal—a real princess—she'd turned into some sort of fishwife!

It isn't me, it's him, she thought, levelling a look of breathless resentment up at his impossibly handsome face. He was the one who was making her act this way, the one who was making her feel…out of control. Because of him she was saying the first thing that popped into her head. She'd lost every vestige of mental censorship; she was saying things she didn't know she felt…

'Oh, God!' Without warning, the adrenalin wave that she'd been riding suddenly broke and she started shaking.

Watching her wrap her arms around herself, an action that didn't disguise the fact she was shaking like a leaf, Kamel felt a sharp stab of guilt. 'You've had a bad experience.' A fact he was a little late acknowledging.

She slung him a look. Anybody hearing him would think he gave a damn. 'I'm fine. Look, it was handy you turned up when you did.' He was the last person in the world she would have wanted to see her in that position, but that didn't alter the fact she had needed saving. 'And if the opportunity ever arises and some ex-girlfriend of yours comes to scratch your eyes out I'll return the favour.' By the time the last syllable had left her lips Hannah was utterly drained; her ironic smile was not weak, it was non-existent.

'So you will rescue me?' He was torn between amusement, astonishment and an uncharacteristic impulse that he firmly quashed. Comforting embraces were so *not* his style.

She felt the colour rush to her cheeks. 'You think that's funny because I'm a woman.' Hopping on one foot while she bent to try and retrieve the shoe that had been sucked into a patch of mud, she turned her head and threw him a look of frowning dislike. 'You going to stand there and watch?'

He held up his phone, his eyes trained on her bottom, the firm, curvy outline very clear against the silk of her gown. 'That really is a good look for you!'

'You dare!' she growled.

Still grinning—the grin made him look normal and nice and far too good-looking—he shrugged and slid the phone back into his pocket before he bent and grabbed the protruded strap of her shoe. It came free with a massive slurping sound.

'Well, Cinderella, you can go to the ball but I don't think that you're going to be doing much dancing in

this,' he said, shaking free the larger dollops of mud
that clung to the heel. His brows suddenly lifted.

'What?'

'I never realised,' he said, his glance transferring
from the wrecked shoe to her foot and back again, 'that
you actually have really big feet.'

Hannah's jaw dropped.

'As for women being weaker…Have you ever *seen* a
tigress protecting her young?' It was not the image of a
tigress that formed in his mind, though. It was Hannah
with a baby in her arms at her breast.

'I suppose you have.' There was an air of resignation
in her response. He'd done all the things she hadn't…
An image that she had seen in a magazine during her
last hairdresser's appointment superimposed itself over
his face: the gorgeous scantily clad model strutting her
stuff at a red-carpet event while her escort looked on
indulgently.

'I have no doubt that a woman can be fierce in defence of what she considers hers.'

'You're not mine,' she blurted, embarrassed by the
suggestion and slightly queasy. In her head the damned
supermodel was now doing things to the man she had
married that Hannah knew she never could…which was
a good thing, she reminded herself.

'And I'm not fierce. I'm…I just like to pay my debts.'

'And you shall.'

Promise, threat…Hannah was beyond differentiat-
ing between the two even in her own head. 'By having
sex with you?'

Anger drew the skin tight across his hard-boned features. 'I have no intention of negotiating sex with my
own wife,' he asserted proudly.

'You think I'm going to have sex with a man I don't like or respect?' She barely spoke above a whisper but her low voice sounded loud in the charged silence.

'You don't have to respect or like someone to want to rip off their clothes.'

'My God, you do love yourself.'

'This isn't love, but it is a strong mutual attraction.'

Heart thudding, she dodged his stare and snatched the shoe from him, grimacing as she slid her foot back in. 'Thank you.' She managed two steps before the heel snapped and threw her off balance. The jolt as she struggled to stay upright caused her chignon to come free, effectively blinding her. She took several more lopsided strides forward before she stopped and swore.

Throwing him a look that dared him to comment, she took off both shoes and threw them in a bush. Hitching her skirt a little higher, she continued barefoot, feeling his eyes in her back.

'Go on, say it!' she challenged him.

'Say what?'

'Say whatever sarcastic little gem you're just aching to say. Go ahead,' she said, opening her arms wide in invitation. 'I can take it.'

Their eyes connected and her challenging smile vanished. She dropped her arms so fast she almost lost her balance. She would have lowered her gaze had his dark, glittered stare not held her captive. The silence settled like a heavy velvet blanket around them. She had to fight for breath and fight the weird compulsion that made her want to…

'You want to take me, *ma belle*?' His eyes cancelled out the joke in his voice.

She could feel the heat inside her swell and she thought, Yes, I do. 'You can't say things like that to me.'

'What do you expect? You are a very confrontational woman.'

'I'm cold.'

'So the rumour goes, but we both know different. What were you doing with a man who wants to put you on a pedestal and worship you from afar?'

'Many girls dream of that.'

'Not you, though. You want to be touched and you looked like you'd seen a ghost when you saw him.' Kamel had made it his business to find out who the man was who was responsible for her shaken look.

Hannah heaved in a deep breath. She *longed* to be touched. She shivered; he saw it and frowned. 'You're cold.'

'Oh, and I was just getting used to the idea of being hot,' she quipped back.

He threw her a look. 'I will explain to the guests that you are feeling unwell. Rafiq will see you to your room.'

On cue the big man appeared. Hannah was getting used to it—she didn't jump, but she did accept with gratitude the wrap he placed across her shoulders.

CHAPTER EIGHT

HANNAH ACTUALLY PERSUADED Rafiq to leave her in the hallway and made her way upstairs alone. It was an area of the house that no guests had entered and it was very quiet. She found herself walking past the door to the guest suite, drawn by a need to experience the comfort of familiar things. She took the extra flight of narrow winding oak stairs hidden behind a door that led up to the next floor.

The attic rooms had been the servants' quarters years before. Later on they became the nursery and more recently a semi self-contained unit, complete with mini kitchen. She opened the door of her old bedroom and stepped inside. The paintwork was bright and fresh but it was the same colour scheme she had chosen when she was twelve. The bed was piled high with stuffed toys, and the doll's house she had had for her tenth birthday stood on the table by the window. It was like being caught in a time warp.

She picked up a stuffed toy from the pile on the bed and flicked the latch on the doll's house. The door swung open, automatically illuminating the neat rooms inside.

She stood there, a frown pleating her brow, and

waited. She didn't even recognise she was waiting until nothing happened. There was no warm glow, no lessening of tension. She didn't feel safe or secure.

In the past, she realised, this room had represented a sanctuary. She had closed the door and shut out the world. But even though the familiar things that had given her a sense of security were still the same—she had changed.

She closed the door of the doll's house with a decisive click. It was time to look forward, not back.

In the guest suite she showered and pulled a matching robe on over her silk pyjamas. Her hair hung loose and damp down her back. Leaving the steamy bathroom, she walked across to the interconnecting door and, after a pause, turned the key. Locked doors were no solution. Hugging a teddy bear had not helped, and hiding from the situation was not going to make it go away. Would talking help? Hannah didn't know, but she was willing to give it a try.

So long as he didn't construe the open door as an invitation to do more than talk.

She cinched the belt of her robe tight and walked across to the bed, trying not to think about the flare of sexual heat in her stomach as she heard his voice in her mind—*You don't have to respect or like someone to want to rip off their clothes.*

'Oh, God!'

She didn't know if the dismayed moan was in her head or she'd actually cried out, but when she opened her eyes there was no room for debate—he was no creation of her subconscious. A very real Kamel stood framed in the doorway, one shoulder wedged against the jamb, as he pulled his tie free from his neck.

'I'm glad that's over.'

He sounded almost human. He *was* human, she realised, noticing the lines of fatigue etched into his face—a fatigue that was emphasised by the shadow of dark stubble across his jaw. So he could get tired. It was a tiny chink in his armour, but she still struggled to see him suffering the same doubts and fears as the rest of the human race, and it went without saying that fatigue didn't stop him looking stupendously attractive. No, *beautiful*, she corrected, her eyes running over the angles and planes of his darkly lean face, a face that she found endlessly fascinating. She compressed her lips and closed a door on the thought. She knew it would be foolish to lower her defences around him.

He pulled the tie through his long fingers and let it dangle there, arching a sardonic brow as his dark eyes swept her face. 'So, no locked doors?'

'That was childish.'

The admission surprised him but he hid it. It was harder to hide his reaction to the way she looked. The only trace of make-up was the pink varnish on her toenails. With her hair hanging damply down her back and her face bare she looked incredibly young, incredibly vulnerable and incredibly beautiful.

There was a wary caution in the blue eyes that met his, but not the hostility that he had come to expect.

'I thought you'd be asleep by now.' The purple smudges under her eyes no longer smoothed away by a skilful application of make-up made it clear she still desperately needed sleep. Kamel reminded himself that her nightmare had been going on forty-eight hours longer than his. He felt a flash of grudging admiration for her—whatever else the woman he had married was, she was not weak.

Hannah absently rubbed the toes of one foot against the arch of the other until she saw him staring and she tucked them under her. She pushed her hair behind her ears as she admitted, 'I felt bad letting you make excuses for me. Was it awkward?' She had probably broken about a hundred unwritten rules of protocol.

'Awkward?' He arched a brow. 'You mean did anyone see you leave with—?'

'I didn't leave with him. He f—'

He held up his hands in a gesture of surrender. 'I know.'

'Me not being there. What did you say?'

'I did not go into detail. I simply told my uncle that you had retired early.' He had actually told Charles Latimer a little more. He had made it clear to his father-in-law that if he wanted his daughter to spend any time under his roof he would guarantee that Rob Preston would not be there.

'Did they believe you?'

He took a step into the room and dropped his tie onto a chair. 'Why should we care?'

The *we* was not symbolic of some new togetherness so the small glow of pleasure it gave her was totally out of proportion.

'So how long were you standing there watching?' She had gone through the scene enough times to realise that Kamel could have heard some, if not all, of the exchange with Rob.

Grave-eyed, she looked up from her contemplation of her hands and heard him say, 'Long enough.'

She ground her teeth in exasperation at this deliberately cryptic response.

'So he cheated on you?'

Oh, yes, he would have heard that bit.

'It happens.'

There was no pity in his voice; Hannah let out a tiny sigh of relief.

'Dumping him on the actual wedding day was a pretty good revenge.' Kamel understood the attraction of retribution, though, being a man to whom patience did not come easily, he struggled with the concept of a dish served cold.

'I didn't plan it.' She looked startled by the idea. 'That's when I found out.'

He looked at her incredulously. 'On the actual day?'

She nodded, experiencing the familiar sick feeling in the pit of her stomach as the memory surfaced. It had been an hour before the photographers, hairdressers and make-up artists were due to arrive. She had knocked on Sal's door under the pretext of collecting the something blue her best friend had promised her, though what she had actually wanted was reassurance—someone to tell her she was suffering from last-minute nerves and it was all normal.

'I walked in on him with Sal, my chief bridesmaid. They were… It wasn't until later that I discovered he'd worked his way through most of my circle.'

She didn't look at him to see his reaction. She told herself she was past caring whether she came across as self-pitying and pathetic, but it wasn't true. She simply didn't have the strength left to maintain the illusion.

The last few days one hit after another combined with exhaustion had destroyed her normal coping mechanisms… What pride she had left had been used up in her encounter with Rob.

'So he slept with everyone but you.'

Her eyes flew to his face. 'So you heard that too.'

He nodded. He had heard, but not quite understood. It was not a new strategy, and she was the sort of woman who was capable of inspiring obsession in susceptible men, though why a man who was willing to marry to get a woman in his bed would then choose to sleep around was more difficult to understand. Especially when the woman in question would make all others look like pale imitations.

'So the only way he could have you was marriage.' Twenty-four hours ago the discovery would not have left him with a sense of disappointment. Twenty-four hours ago he'd had no expectations that could be disappointed—he had only expected the worst of her.

His cynical interpretation caused her cobalt-blue eyes to fly wide open in shocked horror. 'No, I wanted to.' She gave a tiny grimace and added more honestly, 'I would have.' The fact was she simply wasn't a very sexual creature, which did beg the question as to why she couldn't look at Kamel or even hear his voice without feeling her insides melt. 'But he…'

Kamel watched her fumble for words, looking a million miles from the controlled woman reputed to have a block of ice for a heart, and felt something tighten in his chest.

'Apparently he wanted to worship me, not—'

'Take you to bed,' Kamel supplied, thinking the man was even more of a loser than he'd thought.

'I don't actually think he thought of me as a woman. More an addition to his art collection. He likes beautiful things...not that I'm saying I'm—'

'Don't spoil all this honesty by going coy. We both know you're beautiful. So why is it everyone thinks he's the injured party?'

'I'd prefer to be thought a bitch than an idiot.' The explanation was not one she had previously articulated. She was startled to hear the words. It was something she had not admitted to anyone before.

'And your father still invited the man here?' If a man had treated his daughter that way he would have— Kamel dragged a chair out from the dressing table, swung it around and straddled it.

'Oh, it was easier to let him think I'd had second thoughts. They've been friends for a long time and Dad had already had an awful time telling everyone the wedding was cancelled. A lot of people turned up and it was terrible for him—'

'And you were having such a great day...'

Hannah's protective instincts surfaced at the implied criticism of her father.

'You were right. It was my fault. This is my fault, totally my fault.'

He shook his head, bemused by her vehemence, and protested, 'You didn't ask the guy to jump you!'

'No, not Rob. Getting arrested, getting you mixed up in it, terrifying Dad half to death. If he has another heart attack, it would be down to me.'

It was news to Kamel that he had had one. The man certainly hadn't been scared enough to change his lifestyle. 'I think a doctor might disagree. Your father does not hold back when it comes to saturated fat.'

'You're trying to make me feel better.'

He studied her face. 'It's clearly not working.'

'Why are you being nice? It's my fault we had to get married. I should have waited for help. I shouldn't have left the Land Rover. I shouldn't have been there at all.' She shook her head, her face settling into a mask of bitter self-recrimination as she loosed a fractured sob. 'All the things you said.'

'The village did get the vaccines, and the help they needed.'

Lost in a morass of self-loathing, she didn't seem to hear him. 'I couldn't even help myself, let alone anyone else. I was only there to prove a point. I've spent my life playing it safe.' She planted her hand flat on her heaving chest and lifted her tear-filled eyes to his.

'I always played by the rules. I even wanted a safe man... I didn't even have the guts to do what I really wanted.' She shook her head slowly from side to side and sniffed. 'I went to university and did a course I had absolutely no interest in rather than stand up to my dad. I got engaged to a man who seemed safe and solid, and when he turned out to be a total bastard did I learn? No, I got engaged to a man I knew would never hurt me because...I always go for the safe option.'

He let out a long, low whistle. '*Dieu*, I wanted you to take responsibility for your own actions—not the financial crisis, world hunger and bad days in the week that have a Y in them.'

Startled, Hannah lifted her head. Her eyes connected with his and a small laugh was shaken from her chest. 'I just want...' She stopped, her husky voice suspended by tears, her control still unravelling so fast she could not keep pace.

With a muttered imprecation he dropped down to his knees beside the bed and pushed the hair back from her damp face.

'What do you want?'

Her wide brimming blue eyes lifted. 'I just want to be…to feel…not like this.' She gnawed at her lower lip and brought her lashes down in a protective veil. 'Sorry, I don't know why I'm saying this stuff to you.'

Responding to the painful tug in his chest, Kamel stood up and gently pushed her down. Sliding his hand behind her knees, he swung her legs onto the bed, pulling a pillow under her head before joining her.

'Go to sleep,' he said, lowering his long length onto the bed beside her.

'I can't sleep. I have dreams that I'm back in that cell and he is…' She struggled to sit up. A light touch on her breastbone stopped her rising and after a moment she stopped fighting. 'I can't sleep.'

He touched a finger to her lips. 'Move over.' Pausing to slide an arm under her shoulders, he pulled her head back onto his shoulder.

'Why are you being nice to me?' she whispered into his neck—and then a moment later she was asleep.

Kamel, who preferred his own bed, realised this was the first time in his life that he had slept with a woman, in the literal sense. Only he wasn't sleeping and he seriously doubted he would. A state of semi-arousal combined with seething frustration was not in his experience conducive to sleep, especially when there was zero chance of doing anything to relieve that frustration.

On the plus side at least the scenery was rather special. Asleep she looked like a wanton angel. There were probably a lot of men out there who would be willing to give up a night's sleep to look at that face. He was aware of an ache of desire somewhere deep inside him so strong it hurt. Ignoring it didn't make it go away, and not looking at her was not an option because his eyes, like the north arrow on a compass, kept going back to the same place.

So in the end he didn't question it; he just accepted it.

Hannah fought her way out of a dream, struggling to shake off the lingering sense of dread.

'Wake up. You're safe.'

Still half asleep, she opened her eyes, saw his face and sighed. 'I love your mouth,' she said before pressing her own lips to the sensual curve.

'Hannah.' He pulled away.

She blinked, the confusion slowly filtering from her.

'Sorry, I thought you were a dream.' She had kissed him and he hadn't kissed her back. He hadn't done anything. Once was bad, but twice was humiliating.

'I thought you were a bitch.' And that had made the politically expedient marriage not right, but not this wrong. 'I was wrong.'

'Not a bitch.' Great, I feel so much better.

Suddenly she felt very angry. She struggled to sit up. 'So what is wrong with me?' she asked, looking down at him for once. 'I mean, there has to be, doesn't there? I've been engaged twice, and no sex.' Hannah could hear the words coming out of her mouth. She knew she shouldn't be saying them but she couldn't stop. 'Now I'm married, and you don't even want to kiss me!'

With a dry sob she flung herself down and rolled over, her back to him.

It was the sight of her heaving shoulders that snapped

the last threads of Kamel's self-imposed restraint. 'Don't cry,' he begged.

'I'm not crying,' she retorted, sniffing. 'I've just re-alised something. I don't know why I was so bothered about marrying you.'

'I'm flattered.'

Hannah rolled over until she was able to stare straight at him. She had barely registered his dry comment, as her thoughts—dark ones—were turned inward.

'I can't even do sex so what would the point have been of waiting for someone who can give me...*more*?'

Kamel had never felt any driving desire to be a with a woman who considered him her soul mate. On the other hand, being basically told that you were an *all right* consolation prize for someone with low expectations was a bit below the belt even for someone with his ego.

Well at least the pressure is off, he thought. She's not expecting much of you!

His sudden laugh made her look up.

'So you are willing to settle for me?'

A small puzzled indent appeared between her feath-ery brows as she struggled to read his expression. 'Doesn't seem like I have a lot of choice in the matter, does it?' She glanced at the ring on her finger.

'So you are willing to...how did you put it—take one for the team?'

'I thought you'd have been glad to know that you don't have to pretend, that I don't expect—'

'Much?'

This drew an exasperated hiss from Hannah.

'Well, the mystery of why you're a virgin is solved,' he drawled. 'You talked them to sleep.'

With an angry snort Hannah reached behind her for

one of the pillows that had been spread across the bed while she slept.

'I don't think so, angel.'

Somewhere between picking it up and lobbing it at him she found the pillow was removed from her fingers and a moment later she was lying with her wrists held either side of her head, with his body suspended above her.

She could hear a sound above the thunderous clamour of her frantic heartbeat—it was her panting. She couldn't draw enough air into her lungs to stop her head spinning. His mouth was a whisper away from hers; she could feel the warmth of his breath on her lips.

The dark intent shining in his heavy-lidded eyes made the heat prickle under her skin.

'Just—' he ran his tongue lightly across the surface of her lips '—how—' he kissed one corner of her mouth '—much—' he kissed the other corner, smiling as she gave a deep languid sigh and lifted her head towards him '—are you willing—' he kissed her full on her trembling lips before trailing a series of burning kisses down the smooth column of her neck '—to take for the team?'

'I…don't…God…stop…please don't stop!' she moaned, terrified at the thought he might.

Her beating heart stumbled as his beautiful mouth came crashing down to claim her lips. The relief she felt as she opened her mouth to him in silent invitation was quickly consumed by the response of her body to the thrust of his tongue: low in her belly each carnal incursion caused a tight clenching; between her legs the dampness ran hot.

While he kissed her with something approaching

desperation his hands were busy in her hair, on her face, sliding under her nightdress to caress the warm skin of her smooth thighs then reaching to curve over one taut, tingling breast. As he found the loop of the top button and slipped it off his patience snapped and he tugged hard, causing the remainder to tear from the fabric as he pushed the two sides apart to reveal her breasts to his hungry stare.

She arched up into him as he took first one turgid rosy peak and then the other into his mouth, leaving her gasping and moaning; her entire body reached fever pitch in seconds. He pressed a kiss to her belly and the frustration building inside got higher and higher as his finger slid lower and lower, inscribing a tingling line between her aching breasts and then down her quivering belly.

Nakedness turned out not to be inhibiting—it was liberating. She lifted her arms and tugged him down to her. The slow, drugging kisses continued as she arched, pushing her breasts up against his hard chest, frantic for skin-to-skin contact. Her hands ran down the strong, smooth lines of his back, revealing his strength, his sleek hardness.

The liquid heat in her belly had a new urgency as he began to fumble with the buckle on his belt. A moment later she heard the sound of his zipper.

Afflicted by a belated bout of virginal modesty, she closed her eyes, opening them only when he took her hands in his and curled them around the hot, silky, rock-hard erection.

She couldn't prevent the little gasp that was wrenched from somewhere in her chest.

At least make an effort to look like you know what you're doing, Hannah.

The voice in her head was critical but he was not.

A deep feral moan was wrenched from his throat as her fingers began to experimentally tighten then release the pressure around the throbbing column. His eyes drifted shut and he began to breathe hard. Then without warning he took her hand and tipped her back onto the pillows.

She let out a series of fractured gasps that terminated in a higher-pitched wailing moan as he touched the dampness between her thighs.

'This is good?' he slurred thickly as he continued to stroke and torment, making her ache everywhere.

She nodded vigorously and pushed against the heel of his hand. 'Oh, yes...very good.'

He raised himself up, took her hand and, holding her gaze, laid it against his chest. Not looking away from her eyes for an instant, he fought his way out of his shirt and flung it away.

'You're beautiful,' she breathed, unable to take her greedy stare off his tautly muscled, gleaming torso.

Kamel swallowed. He wanted her badly. At that moment he could not think of anything he had wanted more.

'I've wanted to be inside you since the moment I saw you.' He pushed against her, letting her share the relentless ache in his groin.

'I want that too.' Delighting in the discovery of an inherent sensuality, she parted her thighs.

Responding to the silent invitation with a fierce groan, he came over her and settled between her legs. She had expected to tense at that final point of no return, but she relaxed. It was easy, not so painful as she'd imagined—and then as her body tightened around him she felt her blood tingle and squeezed her eyelids tight, just focusing on all the things that were happening inside and Kamel filling her so wonderfully, Kamel moving, pushing her somewhere…

Then just as the itch got too intense to bear, she found out where she was going and let go. She heard Kamel cry out, felt the flood of his release and wrapped her legs around him, afraid that she'd be washed away, lost.

She wasn't. She finished up where she'd started, under Kamel.

Some time later she did recover the power of speech but she couldn't do full sentences.

'Wow!' she said, staring at the ceiling. Beside her, his chest heaving, Kamel was doing the same.

He turned his head. 'For a first effort, I have to say you show promise.'

This time he did not prevent her lobbing the pillow at his head, but in the subsequent tussle it ended on the floor and they ended up in a tangle of limbs.

CHAPTER NINE

WHEN HANNAH WOKE it was light and she was alone.

She felt the bed beside her—it was still warm. She gave a wistful sigh. She hadn't expected him to be there but it would have been...no, *nice* was not part of their relationship. Though yesterday she would have said the same about sex. It was crazy, in a good way, that the area of this marriage she'd thought would be hardest—that she had been dreading—turned out to be the easiest and the most pleasurable.

She gave a voluptuous sigh and smiled. It had been easy, natural, and totally incredible.

She sat up suddenly, her eyes flying wide in dawning alarm. She was assuming that it would be happening again soon and often. But what if last night wasn't going to be something that happened regularly? While she hadn't known what she was missing, celibacy had been easy—but now she did know. She gave an anxious sigh.

It would be...terrible. One night and Kamel was her drug of choice; she was a total addict.

She showered and dressed in record time, wondering if she should just come out and ask him. She was on her way to see Sarah when she literally bumped into him.

He was dressed in running shorts and a tee shirt and looked so gorgeous that she was struck dumb.

'I've been running.'

She nodded, and thought that there really was such a thing as being paralysed with lust. If she'd stayed in bed, would he have walked in? Her eyelids drooped as she imagined him peeling off his top and—

'And you are…?' he prompted.

Hannah started guiltily, the colour rushing to her cheeks. 'I'm going to see Sarah, and Olive and the puppies.'

'Sarah?'

'The cook…but she's more than that. I'll be ready for the flight.'

'I'm sure you will. See you then.'

He actually saw her much sooner. He had showered and was beginning to wade through his emails when he heard her bedroom door slam, quite loudly. A slamming door was not in itself indicative of a problem. He cut off the pointless line of speculation and focused on work. Luckily his ability to ignore distractions was almost as legendary as his reputation for zero patience for those undisciplined individuals who brought their personal lives into the workplace.

Five minutes later he closed his laptop, realising that in the interests of efficiency it would save time if he just went and checked she was all right.

He didn't ask. It was obvious she wasn't.

'What's wrong?'

Hannah stopped pacing and turned around. 'Nothing.'

He arched a brow.

'I can't tell you.' She pressed a fist to her mouth.

He walked over, removed her fist and said calmly, 'What can't you tell me?'

'I walked in on Sarah with Dad, They were...' her eyes slid towards the bed '...you know.'

Kamel blinked. 'You walked in on your father having sex with the cook?'

She covered her ears with her hands. 'Don't say it out loud!'

Kamel fought back a smile. 'It always comes as a shock to a child when they learn their parents have sex.'

'I know my father has sex. I just don't want to see it!'

This time he couldn't fight the smile. 'It's going to be tough for him—'

'No, they didn't see me. That really would be awful. No, the door was half open and...' She stopped, closed her eyes and shook her head, shuddered. 'I backed out and ran.'

'I imagine you did.' His lips quivered.

'This isn't funny,' she protested.

Unable to stop himself, Kamel began to laugh.

A laugh bubbled in her throat. 'I want to delete the image from my mind. I really do.' The laugh escaped.

Five minutes later Hannah was all laughed out, and Kamel was sprawled on the bed, one arm under his head, telling her that when he had walked in he had thought there had been some major disaster.

'Your face! Honestly it was...' He sat up and sighed. 'I should get back to it. I've got a stack of—'

'I'm sorry I stopped you working.'

He gave a sudden grin. 'No, you're not.' He patted the bed beside him and leaned back against the pillows.

Hannah came across the room, hesitating only a moment before she manoeuvred herself to sit straddling him.

'I like your thinking,' he purred, his eyes flaring hot as she pulled the top over her head. 'I like other things even more.'

'Are you all right?'

Hannah shrugged and put down the book she had been holding. Her interest in the novel was feigned but her confusion was not. 'With flying, you mean...?'

A spasm of irritation crossed his face. 'Your father and the cook? It happens—the attraction between people from different backgrounds.'

Her brow smoothed and she laughed. 'You think I didn't know? Or that I have some sort of problem with it?'

His brows lifted. 'You are telling me you don't?'

In defiance of his open scepticism, she shook her head from side to side. 'Beyond the fact that discovering that your parent has a sex life, which is a bit...uncomfortable...no, I like Sarah.'

'And the fact she is the cook?'

'I know you think I'm a snob. She's probably the best thing that has ever happened to my dad. I just wish he... I wish they'd come out into the open about it. I wish...' She caught the expression on Kamel's face and, taking it for boredom, brought her ramble to a juddering stop.

It would be a massive mistake to assume that, because Kamel had seemed to have an endless fascination with her body, his interest extended beyond the bedroom. She knew that any woman would only ever be a substitute for the woman he had lost, Amira. Kamel must have thought nothing could be worse than seeing the woman he loved happy with another man—until he'd found out that there was something much worse.

'You wish?'

I wish I could look at you and not ache. 'Forget it.'

It was sex—fantastic, incredible sex—but she had to stop thinking about it.

'I don't want to bore you.'

He unclipped his seat belt and stretched his long legs out in front of him. 'Don't worry. If you bore me I'll let you know,' he promised.

'I think that Sarah deserves more than to be a secret...' She gave a self-conscious shrug.

'Maybe this Sarah is happy with just sex.'

She looked away. Was there a message, a warning even, in there for her?

'Maybe she is,' Hannah agreed without conviction. She turned her head to angle a curious look at his face. 'You expected me to be devastated to find my father in bed with the cook, didn't you? Sarah has been my father's mistress for the past five years that I know of. Probably longer.

'The truth is I've no idea how Sarah is content to be treated like some sort of...' She stopped, wondering whether that wasn't exactly what she was doing. 'We both worry about her.'

'We?'

'Sarah's daughter, Eve, and I. She's a year younger than me.' She noticed the airstrip below and pressed her face to the window to get a better view. 'Is it far to the villa?'

'Not by helicopter.'

'Helicopter?'

He nodded. 'It beats being stuck in a traffic jam.'

That, she thought, was a matter of opinion.

As the helicopter landed Hannah closed her eyes—but even with them squeezed tightly shut she retained the stomach-clenching image of them falling directly into the ocean.

The pilot landed the helicopter smoothly but Hannah appeared oblivious, her eyes tightly shut, hands clenched into white-knuckled fists. Her lips continued to move, presumably in a silent prayer. Watching her silent but abject terror, he had felt like an inconsiderate monster for subjecting her to what had clearly been an ordeal. He wanted to be irritated with her but she looked so fragile, her big eyes reminding him of a scared child. But she wasn't a child. She was all woman—*his* woman. The reminder should have made him feel resentful— after all, he was paying the price for her stupidity—but instead the thought came with an accompanying shaft of possessive pride.

'You can breathe now.'

Hannah opened her eyes and collided instantly with Kamel's dark, intense stare. The feeling of falling into the abyss didn't go away; if anything it intensified as, with a thudding heart, she fumbled with her seat belt.

'What time is it?' she heard herself ask.

'You have somewhere you need to be, *ma belle*?' His eyes drifted to the wide, full, plump curve of her lips and he felt the barely damped fires of passion roar into life.

She was the most responsive woman he had ever had in his bed. He still couldn't get his head around the fact that the cool, distant virgin had turned out to be

KIM LAWRENCE

a warm, giving woman who held nothing back. In the middle of figuring how long he could wait until he got her into bed again he found himself wondering about the sequence of events that had led her to hide her passionate nature behind a cool mask.

He had never felt the need to look beyond the surface of a beautiful woman, and he had no intention of looking too far now.

'Relax.'

This struck Hannah as ironic advice from someone who, as far as she could tell, never totally switched off, someone who was never *totally* off duty. Duty always came first with Kamel. If it didn't, they wouldn't be married.

While Kamel was speaking to the pilot she took the opportunity to look through the glass without fear of gibbering. The helipad was not, as it had seemed, positioned perilously on the cliff's edge, but several hundred feet away, and screened from the villa by an avenue of trees. Hannah could just make out through the branches the terracotta roof, but the rest of the villa was totally concealed by the lush greenery.

Above the whirr of the blades she could hear the men's voices. She was struggling to catch what they were saying when it happened. Previously it had only occurred when she was in a small space—the lift between floors, or in the pantry in the kitchen—but now there were no walls to close in on her, just glass. Even so, the urge to escape and the struggle to breathe were equally strong.

Her knees were shaking but Hannah was so anxious to get back on terra firma that she didn't wait. She didn't wait for Kamel, who was still deep in conversation with the pilot; she just had to get out of there.

Hannah watched as her luggage was piled onto a golf cart by two men—one of whom she had almost flattened when she missed the bottom step in her anxiety to escape the helicopter. Both men nodded respectfully to Kamel and vanished through an arch cut in the neatly trimmed green foliage.

Hannah could feel Kamel's disapproval—she'd sensed it before but it had upped several notches.

'You should have said that you have a problem with helicopters.' Seeing the surprise in the blue eyes that flew to his face, he smiled. 'Yes, it was obvious.' He took one of her hands in his and turned the palm upwards, exposing the grooves her nails had cut into her palms. 'Any tenser and I think you'd have snapped. Why on earth didn't you say anything?'

'Why didn't you ask?' she countered, wishing he would release her hand, while feeling an equally strong reluctance to break the contact. His thumb was moving in circles across her palm, and each light, impersonal caress sent wave after wave of disproportionate pleasure through her body. But then there was no sense of proportion in her response to Kamel when she thought about how completely and how quickly she had given up control, and it terrified her.

She tensed as his eyes flicked from her palm to her face. 'You have a point,' he conceded. 'Should I call them back?' He gestured in the direction of the now invisible carts. 'I thought you might like to stretch your legs, but if you prefer—?'

'No, a walk would be good.' A night of mind-blowing sex might be better, though. The reciprocal warm glow in his eyes made her wonder if underneath all the politeness an alternative dialogue wasn't just going on in his own head too. But who knew what went on in the mind of a man like Kamel?

She couldn't begin to intellectualise her response to him. How could she be standing here, thinking about him ripping her clothes off?

Shocked and more than a little excited by the thought, she lowered her gaze. 'You don't have to act as though this is a real honeymoon,' she murmured. It was duty for him. And for her it was...all so new she had no name for what she was feeling. But the ferocity of it scared her. 'I know it's window dressing.' It had never crossed her mind that she could want a man's touch this badly, to the extent it was hard to think past it.

'I like touching you.'

For a shocked instant she thought she had voiced her secret longing. 'Oh!'

'The sex wasn't window dressing.'

Experiencing a wave of lust so immense she felt as though she were drowning, she closed her fingers tight around his hand. She swallowed, suddenly unable to meet his eyes, her heart thudding fast in her chest. She felt bizarrely shy. The emotion paralysed her vocal cords and brought a rosy flush to her cheeks.

'We are expected to make a baby, so why not enjoy it?'

The glow faded. Afterwards, with his duty done, would he seek his pleasure elsewhere? His life was all duty—he would probably be glad to escape it.

'It's not far to the villa,' he said as they reached the top of the incline they had been climbing.

Hannah gasped. 'It's beautiful, Kamel.'

'Yes,' he agreed. 'So, you think you might be able to stick it here for a few days?'

How few? she wondered. And what happened after that? But then she closed down that line of thought. Better to enjoy the here and now and not think too far ahead.

'I might cope.' She looked at the sugar-pink painted villa that seemed to cling to the edge of the cliff.

'I even know where the kitchen is here.'

She lifted her brows and tried to look serious but a laugh bubbled through. 'I'm more interested in the pool today.' She mimed a fanning gesture with her hand.

'That sounds good.' He withdrew the vibrating phone from his pocket and looked at the screen. 'Sorry, I might have to take a rain check on that.' You did not hang up on a king, even—or maybe especially—if that king was your uncle. 'I really have to take this. Go have an explore.'

Hannah nodded, lowering her eyes to hide the irrational stab of hurt. It was crazy to mind that she was not at the top of his priorities.

CHAPTER TEN

WHEN SHE SLID open the wardrobes that lined one wall of the dressing room and found they weren't empty, Hannah thought she was seeing an example of Kamel's famed forward thinking.

The beginnings of a frown began to form on her brow as she lifted the top item on the stack of underclothes. Size-wise—not to mention style-wise—it was really not her! A few moments later as she flicked through the row of expensive garments the frown was fully formed and it had become obvious that even Kamel did not think of everything! She felt her self-righteous anger reach new heights as she picked up the faint but distinctive scent that clung to the garments. He thought it was fine to have his wife share wardrobe space with his mistress… maybe the economy appealed to him!

She felt physically sick, but, in the grip of a masochistic urge she could not fight, Hannah stretched out a shaking hand to the neatly folded stacks of underclothes on the shelf. They were not items that could be classed utilitarian or, by any stretch of the imagination, tasteful.

Hannah pushed the lot onto the floor and, with a vengeful cry, grabbed the most tacky, glittering thing she could see. It turned out to be a gold beaded dress with a designer label, and a split so low on the back the wearer couldn't possibly have worn any underclothes.

Had she been this angry when she discovered Rob's multiple infidelities? Hannah was incapable by this point of questioning the degree of her reaction. She was incandescent with rage. Not only did she not want a second-hand G-string, she didn't want a second-hand man!

How stupid had she been to even begin to let down her guard with him, to trust him? Experience had taught her you couldn't trust a man.

Eyes flashing, back stiff, she stalked down the glass-roofed corridor that connected the more modern bedroom wing to the main house and into the open-plan living room where she had left Kamel. The room was empty but the echoing sound of her heels on the terracotta tiles drew a call from outside.

'Come have a swim!'

Responding to the invitation with narrow-eyed determination, she exited the patio doors just as Kamel levered himself from the infinity pool.

Rising in one seamless motion, he stood with the towel he had retrieved from the pool's edge in one hand, but he made no attempt to dry himself. The water continued to stream down his lean brown body, making his skin glisten like polished copper in the sun.

She caught her breath. Not even a full-blown rage could protect her from her visceral reaction to the sight of six feet four inches of dripping-wet Kamel. She was helpless to control her quivering response to the image of earthy power in his broad shoulders, deeply muscled chest, and strong thighs. She swallowed, knowing she was staring but helpless to stop herself. The moisture clinging to his skin emphasised each individual slab of muscle in his flat washboard torso, and he didn't carry an ounce of surplus flesh to blur the perfect muscle definition.

Kamel was all hard, primal male; he represented a physical male ideal combined with an earthy sexuality that had made him a deadly combination—the perfect lover. As she stared at him Hannah could feel her anger slipping away, feel the heat build inside her. She sucked in a short shocked breath, her eyes widening in disgust with herself as she recognised what was happening.

· He looped the towel around his neck and she turned her head slightly to avoid the rippling contraction that moved across his flat torso as he lifted his arm to drag a hand across his wet hair.

She would *not* turn into one of those women who put up with all sorts of crap from a man just because he was…well…good in bed. And Kamel was, in her defence. There were probably not enough superlatives to describe just *how* good he was! She smothered the internal sigh and thought that he'd certainly had enough practice at it. It was not by accident they had dubbed him The *Heartbreaker* Prince!

One corner of his sensual mouth lifted in a lazy half-smile, but there was nothing lazy about the gleam in his eyes. She pressed a hand to her stomach—not that it helped to calm the fluttering.

'I think you're a little overdressed, angel,' he rasped throatily.

The same could not be said of him. The black shorts he wore low on his hips left little to the imagination—and hers was rioting as she raised the level of her stare.

'There are some swimsuits in the pool house.'

She closed her mouth with a firm and audible snap.

Clutching the dress in one hand and her anger in the other, she slung him a contemptuous look that would have frozen a normal man stone dead in his tracks. The man she had married gave a here-we-go-again look and dragged some of the excess moisture from his hair with one hand, sending a shower of silver water droplets over her heated skin.

'I just bet there are, but I'm not too keen on wearing other women's cast-offs—or, for that matter, sleeping with them!'

He responded to her hostility with a long, slow, considering look. *'Right.'*

He didn't add *I see* because he didn't. When she had left him a few minutes earlier the sexual promise in her blue eyes... Well, if she hadn't left when she had, he had been within an undiplomatic hair's breadth of doing the unthinkable—slamming the phone down on his uncle with the explanation, *I need to make love to my wife.*

Acknowledging the strength of that need had been what had driven him to the pool. He hadn't spared his body—the relentless pace through the water should have left him incapable of breath, let alone lust, but the ache was still there, and now she was looking at him as though he had just been found guilty of waging a hate campaign against kittens!

He ground his teeth at the sheer, unremitting frustration of it all. He tilted his head, a dark scowl forming on his wide forehead as he fished for a word that summed up his life before Hannah had come into it. *Centred.*

At another time he might have appreciated the black irony of the situation, but at that moment, with frustrated desire clenched like a knot, the humour passed him by. He had married her, resenting both the sense of duty that made him step up and the woman herself. And now, days later, he wanted her so badly he could barely string a coherent thought together. He was utterly consumed by it.

Not his type…well, that self-delusion had lasted about five seconds! Hannah was every man's type and once you saw the woman behind the cool mask… He shook his head, his fine-tuned steel trap of a mind finding it impossible to rationalise the fascination she exerted for him, the all-consuming need he felt to possess her and to lose himself in her.

It was just sex, he told himself, recognising an uncharacteristic tendency to over-analyse in his train of thought. Why try and read anything else into it? He'd married a woman he couldn't keep his hands off. But there was always a flip side, no heaven without hell. Not only did she have the ability to stretch the boundaries of sexual pleasure, she also had the ability to drive him crazy with her mood swings.

He forced his eyes from her face to the garment in her hand. Her mood seemed out of proportion with a wardrobe malfunction. He struggled to school his features into something that conveyed an interest he did not feel—he was more interested in peeling off her clothes than discussing fashion.

'You want to show me a new dress?'

Her brows hit her hairline. He actually thought she wanted to parade around and ask his approval!

'I suppose you've never seen this before?' Her voice shook almost as much as her hand did as she held out the backless, frontless, totally tasteless garment.

Recognition clicked in his brain. 'I have.' He had

little interest in women's clothes but this one had been hard to forget—as was the evening that had gone with it.

He hadn't been the intended victim or beneficiary of the provocative number. Neither, it turned out, had Charlotte begged him to escort her to the glittering premiere for the pleasure of his company. He and the dress had been part of her revenge on her ex-husband. Bizarrely, although Charlotte had been glad to be out of her marriage, she had resented the fact her ex had moved on too—especially as the woman he had moved on to was a younger version of herself.

'You're angry.' His eyes slid down her body, over the slim curves and long, long legs. She was, he decided, totally magnificent. 'I know because your eyes turn from summer sky to stormy sea when you're mad.'

'It can work once, even twice, but I have to tell you, Kamel, that the staring-deep-into-my-eyes thing has a shelf life,' she lied. 'So don't try and change the subject.'

'What was the subject?' he asked, continuing to stare deep into her eyes, causing major and probably permanent damage to her frazzled nervous system.

'Your girlfriend's choice of clothes. Oh, incidentally, I'm *totally* fine with sharing my wardrobe space with your harem, though I have to tell you that they are not my size!'

'I know,' he said, his fingertips twitching as he transferred his stare to Hannah's heaving breasts. They fitted almost perfectly into his palms, soft, firm and... He took a deep swallow and lifted his gaze. 'Charlotte has had help in that area. They were, I believe, an engagement present from her ex.'

Her chin went up as she enquired in a deceptively soft voice, 'Are you suggesting I need help in that area?'

The icy question drew a low smoky laugh from him. 'You are *perfect* in that area.' The humour faded from his face, leaving a restless hunger. She was perfect. His perfect lover.

The hunger in his stare as much as his flattering words brought hot colour flying to her cheeks. But this heat was mild compared to the surge of sexual warmth that settled deep in her pelvis and spread. Her mask of disdain was rice-paper thin as she gave a sniff and tossed her head.

'I have no interest,' she informed him icily. 'Not in what your idea of perfect is, or the surgical procedures your girlfriend has had, or who paid for them.' Her haughty delivery vanished as the strength of her feelings became impossible to disguise. 'I just have an interest in being treated with a modicum, a bare *modicum* of respect while we are sharing a—' on the brink of saying bed, she stopped herself; the chain of thought already set in motion was less easy to stall '—roof!' she improvised, seeing his muscled body sleek with sweat, his face taut in a mask of need.

'I'm sorry you were upset. I gave instructions for the room to be cleared.'

'*Cleared!*' she parroted, her face twisted in an ironic grimace of disgust. 'I would have thought *fumigated* would have been more appropriate when we're talking about the sort of woman who would wear this!' She directed a look of lip-curling distaste at the garment, which was a perfect example of the adage money couldn't buy class.

'Don't you think you're overreacting to what is, after

all, a simple housekeeping error? I'll speak to someone and it won't happen again.'

'You mean the next time your girlfriend leaves her clothes you'll have them tidied away *before* I arrive? My God,' she flung with sarcastic appreciation. 'I'm one hell of a lucky woman to have married such a considerate man.'

'I will not be seeing Charlotte again.' Though the lady had made it quite clear that she did not see marriage as an obstacle to continuing their relationship.

'I do not want to know her name.' Or hear how good she is in bed, Hannah thought, experiencing a wave of jealousy that felt like a knife between her ribs. She paled and lifted her hands to her ears, squeezing her eyes shut.

Unfortunately neither action blotted out the knowledge that there would be women in slutty outfits sharing his bed in the future. They just wouldn't be called Charlotte.

She drew in a deep shuddering breath, her temper reaching boiling point in the time it took her to drag air into her lungs. 'So you think I'm *overreacting*?' she quivered incredulously. 'I'm curious—are you *trying* to be an insensitive, hateful slob?'

I'm curious—are you trying to look like a tart?

Kamel laughed as he recalled his response to Charlotte in the dress his bride held in a death grip. But then he saw Hannah's face. 'I'm not laughing at you.'

'Oh, you're laughing with me. I feel *so* much better.'

His jaw clenched as he fought to contain his increasing irritation. Sexual frustration had already eaten deep chunks out of his self-control without his dealing with her emotional antics. He took a deep breath and de-

cided he would rise above it and be reasonable, even
if she wasn't!

'I wasn't thinking about you. I was thinking about
Charlotte.'

If Kamel ever found himself faced with an angry
and unreasonable woman he generally removed himself
from that scene. By choice he avoided women likely to
indulge in scenes, but you couldn't always tell and it
paid to have a plan B.

He should have walked. She was asking him to explain his actions, and no woman had ever done that.

Looking into her eyes was like staring straight into
a storm. Though storms were preferable to thinking too
much about the flash of desperate hurt he had seen in
those shimmering depths. Crazily, of all the emotions
he was struggling to contain the one that rose to the
surface—the compelling urge to wipe that hurt away.
It made no sense. It had been her decision to enact a
Greek tragedy when given the same circumstances most
women would have chosen to tactfully ignore it.

'Look. I'm sorry that the room was not cleared. I'll
have t—'

'You're crazy if you think I am going to sleep in that
bedroom with you!'

His jaw tightened. 'You know something? I'm starting to feel quite nostalgic for Hannah the ice queen.'
He jammed his thumbs into the waistband of his shorts
and glared at her. 'Just what is your problem, anyway?
I had a sex life before we were married.' He lifted one
shoulder in a half-shrug. 'Having sex does not make me
some sort of weird pervert. Most people would think
that it makes me a lot more normal than a woman who

is so uptight and controlling that she saves herself for marriage.'

'So now I'm not normal? Well, let me ease your mind on one thing. I sure as hell wasn't waiting for you!'

'And yet, you can't get enough of me in bed.'

'It's the novelty value.'

He clenched his teeth and glared at the gold gown in her hands. 'Give me that damned thing.'

She looked into his dark eyes and felt the answering passions surface. Heart thudding like a trip hammer, she ignored the hand extended to her and shook her head.

'You're being very childish. I have had other women. This can hardly be a surprise to you.'

Of course it wasn't—so why the hell was she acting like this?

'I don't give a damn about your girlfriends!' she contended, snapping her fingers to show how little she cared. 'You can have a damned harem for all I care!'

'I'm glad you explained that. So *this*—' his hand sketched a toe-to-head line in the air '—is someone who doesn't care a jot? If you hadn't explained I might,' he drawled, 'have thought it was jealousy.'

Her reaction to the suggestion was dramatic. The colour that had flooded her face receded, leaving her eyes a deep well of colour.

'This isn't jealousy,' she denied, trying desperately to think of an alternative and failing. 'This is wanting to be treated with respect.'

'Am I asking you to hide in the damned shadows?' The woman, he decided, took irrationality to new uncharted levels. 'This has gone on long enough. Hand it over.'

He caught the hem of the dress and Hannah responded with teeth-gritting determination, pulling it into her chest with such force she heard the sound of fabric tearing. She was clinging on so hard that when he pulled the dress she came with it.

To absorb the impact of her soft body into his, Kamel took an automatic step back and felt his foot hit the edge of the pool just as Hannah lifted her gaze.

She saw the intent gleaming in his dark eyes and shook her head. 'You wouldn't!'

His smile was answer enough.

She hit the water yelling a warning and spluttered as the water filled her nose and throat. His arm was wrapped around her waist as they both surfaced. When the water cleared from her eyes she saw he was laughing. She opened her mouth and Kamel pressed a hard kiss to it before he let go, kicking away from her.

She lifted a hand to her mouth. Thinking only of the kiss and not the fact there were several feet of water beneath her feet, she stopped treading water to stay afloat.

He waited for her to surface, breathless and angry and still, amazingly, clutching the damned dress.

'I'm drowning.'

'No, you're not.' Flipping onto his back, he kicked lazily away from her, still maintaining eye contact.

He was utterly heartless. She hit at the water surface angrily, sending a spray of silver droplets his way. None reached him, and she struck out towards him. Hannah was a reasonable swimmer but her efforts were severely hampered by her sodden clothes, and after a couple of feet she was puffing and panting.

'Stand up.'

Easy for him to say—he was ten feet tall! Cautiously she put a foot down. Her toe found the bottom, and, bouncing along for another few feet, she finally risked attempting to follow his advice.

The water reached her shoulder but it only reached Kamel's waist. He looked like a glistening statue—if cool stone had been capable of oozing the sort of restless vitality he projected. Kamel was not stone or cold. 'You did that deliberately!' she charged, focusing on her fury and not on his body—at least that was the aim.

When the sexiest man on the planet was standing there dripping wet and gorgeous it was hard to ignore.

He shrugged, fixing her with a gleaming amused gaze. 'What can I say? The temptation...' His voice trailed away as his glance dropped. The immersion had left her shirt plastered to her body; the lacy outline of her bra was clearly visible, as were the thrusting projections of her nipples. Heat pooled in his groin and the laughter faded from his heavy-lidded eyes as in his mind he saw himself drawing the ruched rosy peak into his mouth and heard her hoarse cry. He took a step towards her.

'Get away from me!' Refusing to recognise the heart-pounding excitement that made her feel light-headed, she banged the water with the heel of her hand in warning.

His response was a predatory smile. Holding out a hand to ward him off, she took a staggering step backwards and immediately sank beneath the surface. Floating on her back, kicking to stay afloat safely out of reach, she glared at him with eyes several shades deeper than the glittering water.

'That was so childish!' she accused, finding her feet again and stepping into marginally shallower water. 'I could have drowned—you'd have liked that.'

He arched a satiric brow. '*Me*, childish?'

Hannah blinked back at him, an expression of shock filtering into her eyes as their glances connected and locked. Her jaw dropped and her eyes widened as she thought, He's right. Who was the person who had charged in all guns blazing? She turned her glance downwards over her drenched clothes, and felt the clutch of cold, horrified embarrassment in her stomach. This wasn't her. She lifted her eyes, saw the way he was looking at her, and the cold in her belly turned hot and liquid.

'You're right. It is me!' she yelled. The discovery was liberating.

Kamel didn't have a clue what she was talking about and he didn't ask, because she was churning the water, windmilling her hands, sending as much spray over herself as him—and he reciprocated.

Hannah threw herself into the exertion and was not even aware of the point when she began to cry. Blinded by the spray, she didn't realise until her arms and shoulders got too tired to retaliate that Kamel had stopped splashing and he was standing right there, toe to toe with her.

The sun and the water droplets on her lashes gave a shimmering effect to his dark outline.

Everything seemed to slow, even her heartbeat. Her throat closed over, then she stopped breathing completely. She closed her eyes and felt his finger on her cheek. Leaking control from every pore, she opened her eyes. The sexual tension humming in the air had a stronger physical presence than the Mediterranean sun burning down on them.

'Are you crying?'

She shook her head, and wondered how he could tell.

'Come here!' he growled.

Afterwards, Hannah had no clue whether she stepped into him or whether he pulled her into his arms. All she knew was that it felt gloriously right to be there. His dark, hot eyes made her feel light-headed but she couldn't look away as he brushed the strands of wet hair away from her face. She couldn't take her eyes off him.

Kamel watched through eyes narrowed against the sun as the sparkling defiance faded from her blue eyes. He saw the hot glaze of desire drift in, and heard the husky little catch as she drew in a shuddering sigh and reached for his hand—not to pull it away, but to hold it there.

Kamel felt a rise of unfamiliar emotion as he looked down at her, and his fingers tightened around the slim ones that were entwined within his. He felt her shiver and frowned.

'You're cold.'

She shook her head. Turning her face into his palm, she felt anything but cold—she was burning from the inside out. She let out a gasp as Kamel dragged her into his body; the hard imprint of his erection against the softness of her belly drew another gasp, this one fractured. Her hands slid around the nape of his neck into his dark hair.

'Can I be of—?'

Kamel swore and cut across Rafiq's enquiry. 'No, we are fine. That will be all.'

The man bowed and melted away.

'You have a beautiful mouth,' she said, staring dreamily at the sculpted outline.

Kamel's face was a rigid mask of driven need as he

brought his beautiful mouth crashing hungrily down on her soft, parted lips. Hannah's mind blanked as she went limp in his arms, giving herself over completely to the hungry, sensual onslaught of his deep, draining kisses. It felt as though he would drink her dry and she didn't mind one bit. She wanted it.

They were both breathing like sprinters crossing the line when he lifted his head. 'I can't get enough of you,' he confessed huskily.

'You make it sound like a bad thing,' she whispered.

He stroked her face, pulling her in even closer, feeling her breathing become more ragged as he let her feel how much he wanted her. 'Does that feel bad?' he asked.

'Oh, God, Kamel!' It was agony to be this close and yet not close enough, not nearly close enough. 'I feel… you're…' Her moan was lost inside his mouth.

It wasn't until they reached the edge of the pool and she saw her shirt floating on the water that Hannah realised that she was naked from the waist up.

How did that happen? She didn't spend long wondering. Consumed by an elemental hunger that allowed no room for thought, just feeling—layer and layer of hot feeling!—she plastered her aching, swollen breasts up hard against his chest and wound her legs tight around his waist, almost lifting herself clear of the water as she probed Kamel's mouth with her tongue, drawing a deep groan from his throat.

'Just hold on…let me…' He unwound her hands from around his neck, breaking the tenacious grip as he pushed her away from him.

'No…!' She opened her eyes and collided head-on with the heat in his.

Evading the hands that grabbed for him, Kamel

spanned her waist with his hands and lifted her out of the water onto the edge of the pool. A moment later he was beside her, pulling her to her feet.

He lifted her into his arms and began to stride off— not in the direction of the villa, but the grassy area where a tree-lined stream ran through the sloping mani-cured lawn towards the deep forested area that bordered three sides of the property.

'We can't here...someone will see,' she protested half-heartedly.

'This is a paparazzi-free zone, I promise.'

'I wasn't thinking of intruders. People work here.'

She admired his confidence, and because he was kissing her like a starving man she allowed herself to be convinced by it. The simple truth was that she couldn't have stopped even if she had wanted to. And she didn't.

The grass he laid her on was soft against the bare skin of her back; the sun shining through the leafy can-opy above left a dappled pattern on her skin. She lay breathing hard, one arm curved above her head, and anticipation made her stomach muscles quiver as he knelt beside her.

He bent forward, his body curving over hers, every muscle in his body pulled taut as he allowed the image to imprint on his retinas. It was one he knew would stay with him. The hectic flush of arousal on her cheeks, the wanton invitation that curled her soft full lips up-wards—she was sinful temptation personified and it would take a stronger man than he was to resist.

Kamel had no intention of resisting; he just wanted to claim what was his, driven by primitive instincts as old as man.

He could feel her eyes on him as he slid the saturated

skirt down her hips. His actions were made clumsy by
the urgency that burned in his blood and the thin threads
of lace on the tiny pants snapped as he tried to free her
of the bondage.

Stripped of everything, her body was smooth and
pale—so perfect that he couldn't breathe. He touched
her breasts, running his thumbs across the tight peaks
before he cupped them in his big hands.

Hannah closed her eyes, focusing everything on the
sensation as he ran his hands over the smooth curve of
her stomach, feeling the light calluses on his palms.

She raised her arms, reaching out towards him.

Eyes blazing with a need that made him shake, he
knelt astride her, then, holding her eyes, he parted her
thighs. Her skin was cool to the touch but inside she
was hot. He closed his eyes and thrust in deeply, not
holding back as he felt her hotness, her wetness close
around him.

He ran a hand down her smooth thigh. 'Hold me
now.'

Her long legs wrapped around him, locking around
his waist to hold him as they pushed together towards
a release that left them both breathless.

As Hannah gasped her way to cogent thought one
surfaced, rising above the others, swirling in her plea-
sure-soaked brain. For that, she would do *anything*.

Even share him?

Everything in her said that was wrong. Self-disgust
curled in the pit of her stomach.

But what was the alternative? Could there be room
for compromise?

'I understand that there will be women.' The truth

hurt, but she had to be grown up about this. 'I suppose I should not have reacted. If you—'

'Do not say it.' The cool command cut across her hesitant voice. 'I do not need your blessing to sleep with other women.'

She sucked in a taut breath. 'I know you don't need my permission,' she admitted unhappily.

He lifted his head from her breast, struggling against outrage even though a short time ago he would have welcomed her adult attitude. 'Only you could say something like that at a time like this. I am not thinking about other women every second of the day. I am thinking of you. And right now I am thinking of doing this again in bed. Would you prefer to talk or make a baby?'

'But I thought you wanted—'

'How could I know what I want when you insist on telling me? Come with me and I will tell you what I want.'

'That's a plan,' she agreed faintly.

CHAPTER ELEVEN

IT WAS ON the second night of their honeymoon that the telephone rang in the middle of the night. Kamel shifted her off his dead arm and reached for the phone with the other.

'I have to go.'

'What's wrong?'

Kamel put the phone back on the hook. Under his tan he was ashen.

'Your uncle?'

He shook his head. 'No, not that, thank God.'

She was relieved for his sake. She knew how fond Kamel was of his uncle and had also worked out from a few things he had said that he was in no hurry to take the throne. In fact, she had the impression that Kamel inexplicably thought he was not good enough to fill his cousin's shoes.

The few times Kamel had mentioned his cousin, the qualities he said he had possessed—the ones that made him the perfect heir apparent—were qualities that Kamel had too, in abundance!

'There has been an earthquake.'

Hannah gasped.

'Rafiq will stay here with you.'

'Good luck and take care,' she said, struggling to keep her emotions low-key but wishing he had asked her to come with him.

'It's on occasions like this that my uncle must feel the loss of Hakim. It was so senseless. It will never make any sense. He had the ability to—'

Hannah could no longer hold her tongue. 'I'm sure your cousin was a great guy and it's desperately sad he is gone, but I'm damned sure he wasn't perfect. If he had been, he wouldn't have stolen the woman you loved! You're as good as he was any day of the week! Your uncle is lucky to have someone so dedicated.'

There was a long silence, finally broken by his slow drawl.

'So the gossips have been talking? I suppose that was to be expected. Well, one thing they didn't tell you is the difference between me and Hakim is that he *wanted* to be the king. I hate the idea. And he had Amira beside him for support and that made all the difference for him.' Kamel found that lately he was able to think about their incredible devotion to one another without feeling bitter or jealous. It was one burden he no longer carried.

She gasped as though he had struck her and glanced down expecting to see a blade protruding from between her ribs. 'And you have me.'

'Don't worry,' he said, totally misinterpreting her re-action and her flat tone. 'I'm not expecting you to hold my hand.' He paused and cleared his throat. 'Amira was brought up to this life, and she knew the pressures.'

Unable to see the desperate pain and longing she knew would be in his face, Hannah looked away, hearing Raini's words in her head. *A beautiful queen.*

'I may not understand being royal,' she admitted quietly, 'but I do understand that, even though you hate it…' she lifted her gaze to his face and gave a quick smile '…you still put everything into it. That makes you someone who will make a great king one day.' Under the rather intense scrutiny of his dark eyes, she coloured. 'A king should have a level of arrogance that would be unacceptable in any other job.'

This drew a laugh from Kamel, who dropped a kiss on her mouth. Their lips clung…for how many seconds she didn't know, but it was long enough for Hannah to know she had fallen in love. And the man she loved would only ever see her as a pale imitation of the love of his life.

A little over a month after the earthquake, which had not actually caused any loss of life but had flattened a power plant, Hannah was breakfasting alone. She was in no hurry, as the ribbon-cutting ceremony for the opening of a new school had been unexpectedly postponed. When she'd asked why, her secretary had been strangely evasive, but then she was probably reading things into the situation that weren't there.

Like today—just because no one had remembered her birthday didn't mean that she had no friends, that nobody would miss her if she weren't there.

Struggling to divert the self-pitying direction of her thoughts, she picked up her fork and toyed with the smoked salmon and fluffy scrambled egg on her plate. It looked delicious, it smelt delicious, but she was not hungry. Her lack of hunger had nothing whatever to do with the fact it was her birthday and nobody had remembered. Actually, there had been other days this week when she had not been able to face breakfast.

She put down her fork and reminded herself that she was not a child. Birthdays no longer had the same importance, though even last year her father, who always made a fuss of her, despite the memories the day brought back for him—or perhaps because of them— had invited her friends for a pamper spa day. Hannah had known but she had pretended to be surprised.

Practically speaking you could hardly have a spa day with friends who were hundreds of miles away—and her father, it seemed, had forgotten. Out of sight, out of mind? She had rung him two nights on the run and he hadn't picked up or responded to her text messages. Presumably he had decided she was Kamel's problem now. And Kamel had left their bed at some unearthly hour. She had barely been able to open her eyes when he had kissed her and said, 'See you later.'

'How later?' she had muttered, wondering how he managed to expend so much energy during the night and still look fresh and dynamic in the morning. Would she have traded a fresh morning face for the nights of shared passion? Hannah hadn't even asked herself the question. It was a no-brainer.

The prospect of lying in Kamel's arms at night was what made the long and sometimes exhausting days bearable. It had been a steep learning curve and a shock to find herself with a personal secretary and a diary of official engagements. And part of the problem was of her own making. Initially, despite being advised to be cautious by her advisor, Hannah had agreed to lend her name to any worthy cause that approached her. Now she was snowed under by obligations to promote the numerous good causes she had lent her name to, and had been forced to be a little more discriminating.

Not only had she learnt her own life was not to be one of leisure, she had stopped thinking of Kamel's life as one of glitter and self-indulgence. He worked harder than anyone she had ever known, and as for glamour— some of what he was called upon to do was mind-numbingly boring and the flip side of that was the delicate tightrope of diplomacy he trod when he negotiated with men of power and influence.

He never complained, and she never told him how much she admired him. He had never mentioned Amira again but she was still there, the silent invisible presence. They could close the door on the rest of the world at the end of the day, but not his dead love. She was a constant. A perfect ideal that Hannah knew she could never live up to. She also worried about what would happen when those forbidden words slipped out in a moment of passion—so she really struggled to stay in control when they made love. Maybe Kamel guessed what she was doing because sometimes he looked at her oddly.

How would he react? she wondered, picking up her coffee cup. She had taken a sip from the cup before she saw what was concealed behind it: a gold-embossed envelope with her name inscribed in a bold familiar print across it.

She slopped coffee on the pristine white cloth in her haste to tear it open. It did not take long to read the message on the card inside.

Your birthday present is in the kitchen.

He knew it was her birthday and he'd bought her something! Like the child she no longer was, she leapt to her feet with a whoop of delight.

The private jet stood idling. Bad weather had delayed Kamel's flight. These things happened, and there was always a choice. A man could stress about a situation that was outside his control, fret and fume, and metaphorically or possibly literally bang his head against a brick wall.

Or he could not.

Kamel saved his energy for situations he could influence, but today he had struggled to retain this philosophical outlook. By the time his car drove through the palace gates it was almost midnight and he was in a state of teeth-clenching impatience.

He had bought women presents before, typically expensive baubles, and he took their appreciation for granted. The bauble he had bought Hannah had been in a different class. News of the record-breaking price it had fetched at auction had made the news headlines.

It had been a fortnight ago, the same night that Kamel, who normally worked in his office after dinner, had found himself wondering what Hannah did while he worked. He spent each and every night with her, he saw her in the morning and her personal secretary told him what her schedule was for the day. Sometimes they ate together in the evening but after that…? It had not previously occurred to him to wonder what she did with herself in the evenings.

So he asked.

'The princess takes a walk and usually spends some time in the small salon. She enjoys watching television.'

'Television?'

Rafiq nodded. 'I believe she follows a cookery programme. Sometimes she reads…' Without any change
of expression, he had somehow managed to sound re-
proachful as he added, 'I think she might be lonely.'

'That will be all.' Only a long relationship and a respect for the older man stopped him saying more, but
Kamel was incensed that his employee should think
it came within his remit to tell him he was neglecting
his wife!

If she was lonely, all she had to do was tell him. The
trouble was that she had no sense, and could not accept advice. She had taken on an excessive workload,
despite his giving her secretary explicit instructions to
keep her duties light. She had ignored him, she had…
His anger left him without warning, leaving him exposed to the inescapable fact that he had been guilty
of neglect. Outside the bedroom he actively avoided
her. But then logically if they were to be parents there
would, for the child's sake, need to be some sort of mutual understanding outside the bedroom.

Lonely. A long way from home and anyone she knew,
living in a totally foreign environment by a set of rules
that were alien to her. And Kamel had needed someone to tell him that?

She hadn't complained and he had been happy and
even relieved to take her seeming contentment at face
value. Determined to make up for his neglect, he had
gone to see for himself, but any expectation of discovering a forlorn figure had vanished when he'd walked
into the small salon and found Hannah sitting cross-
legged on a sofa giggling helplessly at the screen. She
seemed surprised to see him but not interested enough

to give him all her attention. Most of that remained on the television. Of course, it was a relief to discover she didn't need him to entertain her.

'A comedy?' He sat on the sofa arm and looked around. The room was one that he rarely entered but he recognised there had been some changes. Not just the television and bright cushions, but where a large oil painting had stood there was now a row of moody monochrome framed photographs of rugged mountain landscapes.

On the desk there was a piece of driftwood and some shells beside an untidy stack of well-thumbed paperback novels.

Hannah caught him looking. 'The painting made me depressed and the other stuff is in a cupboard somewhere.'

'What a relief. I thought you might have pawned it.'

She looked at him as though she couldn't decide if he was joking or not. 'Do not let me interrupt your comedy.'

'It's a cookery competition. His sponge sank.'

'And that is good?'

She slung him a pitying look and shook her head. 'If he doesn't pull it out of the bag with his choux buns he's out.'

Kamel had stayed, not because he found the competitive side of baking entertaining, but because he found Hannah's enjoyment contagious. She was riveting viewing. It fascinated him to watch her face while she willed on her favourite, the sound of her throaty chuckle was entrancing, and her scolding of a contestant who, as she put it, *bottled it*, made him laugh.

When the programme finished he was sitting beside

her, sharing the sofa, and it was too late to go back to work. So he accepted her suggestion of a second glass of wine and watched a documentary with her. It was then he discovered that Hannah, renowned for her icy control, cried easily and laughed even more easily. Her aloof mask concealed someone who was warm, spontaneous and frighteningly emotional.

She had been pretending to be someone she wasn't for so long that he wondered if she remembered why she had developed the mask. But then his research into the subject had said that dyslexics developed coping mechanisms.

After that first evening it had become a habit for him to break from work a little earlier and join her. On the night he had taken receipt of her birthday gift he had cut his evening work completely and when he'd entered the salon had been feeling quite pleased with himself as he'd contemplated her reaction when she opened her gift the following week.

'No cookery programme?'

'No,' she'd snuffled, looking up at him through suspiciously red eyes. 'It's too early. This is an appeal for the famine.'

The appeal had been followed by a news programme where the headline was not the famine but an item on the diamond purchased at auction by an anonymous buyer and the record-breaking price it had achieved.

When she'd expressed her condemnation of a society where the values were so skewed that people put a higher price on a shiny jewel than they did on children's lives, he'd agreed wholeheartedly with her view before going away to pass the ring he'd bought for her on to the next highest bidder, and to make a sizeable

donation to the famine appeal. He'd then spent the rest
of the evening wrestling with the problem of what the
hell to buy for the woman who could have everything
and didn't want it!

For a man who had never put any thought into a gift
beyond signing a cheque it had not been easy, but he
considered his solution inspired.

Would Hannah?

At some point he would have to ask himself why
pleasing her mattered so much to him, but that remained
a question for tomorrow. Today things were going rather
well. This marriage could have been a total disaster
but it wasn't.

The sound of music as he walked into the apartment
drew him to the salon. A soft, sexy ballad was playing. The room was empty but the doors of the balcony
were open and the dining table there was laid for two,
with red roses and candles. The roses were drooping,
the candles in the silver candelabra had burnt down,
spilling wax on the table, and the champagne in the ice
bucket was empty, as were the plates.

He was making sense of the scene when Rafiq appeared.

'Where?'

'I believe they are in the kitchen.'

'They?'

'The chef is still here.'

Rafiq opened the kitchen door, but neither his wife
nor the celebrity chef he had flown in to give her a day's
one-to-one teaching session heard him. Could that have
had something to do with the open bottle of wine and
two glasses on the table?

Or the fact they were having a great time? The guy with his fake smile and spray tan was relating an incident with enough name-dropping to make the most committed social climber wince.

Hannah wasn't wincing, though, she was eating it up, with her amazed gasps and impressed ahhs.

Well, she wasn't lonely, and she certainly wasn't missing him.

Scowling, he tugged at his tie and walked inside. He was paying the man to give his wife cooking lessons. He could manage the other things himself.

'Happy birthday.'

At the sound of the voice she had been waiting to hear all evening, Hannah's head turned. She started to her feet just in time, restraining the impulse to fling herself at him.

To his mind, her reaction had all the hallmarks of guilt.

'Have you had a good day?' His eyes slid to the chef, who had risen slowly to his feet.

'Yes, thank you.'

Her response and her demure, hand-clasped attitude reminded him of a child summoned to the headmaster's study, and he felt his temper rise.

'I made us a meal but you—'

'You missed a great meal, really great. This girl is a talent.'

'The girl is my wife.' Kamel had spent the day being pleasant to idiots but enough was enough.

'Hannah is a great pupil. Really talented.'

'Yes, you mentioned that. Well, thank you for stepping into the breach, but I would like to say happy birth-

day to my wife—alone. Shall I have someone show you
to your room or can you—?'

'I'll be fine. Goodnight, all.'

The door closed and Hannah gave a sigh of relief.
'Thank goodness for that.'

Her reaction sent his antagonism down several levels.

'You did not enjoy your birthday present?'

'It was the best birthday present I have ever had! It
was fine before he started drinking and then…' She
shook her head. 'He kept telling the same story over and
over and I couldn't get rid of him. Thank goodness you
came when you did. I was ready to hide in the pantry,
but at least it stopped me brooding. Dad didn't call. I
hope he's all right. Some years he is worse than others,'
she admitted, worriedly.

Kamel shook his head. *'Worse?'*

'Sorry, I was talking as if you knew.'

Kamel struggled to contain his frustration. He had
to drag every bit of information out of her. 'I would
like to know.'

'My mother died when I was born. Well, actually she
died a few weeks earlier. She was brain dead but they
kept her alive until I was strong enough to be delivered.
Dad stayed by her side night and day all that time and
when I was born they switched off the life support. It's
hardly any wonder it was months before he could even
look at me. If it hadn't been for me she'd be alive.'

The fist around his heart tightened as she raised her
swimming blue eyes to him.

'Your father doesn't blame you for your mother's
death.' No father could do that to an innocent child.
It was more likely, knowing Hannah, that she blamed

herself. How had he ever thought this woman was self-ish and shallow?

'Well, if he did I guess he's been trying to make up for it ever since by spoiling me rotten. I wish he'd ring.'

'Your father will be fine.'

Hannah nodded and stood there noticing the lines of fatigue etched into his face. Presumably he'd had a bad day—the same bad day that was responsible for the air of menace he had been radiating when he'd walked in. He'd made her think of a big panther, all leashed vio-lence and tension.

'Come here.'

The rough invitation and the glow in his eyes made her tummy flip. 'Why?'

'I want to make up for missing your birthday.' He wanted to make up for every moment of pain in her life.

'What did you have in min—?' She let out a shriek as he scooped her up into his arms. 'What are you doing?'

He kicked open the door and grinned. 'I am taking you upstairs to give you the rest of your birthday pres-ent. It might,' he added, his eyes darkening as they swept her face, 'take some time.'

CHAPTER TWELVE

HANNAH KICKED OFF her shoes as she walked into the bedroom. Kamel stood, his shoulders propped against the door jamb, and watched as she sat at the dressing table and struggled with the clasp of the sapphire necklace she wore.

He had never imagined that the nape of a woman's neck could be erotic, but he had to accept that some of life's normal rules did not apply where his wife was concerned. When she had walked into the room at his side tonight, making him think of a graceful swan in her slim-fitting white gown, she had been literally shaking with fear but nobody would have guessed as she smiled and charmed everyone present at the formal state dinner.

The fierce pride he had felt as he had watched her across the table, graceful and lovely, had only been matched in the emotional stakes by the rush of protectiveness he had experienced when, during the press-the-flesh session following the formal banquet, when those who were being rewarded for good works got a chance to meet the royals, Hannah's interest in the diverse range of people who lined up to shake her hand had seemed real—as had the fear in her eyes when she had seen the Quagani colonel. The moment had passed and she had recovered her poise, but Kamel had kept an eye on the man. Diplomatic incident or not, he was poised to throw the guy out personally if he so much as looked at Hannah the wrong way.

In the event he had seemed to behave himself. Even so, Kamel intended to make damned sure that in the future their favourite cuddly colonel had his card marked when it came to entry into this country.

'Let me.'

She looked at him in the mirror, unable to disguise the shiver of pleasure as his fingers brushed her neck.

'Thank you,' she said, looking at him through her lashes with eyes that shone brighter than the gems he was removing.

He paused. She seemed about to say something but then, as if she had changed her mind, she tipped her head in acknowledgement as he dropped the necklace into her hand.

'You did well tonight.'

The comment smoothed the small groove in Hannah's brow and she released the sigh she'd felt she had been holding in all night. 'So I passed?'

He didn't return her smile. 'Is that how you saw tonight? As a test?' The idea troubled him. 'You're not being graded, Hannah. No one is judging you.'

Hannah shrugged. She had been here long enough to learn a little of the politics of the place, and she knew that she was resented in certain quarters. More than a few people were just waiting for her to mess up. She would never be Amira, but she was determined to prove them all wrong.

'Especially not me.'

Whatever trust issues he had with Hannah had long gone. He often watched her—which was not exactly a hardship—and found himself wondering how he had ever even for a second thought she was a cold, spoilt bitch!

He was not a man who looked deep inside himself, maybe because he knew that he wouldn't have liked what he'd have seen.

He'd once told Hannah to lose the attitude, but now he saw that it was advice he ought to have been directing at himself. He'd seen marriage as a life sentence the moment when the doors slammed shut. He had not faced his resentment of the role that had been thrust on him. Hannah had made him do that.

He'd never for one second thought that marriage might be better than the life he'd had to let go. He'd put so much effort into seeing himself as someone who had missed out on the chance of happiness when he had lost Amira that when it had fallen at his feet he'd not recognised it.

And yet there was a cloud. Hannah welcomed him into her bed but he sensed a new restraint in her. She was holding back. On more than one occasion he had nearly demanded to know what the hell was the matter—but he'd stopped himself. What if she told him and he didn't like the answer?

His quiet admission that he hadn't been judging her made her throat ache with unshed tears.

'I was dreading it,' she admitted.

'I know.'

'It was strange sitting next to the man who once held my fate in his hands.' Protocol dictated that she was seated next to the daunting Sheikh Malek. 'He could have signed my death warrant.'

'No!'

The explosive interjection made her pause and touch his hand. His fingers unclenched under the light pressure. 'Tonight he was telling me about his rose collection. He invited me to a tour of his rose gardens.'

Kamel let out a silent whistle as he brought his hands up to rest on her shoulders. 'You're honoured. I haven't made that invite yet. It's the hottest ticket in town, I promise you.'

He bent his head and Hannah closed her eyes, but the anticipated kiss did not arrive on her waiting lips. With a disgruntled little frown between her feathery brows, she opened her eyes and saw him digging into the pocket of his jacket.

'I almost forgot. This is yours, I believe.'

Her frown deepened as she shook her head and looked at the small fat brown envelope he held. 'It's not mine.'

He turned it over. 'Well, it's got your name on the front.'

Sliding her finger under the sealed flap, she split it open and angled a questioning look up at him, suspecting this was Kamel's way of delivering a surprise. 'There's no celebrity chef hiding inside, is there?'

Kamel responded to the teasing with a lopsided grin. 'The man's ego wouldn't fit into this room, let alone an envelope.'

Hannah turned the parcel around, feeling an odd reluctance suddenly to open it. 'Where did it come from?'

'Someone saw you drop it, handed it to someone who passed it on to me. I assumed it fell out of your bag.'

Her lips quirked into an amused smile. 'My bag will just about hold a lipstick.'

Her explanation drew a puzzled look. 'Then why carry it?'

'Only a man would ask that question.'

'What is it?' he asked as she tipped the contents of the envelope onto the dressing table.

'I've no idea,' she admitted, staring as several photos clipped together fell out, then, after another shake, a card. 'It says here that...' She read the logo on top of the card and her brows lifted. 'Private investigator!'

Kamel picked up the photos. He did not look beyond the one on the top. A muscle in his lean cheek clenched.

'What's wrong?' she asked, struggling to read his shuttered expression.

'See for yourself.' He slid the clip off the bundle and fanned them out, playing-card style, on the surface in front of her.

Hannah accepted the invitation, and the nausea she had been feeling intermittently all evening resurfaced with a vengeance. There were two people in each grainy print and, even though they had clearly been taken using a telephoto lens and there was some graininess, there was no mistaking one at least of the faces...or the body.

Kamel's mouth twisted in distaste.

'I thought we had all of these.'

Of course, once images made their way onto the Internet they were there for ever, but the person who had taken these had been refreshingly pragmatic. The only thing he'd been interested in was money, not causing embarrassment.

'You knew about these?' She held a clenched fist to her pale lips.

'These were taken long before we were married. You do know that, don't you?' He could have pointed out that the dress she was wearing—when she was wearing one—was the gold number that had been the trigger for their poolside tussle. But he shouldn't have to.

He had not needed to ask Hannah if she had employed a private investigator; he knew she hadn't. He recognised this for what it was—a rather obvious and malicious attempt at mischief-making, one that could only work in a marriage where there was a lack of trust that could be exploited.

'Do you believe me, Hannah? Do you trust me?'

Saying she did amounted to an admission that she loved him. Was she ready to make it?

The realisation that she was came hand in hand with the even stronger realisation that if she didn't move fast she was going to throw up all over his shiny shoes.

She threw him an agonised look, then dashed to the bathroom with her hand pressed to her lips, and slammed the door in his face.

When she finished being violently sick, Hannah got weakly to her feet and washed her face. A look in the mirror told her she looked like death warmed up. She went back into the bedroom.

She squared her shoulders and opened the door. It was time she manned up and came clean. She would tell him that, not only did she trust his word, she trusted him with her life and that of their unborn baby.

She curved a protective hand over her flat belly and whispered, 'Here goes.'

It was empty.

The anticlimax was intense, but it only lasted a moment. She looked back on their conversation before she had made her dash for the bathroom, and she saw the situation from his perspective. He had asked her if she trusted him and she had bolted.

She put herself in his shoes—what was he thinking?

The answer was not long coming. He thought she didn't trust him. The knowledge buzzed in her head and she knew it wouldn't go away until she told him how she felt.

He had to know she wasn't that person. Fuelled by an urgency that infected every cell of her body, that defied logic, she ignored the heels she had kicked off and shoved her feet into a pair of trainers.

The bodyguard standing outside the door moved to one side as she exploded through the door.

'Where is he?'

The steely face betrayed a concern as he looked down at her.

'Shall I get someone for you—?'

'No, just tell me where he went!' she screeched, fighting the impulse to beat her hands on his chest.

After a pause that seemed to Hannah to go on for ever, he nodded to the door that led to the stone spiral steps that in turn led to the side entrance to their apartment.

Hannah's grateful smile shone, causing the big man to blush but she didn't notice. Slinging a 'Thank you!' over her shoulder, she flew down the stairs at record-breaking speed, slowing only when she remembered the baby.

Outside her burst of optimism vanished as she scanned the surrounding area lit by spotlights. Her anxious gaze failed to pick up any sign of movement amongst the rows of fragrant lemon trees that grew in the manicured expanse of green, a green maintained by high-tech underground irrigation.

She was about to concede defeat when she saw a figure who had been previously concealed by a hollow in the undulating ground outlined on the horizon.

'Kamel!'

Maybe he didn't hear her, or maybe he chose to ignore her. Her jaw firmed; she'd *make* him listen, she told herself grimly, or die in the attempt!

In her head she could hear him calling her a drama queen. Tears welled in her eyes and she tried to call his name but nothing came out of her mouth. Swallowing tears and the frustration that lay like a weight in her chest, she willed herself on.

He had vanished from view before she had made it halfway across the grass, but when she reached the top of the rise she had a lucky break: she saw his tall figure enter the massive garage block.

With cruel timing as she came around the building a sports car emerged through the open doors, kicking up a cloud of dust that made her cough as it vanished.

Well, that was it.

Feeling utterly deflated, she stopped to catch her breath, pressing her hand to a stitch in her side. She experienced a moment's panic before telling herself not to be stupid. Pregnant women played sport, rode horses, did things a lot more physically demanding than jog a few hundred yards. Her only problem was she was unfit.

Actually it wasn't her only problem. Why had she hesitated? If she had told him how she felt he wouldn't have needed to be told she trusted him. He'd have known. But, no, she'd been busy covering her back, protecting herself from the man who, whether he had intended to or not, had shown her what love was about.

It had been weeks since she'd admitted it to herself and she'd been too scared to let him see she loved him. She was disgusted by her own cowardice. Maybe it was only sex for him, but she had to know. She *needed* to know. She needed to tell him she was alive and Amira was dead. She had to be brave for their baby.

Hands braced on her thighs, she leant forward to get her breath. It was time to be honest. If she didn't it would be her own insecurity that stretched the gulf that had opened up between them tonight.

She was so caught up with her own internal dialogue that as she straightened up and brushed the hair back from her face she almost missed the figure that emerged from the garage block, the figure carrying the cane. The figure of the colonel...

For a moment literally paralysed with fear, Hannah felt herself dragged back to that room of her nightmares—the bright white light, the stains on the wall that she didn't like to think about and the sinister tap, tap of that cane.

But he wasn't tapping his stick. He wasn't doing anything to attract attention to himself. As he moved towards the staff quarters he looked furtively left and right, then over his shoulder. For a moment he seemed to be looking straight at her and, standing there in the pale ball gown, she felt as though there were a neon arrow above her head. Then he turned and walked away quickly.

It was only after he had vanished that she began to breathe again.

She was ashamed that she'd felt so afraid. He couldn't

hurt her any more. He never had; he'd only been playing mind games. He was harmless really. But harmless
or not, remembering the expression she had caught a
glimpse of earlier that evening when his cold little eyes
had followed Kamel across the room made her shudder.

'Hannah, you're way too old to believe in the bogey
man.' Firmly ejecting the hateful little creep from her
head, Hannah was turning to retrace her steps when she
lost her footing. By some miracle she managed not to
fall, but she did jar her ankle. Flexing her toes and ex-
tending her foot to see the damage, she noticed a dark
patch on the ground. There was a trail of similar spots
leading all the way back to the garage. Unable to shake
the feeling that something was not quite right, she found
herself following the breadcrumb trail of spots. It led
back into the large hangar of a building that housed
Kamel's collection of cars.

She had seen them before and had made a few appropriate noises of approval, though in all honesty her
interest in high-end vintage cars was limited. So long
as the car she drove got her from A to B she was happy.

The lights were off in the building, but as she walked
inside the internal sensor switched them on, revealing the rows of gleaming cars inside. Only one was
absent—the vintage sports car that Kamel had driven
off in. Where it had stood in the empty space the trail
came to an end.

While Hannah's interest in cars was limited, a condition of her being given driving lessons for her sev-
enteenth birthday had been she attend some basic
car-maintenance classes. Some things had stuck with
her, like the unpleasant smell of brake fluid.

She dipped her finger in the pool, lifted it to her nose

and gave a whimper, the colour fading from her face. The images clicked through her head. The hate in that man's eyes, his furtive manner as he'd left the building. Why hadn't she challenged him? Would the little coward dare…?

She didn't follow the line of speculation to its conclusion; she didn't think of the security guard who might have kept a discreet distance but was undoubtedly within calling distance, or even the internal phone on the wall behind her. She just ran.

The palace compound was more like a village or small town than a single residence, and, though it was possible to take a direct route to the heavy entrance gates, there was also a more circuitous route. She had complained recently that Kamel treated it as if it were his own private racing track. He had laughed when she'd closed her eyes and squealed at the last hairpin bend, convinced they were heading straight into a wall.

Without brakes… She shook her head to clear the image and pushed on. On foot it was possible to take a much shorter, direct route. She ought to be able to cut him off before— She refused to think that she was not going to make it in time.

The information did not make it to her lungs. They already felt as though they were going to explode and when she was forced to stop to catch her breath it also gave her body time for the pain in her ankle to register. That was when she remembered the phone in the garage block. She could have rung through to the entrance gate—someone would be there now, ready to warn Kamel. She was trying to decide between the options of going back to the phone or trying to intercept him when she saw a really ancient bike propped up against a wall.

Sending up a silent thanks to whoever had left it there, she climbed aboard and began to pedal through the trees.

Kamel had gunned his way out of the garage.

It all happened so fast the sequence of events was a blur: the car appearing, throwing herself into the road, arms waving, then the crunch of metal as the front of the Aston Martin embedded itself into a tree.

I've killed him!

She felt empty, her body was numb—and then the door of the car was being wrenched open. It actually fell off its hinges as Kamel—large, very alive and in what appeared to be a towering rage—vaulted from the vehicle. The feeling rushed back and she began to laugh and cry at the same time.

'You little fool! What the hell were you doing? I could have killed you!' Looking white and shaken and a million miles from his indestructibly assured self, Kamel took her roughly by the shoulders and wrenched her around to face him. He registered the tears sliding down her face and hissed out a soft curse. How could you yell at someone who looked like that? 'You just took ten years off my life.' If he had no Hannah he would have no life; the blinding insight stretched his self-control to the limit.

'I had to stop you—the car, the brakes...'

His ferocious frown deepened. 'How the hell did you know about the brakes?'

She wiped the tears from her cheeks with the back of one hand and sniffed. 'You knew?'

'I stopped a few yards after I left the garage.' To ask himself what the hell he was doing. Throwing some sort of tantrum because she didn't immediately express unconditional trust? He'd moved the goalposts of this relationship on an almost daily basis. Hell, at the start, he hadn't even wanted a relationship. If he had to work for her trust, he would. 'Or tried to.' He had used the gears to slow down to a crawl, planning to pull over at an appropriate place, which was the only reason he had not hit Hannah.

He closed his eyes and swallowed, reliving the nightmare moment when she had rushed into the road.

'So you knew about what he tried to do?'

'Who tried to do what?'

'The colonel. He cut your brakes and I think he might be the one who sent the photos.'

Understanding softened his dark eyes as he placed a thumb under her chin, tilting her tear-stained face up to him. 'Really sweetheart, that man can't hurt you and I promise you will never have to see him again.'

She pulled away from him. 'No!' she gritted emphatically through clenched teeth. 'Don't look at me like that, and don't even think about humouring me. I am *not* imagining things and it was *you* he was trying to hurt. You humiliated him. I saw the way he looked at you tonight, and then when I followed you he was in the garage and he didn't want to be seen. So when I saw the brake fluid I knew...' She pressed a hand to her chest and gulped back a sob and whispered, 'I had to stop you.'

'You were following me?'

'I just told you—someone tried to kill you.'

'I'll look into it. He will be brought to justice if he

is guilty.' There was no hint of doubt in Kamel's voice. 'You followed me?'

She nodded.

'Why?' He hooked a finger under her chin and forced her to look at him, Hannah met his interrogative dark stare steadily, not trying to look away, feeling weirdly calm now the moment was here.

'Because you asked me a question and you left before I could answer.'

'You ran away.'

'It was that or throw up all over your shoes.'

He stiffened. 'You're ill?'

'Not ill.' For the first time she struggled to hold his gaze. 'You asked me if I trust you and the answer is yes, I do. Totally and absolutely. I know you always have my back—that's one of the things I love about you. Of course, there are an awful lot of things about you that drive me crazy but they don't matter because I love you...' She gave a quivering smile. It hadn't been as hard as she had anticipated, speaking the words that had been locked within her heart. 'The whole package. You.'

This was the moment when in her dreams he confessed his love for her. But this wasn't a dream; it was real. And he stood there, every muscle in his stark white face frozen, tension pulling the skin tight across the bones of his face.

Hannah walked into the wall of pain and kept going, her expression fixed in a reasonable mask. No matter how hard she wanted it, it just wasn't going to happen.

'It's all right. I know that love was not part of the deal. I know that Amira...you will always love her, but it doesn't have to be a deal breaker, does it?'

She felt the tension leave his body. 'Say it again. I want to hear it.'

The glow in his eyes was speaking not to her brain, which was counselling caution, but directly to her heart. It stopped and then soared, and she smiled.

'I love you, Kamel.' She left a gap and this time he filled it.

'*Je t'aime, ma chérie. Je t'aime.* I have been too stubborn, too scared to admit it to myself.'

'Amira…?'

'I loved Amira, and her memory will always be dear to me. But what I felt for her was a thing that… If I thought you loved another man I would not let you go to him. I would lock you up in a tower. I am jealous of everyone you smile at. That damned chef creep…'

'Jealous? You… You're not just saying that because of the baby?' She saw his expression and gave a comical groan. 'I didn't mention that part yet, did I?'

'Baby…there is a baby? Our baby?'

She nodded.

He pressed a hand to her stomach. 'You do know how much you have changed my life?'

'I thought that was exactly what you didn't want.'

He shrugged. 'I was a fool. And you were charming and infuriating and brave and so beautiful. You swept into my life like a cleansing breeze, a healing breeze.'

He opened his arms and, eyes shining, she stepped into them, sighing as she felt them close behind her. 'I love you so much, Kamel. It's been an *agony* not saying it. It got so that I couldn't even relax properly when we made love—I was so scared of blurting it out.'

'So it was not that you had tired of me?'

She laughed at the thought. 'That is never going to happen.'

He put a thumb under her chin, tilting her glowing face up to him. 'You can say it as often as you wish now. In fact, I insist you say it.'

She was giggling happily as he swept her into his arms, and still when the security guard accompanied by a grim-faced Rafiq found them.

'Kamel, stop him. He's calling a doctor. Tell him I'm not ill,' she urged as her husband strode on, refusing her requests to be put down.

'You have had a stressful day and you are pregnant and I think it might be a good idea if a doctor gives you a check-over.'

'And I suppose it doesn't matter what I say?'

'No.'

She touched the hard plane of his lean cheek.

'You're impossible!' she said lovingly.

'And you are mine,' he said simply.

* * * * *

PASSION AND
THE PRINCE

PENNY JORDAN

Penny Jordan, one of Mills & Boon's most popular authors, unfortunately passed away on December 31st, 2011. She leaves an outstanding legacy, having sold over 100 million books around the world. Penny wrote a total of 187 novels for Mills & Boon, including the phenomenally successful *A Perfect Family, To Love, Honour and Betray, The Perfect Sinner* and *Power Play*, which hit the *New York Times* bestseller list. Loved for her distinctive voice, she was successful in part because she continually broke boundaries and evolved her writing to keep up with readers' changing tastes. *Publishers Weekly* said about Jordan, 'Women everywhere will find pieces of themselves in Jordan's characters.' It is perhaps this gift for sympathetic characterisation that helps to explain her enduring appeal.

CHAPTER ONE

LIFTING her head from her camera, through which she had been studying a model posing provocatively in matching bra and briefs, Lily recoiled instinctively from the scene in front of her.

Almost naked male and female models—the girls all fragile limbs and pouting mouths, some of them open in conversation, or drinking water through straws so as not to spoil their carefully applied make-up, and the boys with their gym-toned bodies—stood together as they submitted themselves to the attentions of hovering hair and make-up artists. Fingers tapped away on mobile phones, gleaming tanned skin contrasted with the catalogue client's underwear all the models were wearing for the shoot. Heavy beat music boomed out into the small space despite the fact that some of the models were listening to their own iPods.

In other words it was a normal chaotic studio fashion shoot.

'Has that last male model arrived yet?' she asked the hairstylist, who shook her head.

'Well, we can't hold the shoot any longer. We've only got the studio for today. We'll have to use one of the other male models twice.'

'I can spray on some dye that will darken the blond guy's hair, if you like?' the stylist offered, reaching out to steady the rail containing more underwear to be modelled as it swayed dangerously when one of the models pushed past it.

Looking around, Lily felt her heart sink. She had grown up in this world—until she had turned her back on it and walked away—and now she disliked, almost hated it, and all that it represented.

Given free choice, this cramped, shabby studio with its familiar smell—a mix of male pheromones, sweat, female anxiety, cigarettes and illegal substances that seemed to hang invisibly in the air—was the last place she wanted to be.

Edging past a chattering group of models to get to the door, she put down her camera on a nearby table and went to check the pose of the pretty girl with the wary charcoal-grey-eyed gaze, wondering as she did so how many young hopefuls had entered the industry imagining that they would leave with a contract to model in a top fashion magazine only to discover a much seamier side to modelling. Too many.

This kind of shoot was the unglamorous rump end of what it meant to work in fashion, and a world away from money-no-object glossy magazine shoots.

She hadn't wanted to do this. She was here in Milan for a very different purpose. But she had never been able to resist her younger half-brother's pleas for help and he knew it. Rick's mother—her father's second wife—had been very kind to her when she had been young, and she felt that it was her duty now to repay that kindness by helping her half-brother. She couldn't ignore her sense of duty any more than she could ignore all their late father had been.

She had tried her hardest to dissuade Rick from following in their famous and louche father's footsteps, but to no avail. Rick had been determined to become a fashion photographer.

Satisfied with the model's pose, she went back to the camera—only to frown in irritation as the door to the studio swung open, throwing an unwanted shadow across her shot, along with an equally unwanted suit clad male torso. The missing male model had obviously finally arrived—and ruined her shot by stepping into it.

Thoroughly exasperated, she pushed back the shiny swing of her blonde hair and told him, without removing her gaze from her camera, 'You're late—and you're in my shot.'

It was the sudden silence and the stillness that had fallen over the rest of the room that alerted her to the fact that something was wrong. Her senses picked up on it and reacted by sending a quiverful of tiny darts of anxiety skimming along her spine. She stepped back from the camera and looked up—right into the coldly hostile gaze of the man who had just walked in. A tall, dark-haired, broad-shouldered, expensively suited man, whose body language reinforced the same cold hostility she could see in his eyes along with proud disdain. Against her will Lily could feel her eyes widening as she took in the reality of the man confronting her, her pulse beating unsteadily against her skin.

Whoever this man was, he was obviously no model. Even stripped he would be... He would be magnificent,

Lily acknowledged, her stomach suddenly hollowing out with a sensation that took her completely off guard. If asked, she would have said—and meant it—that she was inured to male good looks, and that as far as she was concerned sexual attraction was a cruel deceit on the part of Mother Nature, designed to ensure the continuation of the species and best avoided. She had grown up in a world in which beauty and good looks were commodities to be ruthlessly traded and abused, which was why her own beauty was something she chose to downplay.

She intended to be crisp, cool and in control as she queried, 'Yes?' But instead of the apology for ruining her shot and the explanation of his presence she was expecting, she received an even more hostile look of silent, angry contempt that raked her from head to toe.

As yet he hadn't so much as given a sideways look at the scantily clad girls who were now, Lily saw after a look at them herself, all gazing at him. And no wonder, she admitted.

He made the young male models look like the mere boys they were, for all their muscles, but then he *was* extraordinarily handsome—handsome, but cold. And Lily suspected judgemental. He exuded an air of raw male pride and sensual power, even if there was a grim harshness about his expression that warned her that whatever had brought him here it wasn't going to be good news—for someone. But not her. He couldn't be here for her, so why did his presence have every one of her carefully rigged inner alarm systems breaking into a cacophony of warning?

She was her parents' daughter, Lily reminded herself.

At some level that had to mean she was as vulnerable to that kind of overpowering male sensuality as her mother had been. And just as capable of using her own beauty for commercial exploitation? Lily struggled to repress the feeling that made her shudder—as though against an unwanted male touch. She would *never* allow herself to repeat her mother's mistakes.

She was here to do a job, she reminded herself, not to give in to her own insecurities.

Whatever had brought him here to this shabby studio it wasn't the prospect of modelling work. His face might be as commanding and as harshly delineated that a hundred thousand ancient Roman coins might have been struck in its patrician and imposing image. It might be the kind of face that could lead vast armies of men into war and entice any number of women into bed. But it was a face that currently bore an expression of such cutting contempt that if it was captured on camera it was more likely to send prospective buyers running for cover than rushing out to buy what he was supposed to be modelling.

Was he going to say anything to break the pool of tense silence he had created?

Lily took a deep breath, and repeated determinedly, 'Yes?'

Another ice-cold look. The man must be close to inhuman, removed from the emotional vulnerabilities that affected the rest of the human race, not to be affected by the tension she could almost feel humming on the air.

'You are the one responsible for this?'

His voice was quieter than she had expected, but

redolent with the same power as his presence and grimly harsh.

Lily gave the studio and the models a brief concerned glance. He was obviously here on a hostile mission of complaint of some kind, and since she was standing in for her half-brother she knew that she was obliged to agree.

'Yes.'

'There's something I want to say to you—in private.'

A rustle of reaction ran through the room. Lily wanted to tell him that there was nothing he could possibly have to say to her, and certainly not in private, but there was a nagging suspicion at the back of her mind that her half-brother might have done something to provoke this man's anger.

'Very well,' she conceded. 'But you will have to make whatever you want to say brief. As you can see, I'm in the middle of a shoot.'

The look of blistering contempt he gave her made Lily take a step back from him, before reluctantly moving forward through the door he was holding open for her. Out of old-fashioned good manners, or more in the manner of a guard determined not to allow his prisoner to escape?

The studio was in an old building, its door sturdy enough to block out the speculative questions Lily knew would be being asked by all the models and stylists inside it. She stood on the small landing at the top of the stairs that led to the studio, keeping as close to the door as she could.

At such close quarters to him there was nowhere to

escape to—he was blocking her exit via the stairs by standing next to them.

'Call me old-fashioned and sexist,' he told her, 'but somehow finding that it is a *woman* who is procuring young flesh for others and profiting financially by doing so is even more abhorrent and repellent than a man doing the same thing. And you *are* such a woman, aren't you? You are a woman who lives off the vanity and foolishness of others, feeding them with false hope and empty dreams.'

Lily stared at him in disbelief. Revulsion filled her at the accusation he had made, accompanied by shock that he should have made it. The thought crossed her mind that he might be some kind of deranged madman—only to be squashed by the message from her senses that this was a man who was perfectly sane.

She pushed her hand into her hair a habitual gesture of insecurity and told him shakily, 'I don't know what all this is about, but I think you must have made a mistake.'

'You're a photographer who seeks out vulnerable young idiots with the promise of a glamorous modelling career that you know is all too likely to destroy them.'

'That's not true,' Lily defended herself, but her voice wobbled slightly as she made the denial. After all, wasn't what he was saying really very much in line with the way she herself felt about the modelling industry?

She took a deep breath, intending to tell him that, but before she could do so he continued grimly. 'Have you no sense of shame? No compunction or guilt about what you do?'

Guilt. Ah, that was the word above all others that

could trigger off an avalanche of dark memories inside
her—a word like a poisoned dart aimed at her unprotected emotions. She had to get away from him, but she
couldn't. She was trapped here with him on the tiny
landing. In her mind's eye she saw the panic he was
causing in her manifesting itself into a wild flight to
escape from him, a desire to curl herself up into a ball
of flesh so small that it could not be seen—or touched.
But that was just in her imagination. The reality was
that she could not escape.

'This world into which you are attempting to drag
Pietro—my nephew—is one of cruelty and corruption
in which young flesh is used and abused by those who
crave its beauty for their own debauched purposes.'

His nephew? Lily's heart was thumping wildly. Every
word he said carved a fresh wound into her own emotions, lacerating the too thin layer of fragility that was
all she had to protect them.

'I have no idea how many young people have fallen
victim to your promises of fame and fortune, but I can
tell you this. My nephew will not be one of them. Thank
goodness he had the good sense to tell his family how
he had been approached with promises of modelling
work and money.'

Lily's mouth had gone dry. She had always particularly disliked this aspect of her father's work, knowing
what painful fires of experience young models could be
drawn into by the unscrupulous. To be accused as she
was being accused now was such a shock that it robbed
her of the ability to defend herself.

'Here's your money back.' The man was slamming
down a wad of euros. 'Blood money—flesh money…

How many of the vilest sort of predators were you planning to introduce him to at this party you invited him to attend with you after the shoot? Don't bother to answer. Let me guess. As many of them as you could. Because that is what this business is about, isn't it?'

Rick had invited the young man to accompany him to a party? Lily's heart sank even further. Rick was a sociable guy. It was normal for him to go out after shoots and have a drink. Besides, it was fashion week, and Milan was full of important people from the top of the fashion tree. It was also full of those at the bottom of that world, though. The kind who...

She could feel a shudder of revulsion gripping her as her skin turned clammy with remembered fear and her heart pounded. She wanted to breathe fresh air. She wanted to escape from the past this man and their surroundings had brought back to her.

'People like you disgust me. Outwardly you may possess the kind of beauty that stops men in the street, but all that beauty does is cloak your inner corruption.'

She had to get some fresh air. If she didn't she was going to pass out. Think of something else, Lily told herself. Think of the present, not the past. Focus on something else.

The effort of trying to refocus her thoughts caused her to sway slightly on her feet. Immediately he came towards her, taking hold of her to steady her. Her brain knew the truth, but her body was reacting to a very different message that had her demanding with fierce anguish, 'Don't touch me.' Her reaction to being imprisoned was instinctive and immediate, ripped from deep within her as she panicked and used her free hand to try and prise his fingers away from her wrist. But all he did was drag her further into his imprisoning hold.

Crushed against his body, Lily waited for the familiar feelings of nausea and terror to flood through her, but instead—unbelievably, and surely impossibly—her senses were sending her messages of an awareness of her captor so unfamiliar to her that they stunned her into a bewildered stillness.

Could it really be happening that, instead of filling her with repugnance, the cool cologne-over-male-warmth smell of him was actually arousing her desire to move closer to its source? How was it that the solid strength of his male body against her own felt somehow right? As though it was something her flesh approved of instead of feared. It was as though she had opened a door and walked into a world that was topsy-turvy—an *Alice in Wonderland* world in which what she'd expected to feel had been replaced by the unexpected. The totally unexpected, she acknowledged as she looked with bewilderment at the way her free hand was splayed out against his chest, her skin pale next to the dark fabric of his suit.

Only seconds had passed—seconds in time but an aeon in terms of her emotions. Now, alongside the confusion of what she was feeling, she had a growing sense of urgency. A desire—no, a *need* to be free from the intimacy of his hold. And not because she feared him, but because she feared her own awareness of him.

There was an odd look in his eyes, a sort of shocked and furious disbelief, as though he couldn't fully comprehend something.

'Let me go.'

The words, echoing from her past, had a galvanising effect on her captor, banishing that look immediately and replacing it with the anger she could now see in his eyes. Anger was better—anger meant that they were enemies and on opposite sides, even though it was obvious to Lily that, whoever and whatever he was, he wasn't used to women rejecting him. His gaze was a dangerous volcano of molten gold, fixing on hers, pinning her beneath it. She could feel herself starting to tremble, weakness filling her. Tiny betraying shivers of sensation rayed out all over her body from its point of contact with his hand. Sexual awareness? Sexual desire? From her? For this man who was a stranger to her—a stranger who had already shown his bitter contempt for her? How could he have such an intense impact on her, sidetracking her away from telling him just how wrong he was about her?

Abruptly he released her, thrusting her from him, turning away from her towards the stairs and taking them two at a time, whilst she gasped for air and tried to turn the handle of the door to the studio with trembling fingers.

She was back—safe in the studio. Only Lily knew that she could never be completely safe with herself ever again. In a handful of seconds and with one automatic and instinctive male movement the protective bubble in which she had wrapped herself to defend herself against his sex had been torn from her. In his hold she had experienced an awareness of him as a man that had struck right at the core of everything she believed about herself, revealing to her a vulnerability she had promised herself she would never know. How could it have happened so quickly and so unexpectedly? So unacceptably? Like lightning striking out of nowhere? She didn't know, and she didn't want to know. She just wanted to ignore it and forget about it.

Numbly, she forced herself to go through the motions of getting back to work.

'What was all that about?' the stylist asked her curiously.

'Nothing. Just a bit of a mistake, that's all.'

A mistake it certainly had been—and the real mistake had been hers.

Her hands trembled as she adjusted the camera. Her very first memories included the feeling of being able to make herself feel safe behind a camera as she played with the equipment in her father's studio, where she had been left so often as a young child, by parents too involved in their own lives to care about hers. Her camera represented security in so many different ways. It was the magic cloak behind which she could conceal and protect herself. But not today. Not now. When she looked through her camera, instead of seeing a model posing, ready for her to photograph, all she could see was an image of the man who had just ripped the security of her self protection from her.

She closed her eyes and then opened them again. Nothing had really happened to alter her life in any way. She might feel as though she had been dragged through the eye of a storm, but that storm had gone now and she was safe.

Was she? Was she really? Or was that just what she wanted—no, needed to believe?

Her mobile beeped to warn her of an incoming text.

Automatically she pressed to read it, scrolling down its length with a jerky uncoordinated touch that betrayed the effect *he* had had on her nervous system.

It was from Rick, telling her that he'd got wind of a terrific opportunity and was flying out to New York to follow up on it.

PS, he'd texted, *bkd studio in yr name. Can u pay the bill for me?*

Lily straightened her body, pushing her hair back off her face. *This* was reality—the reality of her life and her relationships. What had just happened was nothing— and meant nothing. It should be forgotten—treated as though it had never happened.

It didn't matter. It couldn't matter. For some reason a gap had opened up in the protection she had woven around herself and she had slipped into it. Slipped into it—that was all. Not fallen through it, not become lost for ever in it, spellbound by the dark magic of an unknown man's touch.

She had work to do, she reminded herself. Proper work—not stepping in to do Rick's work for him. Her real purpose in being here in Milan had nothing to do with models, or fashion, or anything that belonged to the world that had been her father's. She had her own world and her own place in it. *Her* world. Her safe, protected and protective world—and that world would never admit into it a man who could bewilder her senses to the point where he might take them prisoner.

Marco nodded to his PA, handing over to him the documents he had just signed, his mind on the rather trying and over-emotional phone call he'd just had from his sister. She was hoping, he knew, that he would take her son Pietro onto his personal staff once he had completed his university education, with a view to Pietro eventually being appointed to the board of the family business, which comprised a vast empire of various interests built up by successive generations of Lombardy nobles and merchants.

Marco's own contribution to those assets had been the acquisition of a merchant bank which had turned him into a billionaire by the time he was thirty.

Now, at thirty-three, he had turned his attention and his razor-sharp intellect away from the future to focus it instead on the past, and in particular on the artistic legacy originally created by members of his own family and those like it in financing and sponsoring artists as their protégés.

Marco had never been able to understand quite where his older sister got her emotional intensity from. Their now dead parents had after all been rather distant figures to them, aristocratic and stiffly formal in the way they'd lived their lives. The upbringing of their two children had been left in the hands of nannies and then good schools. Their mother hadn't been the type to fuss over her children in any way, but especially not physically. She had been the opposite of the normal conception of Italian mothers—proud of them both, Marco knew, but never one to hug or kiss them. Not that Marco looked back on his childhood with any sense of deprivation. His personal space, his personal distance from other people, was important to him.

However, he could and did understand the concern his sister had about Pietro—even if his keenly logical brain was not able to accept her defence of her son's reasons for accepting money in return for a so-called 'modelling' assignment. Her poor son needed a more generous allowance, she had told him, adding that it was Marco's fault that Pietro had felt the need to take such a risk, because Marco insisted on Pietro managing on a ridiculously small amount of money. Of course his sister has been quick to assure him that she was grateful to Marco for intervening and going to see the wicked person who had approached her precious son. After all, they both knew what could happen to young innocents who found themselves caught up in the sordid side of modelling.

Marco's gaze fell on the silver-framed photograph on his desk. Olivia, the girl in it, looked very young. The photograph had been taken just after her sixteenth birthday. Her pretty face was wreathed in a shy smile, her dark hair curling down onto her shoulders. She looked innocent and malleable, incapable of deceiving or betraying anyone. Her beauty was the beauty of a still unopened rose—there to be seen, but not yet fully mature. Olivia had never reached that maturity. Anger burned inside him—an anger that grew in intensity as out of nowhere he felt an unwanted echo of the electrical jolt of sexual awareness that had shocked through him earlier in the day, for a woman who should have been the last kind of woman on earth who could affect him like that. It had been a momentary failing, that was all, he assured himself. A consequence, no doubt, of the fact that his bed had been empty for the best part of a year, following his refusal to give in to his mistress's pleas for commitment.

He stood up and walked over to the window. He didn't particularly care for city living—or Milan. But for business reasons it made sense to keep an apartment and an office here. It was only one of several properties in his portfolio—some bought by him and some family properties inherited by him.

If he ever had to choose only one property from that portfolio it would be a magnificent castle built for one of his ancestors who himself had been a collector of the finest works of art.

Marco had been wary at first when he had been approached by Britain's Historical Preservation Trust, with a view to his helping with an exhibition being mounted in an Italian inspired English stately home that would chart the history of the British love of Italian paintings, sculpture and architecture via various loaned artefacts, including plans, drawings and artworks. But the assurances he had received from them about the way in which the whole project would be set up and handled had persuaded him to become involved. Indeed he had become involved with it to such an extent that he had volunteered to escort the archivist the trust were sending to Italy on a preliminary tour of the Italian properties it had been decided would best fit with what the exhibition wanted to achieve.

Dr Wrightington, who had been appointed by the Historical Preservation Trust, would be touring a selection of properties selected by Marco and the trust, and Marco would be accompanying her. Her tour was to begin with a reception in Milan, after which they would visit the first properties on Marco's list—several villas on the banks of Lake Como to the North of Milan. He knew very little about Dr Wrightington other than the fact that the thesis for her doctorate had been based on the long-running historical connection between the world of Italian art and its artists, and the British patrons who had travelled to the great art studios of Rome and Florence to buy their work, returning home not just with what they had bought but also with a desire to recreate Italian architecture and design in their own homes. The tour would end at one of his own homes, the Castello di Lucchesi in Lombardy.

Marco looked at his watch, plain and without any discernible logo to proclaim its origins. Its elegance was all that was needed to declare its design status—for those rich enough to recognise it.

He had an hour before he needed to welcome Dr Wrightington to Milan at the reception he had organised for her in a castle that had originally been the home of the Sforza family—the Dukes of Milan—and what was now a public building, housing a series of art galleries. His own family had been allies of the Sforzas in earlier centuries—a relationship which had benefited both families.

CHAPTER TWO

LILY looked round her small anonymous hotel bedroom. Her bag was packed and she was ready to leave, even though it would be half an hour before the taxi would arrive.

The label on her laptop case caught her eye: Dr Lillian Wrightington. She had changed her surname just after her eighteenth birthday, to avoid association with her famous parents, taking on her maternal grandmother's maiden name.

Even now, over a year after she had been awarded her PhD, it still gave her a small thrill to see that title in front of her name.

Rick couldn't understand why she had chosen the life she had—but then how could he? His memories of their father were so different from hers.

She had had *the* dream again last night, for the first time in ages, knowing that she was dreaming but powerless to wake herself up from it. It always followed the same course. Her father called her into the studio, telling her that she must stand in for a model who had not turned up. The thought of being photographed brought on her familiar fear. She looked for her own camera, wanting to hold it and hide behind it. Then the door to the studio opened and a man came in. His features were obscured, but Lily still knew him—and feared him. As he came towards her she tried to escape from him, calling out to her father as she did so, but he was too busy to pay her any attention. The man reached for her...

That part of the dream had been completely familiar to her. She had dreamed it a thousand times and more, after all. But then something odd had happened—something new and unfamiliar. As the horror and revulsion had risen up inside her, accompanied by anguish that her father couldn't see she needed help, the door to the studio had opened again, admitting someone else, and when she'd seen the newcomer she had been filled with relief, running to him, welcoming the feel of his fingers on her arms, knowing that despite the anger she could feel burning in him his presence would protect her and save her.

Why had she turned the man who had come to the studio Rick had hired and berated her so furiously into her rescuer? It must be because he himself felt contempt for the seedier side of modelling, and therefore at some deep level of her subconscious she had assessed him as a safe haven from those that she herself had learned so very young to fear. And was that the only reason? Lily gave a small mental shrug. What other reason could there be? What other reason did there need to be. Sometimes it was a mistake to dwell on things too deeply and to over-analyse them.

What mattered more was why she had had the dream again, after nearly three years without having it. She suspected she knew the answer to that particular question. The whole ambience of that studio had aroused too many painful unwanted memories. Memories that belonged in her past, she reminded herself determinedly. She was another person now—a person of her own creation and in her own right. Dr Lillian Wrightington, with a doctorate in the influence of Italian art and architecture on the British grand house.

Reception finally called to say her taxi was outside, and she went down to the lobby, wheeling her suitcase behind her. She was, she admitted, slightly apprehensive about meeting the Prince di Lucchesi—but only slightly. Her job as a freelancer archivist connected to the Historical Preservation Trust meant that she had attended enough fundraising events not to feel intimidated at the thought of mingling with the rich and titled. Besides in many cases, thanks to the research for her doctorate, she knew as much about the centuries of skeletons in their family cupboards as they did themselves, she reminded herself wryly.

Other academics might focus on the life of an artist responsible for certain works. She had focused instead on the patrons. Initially that had simply been so she could establish which patrons had been drawn to and bought which artist's work, but then she had found herself becoming increasingly curious about why a certain person had been drawn to a certain piece of art—or a certain artist. Human relationships were at the same time both very simple and very complicated because of the emotions that drove them—because of the mazes and minefields of problems people themselves created to control the lives of others.

She could have researched the Prince online, of course, but Lily was far more interested in men and women who inhabited the past rather than those who lived in the present. The Prince was merely someone she had to deal with in order to achieve the goal she shared with the Trust.

She had still dressed appropriately for the reception, though. First impressions mattered—especially in the world of art and money. Whilst Lily had no interest in fashion *per se*, it would have been impossible for her to have grown up the way she had without absorbing a certain sense of style. Modestly she considered that she was helped in that by her height and her slenderness. At five nine she wasn't particularly tall, but she was tall enough to carry her clothes well. Although normally when she was working she preferred to wear a tee shirt and jeans—a polo neck and jeans if it was cold, along with a fine wool long-line cardigan—for more formal public occasions such as this one she kept a wardrobe of simple good-quality outfits.

For today's reception she was wearing a caramel-coloured dress. Sleeveless, with a high slashed neck-line, it skimmed the curves of her body rather than clung to them. Round her neck she was wearing the rope of pearls that been handed down to her from her great-grandmother on her mother's side. The only other jewellery she was wearing was the Cartier watch that had been her mother's, and a pair of diamond ear-studs which she had had made from the two diamonds in her mother's engagement ring.

After her mother's suicide her father had given her all her mother's jewellery. She had sold it all, apart from the watch and the engagement ring, giving the money to a charity that helped the homeless. Somehow it had seemed fitting. After all her mother's heart had become homeless, thanks to her father's affairs.

She had toned her dress with plain black accessories: good leather shoes and an equally good leather bag. Good quality, but not designer. In her case she had one of her favourite black cashmere long-line cardigans to wear later in the day for the journey from Milan to the world-famous luxurious Villa d'Este Hotel on Lake Como, where the Prince was going to escort her on a tour of some of the wonderful privately owned villas of the region at the invitation of their owners.

It was entirely due to the Prince that she was being given such a rare opportunity to see the interiors of those villas, her employer at the trust had told her, adding that it had been at the Prince's suggestion and his own expense that she was to stay at the exclusive Ville d'Este, which itself had originally been privately owned.

There was no sunshine quite like the sunshine of late September and early October, Lily thought as the taxi negotiated the streets of Milan. Fashion week was almost over, but she still looked over when they passed the Quadrilatero d'Oro—the area that housed some of the world's most famous designer shops—before heading for the Castello Sforzesco palace.

The reception she was attending was being held within the castle, which now housed several galleries containing works of art by Italy's most famous artists. Lily was familiar with the layout of the building, having visited it whilst she had been studying for her doctorate and writing her thesis, and was a great admirer of its collections. However, after the taxi had dropped her off and she had made her way to her destination, it wasn't either the Sforza family's history or its art collections that brought her to a stunned halt in front of the double doors behind which the reception was to be held.

It was the man waiting for her there that brought a shocked, *'You!'* to her lips.

She couldn't believe it. She didn't want to believe it but it was true. He, the man from the studio who had already harangued and insulted her once, was regarding her with an expression that said just how unwelcome to him her presence was as he announced grimly, 'I don't know what you think *you* are doing here.'

Was he daring to suggest that he thought she was pursuing him? Fortunately, before she could give vent to her feelings, Lily realised that he was staring at the suitcase in front of her, where her name was written plainly on the address label.

Focusing on it, Marco read the label in growing disbelief. *Dr Lillian Wrightington.*

Removing his gaze from the label, he looked up at Lily, demanding, *'You* are Dr Wrightington?'

Lily supposed that by rights she should feel a certain sense of satisfaction at his obvious disbelief, but the reality was that it was hard for her to feel anything other than a stomach churning, knee-knocking despair. Not that she was going to let him see that. Not for one minute.

Instead she drew herself up to her full height, tilting her chin firmly as she responded, 'Yes. And you are?'

He didn't like that, she could see. He didn't like it one tiny little bit. Anger blazed like an inquisition fire in the depths of the tawny gold eyes.

'Marco di Lucchesi,' he answered her stiffly.

The Prince? He was the Prince? Her escort for the next two weeks?'

Her leaden feeling of despair threatened to become a bubble of wild, panicked hysteria. Maybe he was just a member of the royal family. Someone sent on the Prince's behalf? Lily sent up a small prayer to fate. Please, please let that be so.

The doors behind them opened and an official came bustling out, saying when he saw Lily's case, 'Permit me to arrange for your luggage to be stored somewhere safe for you until you are ready to leave, Dr Wrightington.'

'Yes. Yes, thank you,' Lily said with a smile, before turning back to Marco to ask, dry-mouthed, 'Marco di Lucchesi? Prince di Lucchesi?'

'I do not use the title.' His curt response blew away her fragile hopes like a tornado attacking soap bubbles. 'If you are ready I will escort you inside and make some introductions for you. Several of the families whose homes you will be seeing are represented amongst those attending the reception.'

Lily inclined her head.

'The Historical Preservation Trust supplied me with a copy of the guest list.'

'Some of the family trees are rather complex. It is not always easy to know who owns what.'

Not for the ordinary English tourist, perhaps, but Italian genealogy where it related to grand houses and villas were her field of expertise. It was a sign of how much seeing him had shaken her that she did not feel like pointing that out to him, Lily acknowledged. Nevertheless she knew that it was war between them, with gauntlets thrown down and challenges made.

Language could be every bit as filled with subtle tex-
tures that held concealed messages as art.

Her suitcase had been wheeled away. Marco was
standing to one side of her, and the doors—her escape
route—were directly in front of her. Refusing to look
at him, Lily headed determinedly for them.

She almost made it—would have made it, in fact,
if at the last minute he hadn't beaten her to the doors,
with Machiavellian timing and a male stride that easily
outpaced her high-heeled gait. He barred her escape by
the simple expedient of placing his arm across the closed
doors.

There was nowhere for her to go—nothing for her to
do other than either stand where she was, a safe couple
of feet away from him, or walk into him.

Walk into him? In a series of images inside her head
she could see the physical contact there had already been
between them. She could feel again her own inexplicable
reaction to it. The ante-room was empty, the air in it
cool, but she could feel perspiration breaking out along
her hair-line. Why had this had to happen? Why had he
had to come into her life?

Wasn't there an even more important question she
should be asking herself? her inner critic taunted her.
Shouldn't she really be asking why he disturbed her so
much? Why his mere presence was enough to cause a
scarily powerful undertow of emotions and sensations
within her?

He'd touched her first. And, like her, he had recoiled at that first contact as though he had suffered
the same shock of sensation and awareness that had
electrified her. That should surely have put them on a

level battleground. But somehow it had not. Somehow he remained in possession of the higher ground.

It didn't matter what he had or had not experienced, Lily told herself protectively. What mattered was what had always mattered to her, and that was maintaining her own security—emotionally, mentally and physically.

Marco frowned. What was that scent she was wearing? It was so delicate and alluring that it made him want to move closer to her to catch its true essence. Which no doubt was exactly why she was wearing it so sparingly, he thought cynically, reminding himself that he had far more substantial and important questions he wanted answers to than the name of her scent.

'Does the trust know about the kind of work you do in your spare time?'

He was threatening her, or at least attempting to threaten her, Lily recognized. Even if he had not put that threat into exact words. Anger and fear burned a caustic path over her emotional nerve-endings. He was wrong about her. He was misjudging her. He probably thought he was far too important for her to risk offending him by standing up to him. She had a right to defend herself, though, and that was exactly what she was going to do—as little as she liked being put in a position where she had to explain herself to him.

'I wasn't working—as such. I was simply doing a favour for…for a friend, and standing in for them at the last minute.' It was the truth, after all.

Marco felt his anger against her grow and burn even more hotly. She was playing with words, using those that suited her and discarding those that did not. Just as she played with the vulnerable young lives of silly young fools like his nephew. 'So the trust doesn't know?'

'There is nothing for them *to* know. I did a favour for...for someone, and—'

'A favour? Is that what you call it? I have a very different name for what you were doing.'

How could this woman, this Dr Lillian Wrightington, be the same woman he had caught trying to bribe his nephew into modelling for her?

It seemed impossible...but it wasn't. Quite plainly Dr Wrightington was a woman who lived two very separate lives. What could possibly motivate a woman highly qualified and presumably able to command a respectable salary to involve herself in such sleaze? The anger and pain he had felt over Olivia's death surged through him. He could taste it in his mouth, feel it burning his emotions.

They had been childhood friends, expected by their families to marry one day. Theirs would have been a platonic union, a business arrangement, and Olivia had assured him that she wanted the same thing, too. Only she'd been leading a secret life, duped into chasing fame as a model, and it cut deep to think that the girl he'd thought he knew had been deceiving him all that time.

Olivia had never found that fame. Drugs and ultimately prostitution had dragged her into the gutter and from there to her death, and her journey there had been facilitated by a woman like the one standing in front of him now. A woman who bought beautiful young flesh for those with a taste for it, and who deceived those who possessed that beautiful young flesh with promises of fame and fortune.

He had trusted both Olivia herself and that woman, but they had both lied to him about their intentions. That knowledge had left a raw wound within him that his pride could not allow to heal. They'd given him their word, their promise, they'd taken his trust and destroyed it. He'd have to be a complete fool—a weak, easily manipulated fool—to trust another woman now. His cynicism burned inside him like vitriol.

'Why do you do it?' he asked grimly.

Lily could feel the icy-cold blast of his contempt like a burn against her skin. It made her want to shrink into herself in anguished pain. What had she ever done to warrant his harshness towards her? Nothing. And yet the knowledge that he felt contempt for her pierced her. What was it about him that made her own emotions react so deeply to him? As though somehow she was hyper-sensitive to him—as though some kind of magnetic link existed between them, enclosing her and making her acutely vulnerable to the force-field of his personality, no matter how hard she struggled to resist the effect he was having on her.

'Why do I do what?'

'Don't pretend not to understand me. You know perfectly well what I mean—that seedy studio, the manner in which you approached my nephew.'

His words brought a guilty flush of colour to her skin, even though she had nothing to feel guilty about.

'I've already told you I was simply doing someone else a favour.'

Far from placating him, her explanation served only to add to his biting contempt.

'I can imagine the kind of *favour* you were attempting to do,' he told her brutally, the fury inside him spilling over. 'Tell me something,' he demanded. 'Does what you're doing never worry you? Do you ever give any thought to the damage and destruction you and your kind cause?'

Lily's heart had started to thump heavily and uncomfortably. She was beginning to feel panicked by his attack. He was advancing into private territory within her that was filled with thinly healed sores. It was incredibly ironic that he should make the assumptions about her that he had. Incredibly ironic and almost unbearable. Only her keenly honed instinct to protect herself stopped her from protesting and from justifying her involvement. Instead, as calmly as she could, she said unsteadily, 'As I've already told you—not that I need to explain or excuse my actions to *you*—I was asked by my...by someone to take over a photographic shoot for a clothes catalogue. Nothing more than that.'

'So what about the young man who was approached in a student bar and offered the opportunity of doing some modelling work in this shoot? Didn't that worry you? Didn't you question your...*friend* about why he had found a model in such a way? There are, after all, model agencies who I am sure have books filled with the names of young men who already know at least some of the pitfalls of the business in which they are involved.'

Lily could feel the sting of his words against her emotions, lacerating and flaying them as effectively as though he had laid a whip to her flesh. The only difference was that the wounds he was inflicting on her she could and must keep hidden from him. In the life she had so carefully created for herself there was no place for the girl she had once been and there never would be. She had cut herself off from her past to protect herself from her own ghosts. She would never look back at them.

Because she was still afraid of them?

Why was this happening to her? She had been so happy, so safe, had felt a real pride in herself and what she had achieved, and now because of one man—this man—who was determined to misjudge her, everything she had was in jeopardy. The desire to give in to her emotions had never been stronger, but Lily knew that she had to overcome that desire. Calmness, logic and knowing the truth must be her weapons in this fight, and she must wield them well if she was to protect herself.

Lily took a deep breath,

'Clothing catalogues don't exactly pay top dollar. My…the person I was helping wanted to keep his costs down. That was why he approached your nephew. No other reason.'

'Do you really expect me to believe that? It's illogical. After all, in addition to paying my nephew your friend also suggested he accompany him to a post-shoot party with some of fashion's big names.'

This was too much. Lily could feel her defences crumbling. She had really had enough. She wasn't at all happy about being put in the position of having to defend her half-brother's behaviour, but neither did she think Marco di Lucchesi's behaviour towards her was in any way acceptable.

He had virtually accused her of acting on behalf of a pervert bent on corrupting the innocence of his nephew. Rick had his faults, but he would only have been trying to impress his potential models—nothing more.

'You're mistaken about Rick,' she insisted fiercely, 'and about me.' When he didn't respond she added impulsively, 'If you want the truth, I feel exactly the same way about the sleazy side of modelling as you do.'

Wasn't that more or less exactly what the owner of the model agency Olivia had worked for had told him when he had gone to her for help in his quest to bring Olivia safely home? When Olivia herself had refused to listen to him? Hadn't the woman told him that she shared his opinion of Olivia's vulnerability and that he could trust her to protect and keep her safe? Eighteen-year-old Marco had foolishly believed her, but she had been lying, and so too was the woman confronting him now. Past experience and the facts told him that.

Why, then, when it should have been the simplest of matters to continue to denounce her, without any compunction and without any kind of emotional reaction himself, was he now discovering that it wasn't? What was stopping him? For some inexplicable reason, and completely illogically, he was actually experiencing an unwanted but undeniable emotional reaction to her deceit. Why? Why should he care that she was a liar who couldn't be trusted? He didn't, Marco assured himself, and told her curtly, 'What you're saying does not add up, therefore it cannot possibly be true.'

Lily stared at him in stunned disbelief. Everything about his body language and the look on his face told her that nothing she could say would change his mind. He was calling her a liar, and he was making it plain that he wasn't going to change his mind—no matter what she tried to say. It was as though he wanted to dislike and distrust her. Very well, she would defend herself by using the same 'logic' on him that he had used against her.

'No one forced your nephew to accept the photo shoot, the money, or the party invitation,' she pointed out, somehow managing to adopt a cool, clear, emotionless voice. 'Instead of harassing me you might do better using your bullying questioning tactics on him. After all, a young man so well connected and coming from such a wealthy family shouldn't need to accept work that pays so little—unless, of course, he had other reasons for accepting it.'

She had hit a nerve now, Lily recognised. He might not have betrayed it in any visible way, but she knew as surely as if the reaction had been hers that inwardly he had recoiled from her challenge.

'What reasons?

His voice was harsh, almost raw with an emotion that was more than anger—as though something had been dredged up from deep within him against his will. Lily could feel herself weakening. Only he was not a man for whom she should feel compassion, she warned herself. In his way he was every bit as dangerous as those he was castigating, if not more so.

Taking a deep breath, she challenged him silkily. 'An uncle who keeps him on too short a rope, perhaps?'

He didn't like it. He didn't like it one little bit. And yet to her surprise, instead of retreating into an angry and arrogant princely silence, no doubt meant to indicate to her that he did not have to explain himself or his actions to someone as plebeian as she, he told her, 'Pietro is a young man with a tendency to behave impulsively and the belief that he is immortal. Traits which in my opinion are the result of a little too much maternal indulgence. If I believe he should be able to manage within his not ungenerous allowance then I do so in the knowledge that one day he will be responsible for managing a far greater sum of money. You may think that to be keeping him on a short rope. I consider it to be encouraging him to respect the benefits of living within his means.'

'Perhaps that is something you should be telling him, not me?' Lily suggested. 'I accept that your nephew is important to you, but what is important to me right now is doing what the Trust sent me here to do.' She looked pointedly at the closed doors he had barred.

'And you can be trusted to carry out that duty, can you? Without disappearing to undertake some very different work on the side for a "friend"?'

'You have neither the right nor any reason to question my commitment to my work.'

'On the contrary, I have both the right—since I am responsible for persuading people to admit you into their homes—and the reason you have already supplied to me.'

'We are keeping people waiting,' Lily reminded him,

anxious to bring their conversation to a close and to escape from him. She looked at the door, but he was standing closer to it than she was and he was watching her.

CHAPTER THREE

THE way Marco was looking at her was making Lily's heart thump raggedly with tension. If only someone would come and interrupt them, bring her torment to an end. But no one did, and she was left with no alternative other than to listen to him.

'I don't accept for one minute that the motives of you or your friend were as altruistic as you would have me believe,' he told her.

'I'm telling you the truth. If you can't accept that then that's your problem.'

'No,' he told her harshly. 'You are *not* telling me the truth.'

His presence encircled her now. She could neither step forward nor back. He had bent his head to speak quietly into her ear, and now a thousand delicate nerve-endings were being tortured by the warmth of his breath. She felt hot and dizzy, with a torrent of sensations cascading through her caused by the fact that he had breached the polite barrier of personal space that should have existed between them.

She had to say something. She had to stand her ground. But she could hardly breathe, never mind that her flesh was almost screaming out a feral cry of panicked fear. She tried to step past him, but he moved even more swiftly, causing her to cannon into him.

Her small gasp grazed the bare skin of Marco's neck, causing an explosion of sensual pleasure to bomb his nerve-endings and race from them along his veins like liquid fire. His response to it was so instinctive and automatic that he was reaching for her before his brain knew what was happening. Frantically it searched for an explanation for what he was feeling. How could he, a man who could quite easily remain impervious to the most blatant of erotic sensual persuasion from the women who had shared his bed, have succumbed so easily to the mere touch of her breath against his skin? What was it about this woman that ripped aside his self-control and induced in him such a primitive male response?

Of course he would release her; there was, after all no purpose in him holding her. No purpose and certainly no desire, he assured himself—and he would have released her too, if she hadn't started to struggle against him, igniting a feeling inside him that came like a thunderbolt out of nowhere to challenge his male pride.

'No!' Panic had filled Lily at the way her body was reacting to the proximity of his body, as though it actually *wanted* that proximity, and she desperately needed to bring it to an end before he realised the effect he was having on her. But now, as she saw the look in his eyes, Lily realised that he had misinterpreted her anxiety as defiance—and she could see too that he intended to punish her for it.

That punishment was swift and shocking. His mouth taking hers in a kiss of blistering male revenge that seared her senses. It had been years since she had last been kissed—and never, ever like this. Never, ever in a way that imprinted everything about the male lips possessing hers on her senses and her psyche, from the texture of his skin to its taste. In a thousand rapid-fire shutter actions his maleness was being matched by her femaleness. Why? What was happening to her?

Lily lifted her free hand in protest, her eyes opening and widening when her fingertips grazed the flesh of his face. She could feel the contrast between the skin of his jaw where he'd shaved and the skin above it. The photographer in her, the artist, wanted to explore the lines of his face, so dramatically perfect. *She* wanted to. Her lips softened and parted. So that she could protest. It had to be for that. It couldn't be for anything else. And that small mewing sound locked in the back of her throat? That was a complaint, she assured herself.

His own eyes were open now, his gaze a danger-ous volcano of molten gold fixing on hers. She could feel herself starting to tremble, weakness filling her, so that she was forced to lean into him. Into him and onto him.

There was a moment in space and time during which it seemed to Lily that their bodies moved together of their own volition—and then abruptly he was pushing her away from him.

What was happening to him? He never normally al-lowed emotion to control his behaviour. Never.

Someone was trying to open the door from the other side. Without looking at one another, never mind speak-ing to one another, they both stepped back from it. As swiftly and determinedly as he intended to step back from what he had felt holding her in his arms, her lips clinging to his, Marco told himself, acknowledging grimly as he did so that he had been right to have doubts about the wisdom of this project. He should have trusted his instincts and refused to get involved. The trouble was when he had had those doubts it had never for one minute crossed his mind just *why* he had been right to have them. It had been the ability of a foreign organisation in a foreign country to do justice to the history of Italy in general and his own family in particular that had made him feel wary about the project.

Now, though, he was having to deal with a far more immediate and personal cause for concern. And that was...

He snatched a brief, hard glance at Lily. On the face of it there was no immediately discernible reason why his flesh should be so aware of hers, or so responsive to it. No discernible reason why his senses should so attuned to her presence, her scent, the shadow cast by her body, the sound of her breathing, the lift of her breasts as she did so. Grinding his teeth against the way his thoughts were running free, he battled to bring them back in order, straining the muscles of his self-control just as controlling runaway horses and chariot would have strained the muscles of an experienced Roman gladiator.

She was attractive enough—quietly and discreetly beautiful, even. In a way that blended perfectly with her current persona whilst being completely at odds with the persona she had revealed in the studio—her real persona, he was sure. And was that the persona to which he was attracted? Like a schoolboy aroused by the thought of the pseudo-wantonness of a naked centrefold model? Was there deep within him a hitherto unknown part that was attracted to and aroused by such a woman? The thought revolted him, and it told him all he wanted to know about his real feelings. A part of him would have preferred that to be the truth rather than having to admit the actual truth—which was that his body was every bit as responsive to her in her present role as Dr Lillian Wrightington as it had been to the streetwise, jean-clad, predatory woman.

So physically he had responded to her? What did that mean? Nothing. Nothing at all. He would not allow it to mean anything.

Holding the door open for her, Marco told Lily in a curt voice, 'I shall be watching you, Dr Wrightington, and if I suspect for any reason that your presence here is compromising the success of this project I shall have no hesitation in getting in touch with the trust and requesting them to replace you with someone else.'

'You can't do that,' Lily protested. Her mouth had gone dry and her heart was thumping unevenly. This project meant so much to her. There'd even been talk of it being covered for a very well thought of TV arts programme. More than the career benefits that kind of exposure would bring her, though, Lily wanted to share with a wider audience the huge impact Italian art brought back to Britain had had on so many aspects of British life—from architecture to literature, from gardening to fashion, and so much more. To be dismissed from this project was the last thing she wanted.

Marco was a powerful man, and one who was already prejudiced against her. What was that sharp stab

of anguish all about? She didn't care what he thought
about her. He could misjudge her as much as he wished.
In fact she was glad that he had. Was she? Was she
really?

Marco was still holding the door open. The buzz of
conversation from the people gathered inside the room
receded like an ebbing tide, until there was nothing left
apart from a rustling silence as everyone looked towards
them.

Whilst she felt uncomfortable, her companion seemed
completely composed and in control, announcing,
'Please accept my apologies for the fact that we are a
little late. The blame is entirely mine.'

And he would be forgiven for it, Lily could tell. The
smiles being directed towards him were both admiring
and respectful. No one, it seemed, wished to question
or query the Prince di Lucchesi.

'I know you are all impatient to talk with our guest of
honour, Dr Wrightington, so I think I shall dispense with
a lengthy speech and just say instead that her scholarship in the subject of the art collected by our predeces-
sors and the architecture of our homes should speak for
itself.'

Had anyone other than her noticed that questioning
'should'? Lily wondered, thankful of the poise she had
learned from observing her mother—before heartache
and prescription pills had destroyed her. It was surprisingly easy to stand tall with a smile pinned to your face
once you'd learned the trick of hiding the reality of what
you were feeling within yourself.

Easy, too, to make small talk as she circled the floor
at Marco's side whilst he introduced her to people with

names that were woven into the very fabric of this part
of Italy's.

'Your Grace.' Lily responded to Marco's introduction
to an elderly duchess with a formidably upright bearing. 'I can't thank you enough for allowing me to see
your villa and your art collection. There is a wonderful
sketch in the archives at Castle Howard of one of your
ancestors, drawn—'

'By Leonardo. Yes, I have heard of it. Although sadly
I have never seen it.'

Lily smiled at her. 'I was given permission to photograph it so that I could show it to you.'

She was impressive, Marco acknowledged reluctantly.
Not just in her knowledge of her subject but also in her
manner—but how much of her was learned and how
much the real woman? Not very much, he decided.

'It will be interesting to compare it with the painting
of my husband's ancestor by Leonardo,' the Duchess
told Lily with a smile.

Normally Lily enjoyed this kind of occasion—the
opportunity to talk with people who shared her interests
and her love of Italian art—but today for some reason,
after less than a couple of hours of mingling with the
other guests, she developed the beginnings of a very
painful pounding stress headache that made her feel
slightly sick.

For *some* reason? She was supposed to be an intelligent woman. The reason for her tension was standing
less than two yards away from her, and right now she
could feel his gaze burning into her back. So the man
running the project here in Italy was hostile to her and
contemptuous of her—so what? She more than most

people was adept at cocooning herself in her own private emotional and mental space and not allowing others to penetrate that space. Adept at it? She was an expert in it, Lily acknowledged wryly. In fact if there was a degree to be had in it she would have graduated first class with honours.

'It will soon be time for us to leave.'

The sound of Marco's voice from directly behind her had Lily almost choking on the sip of wine she had just taken. Not because she hadn't heard him move—she had. She was acutely aware of every single move he made. What she hadn't been prepared for was the warmth of his breath on the nape of her neck, where it was revealed by the soft knot of her drawn back hair. Was it just because he had caught her off-guard that she had felt the shower of tiny darts that had now brought her skin out in goosebumps? Goosebumps of delicious sensual pleasure?

Lily knew that it wasn't. She wasn't even going to begin question how it was that a person who had turned her back on the delights of sexual pleasure should immediately be able to recognise and understand that the degree of sensuality she had just experienced spoke of a vulnerability to the man who had caused it that went far beyond the norm of casual sexual attraction. Some questions were better not asked—especially by someone like her—when they involved someone like Marco.

When a man standing in a group to her right moved, accidentally nudging her arm and causing some of her wine to spill from her glass onto her bare skin, Lily was relieved—grateful, in fact, for the small incident. It distracted her attention and Marco's far too perceptive and sharp gaze from her earlier involuntary shudder of delight.

'I'm so sorry,' the man apologised, telling a passing waiter, 'We need a dry cloth, please.'

'There's no need...' Lily began to say, but the words became locked in her throat as out of nowhere, or so it seemed, Marco himself produced a white cloth, which he placed on her damp arm. He ignored her panicky, 'I can do it myself,' just as he ignored her attempt to move away from him. Somehow he had taken possession of both her nearly empty glass, which he had placed on the tray of a hovering waiter, and her damp arm, his hand and his fingers lean and tanned against the white starched fabric of the cloth. He had good hands, Lily acknowledged. Strong artist's hands. Hands with a powerful male grip that could crush a woman's resistance to their hold should he feel it necessary.

A new quiver forked through her. Not on her flesh this time, but deep within it—a swift, tightening, convulsive sensation that gripped and then relaxed, leaving a far too intimate pulse beating in its place.

Lily was perfectly familiar with the outward signs of sexual arousal. After all she had seen models mimicking them in one form or another for as long as she could remember. Bitterly she recalled how when her father had finished working she would be pushed into the small boxroom off his studio whilst he 'played'. Her father had been of that order of photographers in a certain era who had believed that having sex with models was one of the perks of the job. No, she was no stranger to the signs and sounds of physical arousal, both real and faked, male and female, but when it came to being familiar with her own sexual arousal… That was haunted, poisoned territory that had long ago become an empty wasteland and she didn't go there. She didn't want to go there.

Marco was releasing her.

'It's time for us to go,' he told her. 'The traffic to the airport will be heavy at this time of the day.'

'The airport? We're flying to Lake Como?'

She'd assumed that they'd be driving there.

'By helicopter. It's much the easier way to get there,' Marco informed her, clapping his hands for silence so that he could announce their departure.

'I was already looking forward to introducing you to Villa Ambrosia,' the Duchess told Lily, coming over to say goodbye to her and holding both Lily's hands in her own as she did so, in a gesture of genuine liking and approval. 'But now that I have met you I am looking forward to it even more. She is a delightful girl, Marco,' she added, turning to him. 'Look after her well, won't you?'

Of course Lily didn't dare look at Marco once the Duchess had left them and they were on their own. The Duchess's comment about his looking after her wouldn't have gone down at all well, she suspected.

The museum official who had taken her case and insisted on wheeling it for her escorted them to their waiting car. It would be very easy to get used to such a pampered way of life, Lily thought, remembering ruefully how often she had ended up with an aching back from a bulging bag holding her laptop, her camera, and assorted other necessary paraphernalia for her work.

The traffic was heavy, but the insulated interior

of the luxurious saloon car protected them from the fume-clogged air outside. A glass screen separated them from the driver, and the combination of that and the soft leather of their seats made Lily feel that they were isolated together in a space that was far too intimate.

Not that there was any intimacy between the two of them. Marco had produced his cell phone the minute the chauffeur had closed the door of the car, his brief, 'Please excuse me,' immediately distancing him from her. Because he *wanted* to be distanced from her? Of course he did. He despised her. Lily knew that was true, but she also knew that—like her—he had felt the startling electric connection that had burned into life between them the first time he had touched her. A connection that neither of them wanted.

Now Marco was putting his phone down and turning towards her.

'Just before we left the reception the Duchess asked me if there was any chance that we might be able to spend a couple of nights at her villa as her guests. You obviously made a very big impression on her.'

The stiff hostility in his voice told Lily how little he liked telling her that.

'I've just been checking through our schedule. It would be possible for us to extend the tour to include a short stay with her if you wish to do so.'

So he hadn't been distancing himself from her. He had actually been working on her behalf, or rather on behalf of their shared project, Lily was forced to admit reluctantly. She didn't want to have to feel guilty about misjudging him, but it seemed that she was going to have to admit that she had. Just as he had misjudged her—although she suspected she would never be able to convince him of that. Not after everything that had happened between them. Not that she was going to even attempt to change his mind about her. Why should she want to?

Still, she couldn't help but wonder what had caused such a deep-rooted loathing of what he believed she represented. Whatever it was, she couldn't imagine him ever telling her about it. Everything about him said that he simply wasn't the kind of man who confided in other people. He was too remote for that, too proud, Lily thought tiredly as she forced herself to respond with professional politeness.

'It's very generous of her to make such a kind offer. I'd love to have the opportunity to spend more time studying both the villa and her art collection.'

'Very well, then. I'll e-mail an acceptance of her invitation to her personal assistant.'

The chauffeur swung the car out of the static traffic and into a space he had spotted in the adjacent lane. Automatically Lily put her hand down to stop herself from sliding along the leather seat, but to her embarrassment felt only the hard, unyielding surface of Marco's thigh.

Scarlet-faced with mortification, she snatched her hand away. Was it her imagination or were her fingertips tingling with awareness of the flesh they had accidentally touched? It was certainly her imagination that was providing her with unwanted and dangerous images of charcoal sketches of a taut male thigh. Marco's thigh.

'We'll be at the airport in a few minutes.'

The calmly delivered information should have been

enough to block out such images but somehow it wasn't. Lily kept her face turned towards the car window as they approached the airport. She didn't dare risk looking directly at Marco. Not that he could see what had been going on inside her head, of course. Thank goodness.

From his own corner of the comfortable limousine Marco cursed under his breath at the effect Lily's brief touch on his thigh had had on him. Because he hadn't been expecting it, that was all. There was nothing special about her touch that could have caused that almost violent surge of unstoppable desire from stabbing up his thigh and into his groin. He had been so involved in his business affairs that he hadn't realised until now just how long he had been celibate. Too long. That was what had made him vulnerable to her. Nothing else. His intellect and his emotions were appalled by the very idea that he could find her physically desirable, given what he knew about her. She was a woman whose way of life he had very good reason to abhor—a woman he had already discovered to be involved in the same kind of world that had destroyed Olivia.

Olivia.

Lured away by promises of the fame her beauty could bring her as a top model, Olivia had been seduced by the thought of excitement and adventure far from the safety and security of her sheltered life with her parents.

It had taken him several weeks to discover that she had moved to London. He had pleaded with her to come home but she'd refused. She had told him that she had been taken on by a modelling agency and had been sharing a flat with other young models.

He had gone to see the owner of the model agency and appealed to her for help. She had seemed so sympathetic and understanding, so concerned for Olivia, that he had made the mistake of believing her when she had assured him that he had her personal guarantee that Olivia would be safe in her care, and that she would quickly tire of her new life and decide to return home.

At eighteen, he had been a gullible fool. How that knowledge still burned like acid within him. He'd had no idea that the woman was little more than a procuress, and that far from protecting the girls in her charge she was selling them into a life of drugs and prostitution. That life had led ultimately to Olivia dying from an overdose, alone in a New York hotel room.

He had buried his shame, his gullibility, his guilt deep within himself, making a vow to himself that his days of trusting others were over and that in future he would rely on logic and not emotion to direct the course of his life.

Until now—until Dr Lillian Wrightington, with her lies and her connection with all that he loathed—he had had no difficulty whatsoever in keeping that vow. But now, in the short time that he had known her, she had not only undermined that resolution she had also found a fault line in his defences that was causing all his long-buried vulnerabilities to rise like ghosts to mock and taunt him.

What went on inside the head of a woman like her to enable her to live a double life without guilt, to tell her lies with such passionate conviction?

Against his will Marco found that his gaze was drawn to Lily's averted profile, as though by studying it he might somehow find the answer. Very quickly he realised his mistake. His brain might only seek to study and analyse the facts, but his body was reacting to her on a very different and very dangerous level indeed. And was that reaction outside his control? Of course not, he denied. But he still had to move discreetly in his seat, in order to ease the pressure of his unwanted arousal. And whilst he did so his gaze insisted on remaining fixed on her.

Why? He tried to look away, but a few small wisps had escaped from the soft knot of her hair, catching his attention and sending his senses down a dangerous course at such high speed that to stop them was impossible.

She was looking downwards, that he could see the dark fan of her lashes and the shadows they threw across her face. The downbent angle of her neck revealed the vulnerability of its exposed nape. She had a small beauty spot just to one side of the top bone of her spine, just where a lover would be unable to resist the temptation to kiss it and then work his way along her slender throat to her ear, and then back down again to her collarbone. Her skin would smell and taste of the scent that surrounded her, which reminded him vaguely of roses and lavender. Her bare arms were slender and toned, and lightly tanned. Her wristwatch was slightly loose on her wrist. Her dress might not cling to her body, but he had watched her earlier at the reception as she mingled with the other guests. She must know that the way it subtly hinted at the swell of her breasts and the curves of her waist and hips was far, far more sensually alluring than something tight would have been.

Marco tried to control his wayward thoughts, but doing so was like trying to swim a river at full tide—every effort he made to reach the safety of logic only resulted in him being swept further into the dangerous current of his senses.

The very fact that her dress obscured rather than revealed her body aroused the hunter him, made him want to confirm for himself that the secrets of her body were every bit as pleasurable to his gaze and his touch as he suspected. She was temptation in a dozen different ways. *Deliberate* temptation, Marco warned himself, remembering the manner in which she walked, her posture upright, her head held proudly on the slender stem of her neck, whilst at the same time being so careful not to sway her hips, not to attract attention to her femininity. It only served to build a man's appetite to know more of her. The ache in his body intensified. He needed to think of something else, of someone else, but somehow he couldn't. He couldn't think of anything other than her.

And it wasn't just his own sex she had won over at the reception. The women there had liked her as well. She had seen the approving looks they had given her, and the way in which even the most regal of them had unbent whilst talking with her. The Duchess's invitation was proof of that.

No, he couldn't deny that she was well versed in her subject, and also able to share her own obvious love for it with others, so that they too became enthused.

If he hadn't known about her other life, her other self, Marco suspected that he too might have become an admirer of her familiarity with her subject. And an admirer of her too?

No!

He had never believed in mixing work with pleasure, Marco reminded himself. It always led to complications and problems. But his role within this project was a voluntary one, taken on because of his own pleasure and pride in his own heritage.

No! His answer to his own question was still the same.

He did not want her. He could not want her. But neither could he deny the fact that his body found something physically compelling about her. It was an awkward reality he could well have done without.

Marco forced his thoughts back into the channels where they belonged. They had reached the airport, and the driver was turning off for the private part of the airfield, where expensive-looking executive jets awaited their passengers and owners. He checked his watch. They were running slightly late, but he had e-mailed ahead to warn the helicopter pilot to alter their departure slot. He could see the chopper up ahead of them on the runway, the pilot already on board. The driver brought the limousine to a smooth halt a mere handful of yards away from the helicopter and then got out to open the rear passenger door for Lily, whilst one of the waiting attendants removed their cases from the boot.

After a few words with the waiting concierge whilst she stood to one side, Marco indicated that she should board the helicopter. When she hesitated, Marco frowned. He could see her hand was gripping the hand-rail to the steps, her bones showing through her delicate

skin. Her face had lost some of its colour, and she looked
like someone screwing up every last bit of her courage
to make herself do something that terrified her. Her fear
had somehow stripped her features of their maturity, so
that instead of a grown woman Marco felt he was looking at a terrified child. A terrified child who was staring
blindly into space as though locked away—trapped—in
a world of dreadful fear.

Reluctantly, trying to check himself but unable to do
so, and against all the urgings of his brain, as though
some deep-rooted recognition was overriding his logic,
he felt the most extraordinary and unexpected feeling
of concern and compassion for that child fill him.

'You don't like flying?' he guessed. 'There is nothing to worry about if you haven't flown in a helicopter before. Come…' Why was he behaving like this?
Treating her as though… Before he could stop himself,
Marco was holding out his hand to her.

Without thinking Lily placed her own hand within
Marco's. She felt slightly sick and light-headed, and the
warmth of his hand wrapping round her own was a reassuring comfort she could feel at a distance, as though
she was standing outside herself, observing her own
reactions.

It was crazy to let the thought of flying in a helicopter
affect her like this just because once before someone
had taken her hand, urged her up the steps to a similar
machine. Once before a man had smiled at her and reas-
sured her that she would be perfectly safe—before his
smile had disappeared in an explosion of anger and a
fierce tug on her arm that had dragged her up into the
dark interior of a helicopter.

The hand Marco was holding started to tremble, the small vibrations seizing her arm and then her whole body. Perspiration broke out on her skin, bathing her in an uncomfortable wash of anxious heat.

People were waiting...watching... She must get a grip.

'There is nothing to be afraid of,' Marco repeated. 'But if you prefer—if it makes you feel more comfortable—we can travel by road.'

His voice was calm, his grip on her hand loosening slightly as he stroked his thumb over her frantically racing pulse.

Lily turned her head and looked at him. His eyes were topaz-gold, not pale blue, and nor were they filled with a look of greedy desire that filled her with fear and revulsion. His stance was still and patient, his manner towards her soothingly reassuring, as though...as though he understood. She took a deep breath.

'No. It's all right. I'll be all right now.'

A small tug of her hand freed it from his grip, and an equally small nod of his head gave her the courage to make her way up the steps, to be helped into the machine by the uniformed co-pilot who introduced himself to her and then escorted her to her seat, showing her how to fasten herself properly into it before telling her cheerfully. 'We'll have you up at Lake Como and Villa d'Este in no time at all.'

When the man then fastened himself into the seat next to her, Lily was surprised—until he explained with another smile, 'The boss will be taking the co-pilot's seat up-front. He's a fully qualified pilot, although on this trip he'll just be playing a watching role.'

Somehow she wasn't surprised that Marco was a pilot. He had all the necessary skills, and she could easily imagine him remaining calm and focused, no matter what kind of crisis he was obliged to face.

The last time she had flown in a helicopter she had been fourteen years old. Lily's stomach muscles clenched. It was memories of that trip that had sparked off her reaction to boarding this machine now, but somehow or other Marco had found a way to break through her fear and bring her back to the present. Lily suspected that he would be anything but pleased to know that her senses had decided to recognise him as their protector and saviour. She found it hard to understand herself, given his hostility towards her.

When the shape of his body briefly obscured the light coming in through the glass nose of the machine Lily's heart jerked as though someone had deliberately pulled on its strings. She recognised that seeing him there now, on board the helicopter, was somehow extraordinarily comforting. How could that be when there was such conflict between them? Lily didn't know. She only knew that something deep inside her followed its own path and saw something in him that represented a safe haven.

A safe haven. For so many years of her life she had longed for that—for a presence, a person, who would take her side and protect her. But she had learned then that for her there was no such presence or person, and that she would have to provide her own protection and places of safety.

Now, cruelly, there was every bit as much danger for her in listening to that insistent instinct that was filling her subconscious with powerful images of safety and protection in the form of Marco di Lucchesi. That was because another instinct, every bit as powerful and demanding, was filling her senses and her body with a very different kind of awareness—the awareness of Marco as a man with the power to arouse her sexuality.

Safety and danger forged together in a complete and exact reversal of what she normally thought of as safety and danger.

Until now, until Marco, for her safety had been her own determined separation of herself from her sexuality, her sacrifice of it in order to protect herself from the danger of repeating the errors of her parents' hedonistic lifestyles. Until now and Marco *she* had been the one who was in charge of her security. Now without her being able to do a thing about it, control of her sexuality and her security had transferred itself from her into the hold of a man who despised and disliked her. How could that be? Lily didn't know. What she did know, though, was that she was not likely to be in any danger from her growing sensual and sexual responsiveness to Marco—at least not from him. She might not have known him for very long, but she knew instinctively that he would not allow himself to give in to any desire he felt for a woman he did not like.

She looked out of the window and down at the land beneath them. It was too dark for her to see anything other than the lights from the homes and roads below them.

'Soon be there now.' The co-pilot's voice was kind, but it lacked Marco's note of authority and safety which struck such a strong deep chord inside her. Just being held by him, even when he was angry with her, made her feel… Lily could feel her face beginning to burn as she felt a sudden fierce ache of pure female sexual desire stab through her. She wanted Marco. Oh, the irony of that! An irony that only she would ever know and understand.

They were coming in to land. Lily had imposed a steel band of rejection over what she was feeling, but it melted like snow in the full glare of a midsummer sun when Marco turned round to look at her. If only things were different. If only they were coming here as lovers. If only…

How could such preposterously foolish thoughts have managed to put down roots inside her emotions? Lily didn't know. She was just thankful that Marco di Lucchesi couldn't see them. Very thankful indeed.

CHAPTER FOUR

THEIR flight had been smooth and uneventful—and, given both that and the nature of his perfectly understandable feelings of distrust and contempt for Lily Wrightington, Marco was at a loss to explain to himself just why he found it necessary to hang back now that they could disembark from the helicopter, just so that he could keep a watch over her. Just as hard to explain was the concern he had felt for her during the short flight—to the point where he had had to actively restrain himself from turning round in his seat to check that she was all right.

She *wasn't* a vulnerable child, no matter what emotive mental images his head had produced to that effect. She was a fully grown woman. A deceitful, amoral, not-to-be trusted woman, who preyed on the vulnerabilities of others. But still he descended from the helicopter behind her, silently checking her safety. It was because of the mess it would make of all his carefully constructed plans should she for any reason become unable to complete her part in their planned tour. This concern for her welfare had nothing whatsoever to do with her in any personal sense. Nothing at all.

A chauffeur-driven car was waiting to drive them

the short distance from the helicopter landing pad to the hotel.

Naturally Lily had read up on the place, knowing that they would be staying there, but there were no words or photographs that could do real justice to the sparkling elegance of the rich interior of the hotel foyer, with its crystal chandelier, smooth marble surfaces and gilt furniture that seemed to give everything within it a rich golden glow.

There was no necessity for them to check in. An immaculately dressed receptionist wearing a uniform that looked to Lily as though it might have been tailored by one of Italy's foremost designers asked them to follow her, whisking them upwards and then along several corridors, faithfully decorated in keeping with the villa's history, before coming to a halt outside one of several doors in the corridor.

'We have given your guest a suite overlooking the lake, just as you requested, Your Highness,' the receptionist told Marco, opening the door and then turning back to him to ask, 'If you would like to see the suite…'

Marco shook his head, and then told Lily, 'I'll meet you downstairs in the bar in half an hour. We can run through tomorrow's schedule over dinner.'

Lily nodded her head.

'The porter will be here shortly with your luggage,' the receptionist informed Lily. 'If you require any information about anything, please ask him.'

'Thank you.' The girl had switched on the lights in the room, and although she stepped into it, Lily stayed in the open doorway, watching as the receptionist led

Marco to another door at the far end of the corridor.
It was crazy of her to feel so alone and abandoned—
as though for some reason she needed to know where
Marco di Lucchesi was in case she needed him.

She heard the click of his door closing as Marco
stepped into his own room. The receptionist disappeared
through a pair of doors that led to the stairs. There was
nothing to keep her standing in the entrance to her own
room now.

No, not merely a room, Lily reminded herself as she
closed the door and went to explore her surroundings.
Her suite was the size of a small apartment, and con-
sisted of a large bedroom, a sitting room and two bath-
rooms. The furniture was reproduction Georgian, and
the suite was decorated in toning shades of dark plum
and pale grey-blue, with the bed dressed in the current
boutique hotel fashion with neat piles of cushions and a
carefully folded deep plum silk throw at the bottom of a
padded cream bedcover. Tall glass doors opened from
both the bedroom and the sitting room onto a narrow
balcony just wide enough for a table and two chairs.
Although she couldn't see it now that it was dark, Lily
guessed that the view over the lake would be stupen-
dous. As it was, the sight of the moonlight reflecting
on the dark waters, and the myriad dancing lights from
craft on the lake and buildings on its banks created an
almost magical picture.

A discreet ring on the bell to her room announced the
arrival of the porter with her small case. After thanking him and tipping him, Lily lifted her case onto the
bed and opened it. She'd packed very carefully for this
tour. For the evening she'd brought with her a fine black

jersey tube-shaped skirt, which could be worn long from the waist, ruched up to make a shorter skirt, or worn as a short strapless dress. To go with it she'd brought a matching black jersey body, with three-quarter sleeves and a boat-shaped neckline, a softly draped long-line black cardigan, and a cream silk blouse. Between them she hoped that these items and the costume jewellery she had also brought with her would cover every kind of event she would be expected to attend.

For daytime she had a pair of slimline black Capri pants, a pair of jeans, and several interchangeable tops—along with her trench coat just in case.

For dinner tonight she intended to put the caramel-coloured dress back on and wear it with a black pashmina. Since her hair had already started to escape from its knot, and given the fact that she only had half an hour before she had to meet Marco, it made sense to simply leave it down on her shoulders.

In the bar Marco was just about to sit down to check through their itinerary for the first day of their tour, when he saw Lily approaching the entrance to the room.

She was wearing the same caramel-coloured dress she had worn for the reception, and a black wrap caught up on one shoulder with a gold Maltese cross that picked out the colour of her dress. She looked effortlessly elegant, Marco acknowledged, her hair framing the delicate bone structure of her face in softly styled natural-looking waves.

He wasn't surprised to see so many of the other occupants of the bar, both male and female, turning to give her a second look. What did surprise him, though, was that she seemed oblivious to their admiration, her manner more hesitant than confident—until she saw him, and then she straightened her back and came towards him with her chin tilted challengingly, like someone ready to do battle, he recognised grimly. No one looking at her now would associate her with that seedy studio and her even more dubious reason for being there.

Marco pushed back his chair and stood up.

'Would you like a drink or would you prefer to go straight in for dinner?'

'Straight in for dinner, please,' Lily answered him

'Very well.' A brief inclination of Marco's head brought the *maître d'* over to their table to escort them through into the restaurant

'What do you think of the place?' Marco asked her, observing the manner in which she was thoughtfully studying their surroundings.

'The decor is stunning.' Lily told him truthfully, 'but a woman coming here for a romantic *tête-à-tête* would have to be very careful about what she wore if she didn't want to end up competing with so much rich adornment.'

'To the man who desires her the only clothing a woman needs is her own skin. That is far more erotic to him than anything else could be,' Marco responded.

Lily could feel her face burning from the heat Marco's words had aroused inside her. The heat *and* the desire. She was glad to be able to sit down at the table to which the waiter had shown them, glad of the room's soft lighting and the large menu she had been handed to conceal her hot face.

Behind his own menu Marco was cursing himself for the rawly sensual images their exchange had produced inside his head. His imagination was laying them out before him in loving detail, as though answering a need within him that had demanded them. Lily lying naked against the silk coverlet of his bed, watching him, wanting him. Her skin would be all shimmering translucent perfection, fine and delicate, her nipples a deep rose-pink, her sex covered by soft blonde hair. Her legs would be long and slender, supple enough to wrap tightly around him…

Marco cursed himself silently again—and her. If this had been any other woman—if he had not known what she really was—then he could have dealt with the situation by taking her to bed. She was not, after all, the first woman to arouse him, and nor had he ever been short of eager partners to share his bed, but he had never desired any of them with this kind of intensity. What was happening to him? Why couldn't he control and banish the sensual hunger she aroused in him?

The discovery that he wasn't able to do so was like having a deep, unbridgeable chasm open up at his feet, leaving him vulnerable and desperately trying to cling on to what he had believed to be a perfectly safe landscape. The discovery was demanding answers to questions for which there was no logical answer, stirring up things within him he had not even known were there. And he didn't like it. He didn't like any of it. Marco liked being able to control his responses, not have them controlling him. He liked dealing in facts and logic, not being forced to endure the uncertainty of illogical emotions. Most of all he hated the fact that Lily confused him by refusing to a stay true to type. He knew what she was, and yet she kept on exhibiting behaviour that suggested she was something else. Or that he had been wrong about her. That was impossible. Wasn't it?

The only reason he was even being polite to her was for professional reasons—because of the commitment he had made to the trust's venture. The last thing he wanted to do was spend time in her company. His pride wouldn't let him back out of accompanying her, though. That would be tantamount to admitting that he was afraid of the way she made him feel.

He put down his menu, meaning to ignore her, but against his will his gaze was drawn to her. The restaurant was full, and there were many beautiful, expensively dressed women amongst the diners, but it seemed to him that Lily had a pure elegance about her that made her stand out head and shoulders above the other women. From out of nowhere the thought formed inside his head that a man would be proud to have such a wife—educated, intelligent, beautiful and elegant. Proud? To be married to a woman he couldn't trust? A woman who hid what she really was beneath an outward image?

The waiter was hovering, waiting for Lily to give him her order.

'I'll have the *missoltini* to start with,' she told him, referring to the Lake Como speciality of small sun-dried fish, 'and then the risotto.' Rice had been grown in Northern Italy for centuries, and risotto was very much a dish of the area.

'I'll have the same,' Marco agreed.

When the wine waiter arrived, hot on the heels of the waiter who had taken their food order, Marco glanced at the list and asked Lily, 'How do you feel about the Valtellina? I know it's a red, and we're starting with fish, but...'

Lily laughed a natural trill of laughter for the first time since they had met, unable to conceal her amusement. She liked the fact that Marco was consulting her rather than telling her what he thought they should drink, and she knew perfectly well why he had suggested the Valtellina.

'Leonardo drank Valtellina. If it was good enough for him then it's good enough for me,' she told him.

Marco had suspected that would be her response, which was in part why he had suggested the Valtellina in the first place.

Was that actually a small smile she could see on Marco's face, as though he was enjoying a private joke? Lily wondered. He had a good smile, warm and masculine, revealing a tantalising hint of a manly cleft in his jaw and strong white teeth. Her heart missed a beat of female appreciation of his maleness, followed by a dull, hollow feeling inside her chest. Because his smile was not for her?

She was glad of the arrival of their wine to distract her from the possible meaning behind her emotional reaction to him.

'So that's the itinerary. We'll start off tomorrow morning with a visit to Villa Balbiannello. I've arranged a private tour for you. Most of the villas we'll be visiting are not fully open to the public, as you know.'

Lily nodded her head. Marco was discussing the arrangements for the morning with her over coffee after their meal, and now he added, 'Since we've got an early start in the morning, and I've got some work to do, I'd like to call it a night—unless you want more coffee.'

Was that a stab of disappointment she felt? Of course not. Lily forced herself to shake her head and tell him firmly, 'I won't sleep if I have any more coffee.'

She ought to be tired, not strung so tightly with nervous energy. It had been a long and far from easy day, to put it mildly. The truth was that she felt as though she'd been travelling on an alien emotional rollercoaster from the first moment she had set eyes on Marco.

They had dined relatively early, the restaurant was still full and busy as they left. As they drew level with one table the stunning-looking brunette seated there with several other people, called out to Marco in a very pleased voice. 'Marco, *ciao.*'

Lily wasn't surprised to see him stop as the woman stood up to reveal a perfect hourglass figure in a cream designer dress that showed off her figure to perfection. Politely she left them to it after murmuring a brief 'goodnight', sensing that the other woman's delight at seeing Marco did not extend to her. She removed from her evening bag the plastic keycard to her suite, ready to make her way there.

In the ante-room to the restaurant a large group of people were heading towards the restaurant—fashion people from Milan's fashion week, Lily guessed expertly, easily recognising the mix of expensively suited older men, bone-thin young models, and a handful of very smart women who looked like magazine editors. She had never been comfortable around such people, reminding her as they did of her past. Her stomach was churning anxiously already, her face starting to heat up with nervous dread.

Desperate to get past them as quickly as she could, she started to skirt the group—only to be brought to shocked halt when one of the men stepped out in front of her, blocking her way. Anger, disgust and most shamingly of all stomach-gripping fear washed over her in a nauseating spine-chilling surge. He put his hand on her arm as he smiled his cruel crocodile smile at her, the familiar sour smell of his breath closing her throat against the retching movement of loathing tightening it. Anton Gillman. A man she had every reason to loathe and fear. She wanted to turn and run but she couldn't.

'Lily, what a delicious surprise—and looking so grown up as well. It's been so long. It must be—what? —twelve years?'

It was surely deliberate that he was talking to her in that adult-to-child manner she remembered so well. Because he knew what hearing it would do to her.

The temptation to correct him and tell him that it was thirteen years was dangerously strong. She must not let him know that she even remembered, never mind knew to the exact year how long it had been.

Someone bumped into her, jolting her uncomfortably. Her keycard slipped from her hand. Immediately, before she could bend down to retrieve it, Anton released her and did so for her, carefully studying the number of the suite printed on the card before taunting her softly as he held it out to her. 'If that's an invitation…'

Horror crawled along her veins.

Almost snatching the keycard from him, she said, half choking on her loathing, 'No, it isn't. You know I would never…' She stopped speaking, not trusting herself to say any more.

The people he was with had moved on into the restaurant. She felt hot and cold, as though she was in the grip of a fever.

But instead of annoying him her rejection seemed only to amuse him, because he laughed and shook his head, shook that mane of dark coiffured hair that curled down his neck just as she remembered it

'Ah, you should never say never, my dear Lily. After all, there is a great deal of unfinished business between you and I, and it would give me a great deal of satisfaction to bring it to its proper end—especially in such an undeniably sensual setting.'

Even though she knew he would be able to see and feel the shudder that ripped through her, she couldn't control it. She was fourteen again, and he a grown man, stalking her with one thing on his mind.

'I'm twenty-seven now,' she forced herself to point out to him. The past fought inside her with the present, the child she had been with the woman she now was. 'Far too old to appeal to a man of *your* tastes.'

He was watching her with amusement, and an open sexual greed that had her only increased her panic. 'Ah, but you *do* appeal to me, Lily. You always have. They say there is an extra allure to a lost opportunity. Are you here alone?'

Lily hesitated before saying quickly, 'No.'

She had waited too long before answering him, Lily knew, and his laughter chilled her with horror. It told her that he knew how she felt.

'You're lying to me,' he told her mock disappointedly, confirming her fear. 'How delightfully erotic that you still fear me. That will add a divine extra pleasure to my possession of you. And I shall possess you, Lily, because it is what you owe me. How pleasing that you should come back into my life so fortuitously. You are staying in suite number sixteen, I see.'

From the restaurant Marco watched Lily with increasing contempt. It was plain to him that she and the man knew one another very well indeed, from the way in which they were standing so intimately close to one another. The man was mature, at least twenty years older than Lily, and well dressed in a flashy kind of way.

'Marco,' Izzie Febretti complained at his elbow, 'you are not listening to me.'

'You have a husband who I am sure will be delighted to listen to you, Izzie,' Marco pointed out, adding, 'Please excuse me,' and then walking away from the table. A long time ago he and Izzie had been lovers. Just like Lily and the man with her? Why did that thought stab at him with such vicious fury?

'Anton,' called one of the other men from the restaurant, leaving Lily free to make her escape on trembling legs. But there could be no real relief for her now that she knew not only that he was here in the same hotel but also, thanks to her own folly, he knew the number of her suite. He had enjoyed threatening and frightening her tonight, she recognised, just as she remembered him enjoying threatening and frightening the young girls he had pursued and destroyed.

'An old friend?'

The sound of Marco's curt voice broke the dark spell of fear at seeing Anton Gillman and she spun her round to look at him.

Unable to reply, she swallowed hard and then told him unsteadily, 'If you'll excuse me, I'm…I'm rather tired…so I'll say goodnight.'

Without waiting for Marco to respond Lily hurried towards the lift. She was desperate to escape from the surroundings that Anton Gillman had contaminated with his presence. She had been caught off-guard by his presence and foolishly had allowed him to take advantage of her shock. He had deliberately set out to undermine and frighten her, and he had succeeded. She knew she wouldn't feel safe now until she was locked in her room, Lily admitted.

Marco watched her hurry away. She had been very impatient to go to her suite. Why? Because she had arranged to meet the man he had seen her with there? She hadn't answered him when he had asked her if he was an old friend. Was he more than merely a friend?

CHAPTER FIVE

IT was just over an hour since she had left Marco—
over an hour of sitting on the edge of her bed fully
dressed, with her muscles clenched and her gaze fixed
on the locked door to her room. Beyond that she had
also locked the door to her suite, so that she would feel
safe. Only Lily knew that she did *not* feel safe—that
she could not feel safe as long as Anton Gillman was
in the hotel.

With every minute that had passed since she had
come to her suite her fear had grown. She had tried to
apply reason to the situation, to keep calm and remind
herself that she wasn't fourteen any more, that she wasn't
a girl now and was a woman, but it hadn't made any difference. Her fear had continued to grow until it was out
of her control and had taken her over completely. Anton
knew which suite she was in thanks to her own clumsi-
ness. How could she feel safe there knowing that—even
with her door locked and bolted?

Lily looked at her watch. It was just gone midnight .
The darkest hours of the night lay ahead of her to be got
through—alone and in fear. She dared not even close
her eyes because of the images she knew her memory
would force her to relive. The glass doors to her balcony

rattled in the breeze, causing her to start up in dread, her heart hammering into her ribs.

And then, like a tiny seed of hope pushing its way through the darkness, a new thought emerged as she remembered the dream she had had and how it had made her feel. There was one place where she would be safe. One person with whom she would be safe if only she had the courage to go to him. Marco. She would be safe with him. If she told him about Anton then she would be safe.

Refusing to give herself time to analyse the instinct driving her, never mind apply any logic to it, Lily got up off the bed, flinging open the locked bedroom door and almost running for the main door as though she was already being pursued. She stopped only to grab her bag before opening the door into the corridor and, having checked that it was empty, hurrying down its length to the door to Marco's suite.

Marco had just got out of the shower, reluctantly admitting to himself that it was a relief to be there in the solitude of his room, where he could escape from the effect Lily's presence had on his self control, when he heard the frantic knocking on his suite door—the kind of knocking that overrode logic and sent his body into immediate emergency response. It had him grabbing a towel to wrap around his hips before striding towards the door.

He wasn't sure what he had expected to see when he opened it, but it certainly hadn't been Lily. Even less welcome than her arrival was the fact that she had rushed past him and was now in his room, inside his sanctuary from the conflict she had set raging inside him.

Safety... Sanctuary... Such was the extent of Lily's relief that it was only once she was inside his suite that she took in the fact that Marco's torso and hair were damp and that all he was wearing was a towel.

Her gaze slithered and skittered as she tried to avoid looking at him and couldn't. The swift response of her senses to him momentarily distracted her from her purpose in coming to him.

Marco, a man to whom the right and the ability to control his life was something he took for granted, always chose who was allowed into his life and when. No one had ever dared to challenge that right. It had been unthinkable that they should. He was the Prince di Luchessi. No one broke the rules he had made for the way he lived his life. Until now. Until Lily had come— uninvited and unwanted—into his room. He had to struggle to come to terms with the fact that she had dared to breach his defences. His personal boundaries, like his privacy, were very important to him. People did not cross those boundaries because he did not allow them to do so. He did not want casual physical intimacy with others, because casual physical intimacy could lead to pressure for emotional intimacy. That was something he would never want or give.

His status meant that a good deal of his life was played out in public. That made the privacy he claimed for himself even more important to him. As a lover he considered it his duty to ensure that his partners found pleasure and satisfaction in his arms, but as a man he preferred to sleep alone afterwards. And now here was Lily, intruding into his personal space and looking at him as though...

Did she know what she was doing to him, looking at him like that? Marco wondered grimly. Of course she did. That was why she was doing it. He was not vain about his body—he ate healthily and kept fit without being excessive about it—but that wide-eyed look of dazed, entranced delight Lily was giving him right now, as though his was the most magnificent male form she had ever seen, would boost any man's ego. Never mind what it was doing to his body. But this was a woman who knew all about manipulating others, Marco reminded himself. Whatever Lily had come to his suite for it certainly wasn't because she had been filled with an urgent desire for him, no matter what impression she might be trying to give him right now.

'Why are you here?' he demanded stiffly. 'What do you want?'

The sound of Marco's voice broke the spell that the intimacy of his nearly naked body had spun round her, his curtness bringing Lily back to reality.

'I had to come. Seeing Anton again after so long…so unexpectedly… He knows my suite number. I couldn't stay in my room. He…' Fear and shock disjointed her words.

'Anton?' Marco checked her, and then wished that he had simply told her to leave. After all, he wanted her out of his room. He wanted her out of his *life*, he acknowledged.

'Anton…Anton Gillman.' Just saying his name made Lily shudder. Watching her, Marco frowned, guessing, 'The man you were with earlier this evening, after dinner?'

'Yes,' Lily acknowledged.

'You gave him your room number?'

'No. I dropped my keycard and he saw it. I was afraid that he'd come looking for me…'

'Why would he do that?'

There was a look on her face that caught him off guard. Fear. Raw, naked fear. He could see it in her eyes and hear it in her voice. Against his will it touched a nerve within him. To his own disbelief he could feel himself reacting, weakening, as she aroused in him an instinctive male urge to take that fear from her and to protect her.

He could not and would not allow himself to give in to that urge. He fought against it, insisting, 'He must have a reason.'

Lily shuddered as Marco's words reminded her of exactly what reason Anton did have for persecuting her.

Marco watched as she shuddered and a mental image from the past was resurrected from the place where he had buried it. Time after time Olivia, her face swollen and bruised, had cried out emotionally to him that she wanted him to take her home, away from her latest 'boyfriend' and his physical abuse of her, and then less than twelve hours later she would be telling him that nothing and no one would ever part her from the man she loved, and that his violence towards her was simply caused by jealousy.

Some women were like that. Some women were drawn to men who abused and humiliated them. Some women even enjoyed deliberately making such men jealous, and went back time and time again to them. Was *that* why she was here? Because she knew her ex-lover would seek her out and she wanted him to believe she was with someone else?

It all made sense now, Marco decided cynically. She had come here intending to use him to make another man jealous. And she'd nearly succeeded, he was forced to admit. That knowledge caused him to state harshly, 'I know what you're up to. You came here to me because you want to make this Anton believe that you and I are lovers.'

He had hardened his heart against her now. He knew that look of fear had been faked, for all that he had initially been deceived by it. She was very good at pretence, as he had already discovered, but he was not a naive eighteen-year-old any more, ready to trust a woman just because she was a woman, ready to accept whatever lies she chose to feed him.

Lily stopped pacing to stare at him in despairing disbelief. How could he think that?

'No,' she denied. 'No, that's not true. I'm so scared—' Her body gave another violent shudder at the thought of having to endure any kind of intimacy with the man she loathed and feared so much, but Marco didn't notice. He was too caught up in the defence mechanism within him that refused to allow him to trust her.

She had come here to his room. She had looked at him as though he was the first man she had seen, the only man she wanted to see, and to his own chagrin he had responded to that look. That was a danger he could not allow to exist. Far better and safer to destroy that response by coming to the conclusion that he had than to risk allowing his vulnerability to her. It made sense to punish himself for that vulnerability by facing up to the reality of what she was based on his own assessment of her. It was entirely logical for him to believe that she was trying to manipulate him. If there were holes in the fabric of his argument, if there were fault lines that threatened to bring it down—such as why, for instance, a chance encounter should lead to Lily being willing to stop at nothing to make an ex jealous—then he did not wish to see them.

'You're lying—again,' he insisted, in defence of his argument, and shored it up with a cold, 'But you're wasting your time. Now, if you'd be kind enough to leave, I've got some work to do.'

Without waiting for her response Marco turned his back on her and headed for the door.

Marco had got it all wrong. Panic spilled through Lily. She had to make him understand. She couldn't let him send her back to her room. The ring of the room's telephone had him turning away from the door and crossing the room to answer the call. He was going to abandon her and leave her defenceless, undefended and unprotected, just as her father had done. She couldn't let that happen—especially when somehow she knew deep down inside herself that there was a human being who cared about the welfare of others buried deep within that inviolate image he chose to project.

He had his back to her now, as he reached for the receiver. Her heart banging into her ribs, her actions driven by the adrenaline of fear, Lily ran into the bedroom, pushing the door closed behind her with one hand. She was trembling from head to foot with the panicked need for speed, her mouth dry with anxiety as she climbed into the bed, pulling the bedclothes round her. What she really wanted to do, she recognised, was to hide herself away underneath them, to hide herself away for ever. But of course she couldn't do that. Marco's anger had showed her the contempt he felt for what he thought she was doing. Surely in view of that contempt he would leave her where she was? Lily reasoned. Rather than risk contaminating himself by touching her and physically ejecting her from his room?

She hoped so. Because if there was one thing she did know beyond all other things it was that she could not go back to her suite and stay there all alone, growing more terrified with every second that passed. Men like Anton fed off the fear of their victims. She knew that. But even knowing it she couldn't control her own fear.

The bedroom door opened. Marco stood framed in the doorway, his mouth hard with fury.

'I'm not going back to my own room,' Lily told him defiantly. 'I'm staying here. With you.'

It was those last two words that did it, setting a match to Marco's already tinder-dry fury and making it burn at a white-hot heat. How dared she lie there in his bed and calmly make it plain that she expected him to play along with her little game as though he simply didn't matter? Did she think he was completely without any male instincts? Any male desire, any male susceptibility to the temptation she was offering?

His fury burned through his self-control.

Advancing towards her, he told her savagely, 'He must have been good.'

'What?'

'He must have been good if you are *this* desperate to get him back. Making him jealous and getting him

back is what this is all about, isn't it?' He had reached
the bed now, one hand reaching for the covers Lily had
drawn up protectively over herself.

'No, of course not. Marco, please let me stay,' Lily
begged him, desperately holding onto the bedding.

Marco had grabbed a fistful of the fabric and she
could feel where his bunched knuckles were grazing
the upper curves of her breasts through the layers of
material. By some alchemy of their own her nipples
started to ache and tighten, and a cord of shockingly
hot sweet desire was pulling so taut inside her that she
could feel the pulse of its beat sending out waves of
awareness from deep inside her to the sensitive nerve-
endings lining the soft outer flesh of her sex. A new
form of panic seized her. This wasn't what she should be
feeling. Beneath the bedclothes Lily squirmed sensually,
choking back a small bemused gasp at the speed with
which her sensuality vied with her fear.

'Keep me safe, Marco,' she pleaded.

Marco knew his self-control was on a short rope. He
could feel it straining and stretching against its tether,
that dark well of male desire for her that should not be
there surging savagely into life. Her breath grazed his
cheek, her lips parting as she fought to resist him—to
resist him because she wanted to use him, so that she
could arouse within another man the jealousy she had
already aroused in him.

That knowledge was all that was needed to sever his
hold on his self-control.

The extent of the anger he felt at the thought of her
with another man was so alien to him that it took Marco
several seconds to grasp what it actually was. He was

jealous? Jealous because she wanted someone else? How could that be? It could not be. But it was, Marco knew. Somehow she had conjured up from within him a version of himself he had never imagined might exist. A version of himself that was all primeval male.

The thought of those softly parted lips being possessed by another man ripped at the pride of the previously unknown version of himself she had somehow brought to life inside him. With a smothered oath Marco slid his hand along the soft column of her throat, bending her back against the pillows, telling her thickly, before his mouth closed over hers with angry male possession, 'Very well, then. If you won't leave, why don't we really give him something to be jealous about?'

Marco was kissing her, and immediately nothing else mattered. Immediately no one else mattered. Immediately she was kissing him back as her heightened emotions exploded into a surge of sensual hunger.

At some deep level inside he had known from the first minute he had set eyes on her that it would be like this between them. He had sensed it, felt it and tried to reject it. But now it was too late for him to reject it, or her, any longer. He had known that his senses and his body would take fire from the wild sensuality of her. He had told himself that she wasn't what he wanted. But he had lied to himself, Marco knew. *This* was why she had angered him—because he had known. His hunger for her ran though him like a deep subterranean power, possessing him and driving him. *This* was why she had angered him so intensely—because at some level he had known that she would take him down into this dark intensity of need where he had no control.

Beneath Marco's kiss Lily gasped and moaned. So this was a woman's desire for the man who could arouse that in her—this was her need and her longing, her sensuality stripped bare of its protection, whilst her body ached to be stripped bare of its covering by the hands of the man holding her. No wonder she had feared it and tried to hide herself. No wonder she now wanted to give herself up to it entirely and completely, her body, her senses, her emotions—all that she offered in an almost pagan sacrifice to the man whose touch held her in such thrall.

Instinctively she clung to Marco, needing his strength to sustain her and guide her through such uncharted waters, her senses clamouring for fulfilment of the desires and needs their intimacy had unleashed. Beneath his kiss her tongue-tip hesitantly sought and found his, quickly retreating from the shock of sensation that sent a deep shudder jolting through her body, only to return to stroke against his tongue again, more slowly this time, her heart thudding erratically into her ribs as she savoured the unfamiliar intimacy.

Marco groaned beneath her exploratory touch—a sound of protest against the torment she was inflicting on him mixed with a raw need for deeper intimacy. When her tormenting caresses didn't offer it he took matters into his own hands—literally. He cupped her face, stroking his tongue against her own, his desire driving a sensual rhythm to its movement that nearly brought Lily's heartbeat to a standstill. The rhythm of the movement of Marco's tongue against her own was the rhythm of life—the rhythm that created life itself.

The bedclothes had slipped away from Lily's body.

Marco could feel the soft motion of her breasts rubbing against his bare chest through her clothes. He warned himself not to lose control, but it was too late. Ruthlessly he stripped off her dress and bra, and his body surged in an almost violent sensual reaction to the sight of the soft, shapely curves of pale female flesh, perfectly shaped and tip-tilted, with deep rose-pink nipples that right now were stiffly erect with arousal. Groaning against what he was feeling, Marco tried to fight against the desire burning through him—but the fight was already lost, because he was already reaching out to cup Lily's breasts in his hands, enticed by her open shivers of mute pleasure into driving his tongue even more deeply into the wet heat of her mouth.

How had it happened? How had she gone from abject fear to this? Lily tried to ask herself through the delirious fever that had taken possession of her.

Beneath his towel Marco could feel his body harden. His erection ached and throbbed madly, sending the blood pounding through his veins and with it the unbearable ache and heat of his desire.

Was it her release from fear that had somehow sparked off this torrent of wild female need inside her? This almost frenzied, frantic yearning for everything that Marco could give her? Lily didn't know. She just knew that the feel of his tongue against hers, the stroke of his fingers against her breasts and her nipples as he tugged erotically on their flauntingly aroused hardness, was sending her crazy with longing. Her—a twenty-seven-year-old woman who had never previously experienced the full passion of her own desire.

She reached out for Marco's body, exploring the

muscles in his shoulders, blind with delight at the sensation of his flesh against her hands, stroking her way down his arms to his elbows, then up the solid, flaring V of his torso and all the way down his back, from his shoulders to the barrier of his towel. Her palms were flat against his flesh, the better for her to absorb every sensation against her own skin. Each one of her five senses clamoured to be sated. This was surely what she had been born for, what she had been created a woman for. She could feel the drumbeat of the call of her own desire driving insistently within her.

Marco could feel her hand resting on the small of his back, against the edge of the towel, and her touch was sending wrecking shudders of longing pounding through him.

His tongue twisted against hers, his mouth pressing hungry kisses against the parted softness of her lips. A kind of madness seemed to have possessed him. A voice, words he barely recognised as his own, pleaded and urged between his kisses. 'Unfasten it.'

Unfasten it and touch me. Know me as though I am the first and only man there's ever been.

'Marco...Marco...' His name slipped helplessly from her lips, the sound a driven breath of aching need, and her fingers slipped on his arousal-slick flesh as she worked to obey his demand.

She was a sorceress, a Circe, tempting and entrancing him with the spell of her sensuality, binding him to her, trapping him in the promise of what she was offering with every touch of her hands, every arch of her back against him, every soft breath of response she gave to his touch. She was the hottest, sweetest woman he had ever touched or tasted—the only woman his body felt it could ever or would ever want to know. His desire for her drowned out every instinct that should be urging him to resist her, feeding itself on every beat of her heart against the hand that covered her breast. Her nipple rose tight and hard against his palm, calling to him to stroke its eager arousal with the pad of his thumb, to roll it between thumb and finger so that she arched up against him in wild abandon. The curve of her spine was lifting her body, offering the fruit of his own conjuring for him to take between his lips, to lick and stroke and finally suckle.

The pleasure of Marco's mouth against her breast! Such an almost unbearable pleasure that it made her cry out wildly and then lift her hands to his head to hold him against her body, leaving Marco to complete the task he had set her.

The light coming in through the still open door to the suite's sitting room burnished Marco's naked body, making him look like a living bronze, Lily thought in dazed helpless delight. Her hungry gaze was desperate to absorb every detail of him, from the muscular line of his calf upwards along the powerful strength of thighs that Leonardo himself would have ached to draw, and then higher...

In the shadows of the room the dark maleness of the body hair at the apex of his thighs sent a surge of reaction shuddering through her senses—a woman's awareness of him as a man—and her gaze was drawn to the raw potent evidence of his readiness to possess her. An impulse she would never in a thousand years have expected herself to feel had her reaching out towards him, her fingers drawn to the hot satin slickness of his flesh, her fingertips stroking down the length of its maleness.

As though in retaliation for her wanton sensuality Marco took her hands, pinning them to the mattress either side of her body with his own, leaving him free to take a slow, self-control-destroying journey of exploratory kisses over her stomach and then across her thighs, whilst her body twisted and trembled helplessly beneath his erotic pleasuring. Desire gripped her in sheets of lightning intensity, quivering surges of sharply increasing longing for his full possession of her. Behind her closed eyelids she was already feverishly imagining that final intimacy, her sex turning hot and wet with eager anticipation. Her ability to think or reason logically, to remember what it was that had brought her here, had been suspended by the demand within her for absolute capitulation to her desire.

Marco gazed down at Lily writhing ecstatically beneath him. How was it that he had reached this point, this place, where this woman held the key to all the answers to everything in his life? How was it that just by breathing, just by being, she seemed able to arouse every single one of his senses whilst feeding his desire for more of her?

'Please. Oh, please!'

Lily's sharp, staccato cry of tortured need pierced the heavy sensual accompaniment to their intimacy—the sounds of deeply drawn breathing, of an aroused body moving rhythmically against linen bedclothes, of sensual kisses pressed into flesh drawn taut with desire.

It wasn't *him* she was crying out for. It couldn't be, Marco knew.

As abruptly as though someone had thrown a bucket of cold water over him, that recognition brought Marco back to reality. Releasing Lily, he pushed himself away from her on a savage thrust of anger and revulsion, keeping his back to her. He had no need to look at her to know that she would be watching him with female triumph because he had made his vulnerability to his need for her so very clear. How had he let things get so out of hand? How had he allowed his desire for her to take him down the road to a self-destruction? And, worst of all, how had he allowed his emotions to become entangled in what should have been nothing more than an instinctive male need for sexual satisfaction?

The only comfort he could offer himself now was that at least her behaviour had confirmed what he had already suspected about her, and he need not have any more doubts that he might in some way have misjudged her. And he *had* been beginning to have those doubts, Marco admitted to himself now. He had been beginning to think and to feel…what? That making love to her would be a good idea? he derided himself caustically.

What mattered most of all right now was not making excuses for himself but making it clear to Lily that, far from allowing a need for her he should not have had get out of control, he had in fact been acting out a carefully thought out plan. His pride demanded nothing less.

Inhaling, he expelled the air he'd sucked into his lungs and told her grimly, 'Having sex with someone as a displacement activity because you can't have the man you really want might be the way things are done in the world in which you live, Dr Wrightington, but in my rather more old-fashioned world it's making yourself cheap. Having sex with another man so that you can boast about doing so to an ex-lover is several notches lower down the scale from that, and it doesn't have a name I'd like to utter in a woman's presence—even a woman like you. As a man, I warn you that if you really think having sex with me is going to persuade your ex to take you back then you don't know as much about men as you think you do,' he finished curtly, getting up off the bed.

To Lily, still trying to come to terms with the intense, agonising ache of unsatisfied desire ravaging her body, his words made her feel as though her emotions were being flayed with a whip that left them ripped and bloodied in a torment of humiliation and pain. How could she have allowed herself to be so…so aroused that nothing else had mattered more than Marco possessing her? Not even her own pride and self-worth? Her shame felt like hot tar being poured into those wounds. He had deliberately led her on, deliberately tricked and trapped her into exposing her vulnerability.

She felt sick with shock and shame, and the only defence she was able to utter was a broken, 'That wasn't supposed to happen.'

It hurt her physically inside, as well as emotionally, that he should think so badly of her—but she was in no state to explain that to him. She was too shocked by her own response to him to be able to do anything more than try to take in what *had* happened.

'You're damned right it wasn't,' Marco agreed angrily. He couldn't trust himself to say anything else to her. He couldn't trust himself to stay in the same room with her, he admitted. Because if he did stay he couldn't trust himself not to go back to her. Not to take her in his arms again and make love to her until she was as incapable of wanting any other man as he already was of wanting any other woman.

Furious with himself for that weakness, Marco headed for the door to his suite's sitting room, acutely aware of the need to put some distance between them.

His chest felt tight with the intensity of his emotions—emotions that were totally at odds with his nature. He had never felt like this before, never imagined he *could* feel like this—possessed by the kind of raw, out-of-control male needs, thoughts and desires he had believed himself too much in control ever to know. That it was a woman like Lily who had made him feel them only made the situation so very much worse. How could he, of all men, be reduced to this by a woman he should only despise?

He looked at the closed door to the bedroom. The Marco he recognised, the Marco he had always believed himself to be, would have lost no time in going back into the bedroom and ejecting Lily from his bed, if necessary. However, the Marco he was now simply didn't trust himself to go back into that room with her—because he knew that, far from ejecting her from his bed, he was more likely to end up back in it with her. That, of course, could not be allowed to happen.

How she must be laughing at him, gloating over her hold over him. Marco paced the room, his thoughts feeding his anger, knowing that he could neither escape from it or from her—Lily—the cause of it.

* * *

In the bedroom Lily lay tensely in the bed, watching the door. Marco had been so contemptuous of her, and she couldn't blame him. What on earth had possessed her to behave in the way she had? She, of all people, who had grown up fearing a woman's need to give herself completely to the man she loved because of what it did to a woman. She who had grown up believing that sexual desire was something that at its worst led to abuse and degradation, used by one person to have power over another, and at best took from those who experienced it all control over themselves and their lives. She had always been so glad that she was immune to its call, unconcerned about discovering its allure and power. She had felt safe in her celibate world—a world in which she could breathe the dusty air of the past instead of the high-octane air of a world she had learned to mistrust.

Anton Gillman had brought her a fear that had dominated every aspect of her life—a fear that ridding herself of her virginity the minute she was sixteen, with a boy as clumsy and untutored as she herself had been had calmed to some extent, but not banished for ever. Everything she had done in her adult life had been to keep herself safe from what she had left behind—even her choice of career. She had been too confident that she had succeeded, though. She recognised that now. Too ready to believe that she was safe from the problems she had seen sex cause in the lives of others.

The truth of that had been brought home to her now. Only minutes ago in Marco's room, in Marco's bed and in Marco's arms, she had forgotten everything she had ever learned, too aroused by her own desire for him to recognise or care about her own danger.

She wanted to creep away and hide herself some-where like the child she had once been, hiding in the cupboard off the studio where her father had kept some of his photographic equipment. But there was no hiding place from what was within herself. Her body was still tight with longing. Shamefully, she knew that it wouldn't take much at all for her desire to be reawakened to the point where it was out of her control. Marco's single touch, his briefest kiss, would be enough to do it.

Marco! She had come here to his suite because at some deep emotional level she had felt that he represent-ed the protection and security she had always wanted and never had. But now she knew that Marco was far more dangerous than any threat Anton might make to her.

What would she do if Marcus came to her now and took her back in his arms?

The leap of aching longing that gripped her told her all she needed to know. Not that Marco was likely to do that, of course. He had made that more than plain. But she couldn't get out of the bedroom without going into the sitting room beyond it, and she couldn't do that, Lily knew. If she did she couldn't trust herself not to humiliate herself even more by begging Marcus to take her back to bed.

An instinct she desperately wanted to ignore was trying to tell her that what had happened had *not* been a merely physical act, disengaged from her mind and her emotions. She didn't want to listen to it, and she certainly wasn't going to believe it. Yes, she had been overwhelmed—but that was just because she wasn't used to such an intensity of physical desire. Nothing more.

After all, she had seen what giving everything to one man—wanting him, needing him, loving him utterly and completely—had done to her mother when that one man had grown tired of her and wanted her out of his life. She had seen the pain of that destroy her mother emotionally, and then mentally, and finally physically—until all she had wanted was death. As a child her father had often told her that she was just like her mother. She must not let what had happened to her mother happen to her. She must not repeat her mother's mistakes.

She knew how little what had happened meant to Marco. And she must make sure that it was the same for herself—at least as far as Marco was concerned.

CHAPTER SIX

MORNING. The beginning of a new day. A joy for those who knew happiness, but a misery for those who longed to hang on to the dark hours of the night to conceal their pain, Marco acknowledged as he stood in front of the uncurtained bedroom window, looking out across the lake whilst the sun rose in the sky.

He had barely slept. He was too tall to sleep comfortably in an armchair, and besides his thoughts had been even more uncomfortable than the chair. How could he have allowed himself to be dragged into Lily's grubby, manipulative plans? His contempt for himself was now every bit as great as his contempt for her. How could he have felt any kind of desire for her? How could he have wanted her with such intensity? He had no idea what had caused last night's weakness to overtake him, but he did know that it must not be allowed to happen again.

He rubbed his jaw with his hand, grimacing at the rough feel of his stubble. He needed a shave and a shower. He also needed to get dressed. For that, of course, he needed access to his bathroom, and his clothes. He looked grimly at the closed door between the two rooms, before striding over to it and turning the handle.

Lily was lying motionless in the large bed, all that was visible of her above the bedclothes the tumble of her hair and the curve of her throat. Her body formed a slender shape beneath the covers, She was lying on her side, almost in a small tight ball, as though in her sleep she felt the need to protect herself. *He* was the one in need of protection—especially from the desire she somehow managed to arouse in him. Marco frowned. The very idea of a woman like Lily needing any kind of protection was risible, and he was a fool if he allowed himself to entertain it. Of course she no doubt would love knowing that he was vulnerable to her.

Her clothes—the clothes which last night he had discarded on the floor—were folded neatly on the chair. Marco looked briefly at them, his attention momentarily caught by the sight of her bra, half tucked away beneath her dress. He remembered now how it had struck him as he'd removed it that its plain, practical style was somehow at odds with the kind of bra he would have expected someone like her to wear. Surely something much more sexy and alluring would have been more in keeping with her lifestyle? Or perhaps, like the consummate actress she obviously was, she immersed herself so completely in her chosen part that even her underclothes had to reflect it. Dr Lillian Wrightington must not be allowed to be the kind of woman who wore sensual underwear.

He walked past the bed, the sunlight throwing his shadow across her sleeping face. Immediately her eyes opened, her head turned, the colour coming and then going in her face. Her eyes widened as she looked at him.

'Excellent,' he told her cynically. 'You've got the

"shocked, prim young woman finding a man in her room" look off to perfection. Especially after last night.'

Lily's face burned. He was talking about her passionate response to his touch. He had to be. And she had no way of denying that response or defending herself from whatever judgement he chose to make because of it.

Marco noted her flushed face. She was angry—obviously because he had refused to be taken in by her play-acting. Good.

'Sadly, excellent though your acting ability is, it was wasted on me as an audience since we both know that you knew exactly what you were doing when you came here last night,' he told her, determined to make sure that she knew he wasn't taken in by her. He might have been overwhelmed by his desire for her last night, but there was no way he was going to let her get away with using that weakness against him.

'What's the next scenario in this little drama you're concocting? Ideally, I suppose it should be the arrival of your ex-lover and his realisation that you spent the night in another man's room.'

The initial shock of opening her eyes and seeing Marco wearing only a towel and standing beside the bed looking down at her, had left Lily too stunned to speak. But now she was fully awake—and fully aware of the events of the previous evening. She had embarrassed herself and infuriated Marco. Things had been bad enough between them before, but her behaviour last night would make a workable business relationship between them virtually impossible. The last thing she wanted was Marco thinking that she was going to make unwanted advances to him. She had to assure him that that wasn't going to happen, no matter how uncomfortable that would be for her.

'I'm really sorry about last night.' she began apologetically, but with firm dignity, sitting up in the bed and making sure that the bedclothes were very firmly wrapped around her. No way did she want Marco thinking that her behaviour was sexually inviting. He had, after all, already made it clear that he did not want her when he had left her last night.

'My behaviour was totally… It was inappropriate. It shouldn't have happened. And if possible I'd like you to forget that it did happen, if you can.'

Marco's gaze narrowed. What kind of game was she playing now? Was she hoping to get him to admit that he had wanted her? Her downcast gaze and her pseudo-humble words were just a pose. That 'if you can' was definitely a challenge to him. Did she want to humiliate him with that knowledge, mock him, telling him that he couldn't resist her?

'I should have thought you would be more concerned about letting your ex-lover know that you spent the night here than with expressing regrets to me. Why don't you go and find him now?'

She opened her mouth to refute his accusation, but before she could do so the closed door between the bedroom and the suite's sitting room opened to reveal a hotel maid, her arms piled high with immaculately folded clean towels, accompanied by an older woman, obviously of more senior status, with clipboard and pen in hand. The older woman broke off speaking to the maid to cast with expert glance round the room, with Lily still in its bed and Marco clad only in a towel, before apologising and then making a swift exit.

Marco exhaled in grim irritation, only realising then that he had failed to use the 'privacy' facility for the suite the previous night.

The fact that Lily had flushed a deep pink and was looking acutely mortified and uncomfortable was lost on him as he strode across the sitting room to the suite's door to rectify his omission, coming back towards her to demand, 'What? Nothing to say?'

Lily took a deep breath. On the contrary, she had plenty to say—and she intended to say it.

'I've tried to…to apologise for last night, but it seems that rather than accept my apology you prefer to accuse me…to suggest that Anton was…'

As hard as she was trying to behave in an adult, businesslike manner, Lily's emotions balked at using the word 'lover' with regard to Anton, so great was her fear and detestation of him.

'Was your lover and you now want to make him jealous,' Marco insisted

'No. The last thing I want is for Anton to come in search of me.'

'It's well known that hell hath no fury like a woman scorned. You've quarrelled with him and you want to make him regret that and regret the end of your relationship. You want to make him jealous. You want him to go to your room and think when you aren't there that you're with someone else—and you are prepared to use any means in order to do so. Isn't that the truth?'

'No. I would never stoop to that kind of behaviour,' she told him, her voice trembling slightly with the force of her feelings. 'I came here to you for one reason and one reason only, and that was because I was too afraid to stay in my own room.'

'Why?' When Lily looked away from him instead of answering him Marco challenged her. 'If you're as afraid of this Anton as you expect me to believe there must be a reason.'

There *was* no reason other than the one he had already suggested, Marco was sure, and that was why she couldn't answer him.

He had started to turn away from her, he the victor in their exchange and she the vanquished, when she said in a low, tense voice, 'Very well—yes, there is a reason, and it has nothing to do with me wanting Anton in my life.' A fierce shudder racked her body. 'Quite the opposite. But I can't...I can't talk about it.'

'Why not? Surely I deserve an explanation for your behaviour?'

'Behaviour for which I've already apologised.'

Lily had had enough. She could feel her self-control fraying and giving way under the pressure of her emotions. She bent her head, not wanting Marco to realise how close to the edge she was, how afraid she was that her own actions as much as her words might inadvertently give her away.

'There's no law that says I have to provide you with an explanation of my...of the reasons for what I did as well,' she told him fiercely. 'A...a compassionate man—a man who understands and accepts that other people can sometimes be vulnerable and in need—would know that. But you aren't that kind of man, are you? You're the kind of man who wants to think the worst about others.'

'I'm the kind of man who knows when he's being lied to, if that's what you mean,' Marco agreed acidly, defending himself against the knowledge that he had been far more affected by Lily's outburst than he should have been.

'But you are *not* being lied to,' Lily insisted. 'Perhaps I should be the one questioning you about your motives for refusing to believe me rather than the other way around,' she added perceptively.

Marco felt his heart thud heavily into his chest wall. His glance fell on his watch and his heart gave a surge of relief as he saw his means of escape from what had now become a very dangerous situation.

'It's nearly eight o'clock,' he told her, ignoring her comment, 'and we're due to leave at nine.'

Seated in the privately hired hovercraft next to Marco, Lily warned herself that she was here in Italy to work, and that she must put aside the temptation to let the pressure of her secret thoughts and emotions stop her from doing that. Even though Marco's unjust accusations had hurt her as well as angered her.

After leaving Marco's suite earlier, she had only just made it downstairs in time for the arrival of their transport, having returned to her own suite first, to shower quickly and then change into jeans and a tee shirt, worn underneath her faithful cardigan.

They'd been driven to the first villa on Marco's list, where they'd been given a private tour of its art collection. After lunch at a small, elegant restaurant, where Lily had still been too wrought up by the events of the morning to do her pasta justice, they had gone on to their second villa, where Lily had discussed the loan to the trust of part of a collection of letters written to past owners of the villa by an Englishman who had stayed there in the decade following Napoleon's defeat. The third son of a duke, the Englishman had come to the lakes for his health, and the letters had been written to a young female relation of the family on his return to England as part of his courtship of her. In addition to the letters there were also some sketches he had done for her of his home in Yorkshire.

Aidan Montgomery had died from his tuberculosis before they could marry, and as she'd inspected the documents closely Lily had wondered if the marks on them came from tears cried over the letters by the fiancée he had left behind.

It had been Marco who had noticed her concentration on the stains, and Marco too who had pointed out dryly to her, when she'd voiced her thoughts, that if Teresa d'Essliers had grieved for her fiancé that grief had not stopped her from marrying someone else within eighteen months of his death.

'A diplomatic family marriage,' the curator had told them. 'Her father was a banker who enjoyed gambling with other people's money. Her husband was one of his clients—a wealthy silk merchant who wished to improve his own social status.'

'Will we have time to visit any of Como's silk mills?' Lily asked Marco now, as the hovercraft took them to their next appointment—a villa situated at the side of the lake, with its own landing stage.

Como had been a centre for the production of silk for many centuries. Although the business was now in decline from its heyday, because of the expense of its manufacture compared with silk imported from China, it still produced many of the exclusive silks used by both interior and fashion designers.

'Do you want to visit one?' Marco asked her. His voice was curt as he focused on keeping as much emotional distance between them as he could.

The coldness in his voice made Lily flinch inwardly, but she refused to let him see how she felt, saying as calmly as she could, 'I'd like to. It could help with the exhibition.' When he looked questioningly at her, she explained, 'One of the things we're trying to do with the exhibition is interest a younger audience, and I feel that the more personal detail we can display, the more able they will be to relate to it. I thought that Como's silk business would appeal to them. I have to admit that I'd also love to see something of the archives of those companies who have been producing silk for several centuries. Although it isn't my specific field, I've seen some of the work that's being done on the research and restoration to the decor of the trust's properties, and some of those fabrics are just so beautiful.'

'I'm surprised you haven't mentioned Como's silk industry's connection with the modern-day fashion industry. Surely that would have an even greater appeal to you, with your own involvement in that particular business?'

'What do you mean? What involvement?' Lily's voice was sharp with anxiety.

'I was referring to your other means of income—the photographic studio,' Marco reminded her grimly.

Lily's body almost sagged with relief. For one awful moment she thought that somehow Marco had guessed about her past and her father.

'I've already told you,' she defended herself, 'I was doing a favour for...for someone.'

'That someone being a man, I assume?' Why was he doing this to himself? Why was he deliberately feeding his own jealousy like this? Prior to Lily coming into his life, if asked, Marco would have said and believed that he was not a man who felt jealousy. He had certainly never experienced it with any of his lovers.

But he was experiencing it now, and it galled him like a thorn sticking into his flesh that Lily should be the person to inflame his feelings to such a pitch, to such a destructive emotion. She represented so much that filled him with contempt it should have been impossible for him even to want her, never mind feel about her as he did.

'Yes,' Lily was forced to admit.

If only she had not agreed to help her half-brother. If only she and Marco had met for the first time at the reception and not at that wretched studio. Then what? Then he would have taken one look at her and yearned for her? Was that what she had done? Had she taken one look at him and somehow known what was to happen to her and that she would want him? A deep shudder tormented her body.

What had caused her to look like that? Marco

wondered. So…so *stricken*, somehow, as though she was having to face a terrible, inescapable truth? She was simply trying to arouse his pity, he warned himself. She was, after all, an excellent actress—as he had good cause to know.

Lily took a deep breath, reminding herself that she was a qualified professional with a job to do. She couldn't let herself be hurt even more. All she could do was try to protect herself by pretending that nothing untoward had happened.

'Is that the villa we're approaching now?' she asked Marco, in what she hoped was a calm and businesslike voice.

Marco had to bend his head to look out of the window of the hovercraft, his action bringing him far too close to her for Lily's comfort, making her feel as though she had jumped from one uncomfortable situation into another that was every bit as uncomfortable in a different way. With him this close to her she could smell the clean tang of Marco's soap mixed with the sensual warmth of his body. The hovercraft jolted on the movement of the water, forcing her to lean as far back as she could to avoid coming into physical contact with him. After what had already happened she couldn't bear to have him thinking that she was tempted to take advantage of the opportunity to be close to him.

Men soon tired of women who were too vulnerable to them. They preferred the excitement and the challenge of the chase, the power of winning their trophy. When that trophy became needy and dependent they no longer wanted it. She had seen that so often with her father. She had seen it break her mother's heart and spirit. Better not to love at all than to be destroyed by the pain of loving someone who had grown bored and become indifferent to you.

A strand of hair had escaped from the clip Lily had used to secure it into a soft knot away from her face, and Marco had an aching urge to reach out and lift it from her skin. If he did his knuckles would graze the soft flesh of her throat and she would turn and look at him, her grey eyes dark and questioning, her lips parted for his kiss. He wanted that to happen, Marco recognised on a savage stab of brutal self-knowledge. He wanted to take her in his arms right now and hold her. He wanted to kiss her until she murmured his name against his mouth in a soft plea of arousal and need.

What was happening to him? How could he feel like this about her when everything he knew about her told him that at best he should be wary of her and at worst he should despise her? Earlier in the day, watching her as she'd talked to the curators of the two villas they had visited, listening to her as she spoke with them, he had seen a woman who was a skilled communicator, a woman who knew and loved her subject and who wore her knowledge comfortably, a woman who had been willing to listen respectfully to what the curators had to tell her even when Marco suspected she was far more knowledgeable about the collections and the history of the villas than they were themselves—a woman, there-fore, to whom the feelings of others was important. And yet at the same time she was also a woman to whom the vulnerability of a foolish young man was simply some-thing to be exploited—for money. A woman who was selfish enough to think nothing of using other people to pursue her own desires.

'Yes, it is the villa,' he confirmed as the craft headed for the landing stage. 'I've arranged for the car to pick us up from here after we've viewed the collection. I don't think there'll be time for us to visit a silk mill today. The Duchess will be expecting us, and like most people of her generation punctuality is important to her. She loves entertaining, and I wouldn't be surprised if she's made arrangements to that effect for this evening—probably for a dinner party. However, if you'd rather not be involved, I'll have a word with her and tell her that you have work you want to catch up on. I expect you will have reports you want to file with the trust.'

She did, it was true, but Lily suspected his suggestion sprang more from his wish not to have to endure any more of her company than he had to rather than any concern for her.

'There's no need for you to do that. Being involved with the villa owners is part of my job. Besides, I imagine that the Duchess has some fascinating stories to tell about her family history and the villa. However, if that is a polite way of telling me that you don't want me there…?' she challenged Marco, determined to let him know that she had guessed the real reason behind his offer.

'It isn't,' he denied. 'I merely thought you might wish to have some time to yourself.'

'I'm here to work. And that work includes listening to what those connected with the villas have to say,' Lily told him firmly.

* * *

It was a little later than Marco had allowed for on their schedule before they were able to leave the third villa. It had been in the same family for several generations, having originally been built for one of Napoleon's favourite generals, and in addition to agreeing to loan the trust several valuable pieces for its exhibition the owner, an elderly Italian who spoke impeccable English, had allowed Lily to take photographs of the interior of the villa, which would also be put on display—a coup indeed, as she was fully aware.

Watching Lily with her camera, Marco could see her professionalism—but instead of admiring it, as did the Visconte, whom she had charmed completely with her interest in his family history, her expertise brought back all Marco's doubts about her and his disdain for what he believed she was.

He would be glad when this task was over and he could return to his normal life and put Dr Lillian Wrightington out of his mind for ever. And out of his heart? The sneaky little question was slid under his guard so dextrously by that taunting inner voice he literally stopped in midstride as he fought to deny the unjustifiable allegation. She meant nothing to him. Nothing, that was, apart from the fact that he didn't trust her and last night she had aroused him to the point where nothing had been more important than possessing her. So he had desired her? Physical desire alone meant nothing. His emotions weren't engaged with her. That was impossible. Wasn't it?

Then how did he explain away his anger and jealousy?

Marco welcomed the distraction from his inner

thoughts provided by the necessary formalities involved in taking their leave of the Visconte and thanking him for his kindness.

As their chauffeur-driven car purred up the drive to the Duchess's home, through the most beautiful formal Italianate gardens, Lily was uncomfortably conscious of Marco's silence. He had barely spoken to her since they had left the previous villa, and she had felt too aware of coldness of the stone wall of his silence to want to break it.

The front of the elegant Palladian-style villa was basking in the last of the early October sunshine beneath a clear blue sky, and as always when she was in the presence of a beauty that stirred her senses Lily felt her emotions rise up in humble awe. It didn't make any difference to her reaction if it was nature that was responsible for that beauty or the skill of a human artist—the effect on her was the same.

Unable to stop herself, she murmured more to herself than Marco, 'This is just so beautiful.'

Somehow the emotion in Lily's voice managed to find a faint hairline crack in Marco's defences that he hadn't known was there. The moisture he could see glinting in her eyes couldn't possibly have been faked, he knew, even though he wanted to believe that it was. A fresh surge of jealousy spiked through him—but not over another man this time. 'Both the setting and the villa do please the eye,' he told her in a dry voice. 'But I like to think that my family's *castello* can rival the villa for catching at the heart. You'll have to give me your opinion when you've seen it.'

The di Lucchesi *castello*. The place from which Marco's family sprang. The place where his ancestors would have taken their wives and sired their children. Children. Lily's heart rocked perilously inside her chest, pierced by an agonised ache of pure female longing and envy. One day Marco would take a bride to his *castello*, and one day she would give birth to his child, his children there. But that woman would not be her. What was she doing, allowing herself to accept thoughts and feelings that could only cause her pain and make her suffer? That mattered to her? Then that must mean…

Lily didn't want to think about what it could mean. It was a relief when the car came to a halt and she knew that she'd soon be able to escape from Marco's presence and the effect he was having on her.

The Duchess herself came down the stone steps leading up to the villa to greet them, welcoming them with warm smile before telling the chauffeur that her housekeeper had a meal ready for him, if he wanted to drive round to the courtyard at the back of the villa.

Such kindness and concern was not always displayed by those in the Duchess's elevated social and financial position, Lily knew, and her heart warmed even further to their hostess as she slipped her arms through both Lily's and Marco's, telling them as they headed for the steps, 'There's no need for the two of you to be bashful or feel you have to be discreet.' She pulled a face and laughed. 'All that creeping around in the middle of the night, terrified that one might step on a creaking floorboard and be discovered. I remember it well. But times have changed, and I like to think that I have changed with them. So, once my housekeeper informed me that her sister—who works at Ville d'Este—had told her the two of you had been sharing a room there, I instructed her to make up my favourite guest suite for the two of you.'

CHAPTER SEVEN

LILY couldn't speak. She couldn't even think properly. She couldn't do anything other than look at the Duchess in mute disbelief as she continued, 'I'm sure you'll like it. It has the most wonderful view over the lake. My late husband and I used to stay in it when we came to visit before my father died. When I inherited it my husband insisted that we replace the rather small double bed with something larger and more comfortable.' The Duchess gave a fond sigh. 'I have so many happy memories of being young here. New love—it is so special. I well remember the first time I saw my late husband. I fell in love with him the minute I set eyes on him. He, though, I'm afraid to say, did not return my feelings for a full twenty-four hours after we had met,' she told them drolly, adding, 'I hope that your brief stay here will give you both some memories that you too will come to cherish.'

All the time she had been talking them they had been climbing the steps. Now they had reached the top, and Lily's heart was pounding—but not because of any exertion involved. Had she understood the Duchess correctly? Had she instructed her housekeeper that she and Marco were to share a bedroom—and a bed? Lily tried to look at Marco, but the Duchess was linked between them, beaming first at Marco and then at Lily, obviously very proud of what she had done and no doubt thinking she was doing them both a favour.

'I have to say, Marco,' the Duchess continued blithely, 'I think that Lily is the perfect girl for you. You both feel so passionately about Italian art and history, and my late husband always used to say that shared interests remain a strong bond between a couple long after the first flush of romance has faded. Ah, good—here we are. Do come in and admire my ancestors, Lily. I hope I may call you Lily? After all we are practically family already, since Marco and I are distantly related.'

The villa's hall was round, with a wonderful balustrade stairway rising exactly opposite the front door then branching off to form a round gallery landing. The design was repeated on each of the three floors, so that it was possible to look up from the ground floor and see the stained glass dome of the cupola several floors above them.

'When the sun is overhead, the light from the stained glass makes the most magical patterns. When we were children my brother invented a game whereby we had to chase the moving pattern of a certain colour all the way up and down the stairs. He was older than me, and he always won. He should have inherited the villa, of course, but he was killed during the Second World War. He was only nineteen.'

Lily was listening to the Duchess, but at the same time she was tense with inner anxiety as she waited for Marco to explain to her that there had been a mistake and they were not a couple. Only he said nothing, and now the duchess was exclaiming, 'Ah, here is my housekeeper, Berenice. She will show you to your room. I hope you don't mind, but I have taken the liberty of organising a small reception here tonight. Just some old friends I know will enjoy meeting you, Lily. They all have connections with the area and its villas, so don't be shy about asking them any questions you may have. We'll meet again in the main salon.'

Their room.

Lily gave Marco an imploring look but still he said nothing, and continued to say nothing until they were alone in the villa's best guest suite. Lily asked him anxiously why he had not corrected the Duchess's misapprehension about their relationship.

'If you had not come to my room last night we would not be in this situation.'

Marco's uncompromising statement couldn't be denied, but Lily still shook her head as she paced the elegant suite. Marco stood in front of one of the room's long sash windows, his head turned so that he was half looking out across the lake and half looking back into the room.

'I know why the Duchess thinks that we are a couple, but you could have told her the truth. You could have explained to her...'

'I could have explained what? That you came to my room seeking to use me—either to protect you from your ex or to make him jealous? Is that really what you would have wanted me to say to her?'

Without giving her the chance to answer, Marco gave a dismissive shake of his head, telling her grimly, 'Anyway, she likes you. She wouldn't believe me.'

He didn't have to say that he neither understand nor shared the Duchess's feelings. The tone of his voice said it for him.

She mustn't allow herself to feel hurt yet again, Lily warned herself. But it was too late. The pain was already flooding through her.

'She's a romantic,' Marco continued. 'She would simply think that I was trying to hide our relationship from her.'

'We haven't *got* a relationship,' Lily told him. Tears were threatening to clog her throat.

'The Duchess believes that we have. And not just a sexual relationship. She's managed to convince herself that we've fallen in love with one another.' The derision in Marco's voice made Lily's face burn. 'If she knew you rather better, of course, she'd know that was impossible.'

Lily swallowed on the misery his caustic comment brought her.

'No. We can't say anything to her,' Marco told her. 'For her own sake. Were we to insist to her now that there isn't a relationship it would result in either her not believing us or in her embarrassment for misjudging the situation if she does believe us. Neither of those situations is acceptable to me. It will make things easier all round if we simply accept the situation as it is. After all, we're only here for two nights.'

'Two nights!' She couldn't share a room and a bed with him for two nights, feeling the way she did about him. 'What if sharing a room with you isn't acceptable to *me*?' she demanded.

Marco turned round fully to look at her.

'Do you really expect me to believe that after last night?' he challenged her. 'After all, you didn't have any objection then—in fact it was what you wanted.'

Lily's heart missed a beat. Was Marco hinting that he knew there had been a time last night when what she had wanted from him had been much more personal and intimate than merely the protection of his presence? She hoped not. It was humiliating enough that *she* knew how she felt about him, without the added humiliation of having to deal with the fact that he knew as well.

'That was different,' she defended herself, adding emotionally in her growing panic, 'I don't *want* to share a room with you.'

'Do you think I want to share one with you?' Marco asked her grimly. 'You are the one who is primarily responsible for the situation we now find ourselves in, not me. I suppose I should have expected this kind of selfishness from you. After all, a woman who tries to use one man to make another jealous has to be innately selfish.'

She could tell him the truth. She could make him feel thoroughly ashamed of himself for the way he was mis-judging her, Lily knew. But it was clear he only wanted to believe the worst of her, and she was not about to tell him her darkest, most painful secret only to have him coldly dismiss her as an accomplished liar.

How could she have allowed herself to become en-tangled—trapped—in this situation? She knew where her vulnerabilities lay. She knew where she was weak. If she'd thought more carefully and clinically about the way he had made her feel that first time she had seen him at the studio, she could have... She could have

what? Walked away from the work she had been paid
to come here and do when she'd recognised him at the
reception? When she prided herself on her professionalism? Hardly.

'I will not have the Duchess embarrassed or upset
by you causing a dramatic fuss about something that,
after all, means very little in this day and age,' Marco
warned her. 'And who knows? If your ex gets to hear
about it perhaps it will have the desired effect and bring
him back—although as a man I'd have to caution you
against encouraging a man to be jealous. It makes for a
relationship based on distrust, and no man who values
himself can or should compromise where trust is concerned. That can be very dangerous.'

'You sound as though you're speaking from experience.' The words were out before Lily had time to think
about what she was saying.

Their effect on Marco was immediate. What was it
about her that led to him revealing things about himself to her—private, fiercely guarded things he would
never normally dream of revealing to anyone. His face
hardening, his voice chilling, he told her, 'I've certainly
got enough experience to know not to trust *you*.'

Lily flinched, stung by his icy words. She hadn't
lied to him, but he had made it plain that he had no
intention of believing her. Had he in the past been hurt
by someone—a woman he'd trusted who had lied to
him—and now he refused to trust any woman? He must
have cared a great deal for her, whoever she was. A very
great deal. The man he was now wouldn't let any woman
close enough to do that to him. A horrible feeling of
desolation sucked the strength from her. It was stupid,

foolish, self-destructive of her to care because Marco had once loved someone so much.

Marco frowned. Why was Lily looking so stricken? She'd been perfectly happy to share a room—and a bed—with him when it had suited her. Now she was looking as though the very thought of doing so was destroying her, and she was obviously rejecting it—and him—in favour of another man. Any sympathy Marco might have been tempted to feel for her vanished.

'Do you understand?' he demanded.

Blindly Lily looked at him. He might not have any compassion for her, but obviously the Duchess's feelings were important to him, so there must be some humanity within him somewhere—even if he seemed intent on concealing it from her.

'Yes, I understand,' she confirmed emotionlessly.

She understood that he loathed and despised her. She understood that there had been a woman in his life who had destroyed his ability to trust. But what she did not understand was why her silly heart persisted in aching with a need that could only destroy her. And tonight she was going to have to share a room with the cause of that need and somehow keep it hidden from him. If she could.

But what if she couldn't?

What if, like the last time she had shared a bed with him, she let her feelings get out of control? Panic filled her.

'We can't share a room,' she insisted. 'I wouldn't feel...'

'What? Safe?' Marco derided her.

Lily couldn't look at him—dared not look at him

just in case he could somehow see what she was really thinking. The truth was that she was indeed afraid that she wouldn't feel safe. Not because she was afraid that she couldn't trust Marco, but because she feared that she couldn't trust herself. She certainly wasn't prepared to admit that to him, though.

'I've just told you we have no other option than to be thankful that it's only for a couple of nights,' Marco said, adding sardonically, 'Allow me to play the gentleman and offer you the bed.'

He wasn't going to be persuaded or argued into changing his mind about the suite, she could tell. And in reality what legitimacy did she actually have to keep on trying to insist that he did so? She liked the Duchess herself, and knew that Marco's comment about her potential embarrassment was justified. She was going to have to accept the fact that, despite her misgivings and her fears they would be sharing the suite, she acknowledged.

'You have the bed this time,' Lily muttered. 'I'd rather have the sofa in the sitting room.'

A brief knock on the door had Marco going over to open it to admit the housekeeper, escorting a young man who was carrying their luggage.

'If there's anything you require for the evening, just dial ten on the telephone on the desk,' she told them.

It was Marco who tipped the young man, whilst Lily was still looking round for her handbag, his gesture winning him an approving look from the housekeeper before the two of them exited the room.

'We've got just over an hour before we're due downstairs for the Duchess's reception. Since the suite seems only to have one bathroom, you can use it first if you wish,' he offered distantly, without looking at her.

Lily nodded her head. She wanted to wash her hair, and although it was easy to dry and style it would take her longer to get ready than it would Marco, so it made sense for her to use the bathroom first.

Even so, she didn't linger under the shower, washing her hair and herself as quickly as she could before pulling on one of the luxurious bathrobes provided for their use. She'd taken her small case into the bathroom with her, hanging up her black jersey skirt to make sure it wasn't creased, and was just straightening up, having removed clean underwear from her case, when there was a sharp knock on the door.

Still holding her undies, she opened the door.

'I just wanted to check that you don't need anything ironed,' Marco told her.

'No. My skirt is jersey,' Lily replied, half gesturing towards the sliver of matt black fabric hanging on the glass door of the shower area, not realising until Marco bent down to retrieve them that her briefs had slipped out of her grasp.

Pink cheeked with embarrassment, Lily took them from him when he handed them to her, balling the nude fabric in her hand as she did so. Why, when she preferred and always wore plain, smooth underwear, was she suddenly now wishing that what Marco had retrieved for her had been something far more sensual? A pretty, feminine wisp of silk and lace, perhaps—the kind of underwear worn by the kind of women she imagined Marco preferred. Beautifully, sexually confident and alluring women for whom it was second nature to dress their bodies in provocative sexy undies.

'I'll be finished in here in five minutes,' she told Marco, pointedly looking at the door.

Nodding his head, he stepped back so that she could close it.

Why had Lily been so embarrassed about him seeing her underwear, Marco wondered as he waited for the bathroom. It was illogical, given what he knew about her. Illogical and out of character for any woman of her age, never mind the kind of woman she was. Another act? If so, why? It wasn't something she could use to bait her ex.

Against his will Marco recognised that something about her reaction, coupled with the plain neatness of that pair of nude briefs she had tried to conceal in her hand, had challenged his assessment of her. Why? And why should he care if it had? He cared because somehow she had activated a rebellion within him he hadn't previously known could possibly exist—a dangerous, unwanted rebellion that wanted to overthrow the laws he had laid down about refusing to give people the benefit of the doubt, about distrusting them instead of trusting them. That rebellion was now allowing emotion to get a foothold within him. That rebellion was now constantly challenging his logic and experience. It was urging him to break his own rules. And, worse, it had joined forces with his natural male desire, and together they were trying to undermine the fortifications that protected him. Together they provoked and taunted his beliefs— beliefs he knew to be true. Together they whispered to

him that it wouldn't hurt to allow himself to enjoy the
pleasure that intimacy with Lily would bring.

He must not allow them any freedom.

'The bathroom's free now. I'll finish getting dressed in
the sitting room.' Lily took care not to look directly at
Marco as she hurried past him with her case and her
skirt, her body firmly wrapped up in its bathrobe. In
a household as well organised as this one was she was
pretty sure there would be a hairdryer in one of the
dressing table drawers, but right now, whilst Marco was
safely out of the way in the bathroom, the first thing she
intended to do was get dressed.

The smooth line of her long skirt and the boat-necked
top she was wearing with it proved the sartorial wisdom
of her smooth nude underwear, Lily tried to comfort
herself five minutes later, as she studied her reflection
critically in the full-length bedroom mirror. With just
this kind of event in mind she had brought with her
two very definite pieces of statement jewellery—a wide
collar of beaten silver that lay perfectly against her collarbone, and a silver cuff that went with it. She had come
across them in Florence, when she had been there on
business. She had fallen in love with the jewellery on
sight, and she hadn't been surprised when the young
girl who had made it had told her that she had been
inspired by an exhibition of Saxon jewellery she had
seen in England.

Lily found a hairdryer, as she had expected, in
one of the dressing table drawers, turning her head
upside down so that she could blow her hair dry
quickly from the roots. She had just finished doing so

when Marco walked back into the bedroom, wearing a towelling robe.

Lily could feel her skin overheating again. Why? She was no stranger to the naked male body in all its artistic forms, and Marco was far from naked. *The* naked male body, perhaps, but not *this* male body. Not Marco's male body. It was ridiculous for her to feel so oddly breathless and aware of him. She had spent last night in his bed, after all. This was different, though. This sharing of a room whilst they got ready together was a very specific intimacy that was doing things to her senses and her emotions that filled her with an aching emotional yearning. For intimacy with a man—any man? For the kind of relationship with a man that provided that intimacy? Or for that intimacy and that relationship only with Marco?

The hairdryer slipped out of her grasp and fell to the floor. As she reached for it so did Marco, their hands touching. For a second neither of them moved. If they were really a couple, and really intimate, instead of removing his hand from hers Marco might have removed the hairdryer instead, before going on to take her in his arms. A bolt of shocked delight jolted through her body, causing her hand to shake as she struggled to grip the hairdryer.

'We've got fifteen minutes,' Marco told her, his breath warm against her forehead as he bent towards her. His words caused her to jerk upright, her eyes widening, before logic warned her that he was simply reminding her of when they needed to be downstairs—not suggesting to her that they had fifteen minutes in which to attempt to quench the sensual desire that had started to pulse inside her, conjured up into life out of nowhere by her own thoughts.

It was discomfiting to realise that there could be so much hidden sensuality in even the most straightforward of comments for a person whose senses and body yearned for that sensuality.

'I'm almost ready,' Lily managed to tell him. Almost ready to go downstairs, but completely and utterly and eagerly ready to stay right here and be made love to by him.

Stop it at once, she warned herself. She was behaving as though... As though she had forgotten everything she had ever learned—as though she had no concern whatsoever for her own future emotional security and peace of mind.

Standing up, she swept her hair back off her face, securing it with a neat band before twisting it into a sleek knot from which she pulled a few soft loose tendrils, all without needing to look in the mirror. She only realised that Marco had been watching her when she turned to see him looking at her.

'What's wrong?' she demanded anxiously.

Her father had always been very critical of her mother's appearance. As a little girl Lily had often watched her mother getting ready to go to parties, and she could remember how her father's comments had often resulted in a row that ended up with her mother refusing to go out. Criticising the woman they purported to love was a trick used by some men to control that woman's self-confidence and make her all the more dependent on him, and she despised herself for allowing herself to be affected by Marco's amusement now. It was too late, though, to retract her question

'Nothing's wrong,' Marco answered her curtly. As though the admission was being dragged from him, he continued, 'I was just thinking how easy you made that look.' He paused, and then, as though the words were being spoken of their own volition rather than his, added, 'And how very beautiful you look.'

Marco looked almost as shocked by the fact that he had paid her a compliment as she was herself. Lily swallowed hard, her own voice husky as she responded.

'Thank you.' His admission deserved an admission of her own from her. 'My father would never have said that to my mother. I don't think I ever heard him tell her she was beautiful, even though she was—' She broke off, shaking her head.

'Your father?' Marco questioned, causing Lily to retreat back into her normal reticence about her background. She had said too much. She shook her head.

'My mind was wandering, I'm afraid. Silly of me. And now we've only got ten minutes. I'll leave the bedroom to you, so that you can get dressed. I can finish getting ready in the sitting room.'

She was gone before Marco could stop her to pursue the matter further, and she had been right. They did only have ten minutes left.

He joined Lily in the sitting room with three minutes to spare, looking so formidably handsome and male in a dark suit worn with a dark blue shirt with a fine white line and a toning tie that Lilly felt herself flooded with conflicting emotions. He filled her with a desire she had never expected to feel, but at the same time he also filled her with anxiety and dread because of that desire.

Lily looked like a pagan princess, Marco thought, and a shocking of the surge of possessive wanting filled him, seized him, at the sight of her in her plain black outfit adorned with that almost barbarically splendid jewellery.

There would be women here this evening who would be wearing family heirloom jewellery worth a fortune, but it would be impossible for them to outshine the dramatic simplicity of Lily's appearance. Any man would be proud to stand at her side. And any man would ache for the evening to be over so that he could have her all to himself. Was that how he felt? Possessive and bitterly jealous because she preferred someone else?

Lily's, 'We're going to be late,' had him nodding his head and then going to open the door for her.

They reached the main salon—a large double-aspect room, decorated very much in the French Empire style in shades of rich gold and French blue, with two enormous chandeliers throwing out brilliant prisms of light—only seconds ahead of the Duchess's guests. There was no more time than to accept a glass of chilled champagne from one of the several formally attired waiters starting to circulate around the room.

Introduced by the Duchess to a dozen or more of her guests within as many minutes Lily was soon struggling to keep a mental note of their names. However, she wished that all she had to bear was that awkward confusion when the Duchess called Marco over to join them and then began introducing them virtually as a couple.

Since he obviously already knew some of the guests Lily expected Marco to do something to correct this error, but he did nothing about it at all, instead staying at her side whilst the Duchess beamed with obvious pride in having 'outed' their relationship. He was obviously very fond of the Duchess, and determined not to embarrass her by revealing the truth in public, Lily recognised. Whilst she could understand that, it certainly didn't make her position any less difficult to bear. Having Marco behave as though they were indeed a couple, having him standing so close to her, adopting a protective manner towards her that she knew was fictitious, brought her to a sharply keen knife-edge of painful awareness of just how much the inner vulnerable core of her longed to have the right to this kind of closeness with him.

Of course he was sophisticated and urbane enough to carry off their supposed relationship with cool self-confidence. He was that kind of man—totally at home in his surroundings and totally in control of himself. And of her? She had known him for less than a handful of days but in that time he had changed not just her beliefs about what she wanted out of life, but her perception of herself as well.

When she was confronted by the feelings aching through her now she came face to face with a part of herself she had thought locked away for ever. Somehow, though, despite it being pushed away, ignored by her and denied, Marco had the power to bring it to life within her. There was no point, though, in indulging in hopeless, self-destructive daydreams and fantasies. Lily knew that loving Marco was dangerous for her and could only bring her misery and pain.

'You need a fresh glass of champagne. That one's gone flat, by the looks of it.'

Marco was holding out a fresh glass to her and smiling as he did so. A faked smile, of course—how could it not be?—but her heart couldn't help yearning and wondering what it would be like to have Marco *really* smile at her like that, with a smile that was full of tenderness and more than a hint of sensual promise of the pleasure that would be theirs once they were on their own. A lover's smile, in other words.

Her hand trembled as she reached for the glass he was holding out to her. To disguise her vulnerability she took a quick sip of it, almost choking on the bubbly liquid in shock when she felt a hand on her arm and heard a familiar female voice exclaim, 'Lily—little Lily! Darling girl, you look *so* like your dear mother. I'd have recognised you anywhere. I couldn't believe it when I saw you. I had to ask Carolina to bring me over.'

Somehow Lily managed to smile back at the elegant mature woman now standing with the Duchess, smiling at her.

'I could hardly believe it myself.' The Duchess laughed. 'There I was, telling one of my closest friends about Marco's lovely new girlfriend and the exhibition she is organising, and when I pointed you out what should Melanie say but that she recognised you? She knew you as a little girl but lost touch with you.'

Lily was acutely conscious of Marco standing next to her, listening to everything that was being said. If there was anything that could cause her even more emotional distress and dread than recognising how vulnerable she was to Marco then it was this. Someone from her past with its memories that she had fought so hard to leave behind her.

Marco could see how shocked Lily was. Shocked in a way that suggested she had been dealt some kind of almost physical blow. She was trying hard not to show it, but he had heard her indrawn agonised breath and seen the colour leaving her face. Why? Because the Duchess's friend had known her as a little girl? *Why*?

She was trapped, Lily thought helplessly. She couldn't simply turn and run away, no matter how tempted she was to do just that. It wouldn't have been so bad if Marco hadn't been with her. She would still have felt shocked. She would still have felt the pain that seeing Melanie had brought her. But that pain would have been much easier to bear without Marco's presence.

And now, instead of running somewhere to hide, she had to smile as though she meant it and say with as much composure as she could to the woman standing with the Duchess, 'Melanie, how lovely to see you again.'

Melanie Trinders had been a close friend of her mother. They had modelled together, and Melanie had been a regular visitor to their home.

Lily had tried to sound cool and slightly remote, but her attempt to put some emotional distance between them had no effect whatsoever on her mother's old friend. Lily was immediately embraced—wrapped, in fact—in the warmth of expensive cashmere and even more expensive scent, and subjected to a fond continental exchange of kisses before being held at arm's

length by the elegant and still beautiful late middle-aged
woman dressed in a scarlet designer dress that fitted her
model-svelte figure like a glove.

'To think that when you invited Harry and me here
tonight I had no idea that your guest of honour was going
to be my dear Petra's daughter. And such a clever and
beautiful daughter. Petra would have been so proud of
you, Lily. Proud of you and happy for you,' she emphasised, giving Marco a meaningful look before turning
back to Lily. 'Emotional happiness was always so important to your mother. I could never understand what
she meant about the importance of love until I met my
Harry.'

Smiling at the Duchess, she told her friend, 'Carolina,
this is such a wonderful coincidence. Lily's mother was
one of my closest friends. We modelled together.' She
gave a small sigh. 'A lifetime ago now. Petra was younger than me, and such a lovely girl.'

Melanie turned back to Lily, still holding her hands.
'Lily, you are the image of her. I remember when you
were born. Your father was still furious with your mother
for having a baby. He didn't even go to see her when she
was in hospital—just as though he had nothing at all
to do with your arrival into the world. He bullied her
dreadfully to lose weight, of course, so that she could
go back to modelling.'

'Your mother was a model?' Marco demanded, his
mistrust and suspicion returning along with his angry
contempt. If Lily's mother had been a model that meant
she would have even more cause to know just what could
happen to the unwary—and yet she had still tried to
inveigle his nephew into it. The loathing he felt for the

kind of people who had brought about Olivia's destruction surged through Marco's veins.

'Not just a model, but *the* model of her time—just as Lily's father was the photographer of his generation. I'm not surprised to hear from Carolina that you use photography in your own work, Lily. I can still remember watching you playing in your father's studio as a little girl. Even then you preferred taking photographs rather than being in them. Your father was a genius with the camera and a wonderful success in the fashion world.' She looked at Marco. 'Given your relationship with Lily, though, I'm sure that she will have told you that whilst her father was brilliantly successful as a photographer he was a disastrous husband and father. I understand his second marriage broke up as well, Lily?'

Melanie had obviously taken Marco's fixed concentration on what she was saying as a sign that he wanted to hear more, Lily decided miserably. Because without waiting for Lily to answer she continued, 'I can remember going into the studio and seeing Lily playing there on the floor. You were such a sweet-natured, pretty child, Lily, and you could have been the perfect child model. No wonder Anton wanted all those pictures of you.'

Champagne nearly spilled from Lily's glass as she made a sudden rejecting movement she couldn't control. Her hand was trembling uncontrollably, her stomach heaving with sick dread, and she looked towards the door, desperate to escape.

Something was wrong. Something was *very* wrong, Marco was forced to recognise, and the rebellion within him rose up and totally overwhelmed the weakened force of his determination to remain distant from Lily. It was that rebellion and not he himself that had him moving towards her, putting himself between her and the others to shield her, taking hold of her arm to steady her, taking charge and obliterating any resistance. Lily looked numbly at him, like a hunted, tormented creature in fear for its life, caught in a car's headlights.

'Anton liked photographing her, then, did he?' the rebellion in him asked conversationally, mercilessly silencing what he thought of as his real self when it tried to protest that it didn't want to get involved.

'Oh, yes,' Melanie agreed. 'He always said she had real model potential...'

Lily struggled to subdue the sound of protest and anguish rising in her throat. She looked ill, Marco recognised. Bruised and defeated and agonised.

'I was so sorry when I heard about your mother's death, Lily,' Melanie added in a much more sombre voice. 'Such a dreadfully sad thing to happen.'

'She was never able to come to terms with her divorce from my father,' Lily responded in a strained voice, somehow managing to drag herself back from the edge of the dark, greedy chasm of fear that had opened up at her feet.

The other woman patted her arm and then excused herself, explaining, 'I must go—my husband will be looking for me. Stay in touch, Lily darling.'

The Duchess too had moved away to talk to another guest, leaving Lily alone with Marco in their own little pool of silence.

Marco was still looking at her, even though he had now released her arm, and Lily could imagine what he was thinking. Draining her glass, she turned to him and spoke in an empty voice.

'My mother committed suicide—drink and prescription drugs. Oh, yes,' she added fiercely when he didn't speak, 'I *do* know what the modelling business can do to those who are too vulnerable for its cruelty. I've experienced it at first hand. That's why...'

Without waiting to see what his response was she stepped past him and walked away, her head held high and half blinded by the tears she knew she dared not shed. She didn't stop in her headlong flight until she realised that she'd lost her way and was in a small anteroom, thankfully all on her own. She wanted fresh air—fresh air and privacy—and the self-indulgence of crying for a mother and a childhood that were long gone. But she wasn't here to indulge herself, she reminded herself sharply. She was here to work. But the floodgates had been opened and there was no holding back the memories now.

CHAPTER EIGHT

SHE knew who the hands on her shoulders belonged to without needing to turn round.

Marco. It couldn't be anyone else.

And the reason she knew was because...because she would know him anywhere. Because with her emotions exposed to the painful air of recognition by Melanie's revelations she had committed the worst self-injury of all. Because there were no other hands she wanted to hold her, only his.

When had her emotions become entangled with her desire for him? When had they melded together to create the most eternally binding human cord of all? Love. Ah, how the mere thought of it threatened pain. She couldn't love Marco. He was turning her round and wrapping his arms around her, holding her as carefully as though she might break. Out of pity, she told herself fiercely. Out of pity—nothing else. And pity wasn't what she wanted from him. She knew that now. She tried to break free but he wouldn't let her go

'You're right,' she told him, as though he had made the statement. 'I'm here to work, not to behave like a silly fool who can't control her emotions.'

The rebellion that had begun as a small protest he

could easily control had become a raging force for change within him, directing him into responses that should have felt awkward and unwelcome but which instead seemed to come fatally easily. It seemed the most natural thing in the world for him to demand, in a voice that was low and rough with something that could have been self-condemnation, 'Why didn't you tell me any of this before.'

'Tell you what? Tell you that my father was a photographer? Tell you that my mother was a model? Tell you that between them the world of modelling and my father destroyed her, and that because of that I've…?' Lily's voice thinned out to become brittle and self-derisory. 'Why should you want to know? Why should you or anyone else care?'

Marco could hear the pain she was trying to control. It seared through him, burning through the restraints he had wrapped around his own emotions. An answering pain mixed with yearning and an entirely male desire to hold and protect her spilled over. To say what he had felt listening to Melanie's revelations had been shock didn't come anywhere near describing the effect those revelations had had on him. They had pierced the seal he had placed on his own emotions, exposing them to the raw reality of another person's pain. Lily's pain.

Now he felt as though he was at war with himself— with one part of him wanting to comfort her and the other defensively wanting him to ignore what had happened, desperately wanting him to ignore the voice inside him that was telling him that he and Lily shared a unique bond forged in pain. Deep within himself emotions he couldn't afford to let himself feel were struggling to find a voice. The scar tissue he had forced to grow over them was being ripped from old wounds, and against the pressure of his denial the words came out.

'I once knew a girl who became a model.'

His harsh and reluctant admission caused Lily to look at him in surprise. Something in the way he had spoken as much as the words themselves jerked her out of her own distress to register his need. She lifted her hand, as though she was going to reach out and touch him, and then let it drop again, saying uncertainly, 'She was important to you?'

'Yes.' Another admission was wrenched from him; another clamp removed from the resolve-clad box in which he had locked away his right to feel emotional pain. 'We were to have been married.'

Married? Marco had been going to *marry* someone?

'She's dead now. That sordid world killed her.'

Sometimes there were things that were too painful to know, Lily acknowledged, and this was one of them. She was still in Marco's arms, but now she felt she had no right to be there and that the sanctuary they provided rightly belonged to someone else.

'I'm so sorry.' She tried to step back from him, but instead of releasing her his hold on her tightened. He was so lost in his pain that he was barely aware he was holding her, Lily suspected.

'I couldn't protect her and she died. I tried, but I failed.' Now that the seal damming his past had been pierced the feelings he had locked away for so long flooded past his defences, leaving him powerless to stop

himself from revealing the self-contempt he had always
tried to keep hidden.

'We grew up together. A marriage between us was
what our families had always hoped for. It seemed the
right thing to do. We got on well together. She understood the demands of my position. I thought that she
knew me and I knew her. I believed I could trust her with
anything—my hopes, my doubts, our future together. I
believed she trusted me, but I was wrong.'

'I'm sorry,' Lily repeated

'She'd always told me she was happy with our parents' plans for our shared future. I didn't know that she
wasn't. She lied to me.'

'Perhaps she didn't want to hurt you and was trying
to protect you?' Lily suggested gently, wanting to ease
his pain.

Marco looked at her.

At no time had anyone—not Olivia and not even
himself—suggested that Olivia might have wanted to
spare him pain. Lily's words, her gentleness and her
concern for him, felt like the comforting and healing
effect of warm sunlight on an unbearably dark, cold
place. But he was giving in to something he must not
give in to. He was letting the dangerous sweetness that
Lily had brought him overwhelm reality. There were
still anomalies in Lily's way of life that logic insisted
did not add up

'We'd better get back to the reception. The Duchess
will be wondering where we are,' Lily warned him.

'In a minute. First I want you to explain to me what
you were doing working in that photographic studio,
given what Melanie said about your childhood. I would

have thought that it would be the last place you'd want to be after what. I've now learned about you.'

'I was standing in for my half-brother,' Lily admitted. Now he knew about her parents she felt strong enough to tell him the truth, and then at last he would believe her. 'My father married a second time. My stepmother was very kind to me. She's remarried now—my father died ten years ago—but my half-brother has turned our father into a hero figure and wants to follow in his footsteps.'

She gave a small sigh. 'He texted me asking me to stand in for him because he knew I was in Milan. I hadn't realised then that he'd asked your nephew to model for him.'

She was telling him the truth, Marco recognised on an unsettling surge of uncomfortable guilt. 'Why didn't you tell me any of that before?'

'I didn't think you'd believe me,' Lily told him wryly.

'I probably wasn't ready to listen even if you had. I'm sorry I misjudged you. '

'Something like that,' Lily agreed. It was impossible for her to tell him now that she had wanted to keep a distance between them because she had feared the effect he had on her. After all, now she not only knew that he did not reciprocate the desire she felt for him, she also knew he was still mourning the girl he had expected to marry.

She started to walk towards the door, conscious of her duty to the Duchess and her work, but came to an abrupt halt when Marco caught up with her and asked, 'And Anton? Tell me about him?'

Lily's breath escaped in a soft hiss of anxiety. 'There's nothing to tell.'

She was lying, Marco knew, but instead of feeling the sense of condemnation against her he would normally have felt instead he felt an unfamiliar stirring of—of what? Curiosity? Or was it something more personal than that? Something that was in fact concern for her?

Whilst he battled with his own thoughts Lily continued walking back to the reception. She looked so vulnerable and so determined to be strong. No one should have to find strength on their own, without someone who cared about them to help them. He knew the desolate wilderness that place was. He couldn't let Lily struggle in it. He strode after her, catching up with her to put his hand under her elbow so that they re-entered the reception together.

Lily didn't know whether to feel relieved or embarrassed when she realised that the Duchess had put their disappearance down to a desire to be alone with one another. Of course it was true that the presence of Marco's arm around her was hardly likely to convince the Duchess that she had got things wrong, but somehow Lily found it foolishly impossible to move away from his pseudo-lover-like hold.

The rest of the evening passed in something of a tired blur for Lily after the emotional trauma of the day. Of course she managed to stop dwelling on her own feelings when the Duchess showed her and Marco over the long gallery housing the villa's art collection, her professionalism cutting in whilst she made notes and took photographs.

'No wonder you're so professional—you must have been handling these things practically from your cradle,' Marco commented at one point, picking up her camera.

'Practically,' Lily agreed. 'Not that I ever had much of an interest in fashion. It was always art that fascinated me.'

'Not modern art, though?'

'The past feels more comfortable, more established. I feel safer there,' Lily told him, only realising when she saw the way he was looking at her just what she might have betrayed.

'Safer?'

'With art of the past there's no need for me to trust my own judgement,' she defended herself.

'Safety and your desire for it seems to be a recurring theme in your life.'

Lily could feel her heart hammering heavily into her ribs.

'The price of having parents who quarrelled a lot and being over-sensitive to that quarrelling, I expect.'

She was glad that the Duchess was there, to keep the conversation from getting too personal, glad too of the other guests who'd been invited to join them for dinner, so that conversation around the dinner table was kept general.

Inevitably, though, the evening came to an end, and she smiled a goodnight at the Duchess before walking up the stairs and then along the corridor with Marco to the guest suite.

'You can use the bathroom first if you wish,' she said, as soon as they were inside the sitting room. 'I've got some notes I want to type up, so I'll be working for a while.'

Marco nodded his head.

He wasn't anywhere near as immune to her as he should be—as he wanted to be, as he must be. Just because she had shown sympathy toward him over Olivia that did not mean... It didn't mean what? That she wanted him? He could *make* her want him. They both had a shared history of pain, and a shared need to have that pain assuaged. He could assuage it. He could hold her and take her and show her that there was far more pleasure to be found in his arms than in the arms of a man she feared as well as desired.

What was he thinking? All the old habits and teaching rose up inside him, warning him against allowing her to get under his guard. They might have some common ground, but that did not mean that he could trust her.

'I'll say goodnight, then,' he told her curtly, opening the communicating door between the two rooms.

'Yes. Yes. Goodnight,' Lily returned.

It was true that she had work to do, Lily reminded herself, smothering a yawn after the door had closed, leaving her alone in the sitting room to their suite. She sat down at the small pretty desk and opened her laptop, connecting her camera to it so that she could download the photographs she had taken.

Normally within seconds of starting on a task like this she would have been so absorbed in her work that she'd have been oblivious to anything and everything else, but tonight for some reason, even though she was focusing on the photographs she had taken, her real attention was on the mental images stored inside her head—images of Marco from earlier in the evening. Marco smiling at her as the Duchess introduced them as a couple. Marco steadying her arm when shock had jolted through her, Marco telling her about the love he had lost.

Lily rubbed her eyes and got up, walking up and down and trying to clear her head. Her eyes felt gritty and dry. Her head was beginning to ache. She was tired, but she dared not risk going through the bedroom to the bathroom to get ready for bed until she was sure that Marco was asleep. Perhaps she could just lie down on the sofa for a few minutes…

Marco looked at his watch. Was Lily still working? It was over an hour since he'd come to bed, and she'd looked tired when they'd come upstairs. It was concern for the efficient execution of the tour that was getting him out of bed now, not his concern for Lily herself, he assured himself as he pulled on a bathrobe and opened the communicating door.

Lily's laptop was still open on the desk, quietly humming, but Lily herself had fallen asleep on the sofa, fully dressed.

Why hadn't she made herself properly comfortable? He told himself that what her obvious discomfort was arousing in him was merely irritation. Why should he be concerned for her, after all? He switched off the laptop, intending to walk away and leave her where she was, but something beyond his control made him go back to look down at her a second time. She couldn't possibly sleep properly where she was. At the very least she'd probably wake up with a stiff neck, and that was bound to effect her ability to work—which was why she was here. Sofas and chairs were not designed to be slept on, especially elegant antique pieces—as he knew to his cost.

Conversely, the bed in the bedroom was vast, with plenty of room for two people to sleep in it without having to go anywhere near one another. It seemed un-gentlemanly to leave her where she was, as though doing so broke his own expectation of courtesy for someone who was, after all, in his care.

He reached down to wake her up, and then stopped. She would only argue with him and insist on staying where she was, insist that he had the right to the bed. It would be far more expedient to simply pick her up and carry her to the bed than to get involved in an argument in which they'd both fight to be the one to do the right thing.

When he lifted her in his arms she made a small sound that had him catching his breath thinking she was going to wake up, but she merely turned into his body. The sensation of her warmth lying against him sent his heart hammering into his ribs. What was the matter with him? He wasn't so unable to control his needs that he was now afraid of even this kind of intimacy with her, was he?

He felt Lily snuggle deeper into his hold, exhaling a small sigh of pleasure as she did so. Pulling back the covers, Marco placed her down on one side of the bed, and then removed his robe so that he could get into the opposite side of the bed and switch off the bedside lamp. He saw Lily frown in her sleep and move, seeking

the warmth that she'd lost. Marco lay on his own side
of the bed, his muscles coiled tightly with tension as
he willed Lily not to breach the distance he had put
between them.

But no amount of willing Lily to stay where she was
on his part had the power to come between Lily herself
and the need that sleep and his touch had awakened in
her. She moved towards him, sighing softly when she
found him, curling up against him with her hand on
his arm, her head on his chest. He wanted to push her
away, but somehow he couldn't. Somehow that rebellion
inside him was overriding the instinct that told him that
allowing such intimacy between them was dangerous.

He had never slept with a woman so intimately—
never allowed himself to gather anyone into his arms
and simply hold them. He had never wanted to—until
now. Such intense intimacy was not something he felt
comfortable with. His parents had lived with a great deal
of formality. They had always had separate bedrooms.
But right now holding Lily so close to him was exactly
what he wanted. He drew her closer and felt the tightening of an unfamiliar ache around his heart. Now he
knew why he had always rejected this kind of intimacy.
He had rejected it because it was dangerous. Because it
made you vulnerable to the woman you were holding.
Because once you had known it you would never want
to be without it—or without her.

Soft morning light filtered in through the room's cur-
tains, caressing the faces of the two people sleeping
together in the centre in the large bed. Lily was held
within the protective curve of Marco's body, his arm

round her. She was oblivious to the intimacy she had
sought—and found—during the night hours whilst she
had slept.

Marco woke first, his senses enjoying the knowledge
that he was holding Lily before he was properly awake
and his brain kicked in to tell him what that meant.
When it did, though, he still didn't release her or move
away from her. He was trying to work out exactly what it
was about holding her that made the intimacy seem not
just right but also necessary, he told himself, defending
his reluctance to put any distance between them.

She looked so beautiful. She *was* beautiful—inside
and out. She was everything any man could ever want in
a woman, and the man who had let her go was a fool to
have done so. Marco's heart slammed into his ribs, and
the small involuntary movement he made, as though in
denial of his own thoughts and the reality of what they
meant, woke Lily from her sleep.

If she kept her eyes closed perhaps she wouldn't have
to wake up, and then she could hold on to her wonderful
dream of being held safe in Marco's arms. Mmm… In
her imagination she was there still, and she could feel
his heart beating against the hand she had placed on his
bare chest. She *could* feel his heart beating beneath her
hand. Lily's eyes flew open. She was in bed with Marco
and he was holding her. How had that happened? Had
she somehow sleep-walked into the bedroom and got
into bed beside him? She hoped not.

She looked at Marco, who immediately released her
and removed himself from the bed, reaching for his robe
as he did so, telling her with a dismissive shrug, 'You
didn't look very comfortable sleeping on the sofa, so I

brought you here. I thought there was more than enough
room in the bed for both of us.' His voice was terse,
his manner distant. He disappeared into the bathroom
before she could say anything.

Thankfully, Lily realised she was still fully dressed.
She was uncomfortably aware that she must have been
the one to initiate their sleeping intimacy, given the
way she had been dreaming about him. Why hadn't he
demanded an explanation of her behaviour? Perhaps
because he was so used to sleeping with eager women—
women he couldn't love because he loved a girl who was
now lost to him for ever—who longed to be close to
him that what she had done had barely registered with
him.

Lily's heart felt very heavy indeed.

They'd had a very busy full day, visiting two more villas
in the morning and stopping briefly for a light lunch
before continuing on to visit a private villa on one of
Lake Como's small islands. Yet no amount of busyness
was enough to push out of her thoughts everything that
she'd felt on waking up in Marco's arms this morning.
It was like holding a special golden treasure whose existence was enough to fill her with happiness. Her treasure, though, was fool's gold—because it meant nothing
to Marco. *She* meant nothing to Marco.

It was now late in the afternoon, and they had stopped
in a pretty lakeside town for a cup of coffee at Marco's
suggestion, prior to their return to the villa.

Marco had just gone inside the café to pay their
bill, and she was sitting drinking in the relaxing scene
around her, when to her horrified disbelief she saw

Anton Gillman on the other side of the road. She had assumed and hoped that he had left the area, with the rest of the fashion pack and returned to Milan, but obviously she had been wrong. Lily shrank back in her chair, hoping that he wouldn't look across the road and see her. For a moment she thought that he wouldn't, and that she was safe, but then the woman seated at a table close to their own got up, her small lap dog barking shrilly. The sound caught Anton's attention so that he glanced towards the café. There was nowhere for her to hide, no hope that he wouldn't see her, and Lily knew that he had when she saw him start to cross the road and come purposefully towards her. It was the worst kind of cruel coincidence.

Lily shuddered to see the admiring looks he was attracting from the woman with the yapping dog. She was quite obviously impressed by his air of authority, his expensive suit and his immaculate grooming. If only she knew the truth about him and his sexual tastes she wouldn't be so interested in him or so admiring.

Lily wasn't impressed, though. She was a teenage girl again, sick with fear and loathing because she knew what he wanted from her.

He was smiling at her—that taunting, cruel smile she had never been able to forget.

'Lily, my lovely.' His voice caressed her as his knuckles stroked along her jaw, and his gaze registered her immediate terrified recoil from him. 'Delicious that you've remained so...sensitive. I shall enjoy discovering just how sensitive when I finally persuade you to give in to me.'

* * *

Inside the café, waiting to pay their bill, Marco saw the tall dark-haired man approaching Lily and recognised him immediately. Her ex-lover. Anger and jealousy surged over him. There were two people ahead of him in the queue to pay, one of them an elderly man who obviously couldn't see very well, and who was struggling to find the right money. Marco saw the man lean towards Lily, who was out of view. The intensity of the emotion that exploded inside him scorched the truth of his feelings into him. He was jealous. He was jealous of another man's right to claim Lily's attention and to claim Lily herself because... Because she meant far more to him than he had previously allowed himself to admit?

The elderly man was still fumbling with his money, and the woman behind him in the queue was tutting in her impatience, but Marco was oblivious to them both. How had it happened? How could it be that Lily had become so important to him? He didn't know. He only knew that she was—just as he knew that this was the last thing he had ever have wanted to happen. He had built a life that depended on him not becoming emotionally involved with others, on not allowing himself to become emotionally dependent on anyone. How had Lily managed to slip beneath his guard and touch that place within him where he was so dangerously vulnerable? His formidable inner defences were warning him to step back from the danger that now lay ahead of him, to turn round and walk away from it—and from Lily herself.

It was illogical for her to feel so afraid, Lily tried to reassure herself. Anton couldn't do anything to harm her now. She was an adult, not a teenager, and they were in public. She was in command of her own life. But some fears could not be controlled with mere reason, and this one had lived privately hidden within her for a very long time.

'Why don't we take a little walk, you and I?' Anton suggested. 'I'm sure your companion won't mind, *Dr* Wrightington.'

Lily's stomach swooped sickeningly. He'd been checking up on her, asking questions about her.

'I'm not going anywhere with you.'

Too late she recognised it was the wrong thing to say, with its echoes of past refusal.

Where was Marco? Why hadn't he come back? What if he didn't come back?

She looked frantically into the café willing Marco to see her and come to her rescue, but she couldn't see him because of the customers blocking her view. She was alone with Anton. Abandoned by Marco just as she had been abandoned by her father. There was no one to support her, no one to protect her.

Hadn't it always been that way? Hadn't she always had to protect herself? Hadn't she always been alone and uncared for by those she'd longed so much to love her? Her mother, her father, Marco… She was so afraid, so alone. She had to get away, to escape. She stood up, her abrupt movement causing her chair to scrape on the stone beneath it with an ugly grating sound, and her panic increased when Anton took advantage of her fear to take hold of her arm.

In the shop the elderly man had finally paid his bill,

scooping up his change with quivering hands, and now the woman was handing over her money.

Marco looked towards the table where he had left Lily. She was standing up now, the man with her taking her arm. They were standing close together. Had Lily forgotten that the man holding her, the man she was about to give herself to, had already let her down once? If so, then perhaps he should remind her. And risk being told that he was interfering where his interference wasn't wanted, as it had been with Olivia? Risk being accused of trying to ruin her life?

In his mind's eye Marco could see his eighteen-year-old self, humiliated and shamed. He would not be endure that kind of humiliation again.

Turning his back on the scene being played out beyond the interior of the café, Marco continued to wait to pay their bill.

'Ah, poor Lily—still so afraid of me. How delicious and erotic…even more so now than when you were younger. There is nothing quite like a little bit of fear to add spice to…things.'

Something snapped inside Lily. Instinct and need pushed aside the rules of modern-day life that told her it was her duty to herself and others not to make a nuisance of herself, not to ask anything of anyone, not to expect others to help her or to forge an emotional bond with her that meant she could turn to them in need. In a last despairing surge she turned towards the interior of the café. She could see Marco now. He was paying their bill.

'Marco…'

The anguished, almost sobbed sound of Lily's voice calling his name drew Marco's gaze in her direction. She was looking at him—looking for him. Her free arm—the arm her companion was not holding—was stretched out toward him. She needed him. Lily *needed* him!

Throwing down a note over twice the value of the coffees they had just had, Marco ran towards the door.

Lily exhaled in relief. Marco had heard her. He was going to help her.

He reached her, grasping her free hand, holding it safe.

'Make him go away, Marco,' she begged him wildly, unable to control her distress. 'Please make him go away.'

'You heard Lily,' Marco told Anton, confronting her persecutor and impaling him with a coldly hostile look of warning.

Anton didn't move, saying mockingly instead, 'Naughty Lily. You never told me that you have a new... protector.'

Whilst Lily flinched Marco didn't shift his concentration from the other man's face. No matter what the relationship between Lily and this man might have been before, it was to *him* that she was now appealing for rescue and refuge, and Marco's nature and upbringing would not allow him to deny her either.

'Any decent man would consider it his duty to protect a woman from your sort,' Marco told Anton curtly. 'And let me warn you that my protection of Lily will extend beyond this incident. You would be well advised to keep away from her in future. In fact, I'd advise you to leave Italy today."

The smirking self-confidence with which Anton had greeted Marco's arrival had evaporated now into blustering protest as he complained, 'You can't make that kind of threat.'

'I'm not threatening you,' Marco assured him. 'I'm simply giving you some advice as a result of your own behaviour.'

Lily listened to their exchange with gratitude and awe. Marco was being magnificent. He was so completely in control, so completely the master of the situation, completely demolishing Anton who, having released her when Marco arrived on the scene, was now backing off, eventually turning his back on them to disappear into the crowd. She looked at Marco. He was standing rather stiffly to one side of her, looking away from her.

Marco knew something had happened to him. Something that threatened his defences. His throat felt raw and tight—with tension, nothing else, he assured himself. He looked back at Lily. She looked stricken, but she didn't say anything. Her face was paper-white as she turned away from him, dignified in defeat, her manner that of a weary combatant struggling to pick up her weapons and continue to fight on alone. She looked alone. He knew all about how that felt—how it hurt, how the heart hardened around that hurt.

She was trembling violently, her manner that of someone too traumatised to be able to behave rationally. Whatever had happened between her and her ex whilst Marco had been paying their bill had plainly affected her very badly. He stepped towards her, and then checked himself and stepped back. He wanted to cross the chasm that separated him from obeying his instincts but years of denying those instincts, had laid down rules inside him that had to be obeyed. The voices of his inner rebellion were growing stronger, urging him to join them, but he couldn't. Because he was too afraid. Afraid of being deceived and betrayed. Out of nowhere, out of nothing he could understand, something inside him rejected that possibility, stating clearly and firmly that Lily wouldn't do that to him.

All around them people were going about their business, but for Marco his world had come to a halt and was now poised trembling on the brink of something momentous. *Lily.* His heart pounded and surged inside his chest cavity, as though trying to break free of unwanted bonds. Lily. She had turned to him. She had wanted his help and she had trusted him to give it. Trust. Trust was a rare and precious gift when it was exchanged between two people. Lily had offered him the gift of her trust, and that gift demanded surely that he reciprocate in kind. Trust Lily? Trust anyone with his own vulnerabilities? He couldn't. He scarcely trusted himself with them. That was why he had had to lock them away.

A car horn sounded in the traffic and the moment was gone, banished by the demands of the real world. The danger had passed. The path he had laid down for himself had forked, and briefly he had been tempted to take the wrong fork, but thankfully he had recognised the folly of doing so. Practicality reasserted itself within him, much to his relief—if for no other reason than because it was easier to deal with practical matters than it was for him to deal with emotions.

They had finished their work for the day and, whilst he'd intended to take Lily on a tour of a silk mill as she'd requested, it was plain to Marco that right now she was in no state to do anything. The best thing he could do was get her back to the privacy of the Duchess's villa.

She didn't speak as they were driven back to the villa, simply sat stiffly at his side, her stiffness occasionally broken by the tremors that shook her body.

The Duchess was out visiting friends, and Lily made no objection when Marco suggested that she might want to rest in their room, letting him guide her up the stairs and along the corridor to their suite, where she subsided onto the bed, sitting tensely at its edge as she spoke for the first time. 'Please don't leave me here on my own,' she begged.

'You're safe now, Lily,' Marco responded. 'He can't come back into your life now—unless you choose to ask him to do so.'

'Ask Anton into my life?' Lily shuddered. 'Never. *Never...*'

'You must have cared for him once.' The cool words, a product of his suspicion and refusal to trust, were forced into the open by those voices within him that warned he had already let down his guard far too much, and that now was the time to rectify that mistake whilst he still could.

But they made Lily flinch visibly, causing him to feel an unexpected stab of guilt as she denied emotionally, 'No. Never. I disliked him from the start. But he was my father's friend and I couldn't avoid him.'

She had met the other man through her *father*? Even

the logical, searching, suspicious voice within him had to accept that that changed things—but it still insisted on reminding her, 'You were lovers.'

CHAPTER NINE

LILY raised her head and looked up at Marco, revulsion darkening her eyes. Marco's words had filled her with anguish and fear, flooded her mind with memories that undermined her already shaky self-control.

She had kept her secrets to herself for so long—refusing to unburden herself to anyone, bearing the horror of them alone—but now suddenly everything was too much for her. She couldn't go on any longer. She couldn't bear the pain and the guilt any more.

She was shivering and trembling, lost in the grip of her emotions and the past.

'*No!*' she told Marco vehemently. 'No. I would never let him even touch me.' She shuddered. 'I hated him—loathed him.' The words gathered speed, spilling out of her in jerky uncoordinated sentences. 'He kept saying things to me…looking at me…even though he knew how much I hated him. That just made him laugh. He said that he'd get his way in the end and that I wouldn't be able to stop him. I told him I'd tell my father, but he just laughed at me. I was only fourteen, and my father…'

She shuddered again and Marco listened, every word she uttered a fresh lash of anguished guilt against new emotions still raw from having the protective cover he had used to smother them ripped from them. Whilst he had been clinging to his refusal to trust her she had been at the mercy of her tormentor.

Like a river dammed from its original course and now returning to it, feelings, emotions and awareness were starting to flow back over dry, parched land that was now struggling to cope with the flood, whilst the other course fought desperately to hold on to its supremacy. As always when his emotions seemed to threaten him, Marco took refuge in practical action, going to the cabinet in the sitting room and opening it, pouring Lily a small glass of brandy which he took back to her, instructing her, 'Drink this.' When she hesitated, he assured her, 'You're in shock and it will help you.'

Nodding her head, Lily tilted the glass to her lips. The fiery liquid burned its way down her throat, warming her stomach, leaving her feeling slightly light-headed.

Why had she told Marco what she had? She wished desperately that she hadn't, but it was too late to deny her admission now. She stood up abruptly, ignoring the dizzy feeling that instantly seized her as she paced the floor at the end of the bed, lost, trapped in a world of fear and despair.

Marco felt the full weight of the enormity of what she had said to him. She was carrying a terrible burden of emotional pain. He could see that now. A burden of pain *he* had reinforced by his cruel misjudgement of her. Like a blind man trying to seek his way in unfamiliar territory he tried to understand what he should do—for her, not for himself, because it was her need that mattered to him now. Comforting her was far more important to him than protecting his own emotional distance. He wanted to help her, he recognised. He wanted to comfort her, wanted to love her. *Love* her? He wanted to *love* her.

Quickly he pushed the admission away. There were things that Lily needed to say. Things she had kept locked away inside herself for a very long time, and he knew all about the darkness that could cause.

'Tell me what happened, Lily,' he urged her gently. 'Tell me about him…Anton.'

Lily looked at him, as though properly registering his presence for the first time. 'I can't,' she answered him. 'You wouldn't understand. You think I'm a liar.'

Her words struck like a blow against his conscience.

'I *will* understand and I *will* believe you,' he promised her, adding quietly, 'You said it was your father who introduced you to him?'

'Yes. Anton owns one of the magazines that used to commission my father. He used to come to my father's studio.'

'And that was where you met him?'

'Yes. I didn't like him right from the start. There was something about him.' Lily closed her eyes, but she couldn't blot out the memories and the images she didn't want to see. 'He knew that I didn't like him. I could tell. It amused him. He enjoyed…he liked frightening me. And I *was* afraid of him. He made me afraid of him. Just by looking at me sometimes. I used to have nightmares about him looking at me.'

Marco swallowed down on the angry pity her words had produced.

'What about your parents? Your mother…?'

'My mother was dead by then, and my stepmother

had left my father, taking Rick with her. I was at boarding school, so most of the time I was...I didn't have to see him. It was just during the school holidays, when I was staying with my father.'

'Didn't you tell him how you felt?'

'I couldn't. He wouldn't have understood. My father... Well, you heard Melanie. He never really wanted children.'

Maybe not, but having had them surely he must have accepted that it was his duty as a father to protect his child? Marco thought grimly, but he didn't want to upset Lily even more by saying so.

As though she sensed what he was thinking, and his criticism of her father, she told him quickly, 'They were friends—and not just that. My father worked for Anton. As you know, my father was a photographer. He worked for several upmarket magazines, doing modelling shoots. He and the people he mixed with were very cutting edge. They lived a certain kind of lifestyle. I suppose the best way to sum it up is to say that it was a...a sex, drugs and rock and roll lifestyle.'

'And Anton also lived that lifestyle?'

'Yes. He was—still is, I suppose—a very wealthy man. A very important man in the fashion world. His magazine is hugely influential. Being commissioned to photograph fashion shoots for it was an accolade. It could make or break a photographer. My father lived for his work. It gave him the kind of high that other people get from drugs. He was very creative, a genius in his field, and he would get angry and impatient with people who got in the way of him fulfilling his talent.'

'Meaning that he didn't have much time for those close to him?' Marco guessed.

'My stepmother was better at dealing with him than my mother, but even she lost patience with him in the end. Rick, my half-brother, worships the memory of our father and wants to follow in his footsteps—but of course he never really knew him properly.'

'Unlike you. So, Anton and your father were friends?'

'Yes. I remember the summer I was fourteen he seemed to be at the studio all the time. When Dad wasn't there he'd ask to take some…some nude shots of me, and I refused. I remember Dad being furious with me when I tried to tell him.'

'Why? What did he say?'

'He refused to believe me—accused me of attention-seeking. Being just like my mother. It was a horrible holiday. Dad refused to speak to me, and then just before I went back to school my stepmother told me that she was divorcing him. I liked her. I still do. She was kind to me—that's why I feel I owe it to her to keep an eye on Rick, as well, of course, as because he's my half-brother. She's remarried now, and she lives in California. She's always inviting me out to stay but I haven't managed it as yet.

'Rick always says that it isn't fair that Dad taught me to use a camera but died before he could teach him. I couldn't have *not* learned, really. Well, I couldn't have had him for a father and not learned how to take a photograph. I always preferred to photograph things, though, not people. It felt safer, somehow. The camera catches things that the naked eye doesn't always, you see. My mother…. Well, in some of the last photographs of her I think you can see how desperate she was, how alone she felt. I wish I'd been able to help her.

'Anyway, after that whenever I came home from school for the holidays Anton always seemed to be there, at the studio, and I noticed…' She paused.

This was so difficult.

'You noticed?' Marco repeated, his voice so devoid of emotion that its calmness steadied her.

She still couldn't look at him, though, so she went to stand in front of the window as she told him in a low voice, 'I noticed that the models my father was being asked to photograph for Anton's magazine were getting younger and younger. That wasn't entirely unusual for the time. The modelling world was changing, and the demand was for younger girls. But Anton's magazine seemed to use more of them than anyone else. There was one girl—Anna. She was so pretty, so very pretty, and young—only fifteen. I really liked her. She wasn't like the other models. She was still at school, like me, but I was at boarding school in the country and she was at a London day-school. Her mother was a dancer and her parents were divorced too. Her father didn't approve of her modelling. She told me that her agent said she thought she'd be doing a *Vogue* cover by the end of the year, only she didn't.'

Her voice became suspended. 'I'm sorry. I can't… It was so awful, so horrible.'

'What happened, Lily?'

Marco suspected he knew what she was going to say, and he was appalled.

'It's the reason I still hate going in helicoptors—because

we travelled to the shoot in one that day.' She shuddered at the thought. 'I still feel so guilty because I never said anything,' she told him in a ragged voice, turning round from the window to look at him, her face ravaged by her emotions.

Marco knew all about guilt, and how it ate away at a person. He went to her, wanting to reach out and hold her, but he was held back by his own demons. They told him that if he held her now he would be making a commitment that would bind him to her for ever, and that was a risk he must not take.

He saw Lily's shoulders lift as she breathed in, taking the kind of breath that someone facing an enormous physical challenge needed to take.

'Anna said that Anton had raped her and she thought she was pregnant. She said that Anton had been coming to the studio to see her, and he'd sent my father away on some pretext so they'd be alone together. She cried when she told me. She said it had been awful and that she was afraid to tell her mother.'

Lily took another deep breath to steady herself.

'That was the day before I was going back to school. I never saw her again. When I asked my father about her he said that Anton had told him she'd stopped modelling because she'd fallen down the stairs to her mother's flat and broken her leg. I wrote to her, but she never wrote back to me. Her mother wrote instead, saying that Anna had gone to live with her father and her stepmother.'

Her voice broke, and Marco could only guess at what she was feeling.

'That was at half-term,' she told him. 'At the start of the Christmas holiday Anton was still always there at the studio.' Her voice grew stronger. 'And then one day, after he and my father had gone out to lunch together, Anton came back but my father didn't.'

Lily swallowed hard.

'It was everything I'd dreaded, but worse. He told me what he wanted to do to me—what he was going to make me do to him.'

Marco's contempt for the other man turned to white-hot rage.

'I told him I'd tell my father, but he just laughed at me. He told me that he had a thing about virgins—young virgins. It was horrible—sickening. I was so afraid that I ran out of the studio. I didn't know what to do or where to go. I had a key to my father's flat, but I was afraid to go there in case somehow he, Anton was there.'

Marco closed his eyes against the anger boiling up inside him—against the man who had wanted to abuse her, against her father, against the whole of his sex for being what it was, but most of all against himself for not recognising her fear and for not protecting her from it.

Marco was so silent, so unmoving. Why didn't he say something? Didn't he know how much she needed comfort from him? How much she needed *him*? Defenceless and drained, Lily could only hold out her arms to him in supplication and beg, 'Hold me, Marco. Please hold me.'

Lily's words shocked through Marco. Hold her? He couldn't. Everything he had taught himself to be recoiled from the thought of such intimacy. He feared the private wounds within himself it might reveal, searing him just as her anguished plea had seared his emotions—those emotions he had fought for so long to deny. If he touched her now he was afraid that he would take her to himself, crush her to himself, and never want to let her go.

Marco was turning away from her—no doubt filled with contempt for her and for her weakness, Lily recognised mutely, and her pent-up breath escaped on a sound that was humiliatingly close to a small sob.

Lily was crying? He had made her cry?

Marco turned round, and from doing that took a step towards her, ignoring the mental lashing of his brain that urged him to stop. How could he when his heart was aching with remorse and longing?

Lily watched him without speaking, and for a moment Marco thought that she was going to ignore him and walk away from him. Part of him hoped that she would. But then she made a suppressed sound of desperation and almost flung herself against him, wrapping her arms around him, resting her head on his chest, her body trembling against his.

Slowly, awkwardly, uncomfortably, he lifted his own arms and placed them round her. Defeat. Surrender. The giving in of his will to his emotions. It should have felt wrong. *She* should have felt wrong. But instead it felt— she felt... Marco understood as he held her close. It felt as though she completed him. He breathed in and then exhaled slowly and deeply, as though he was releasing a burden he had carried for far too long.

She felt so delicate within his hold, and holding her now, as a woman, Marco could only ache for the fragile, vulnerable girl she must have been. Olivia had never felt like this—but then he had never held her like this. He had never held her at all, really. On those rare occasions

when he had kissed her she had never aroused in him
a hunger for her, as Lily had done, Marco recognised.
Never made him want her and then want equally to
reject that wanting because it made him feel vulnerable. Their relationship had been more one of brother
and sister than two young people who would one day
be husband and wife.

But it was Lily who needed to be the focus of his
thoughts now, not Olivia, and most certainly not his own
self-centred fear of losing face through his damaged
pride.

'And the rest of that Christmas holiday?' he pressed
her. 'What happened?'

'I went back to school,' Lily told him, her voice muf-
fled as she kept her face pressed to his shoulder, 'I knew
I'd be safe there. There were always some girls there
who had to stay at school in the holidays. It was lovely.
We had a proper Christmas dinner, and the teachers took
us to the theatre and museums. It was like being part of
a…a family, and I felt…I knew that I was safe.'

Just as she did now, here with Marco, Lily knew,
lifting her head from his shoulder to look at him as she
told him, 'I'm so grateful to you for…for being here for
me, and for helping me. Thank you.'

She leaned forward, intending to kiss his cheek, but
he turned his head in such a swift recoil that her lips
brushed his instead, causing him to recoil even further
and step back from her.

Mortified, Lily apologised. 'I'm sorry. I didn't
intend… I shouldn't have asked you to hold me. It was
thoughtless of me when I know that what I told you

must have made you think of the girl you were going to marry.'

His response was gruff. 'I was thinking of her, yes.' *But not as much as I was thinking of you,* Marco added to himself privately. *Not as much as I shall be thinking about you for ever.*

It was her own fault if his answer had hurt her—her own fault because deep inside herself she must have known that she was falling in love with him, Lily castigated herself. She wouldn't have burned for him in the way that she had if it hadn't been for that love. The look on his face made her feel as though her heart was being wrung out and weeping in pain. It was time for her to move on.

'It's been illogical of me to be so afraid of Anton. I'm an adult now, and he can only intimidate me through my fear if I keep that fear,' she told him, trying to make sure her voice sounded purposeful and friendly instead of betraying her aching need for him. 'And what makes that fear even more illogical is that I made sure that I lost my virginity and so removed what it was about me I believed Anton desired the minute I reached my sixteenth birthday.'

Marco bowed his head. He had lost his own virginity at sixteen himself, to an older girl who had seduced him with enthusiasm and what to him at that age had seemed a great deal of expertise, but it had been an emotionless experience.

'It was a goal I'd set myself—a bridge I had to cross and then burn behind me to keep me safe from Anton,' Lily continued. 'As my birthday is in May, it had to be during term-time. At a dance with the boys from a nearby public school a boy asked me to dance who I remembered from the Christmas Dance. I'd liked him because he was quiet and shy. We did the deed with a good deal of fumbling and uncertainty on both sides, more at my instigation than his. It was a practical necessity rather than an...an act of mutual desire, and I have to say that nothing about it has ever made me feel I want to repeat it.'

Marco's heart jolted. It was wrong, so wrong, that all either of them had known of sexual intimacy was a cold, emotionless coming together—even if in the years since his first encounter he had acquired all the necessary physical skills to please his partners. Together they could share something unique, give one another something that neither of them had experienced with anyone else—something that he now knew he would never want to experience with anyone other than her.

Marco considered himself to be a modern man, and indeed something of a pragmatist, but right now, against any kind of logic, there was something inside him that was asking if it *was* merely circumstance that had brought them together.

What was he thinking? That they had been fated to meet? That it had been written into their lives from birth—preordained, in fact? Was that what he wanted to believe? Was that what he wanted to trust, to give himself over to? Just as he yearned for Lily to give herself over to him?

The walls within which he had imprisoned his emotions were crashing down around him and there was no place left for him to hide from them. He must confront them and accept what they were telling him about himself—if he dared.

Lily's hesitant, 'Can I ask you something personal?' had him giving her a wary look before nodding his head.

'Is it just because I was involved in the modelling world that you don't trust me? Or is it because of her... your....your girl as well?' Why was she persisting in adding more pain to the pain she was already enduring? What difference would it make?

None at all. And yet she found herself exhaling unsteadily when Marco agreed brusquely, 'Yes.'

Lily nodded her head, and was about to turn away when Marco added with even more brusque reluctance, 'And it's *didn't*—not don't. I *didn't* trust you—not I don't,' he elucidated, crossing the floor and opening the door, before she could say anything, leaving her to stare after him.

Did he mean that he trusted her now? And if he did... Stop it, Lily warned herself. Stop building impossible hopes out of nothing, because it'll only backfire on you.

CHAPTER TEN

IT WAS over an hour since Marco had left her alone in their suite. An hour in which she had gone over and over their conversation. What had possessed her to say that about there not being anyone since that boy? What had she hoped for?

Did she really need to ask herself that question? She had wanted him to take her back in his arms. She had wanted him to take her to bed and show her—give her, share with her—all the sensual pleasures she knew she would find there with him. She had wanted to give him her love—even if he had no love to give her because he loved someone else.

He loved someone else, but she knew instinctively that, being the man he was—the kind, caring man he sought to hide beneath an outward mask of disdain and arrogance, the man who had rescued her from Anton—were she to ask him, plead with him, beg him to give her what she had never had, his compassion—the compassion she had now discovered the he possessed—would lead to him giving in and giving her what she wanted.

She would do that? She would humiliate herself like that when she knew he loved someone else?

But didn't she have the right to know him as her

lover? Didn't she have the right to create memories with him and of him that she could hold long, long after she could no longer hold him? She was on the pill—prescribed by her doctor because of problems she'd been having with her periods—so there was no question of an accidental pregnancy, and something told her that a man like Marco would always place sexual health high on the list of things that were important to him.

She had always sworn not to get sexually involved, in case it led to her falling in love and suffering the pain she had seen her mother go through.

She was already in love with him, though, so that argument no longer held good. She was going to suffer the pain of not being loved by him whether or not they were lovers.

Lovers. Her and Marco. Wasn't that really what she had wanted right from the start?

It was too late now. He had gone. But he would come back, Lily reminded herself, and when he did…

When he did she must think about her pride and do nothing, she warned herself.

Marco hesitated outside the suite door. It was over two hours since he had left Lily to rest, and he wanted to warn her that the Duchess had asked if they would mind dining alone this evening, without her, as she had an engagement she'd overlooked. If Lily preferred she could eat alone in the suite. She was bound to have a reaction to what she'd gone through in telling him about her past, and she might prefer to be alone.

With his admission to Lily that he trusted her the last of his barriers against her had been swept away—kicked away by himself, he acknowledged, because he no longer wanted or needed them. What he needed and wanted was Lily's love, Lily's presence in his life. He had been so wrong about her. Could he bring himself to tell her that? Could he bring himself to let her see his vulnerability and his need? Could he really believe the inner voice that told him he could place his trust in her?

Lily watched as the handle to the suite door turned, her heart lifting and then plummeting downwards in a high dive, the sensation inside her chest echoing the tension of the high-risk strategy she intended to adopt. After all, what had she got to lose?

Her heart? She'd already lost that. Her pride? She didn't care about it. Right now all she cared about was creating enough memories to sustain her through the rest of her life from the handful of hours that were all she would have of Marco. She'd made her plans. If he agreed then later, afterwards—tomorrow morning, in fact—she intended to leave the villa for the airport and England without completing their tour. That way Marco would be spared the embarrassment and awkwardness of her continued company, and she would be spared having to face the reality of his lack of love for her. Her last memories of him would be those of lying in his arms as his lover.

She didn't think she'd be letting the trust down. She had enough information and commitment already for the exhibition. Of course leaving tomorrow did mean that she'd never get to see Marco's home...

If she did have any regrets they were superficial—a wish that she could have dressed herself for Marco in something more sensually provocative than the bathrobe she was wearing under which she was naked. She hadn't forgotten his reaction to her sensible undies. Better not to wear them than risk putting him off with their practicality and lack of feminine allure.

The door was opening. Her mouth might have gone dry with tension, her heart might be pounding erratically against her ribs, but she was ready.

Ready and oh, so willing and wanting. A small final mental prayer that things would go well, and then she was positioning herself so that she would be the first thing Marco saw when he walked into the room.

When he did, though, his reaction wasn't what she'd hoped for. She'd somehow envisaged them looking at one another and then her slipping out of her bathrobe and going to him in a shared intense silence. Instead Marco seemed to be avoiding looking at her.

Why hadn't he knocked on the door first? Marco asked himself savagely. If he had he would have saved himself the agony of knowing that Lily was probably naked under that bathrobe, and everything that that knowledge was doing to his self-control. He could almost feel the satin softness of her skin beneath his touch his need for her was so intense. He could almost see her, feel her, taste her, and his body was reacting as though he had. Molten, hot pent-up desire—the kind of desire he had never imagined he could allow himself to feel—was surging through him, taunting him and tormenting him as it swept away his self-control.

He ached for her—and not just physically. His desire for her was passionately emotional. It filled him not just with a need to bind them together in the physical act of love but also with a hunger to bind them together with words as well—the kind of words he had always sworn he would never utter. Words of longing and giving. Words of pleasure and promise. Words that would humbly offer up to her the poor gift of his love and somehow magically win from her the sweet prize of hers.

Words that would give his emotions expression and free them from their imprisonment. The same words that had always been his adversaries, bringing a danger that could rob him of his defences, would now become his aides in the battle to win Lily's heart.

Marco still hadn't moved or spoken, but it wasn't for nothing that Lily had her doctorate. It took her only a handful of seconds to mentally reorganise her plan and see a way of using Marco's silence as a way of taking charge and setting her own agenda.

She paused to steady her nerves, and then told him, 'I'm so grateful to you, Marco, for helping me to come to terms with…with things, and to leave my past behind and walk freely into my future.'

A future he wanted to share with her, Marco recognised as he listened to her.

'I've got a favour to ask you,' Lily continued.

'If I can help, then you have my word that I will,' Marco responded.

Lily's heart somersaulted. He might not say that when he knew what the favour was.

'I know that you aren't the kind of man who likes to leave a task only partially completed,' she said sedately, 'so I'm hoping…'

Marco waited.

'The thing is…' Lily paused. Did she really have the

courage to do this? Thinking about the consequences if she didn't, of all that she would never know or have, was all she needed to convince her that she did.

'Well, the fact of the matter is, Marco, that helping me to get over the effect Anton had on me isn't just about listening to me talking about it. I need your help with something else.'

'Something else?'

Did she want him to pursue Anton and punish him as he deserved for what he had done? He was certainly willing to do so if that was what she wanted.

'I want you to take me to bed and make love to me, please, Marco.'

When she heard the breath he expelled from his lungs, Lily told him quickly, 'I know—I know it's a lot to ask of you. But you are the only person I can ask. You must see that.'

Oh, what a perfidious creature she was—and far more adept at using all the tricks that Eve had given her sex than she had ever imagined.

'If you won't, then how will I ever be able to live a normal life? I've only had sex once, with a boy who was even more nervous about it than I was myself,' she reminded him. 'How can I ever be a proper woman, the woman I really want to be, if I don't even know what it means to be a woman sexually?'

She could see him shaking his head. He was going to refuse.

But instead he said hoarsely, 'You'd trust me to do that…to show you…give you…?'

Lily had never seen him respond so emotionally before, and her heart turned over.

'I trust you completely, Marco. I've never known anyone I could trust more.'

He was looking at her now with something unfathomable and almost tortured in his eyes. Holding her breath, Lily walked towards him, and then, when she was close enough for him to touch her, she let the bathrobe slip to the floor.

'Lily…'

Was the way he said her name a protest or a sign that he was giving in? Lily didn't know, but she did know that she could feel his breath against her lips, and that he wasn't stopping her when she placed her hands on his shoulders and her mouth against his.

'Lily.'

He said her name again. Against her lips this time, taking them beneath his own when they parted, drawing her naked body close to his. She could feel the unmistakable hardness of his arousal and a thrill of relief went through her. It had begun—the journey that would take her from her past to her future, through heartache to a pleasure beyond which lay even more heartache. But she wasn't going to think about that now. For now she was only going to think about Marco, and loving him.

CHAPTER ELEVEN

THEY were on the bed, lying naked there together, and the soft sound of Lily's sighs of pleasure was floating on the air as Marco kissed his way from her shoulder to her ear, causing shimmering showers of lightning pleasure to burst into brilliant life inside her. The touch of his fingertips against her skin as he caressed her provoked a counterpoint sensual response of pleasure, bringing her body to singing, delirious life wherever he touched it. His deliberately slow and careful arousal of her was thrilling it and her with starbursts of erotic delight.

Beneath that pleasure, though, Lily was conscious of a deeper, sharper, keener hunger that had fed on and grown with each small measure of sensual delight until it was beginning to rage fiercely inside her. It was this hunger that she had always feared—this need within her to burn at such an intense heat with love for her lover that her feelings for him could destroy her. The need she had for Marco would never be satisfied by sensual pleasure alone, she knew. It went deeper than that. But for now she would think only of this pleasure and this intimacy, because it was for now that it and Marco would be hers.

* * *

Her response to him was magical—a miracle, given what she had endured. Marco struggled to contain and control his own desire for her so that he could concentrate on her experience and her pleasure. He wanted this to be perfect for her. He wanted it to be everything she hoped it to be. He wanted every touch, every sensation she had to show her a fulfilment that would set her completely free from the past.

He cupped her shoulder, stroking her warm, soft skin and then her breast, feeling her shudder and arch her body against his hand, her nipple taut and flushed with desire, her own hands reaching for his shoulders. He kissed the valley between her breasts and then the soft, sweetly fragranced slope, stroking his tongue against her nipple.

Immediately she cried out, her nails digging into his back and her eyes wide with wonder and delight as her breathing accelerated into unsteady swiftness. His own body ached and pulsed, his groin tightening with his need to grind it against her softness in an attempt to reduce the pressure of his desire. But this wasn't about his satisfaction. Not even when he took the hard peak of her nipple into his mouth to suckle it slowly and Lily responded by crying out and gripping his hips, pulling him down against her open thighs. Her actions turned the soft, slow suckle of his mouth on her breast into a fiercely insistent rhythmic demand that came perilously close to making him lose control.

This was what she wanted, Lily acknowledged triumphantly as her body answered the demand of the sexually explicit rhythm Marco was driving into her with the possessive heat of his mouth. Deep within her that same rhythm was pulsing its own growing need, telling her to wrap her legs around him and draw him down against her body.

His need to possess her, to claim her and fill her, had become an insistent drumbeat inside his body, but Marco knew that he could not give in to it. Not yet. Not until he had given Lily all the pleasure she deserved.

It was hard for him to go slowly and give her the time he thought she needed as he kissed his way down over her quivering stomach, following the path already taken by his hand which was now covering her sex. He stroked the soft mound with the pad of his thumb, and then when she gasped and moaned his name carefully caressed apart the neatly folded lips covering the swollen wet heat of her sex whilst he kissed the inner flesh of her thigh. He felt the shocked tremors of delight that ran through her.

Lily gasped in raw, agonised ecstasy. She couldn't bear it. She could not bear any more of the pleasure that was shooting through her in fiery waves, driving her higher and higher with every erotic touch of Marco's fingers and then his tongue-tip against the eager point of her desire. But even as she cried out her protest the dam broke, sending a series of pulsing quivers of release cascading over her.

Held fast in Marco's arms, Lily clung to him as the last surges of pleasure filled her. Her voice thick and soft with emotion, she whispered her gratitude to him. 'It was wonderful—everything I hoped for and more.'

Smoothing the damp hair back off her face, Marco smiled. 'That was just the beginning.' He loved her so much. Would always love her, he knew.

He kissed her slowly and deeply, taking time to re-build her need until he was sure that her desire matched his own. Then he entered her slowly, carefully but firmly, stopping when he felt the shudder jolting through her.

But Lily shook her head and begged him fiercely, 'Don't stop. Please don't stop now, Marco. I want you so much. I want this so much.' She moved her body against his, gasping with pleasure when he responded, and she felt herself tightening around him, taking him, claiming him. The headiness of her own sense of wonder and triumph dazed her senses and filled her with erotic excitement.

She was all and everything he had been born for, Marco thought as he drove deeper and deeper into her, knowing she was moving with him, knowing that this time their journey was one they were sharing. Their discovery that their desire for one another, like their pleasure in one another, had no limits was a shared knowledge that had them exchanging kisses and touches and murmured words of praise and arousal until Marco felt his body tighten and surge and knew that he couldn't hold back. But even as the first pulse of his orgasm overtook him he felt Lily's flesh tighten round him, her cry of orgasmic relief mingling with his own.

Marco was still holding her close, his arms wrapped tightly around her. Hot tears scalded Lily's eyes. She had thought that knowing him like this would make her feel better, but instead it had made her feel worse. The tears spilled down onto her cheeks.

'You're crying. Why…?'

'Because I love you.'

The words had escaped before she could stop them,

and now Marco was looking down at her, his own expression unreadable.

'I'm sorry,' she apologised. 'I know you don't want to hear that. I never meant to say it.'

Marco was holding her even more tightly, and his voice against her ear was raw with emotion as he murmured, 'You're wrong. I do want to hear it. There's nothing I've wanted to hear more than that my love for you is returned.'

Lily pulled back so that she could look into his eyes. What she could see in them told its own story, but still she had to whisper, 'You love me?'

And then she gasped with joy when Marco whispered back, between fiercely passionate kisses, 'Yes, yes—yes a thousand times. I love you and I always will. Lily, you've freed me from the prison I'd built round myself. You've shown me, taught me to trust in my emotions as well as to trust you. You've made me complete. You've healed me and made me whole. I love you for all those reasons, but more than that I love you because I cannot do anything else *but* love you. You stole my heart the first time I saw you, even though I didn't know it then. I fought against loving you. I tried to deny what was happening to me. I told myself that I would be a fool to let myself be controlled by my feelings. I told myself that I couldn't trust you.'

'Because of her? Because she hurt you so very badly?' Lily guessed, cupping his face in her hands and kissing him tenderly. 'I knew there must have been something—someone who had made you want to lock away your feelings.'

Marco removed one of her hands from his face and slowly kissed each finger.

'It wasn't Olivia's fault—not really. My parents were caring, but of the old school. Physical intimacy wasn't something they encouraged. Such behaviour wasn't something they considered princely. When my governess took me down from the nursery to see them before I went to bed I had to bow to my mother and shake hands with my father.'

Lily's soft, compassionate, 'Oh, you poor little boy!' was all the balm that childhood ache needed.

'My governess and my school taught me that emotions were something that had to be controlled, not given in to. As a future prince I must be in control of them, not the other way around. I learned that emotions were dangerous. They certainly made me feel awkward, and contemptuous of the weakness of that awkwardness whilst I was growing up. Looking back now, knowing how I feel about you, I can see so much more clearly why Olivia might have wanted to rebel against that upbringing—and hers was much the same as mine. I should have been kinder to her—more understanding. What made it worse was that the woman in charge of the model agency that had hired her pretended to be on my side. She assured me that Olivia would be safe, and because of what I believed to be my right to having my opinions treated as important I was stupid and arrogant enough not to even question that she might be lying to me—which she was.'

That still galled him, Lily could tell. And why not? It would gall any man of pride. Marco was a proud man, and in her opinion he had a right to that pride, she decided lovingly. There was more than injured pride in his voice, though—much more. There was also pain and regret and guilt, and it made Lily's heart ache for him.

'She procured young models for men under the guise of finding them work.'

'And that was why you thought what you did about me?'

'Yes,' Marco admitted. 'I told myself that you were two of a kind and kept on telling myself that—even when deep inside I knew you were nothing like her. But by then, of course, I had another and far more personal reason for not wanting to trust you. So I punished you for my mistakes and my own weakness. I misjudged you in so many different ways—over Pietro, over Anton— because I wanted and needed to misjudge you. It was easier and safer than acknowledging what I really felt about you. I thought I was being strong, but in reality I was being weak.'

'Not weak, Marco. You could never be weak. You were doing what you had taught yourself to do. What loving Olivia and losing her in such a terrible way had taught you to do,' Lily told him sympathetically.

Marco shook his head.

'No,' he said quietly. 'I didn't love her. At least not in the way that you mean. She was more like a sister to me than a future wife. I have only loved and will only love one woman, Lily, and that woman is you.'

He meant it, Lily could see.

'I was so afraid of loving you,' she admitted. 'I was afraid of being like my mother and loving a man who would only hurt me. And when you were so contemptuous of me, when you wouldn't believe me...'

'I hurt you,' Marco groaned, kissing her again. 'I hurt you because I was locked in a world where my emotions weren't allowed to exist. But you aroused them, and when you did I had to reject what you were making me feel. I had to tell myself that I couldn't trust you because I knew I couldn't trust myself to resist you.'

'But you saved me from Anton even though you didn't trust me.'

'You were so afraid. I couldn't turn my back on you.'

'And that is the man you really are, Marco. A man who can't turn his back on those in need even when he believes he has very good reason to reject them.'

'You give me credit where I don't deserve it.'

'No. You don't give yourself credit here, and you *do* deserve it.'

'I love you so much. So very much. I want you to marry me, Lily. I want us to be together for always. I want us to give our children—the children we shall create in our love for one another—the childhood that we never had.'

'Yes, I want that too,' Lily whispered beneath his kiss, as her senses and her body flowered into fresh eager longing beneath his touch.

EPILOGUE

THE final sound of the bells ringing out from the *castello's* chapel to announce their marriage were dying away, and the rose petals Lily had insisted on, instead of vulnerable doves being released, as their wedding planner had wanted were still drifting down from a perfect blue spring sky. The gentlest of breezes brushed the slender column of her wedding dress, its silk embossed with a traditional family design and especially made for her at the silk mill in Como in which Marco had an interest.

It had been a perfect day—but then every day since the day Marco had told her he loved her had been perfect in its own individual way.

'So many generations of your family have married and lived here,' Lily said as they stood arm in arm, watching their wedding guests.

'And hopefully many more will,' Marco told her, his hand resting deliberately against her body, where earlier that week the test Lily had done had confirmed their first child was already growing. A baby that would be born seven months into their marriage.

'I just hope we've done the right thing letting Rick take the photographs and video of the wedding,' she

admitted to Marco, watching her half-brother photographing a group of pretty girls who were amongst the
wedding guests.

Pietro, Marco's nephew, was assisting him. Once the
misunderstanding over his modelling had been cleared
up the two young men, so close in age, had become good
friends, and were now work colleagues.

'It was very generous of you to fund the film Rick's
going to make about the California wineries. His mother
has told me that she intends to keep an eye on both him
and Pietro whilst they are over there working on it.'

'Your brother is a good man at heart. But enough of
family. I can't wait for us to leave for our honeymoon,
so that I can have you to myself and show you and tell
you how happy you've made me today, Lily. The hap-
piest man in the world and the luckiest.'

'We've both been lucky,' Lily whispered back. 'Lucky
to have found one another. Oh, Marco if we hadn't…'

'We had to,' Marco told her. 'We were destined to
meet and love one another. Destined to be together, and
we always will be.'

PRINCE OF
SECRETS

LUCY MONROE

Lucy Monroe started reading at the age of four. After going through all the childrens' books at home, her mother caught her reading adult novels pilfered from the higher shelves on the bookcase... alas, it was nine years before she got her hands on a Mills & Boon Romance her older sister had brought home. She loves to create the strong alpha males and independent women who people Mills & Boon books. When she's not immersed in a romance novel (whether reading or writing it), she enjoys travel with her family, having tea with the neighbours, gardening and visits from her numerous nieces and nephews.

PROLOGUE

"WHAT AM I looking at?" Demyan asked his uncle, the King of Volyarus.

Spread before him on the behemoth antique executive desk, brought over with the first Hetman to be made Volyarussian king, was a series of photos. All were of a rather ordinary woman with untamed, curly, red hair. Her one arresting feature was storm-cloud gray eyes that revealed more emotion in each picture than he would allow himself to show in an entire year.

Fedir frowned at the pictures for several seconds before meeting Demyan's matching espresso-dark gaze.

Those who mistook Demyan for Fedir's biological son could be forgiven—the resemblance was that strong. But Demyan was the king's nephew and while he'd been raised in the palace as the "spare heir to the throne," three years older than his future king, he'd never once gotten it confused in his own mind.

Fedir cleared his throat as if the words he needed to utter were unpalatable to him. "That is Chanel Tanner."

"Tanner?" Demyan asked, the coincidence not lost on him.

"Yes."

The name was common enough, in the United States, anyway. There was no immediate reason for Demyan to

assume she was related to Bartholomew Tanner, one of
the original partners in Tanner Yurkovich.

Except the portrait of the Texas wildcatter hanging in
the west hall of the palace bore a striking resemblance to
the woman in the pictures. They shared the same curly
red hair (though Bartholomew had worn it shorter), high
forehead and angular jaw (though hers was more pleas-
ingly feminine).

Her lips, unadorned by color or gloss, were a soft pink
and bow-shaped. Bartholomew's were lost beneath the
handlebar mustache he sported in the painting. While his
eyes sparkled with life, hers were filled with seriousness
and unexpected shadows.

Bartholomew Tanner had helped to found the company on which the current wealth of both Volyarus and
the Yurkovich family empire had been built. At one time,
he had owned a significant share in it as well.

"She looks like Baron Tanner." The oilman had been
bequeathed a title by King Fedir's grandfather for his
help in locating oil reserves and other mineral deposits
on Volyarus.

Fedir nodded. "She's his great-great-granddaughter and
the last of his bloodline."

Relaxing back in his chair, Demyan cocked his brow
in interest but waited for the king to continue rather than
ask any questions.

"Her stepfather, Perry Saltzman, approached our office in Seattle about a job for his son." Another frown,
which was unusual for the king, who was no more prone
to emotional displays than Demyan. "Apparently, the boy
is close to graduating university with honors in business."

"Why tell me? Maks is the glad-hander on stuff like
this." His cousin was also adroit at turning down requests
without causing diplomatic upset.

Demyan was not so patient. There were benefits to not being raised a Crown Prince.

"He is on his honeymoon." Fedir's words were true, but Demyan sensed there was more to it.

Otherwise, this could have waited. "He'll be back in a couple of weeks."

And if Mr. Saltzman was looking for a job for his son, why were there pictures of his stepdaughter all over the conference table?

"I don't want Maks to know about this."

"Why?"

"He will not agree to what needs to be done." Fedir ran his fingers through hair every bit as dark as Demyan's, no strands of gray in sight. "You know my son. He can be unexpectedly...recalcitrant."

For the first time in a very long while, Demyan had to admit, "You've lost me."

There was very little his cousin would not do for the country of his birth. He'd given up the woman he wanted rather than marry with little hope for an heir.

Fedir stacked the pictures together, leaving a candid shot on top that showed Chanel smiling. "In 1952, when Bart Tanner agreed to help my grandfather find oil on or around the Volyarussian islands, he accepted a twenty-percent share in the company in exchange for his efforts and provision of expertise, a fully trained crew and all the drilling equipment."

"I am aware." All Volyarussian children were taught their history.

How Volyarus had been founded by one of Ukraine's last Hetmans, who had purchased the chain of uninhab-ited and, most believed, uninhabitable islands with his own personal wealth from Canada. He and a group of peasants and nobles had founded Volyarus, literally meaning free from Russia, because they'd believed it was only a matter of time before Ukraine fell under Russian rule completely.

They had been right. Ukraine was its own country again, but more people spoke Russian there than their native tongue. They had spent too many years under the thumb of the USSR.

Hetman Maksim Ivan Yurkovich the First had poured his wealth into the country and become its de facto monarch. By the time his son was crowned King of Volyarus, the House of Yurkovich's monarchy was firmly in place.

However, the decades that followed were not all good ones for the small country, and the wealth of its people had begun to decline, until even the Royal House was feeling the pinch.

Enter wildcatter and shrewd businessman Bartholomew Tanner.

"He died still owning those shares." Fedir's frown had turned to an all-out scowl.

Shock coursed through Demyan. "No."

"Oh, yes." King Fedir rose and paced the room, only to stop in front of the large plate glass window with a view of the capital city. "The original plan was for his daughter to marry my grandfather's youngest son."

"Great-Uncle Chekov?"

"Yes."

"But…" Demyan let his voice trail off, nothing really to say.

Duke Chekov had been a bachelor, but it wasn't because Tanner's daughter broke his heart. The man had been gay and lived out his years overseeing most of Volyarus's mining interests with a valet who was a lot more than a servant.

In the 1950s, that had been his only option for happiness.

Times had changed, but some things remained static. Duty to family and country was one of them.

King Fedir shrugged. "It did not matter. The match was set."

"But they never married."

"She eloped with one of the oilmen."

That would have been high scandal in the '50s.

"But I thought Baron Tanner left the shares to the people of Volyarus."

"It was a pretty fabrication created by my grandfather."

"The earnings on that twenty percent of shares have been used to build roads, fund schools... *Damn*."

"Exactly. To repay the funds with interest to Chanel Tanner would seriously jeopardize our country's financial stability in the best of times."

And the current economic climes would never be described as that.

"She has no idea of her legacy, does she?" If she did, Perry Saltzman wouldn't bother to ask for a job for his son—he'd be suing Volyarus for hundreds of millions. As one of the few countries in the world that did not operate in any sort of deficit, that kind of payout could literally break the Volyarussian bank.

"What's the plan?"

"Marriage."

"How will that help?" Whoever she married could make the same claims on their country's resources.

"There was one caveat in Bartholomew's will. If any issue of his ever married into the Volyarussian royal family, his twenty percent would revert to the people less a sufficient annual income to provide for his heir's well-being."

"That doesn't make any sense."

"It does if you know the rest of the story."

"What is it?"

"Tanner's daughter ended up jilted by her lover, who

was already married, making their own hasty ceremony null."

"So, she still could have married Duke Chekov."

"She was pregnant with another man's child. She'd caused a well-publicized scandal. He categorically refused."

"Tanner thought he would change Great-Uncle Chekov's mind?"

"Tanner thought *her* son might grow up to marry into our family and link the Tanner name with the Royal House of Yurkovich for all time."

"It already was, by business."

"That wasn't good enough." King Fedir sighed. "He wanted a family connection with his name intact, if possible."

"Family was important to him."

"Yes. He never spoke to his daughter again, but he provided for her financially until she remarried, with only one caveat."

"Her son keep the Tanner name." It made sense.

"Exactly."

"And he presumably had a son."

"Only one."

"Chanel's father, but you said she was the only living Tanner of Bart's line."

"She is. Both her grandfather and father died from dangerous chemical inhalation after a lab accident."

"They were scientists?"

"Chemists, just like Chanel. Although they worked on their own grants. She's a research assistant."

The woman with the wild red hair in the pictures was a science geek?

"And no one in the family was aware of their claim to Tanner's shares?"

"No. He meant to leave them to the people of Volyarus. He told my grandfather that was his intention."

"But he didn't do it."

"He was a wildcatter. It's a dangerous profession. He died when his grandson was still a young boy."

"And?"

"And my grandfather provided for the education expense of every child in that line since."

"There haven't been that many."

"No."

"Including Chanel?"

"Yes. The full ride and living expenses scholarship she received is apparently what gave Perry Saltzman the idea to approach Yurkovich Tanner and trade on a connection more than half a century old."

"What do you want me to do? Find her a Volyarussian husband?"

"He has to be from the Yurkovich line."

"Your son is already married."

"You are not."

Neither was Demyan's younger brother, but he doubted Fedir considered that fact important. Demyan was the one who had been raised as "spare to the throne," almost a son to the monarch. "You want me to marry her."

"For the good of Volyarus, yes. It need not be a permanent marriage. The will makes no stipulations on that score."

Demyan did not reply immediately. For the first time in more years than he could remember, his mind was blank with shock.

"Think, Demyan. You and I both know the healthy economy of Volyarus sits on a precarious edge, just like the rest of the world's. The calamity that would befall us were we to be forced to distribute the funds to Miss Tanner would be great."

"You are being melodramatic. There's no guarantee Maksim the First's duplicity would ever be discovered."

"It's only a matter of time, particularly with a man like Perry Saltzman in the picture. His kind can sniff out wealth and connections with the efficiency of ferrets."

"So, we deny the claim. Our court resources far exceed this young woman's."

"I think not. There are three countries that would be very happy to lay claim to Volyarus as a territory, and the United States is one of them."

"You believe they would use the unclaimed shares as a way to get their hands on a part of Volyarus."

"Why not?"

Why not, indeed. King Fedir would and, come to it, Demyan wouldn't hesitate to exploit such a politically expedient turn of events himself.

"So I marry her, gain control of the shares and dump her?" he asked, more to clarify what his uncle was thinking than to enumerate his own plans.

He would marry one day. Why not the heir to Bartholomew Tanner? If she was as much a friend to Volyarus as her grandfather had been, they might well make an acceptable life together.

"If she turns out to be anything like her grasping stepfather, yes," Fedir answered. "On the other hand, she may well be someone you could comfortably live with."

The king didn't look like he believed his own words.

Frankly, Demyan wasn't sure he did, either, but his future was clear. His duty to his country and the well-being of his family left only one course of action open to him.

Seduce and marry the unpolished scientist.

CHAPTER ONE

DEMYAN SLID THE black-rimmed nonprescription glasses
on before pushing open the door to the lab building. The
glasses had been his uncle's idea, along with the gray
Armani cardigan Demyan wore over his untucked dress
shirt—no tie. The jeans he wore to complete the "geeky
corporate guy" attire were his own idea and surprisingly
comfortable.

He'd never owned a pair. He'd had the need to set the
right example for his younger cousin, Crown Prince to
Volyarus, drummed into Demyan from his earliest memory.

He'd done his best, but they were two very different men.

Maksim was a corporate shark, but he was also an adept
politician. Demyan left politics to the diplomats.

For now, though, he would tone down his fierce personality with clothes and a demeanor that would not send
his prey running.

He knocked perfunctorily on the door before entering
the lab where Chanel Tanner worked. The room was empty
but for the single woman working through her lunch hour
as usual, according to his investigator's report.

Sitting at a computer in the far corner, she typed in
quick bursts between reading one of the many volumes
spread open on the cluttered desktop.

"Hello." He pitched his voice low, not wanting to startle her.

No need to worry on that score. She simply waved her hand toward him, not even bothering to turn around. "Leave it on the bench by the door."

"Leave what, precisely?" he asked, amused in spite of himself by her demeanor.

"The package. Do you really need to know what's in it? No one else ever asks," she grumbled as she scribbled something down.

"I do not have a package. What I do have is an appointment."

Her head snapped up, red curly hair flying as she spun her chair to face him. "What? Who? You're Mr. Zaretsky?"

He nodded, impressed by the perfect pronunciation of his name.

"You aren't expected for another half an hour." She jumped to her feet, the pocket of her lab coat catching the edge of a book and knocking it to the floor. "And you're going to be late. Corporate types interested in funding our research always are."

"And yet I am early." He crossed the room and picked up the book to hand to her.

Taking it, she frowned, her small nose scrunching rather charmingly. "I noticed."

"Eventually, yes."

Pink stained her cheeks, almost washing out the light dusting of freckles. "I thought you were the delivery guy. He flirts. I don't like it, so I ignore him if at all possible."

The woman was twenty-nine years old and could count the number of dates she'd had in the past year on less than the fingers of one hand. Demyan would think she might welcome flirting.

He did not say that, of course. He gave her the smile

he used on women he wanted to bed. "You have no filter, do you?"

"Are *you* flirting with me?" she demanded, her gray
eyes widening in shock.

"I might be." Awkward and this woman were on very
friendly speaking terms.

Her brows furrowed and she looked at him with evident
confusion. "But why?"

"Why not?"

"I'm hospitably inept, not desperate."

"You believe you are inept?"

"Everyone believes I'm *socially awkward,* particularly my family. Since not one of them has trouble making friends and maintaining a busy social life, I bow to
their superior knowledge in the area."

"I think you are charming." Demyan shocked himself
with the knowledge that he spoke the truth.

An even bigger but not unwelcome surprise was that
he found the geeky scientist unexpectedly attractive. She
wasn't his usual cover model companion, but he would
like very much if she would take off her lab coat and give
him the opportunity to see her full figure.

"Some people do at first, but it wears off." She sighed,
looked dejected for a few short seconds before squaring
her shoulders and setting her features into an expression no
doubt meant to hide her thoughts. "It's all right. I'm used
to it. I have my work and that's what is really important."

He'd learned that about her, along with a great deal else
from the investigation he'd had performed on top of the
dossier his uncle had provided. "You're passionate about
your research."

"It's important."

"Yes, it is. That is why I am here."

The smile she bestowed on him was brilliant, her gray

eyes lighting to silver. "It is. You're going to make it possible for us to extend the parameters of our current study."

"That is the plan." He'd determined that approaching her in the guise of a corporate investor was the quickest way to gain Chanel's favor.

He'd obviously been right.

"Why are you here?" she asked.

"I thought we'd been over that."

"Most corporations donate without sending someone to check our facility over."

"Are you offended Yurkovich Tanner did not opt to do so?"

"No, just confused."

"Oh?"

"How will you know if this is a good setup or not? I mean, even the most fly-by-night operation can make their lab look impressive to a layman."

"The University of Washington is hardly a fly-by-night operation."

"No, I know, but you know what I mean."

"You really have no filter, do you?"

"Um, no?"

"You as good as called me stupid."

"No." She shook her head for emphasis.

"The implication is there."

"No, it's not. No more than I consider myself stupid because I could stare at my car's engine from dawn to dusk and still not be able to tell you where the catalytic converter is."

"It's under the engine."

"Is it?"

"Point taken, but you knew your car exhaust system has one. Just as I know the rudimentary facts about lab research."

"I know about the catalytic converter because my mother's was stolen once. I guess it's a thing for young thugs to steal them and sell them for the precious metal. Mom was livid."

"As she had a right to be."

"I suppose, but getting a concealed weapons permit and storing a handgun in her Navigator's glove box was taking it about sixty million steps too far. It wasn't as if she was in the car when they stole the thing."

Demyan felt his lips twitching, the amusement rolling through him an unusual but not unwelcome reaction. "I am sure you are right."

"Is English your second language?"

"It is." But people rarely realized that. "I do not speak with an accent."

"You don't use a ton of contractions either."

"I prefer precise communication."

Her storm-cloud gaze narrowed in thought. "You're from Volyarus, aren't you?"

He felt his eyes widen in surprise. "Yes."

"Don't look so shocked. My great-great-grandfather helped discover the oil fields of Volyarus. Did you really think I wouldn't know that the Seattle office of Yurkovich Tanner is just a satellite? They paid for my university education. It was probably some long-ago agreement with Bartholomew Tanner."

She was a lot closer than was comfortable to the truth. "He was bequeathed the title of baron, which would make you a lady."

"I know that, but my mom doesn't." And from Chanel's tone, she didn't want the older woman finding out. "Besides, the title would only pass to me if I were direct in line with no older sibling."

"Do you have one?" he asked, knowing the answer but following the script of a stranger.

"No."

"So you are Dame Tanner, Lady Chanel, if you prefer."

Her lovely pink lips twisted with clear distaste. "I prefer just Chanel."

"Your mother is French?" he asked, continuing the script he'd carefully thought out beforehand.

Demyan was always fully prepared.

"No. She loves the Chanel label, though."

"She named you after a designer brand?" His investigators had not revealed that fact.

"It's no different than a parent naming their child Mercedes, or something," Chanel replied defensively.

"Of course."

"She named me more aptly than she knew."

"Why do you say that?" he asked with genuine surprise and curiosity.

He would have thought it was the opposite.

"Mom loves her designers, but what she never realized was that Coco Chanel started her brand because she believed in casual elegance. She wore slacks when women simply did *not*. She believed beauty should be both effortless and comfortable."

"Did she?"

"Oh, yes. Mom is more of the 'beauty is pain' school of thought. She wishes I were, too, but well, you can see I'm not." Chanel indicated her lab coat over a simple pair of khaki slacks and a blue T-shirt.

The T-shirt might not be high fashion, but it clung to Chanel's figure in a way that revealed her unexpectedly generous curves. She wasn't overweight, but she wasn't rail thin either, and if her breasts were less than a C cup, he'd be surprised.

That information had not been in her dossier, either.

"You're staring at my breasts."

"I apologize."

"Okay." She sighed. "I'm not offended, but I'm not used to it. My lab coat isn't exactly revealing and the men around here, well, they stare at my data more than me."

"Foolish men."

"If you say so."

"I do."

"You're flirting again."

"Are you going to try to ignore me like the delivery man?"

"Am I going to see you again to ignore you?"

"Oh, you will definitely see me again."

As hard as Chanel found it to believe, the gorgeous corporate guy had meant exactly what he said. And not in a business capacity.

He wanted to see *her* again. She hadn't given him her number, but he'd called to invite her to dinner. Which meant he'd gone to the effort to get it. Strange.

And sort of flattering.

Then he'd taken her to an independent film she'd mentioned wanting to see.

Chanel didn't date. She was too awkward, her filters tuned wrong for normal conversation. Even other scientists found her wearing in a social setting.

Only, Demyan didn't seem to care. He never got annoyed with her.

He didn't get offended when she said something she shouldn't have. He didn't shush her in front of others, or try to cut off her curious questioning of their waiter on his reasoning behind recommending certain meals over others.

It was so different than being out with her family that

Chanel found her own awareness of her personal failings diminishing with each hour she spent in Demyan's company.

She'd never laughed so much in the company of another person who wasn't a scientist. Had never felt so comfortable in a social setting with *anyone*.

Tonight they were going to a dinner lecture: *Symmetry Relationships and the Theory of Point and Space Groups*. She'd been wanting to hear this particular visiting lecturer from MIT for a while, but the outing had not been her idea.

Demyan had secured hard-to-come-by tickets for the exclusive gathering and invited her.

She'd been only too happy to accept, and not just because of the lecture. If he'd invited her to one of the charity galas her mother enjoyed so much, Chanel would have said yes, too.

In Demyan's company, even she might have a good time at one of those.

Standing in front of the full-length mirror her mother had insisted Chanel needed as part of her bedroom decor, she surveyed her image critically.

Chanel didn't love designer fashion and rarely dressed up, but no way could she have been raised by her mother and *not* know how to put the glad rags on.

Tonight, she'd gone to a little more effort than on her previous two dates with Demyan. Chanel had felt the first two outings were flukes, anomalies in her life she refused to allow herself to get too excited over.

After all, he would get that glazed look at some point during the evening and then not call again. Everyone did. Only, Demyan hadn't and he had—called, that is.

And maybe, just maybe, she and the corporate geek had a chance at something more than the connection of two bouncing protons.

He understood what she was talking about and spoke in a language she got. Not like most people. It was the most amazing thing.

And she wanted him. Maybe it was being twenty-nine or something, but her body overheated in his presence big-time.

She'd decided that even if their relationship didn't have a future, she wanted it to have everything she could get out of it in the present.

Both her mother and stepfather had made it clear they thought Chanel's chance of finding a lifelong love were about as good as her department getting better funding than the Huskies football program.

Nil.

Deep inside, Chanel was sure they were right. She was too much like her father—and hadn't Beatrice said she'd married him only because she was pregnant with Chanel?

Chanel wasn't trapping anyone into marriage, but she wouldn't mind tripping Demyan into her too-empty bed.

With that in mind, she'd pulled out the stops when dressing for their dinner tonight. Her dress was a hand-me-down Vera Wang from her mother.

It hadn't looked right on the more petite woman's figure, but the green silk was surprisingly flattering to Chanel's five feet seven inches.

The bodice clung to her somewhat generous breasts, while the draping accentuated her waist and the line of her long legs.

It wasn't slutty by any stretch, but it was sexy in a subtle way she trusted Demyan to pick up on. She would usually have worn it with sensible pumps that didn't add more than an inch to her height.

But not tonight. Demyan was nearly six-and-a-half feet

tall; he could deal more than adequately with a companion in three-inch heels.

Chanel had practiced wearing them on and off all day in the lab.

Her colleagues asked if she was doing research for a physics experiment. She'd ignored their teasing and curiosity for the chance to be certain of her ability to walk confidently in the heels.

And she'd discovered it *was* like riding a bike. Her body remembered the lessons her mom had insisted on in Chanel's younger years.

The doorbell rang and she rushed to answer it.

Demyan stood on the other side, his suit a step up from his usual attire on their dates, too.

He adjusted his glasses endearingly and smiled, his mahogany gaze warm on her. "You look beautiful."

Her hand went to the crazy red curls she rarely did much to tame. Tonight she'd used the full regimen of products her mother had given her on her last birthday, along with a lecture about not getting any younger and looking like a rag doll in public. "Thank you."

"Do we have time for a drink before we leave for the dinner?" he asked, even as he herded her back into the small apartment and closed the door behind him.

"Yes, of course." Heat climbed up her neck. "I don't keep alcohol on hand, though."

The look in his eyes could only be described as predatory, but his words were innocuous enough. "Soda will do."

"Iced green tea?" she asked, feeling foolish.

Her mother often complained about the food and drink Chanel kept on hand, using her inadequacies as a hostess to justify the infrequent motherly visits.

Demyan's eyes narrowed as if he could read Chanel's thoughts. "Iced tea is fine."

"It's green tea," she reiterated. Why hadn't she at least bought soda, or something?

"Green tea is healthy."

"Lots of antioxidants," she agreed. "I drink it all the time."

He didn't ask if the caffeine kept her up, but then the man drank coffee with his meals and had gotten a large-size fully caffeinated Coca-Cola at the movie.

"I keep both caffeinated and decaf on hand," she offered anyway.

"I'll take the caffeine. I have a feeling we'll be up late tonight." The look he gave her was hot enough to melt magma.

Suddenly, it felt as if all the air had been sucked out of her apartment's cheerfully decorated living room. "I'll just get our tea."

He moved, his hand landing on her bare arm. "Don't run from me."

"I'm not." How could two simple words come out sounding so breathless?

His hand slid up her arm and over and down again, each inch of travel leaving bursts of sensation along every nerve ending in its wake, landing proprietarily against the small of her back. "I like this dress."

"Thank you." Somehow she was getting closer to him, her feet moving of their own volition, no formed thought in her brain directing them.

"You're wearing makeup."

She nodded. No point in denying it.

"I didn't think you ever did."

"I stopped, except for special occasions, after I moved away from home."

"An odd form of rebellion."

"Not when you have a mother who insists on image

perfection. I wore makeup from sixth grade on, the whole works."

"And you hated it."

"I did."

"Yet you are wearing it now." The hand not resting on her back came up to cup her nape. "For the visiting MIT professor?"

"No."

"I didn't think so." Then Demyan's head lowered, his mouth claiming hers with surprisingly confident kisses.

And she couldn't think at all.

Sparks of pleasure kindled where their lips met and exploded through her in a conflagration of delight. It was only a kiss. He was barely touching her, just holding her, really. And yet she felt like they were in the midst of making love.

Not that she'd actually done the deed, but she'd come close and it hadn't been anything as good or intimate as this single kiss. She'd been naked with a man and felt less sensation, less loss of control.

Small whimpers sounded and she realized they were coming from her. There was no room for embarrassment at the needy sounds. She wanted too desperately.

She'd read about this kind of passion, but thought it was something writers made up, like werewolves and sentient beings on Mars. She had always believed that this level of desire wasn't real.

Before meeting Demyan.

Before this kiss.

The hands on her became sensual manacles, their hold deliciously unbreakable. She didn't *want* to break it. Didn't want to take a single solitary step away from Demyan.

Their mouths moved together, his tongue barely touching hers in the most sensual kind of tasting. He used his hold on her nape to subtly guide her head into the position he wanted and she found it unbearably exciting to be mastered in this small way.

Demyan was one hundred percent in control of the kiss, and Chanel reveled in it with every single one of her sparking nerve centers.

The hand on her waist slid down to cup her bottom. He squeezed. The muscles along her inner walls spasmed with a need she'd never known to this intensity.

She'd been tempted to make love before, but never to the point of overcoming the promise she'd made to herself never to have sex—only to ever make love. In her mind, that had always meant being married and irrevocably committed to the man she shared her body with.

For the first time, she considered it could well mean giving her body to someone she loved.

Not that she loved Demyan. How could she? They barely knew each other.

The feelings inside her had to be lust, but they were stronger than anything she'd ever considered possible.

He kneaded her backside with a sensual assurance she could not hope to show. She tilted her pelvis toward him, needing something she wasn't ready to give a name to. Her hip brushed the unmistakable proof of his excitement; they moaned into one another's mouths, the sounds adding to the press of desire between them.

The knowledge he wanted her, too, poured through her like gasoline on the fire of her desire.

Her hands clutched at his crisp dress shirt as she rocked against him, wanting more, needing something only he could give her. He rocked back against her, the sounds coming from him too feral and sexy for the "normal corporate guy" he was on the outside.

The disparity so matched her own newly discovered

sexual being inside the science geek, the connection she felt with him quadrupled in that moment.

Without warning, he tore his mouth from hers and stepped back, his breathing heavy, his eyes dark and glittery with need. "Now is not the time."

Her own vision hazy with passion, all that she saw in focus was his face, the expression there an odd mixture of confusion and primal sexual need that could not be mistaken.

Even by someone as socially inept as she was.

Why was he confused? Didn't he realize how much she wanted him, too?

"We don't have to go to the dinner." She stated the obvious.

CHAPTER TWO

"No. WE WILL GO." He took a deep breath, like he was trying to rein in the passion she so desperately wanted him
to let loose.

On her.

What would it be like to be the center of the storm she
could see swirling in his intent gaze?

Shivering, she knew with absolute certainty that was
one query she wanted answered.

"Do not look at me like that," he ordered.

"Like what?"

"You want to be naked," he gritted out as if it was an
accusation.

Though how could it be? With the erection pushing so
insistently against his dinner trousers, there could be no
question his body was on board with hers in the desire
department.

More to the point, *she* wanted *him* naked, but she didn't
have the moisture in her mouth to say so. She simply nodded a hazy agreement.

"No. We have the dinner. Sex…" He shook his head as
if finding something difficult to comprehend. "Sex will
come later."

"Please tell me you aren't into delayed gratification."
She'd found her voice and cringed at how blunt she'd been,

not to mention needy sounding. "It's just that I don't get a lot of gratification at all. I don't want to put it off."

She snapped her mouth shut, biting her lips from the inside to stop any more untoward words from escaping.

Instead of reassuring her that it would be perfectly okay to miss the lecture, and dinner, and anything else that stood between them and making love, he seemed amused by her words. Darn it.

Demyan's mouth curved slightly and the need in his eyes receded a little. "Rest assured when we make love, you will not feel in any way ungratified."

Chanel usually objected to the euphemism of lovemaking for what was essentially a physical act between two people. An act she had heretofore refused to indulge in completely. They weren't in love, so how could they make love?

Only, she found the words of objection stuck in her throat. In fact, she could do nothing but agree with his assertion. "I'm sure."

He might be something of a corporate geek, but his confidence in his sexual prowess was too ingrained not to be well based.

Demyan helped Chanel into her seat, his head still reeling from how quickly he'd lost control with her back at the apartment.

He'd very nearly taken her right there in the living room. No finesse. No seduction. Just raw, consuming, *needy* passion.

Demyan did not do consuming. He did not do need.

Raw exposure of desire was for other men. He didn't hold back, but he didn't lose control either. He was known for showing maximum restraint in the sexual realms, bringing his partners to levels of pleasure they showed great appreciation for.

He did not lose it over a simple kiss.

His tongue had barely penetrated Chanel's mouth. With two layers of clothing between them, their bodies had not been able to touch intimately. He'd still been so close to coming, he'd had to pull away before he shamed himself with a reaction he'd never even evinced in adolescence.

The plan had been to give *her* a small taste of passion before leaving the apartment, to flirt with Chanel in subtly sexual ways over dinner and then leave her after a make-out session that left her wanting more.

Gaining her acquiescence to a hasty marriage with the prenuptial agreement the royal family's lawyers had already drawn up required strict adherence to his carefully thought out strategy.

The plan was to keep her reason clouded by emotion, unfulfilled lust built into consuming desire being the primary element.

He didn't plan to consummate their relationship for another week, at least. He wanted her blinded by her own physical wants, ready to commit to him sexually and emotionally.

Instead, he felt like an untried boy gasping for the chance to feel up under her skirt.

"Are you okay?" Chanel asked, worry in her tone.

Shaking off the disturbing thoughts, he gave her his most winning smile. "Of course. I am here with you, aren't I?"

"Don't say things like that." Her frown was far too serious for his liking.

"Why not, when they are true?"

"They don't *sound* true." There was too much knowing

in her gray eyes for his comfort. "That smile you give me sometimes, it's just like a plastic mannequin."

How odd that she should claim to know the difference. No one doubted his sincerity.

A smile was a smile. Except when it wasn't. As he well knew but had not expected his less-than-socially-adept companion to. Taken aback, he sat down, noting as he did so the interested looks of their neighbors.

He turned the smile on them. "What do you say? Am I sincere?" he asked an older woman wearing something he was sure fit a lecture hall better than a formal dinner hosted in the Hilton ballroom.

Her returning smile was the besotted one he was used to getting from women. Even academics. "Very. Perhaps your companion can't help her insecurities. Women like us don't usually snag such lovely escorts."

Chanel made a small, almost wounded sound next to him.

Before he could respond to it, the short, rather round man beside the older woman puffed up like a rooster. "Is that meant to imply that I am not as imposing?"

The woman looked at her date, and the smile she gave him shone with the kind of emotion Demyan found incomprehensible. "No, you are not, and that's exactly the way I love you. I would not have married you nearly forty years ago and stayed this long otherwise."

Feathers suitably smoothed, the man relaxed again in his chair, even deigning to give a somewhat superior smile to Demyan before turning to his wife. "Love you, too, m'dear."

The older couple became obviously lost in a moment Demyan felt uncomfortable witnessing. He turned his attention to Chanel, only to find her frowning, her expression sad and troubled.

"What is it?"

"She's right. You don't belong with me."

"That is not what she said, Chanel." He put his hand on the green-silk-clad thigh closest to him. "I would say there is great evidence to the contrary."

"What do you mean?"

He did not answer, but his expression was as meaningful as he could make it.

He could tell the exact moment all the tumblers clicked into place in Chanel's scientific brain.

Her eyes widened, color surging up her neck into her face. "That's just chemistry. A kiss hardly constitutes a claim."

On that, he could not agree. Loss of control or not, their kiss had been a definite claim-staking on his part. "I'm surprised a woman of your education would declare there was anything *mere* about chemistry."

"We're *here*."

"And?"

"And if the chemistry was so amazing, we wouldn't be."

He couldn't believe she'd said that. He'd damn near ruined a pair of Armani trousers because of the heat between them.

They were not back at her apartment making love for two important reasons only, and neither had a thing to do with how much he'd wanted what she offered so innocently.

Making love tonight wasn't according to plan. Even if it had been, Demyan would have changed the plan because he'd needed the distance from his passion.

He couldn't tell her that, though. Not even close. "I thought you wanted to hear this lecture."

"I did."

He let one brow quirk.

"I do," she admitted with the truculence of a child, made

all the more charming because he was fairly certain she had not been a truculent child.

Just a very different one than her mother had expected her to be.

From everything he'd learned about her, both from the investigative dossier and herself, Chanel Tanner took after her father, not her mother. Not even a little. Mrs. Saltzman had clearly found that very trying when raising her daughter.

An hour later, Chanel looked up from the furious notes she'd been taking for the past twenty minutes on her smartphone. "I'm enjoying myself. Thank you."

A genuine smile creased his lips. "You're welcome."

He liked seeing her like this, enthusiastic, clearly in her element.

"Dr. Beers has made at least two points I hadn't considered before. They're definitely worth additional consideration and research." Chanel glowed with satisfaction Demyan found oddly enticing.

He liked this confident side of her.

Afterward, Demyan made sure she got the opportunity to talk to not only the visiting lecturer but also the head of the university department overseeing her lab's research.

Her boss, who had attended the dinner as well, kept shooting her accusing glances from across the ballroom.

Demyan observed, "The head of your research is not happy to see you here."

"He doesn't like any of his assistants to make connections outside the department." Chanel didn't sound particularly bothered by that fact.

"That is very shortsighted."

"He's a brilliant scientist, but petty as a human being." She shrugged. "I have no aspirations to run my own lab."

"Why not?"

"Too much politics involved." She looked almost guilty. "I like the science."

That sounded like what Demyan knew of her father. "Why the frown?"

"My mother and stepfather would be a lot happier if I had more ambition, or any at all, really."

"Yes?"

"When Yurkovich Tanner offered my schooling scholarship, they made it clear I could attend any school I wanted to."

This was not news to Demyan, but perhaps she would explain why she'd opted for a local state school when she'd had the brains, the grades and the SAT scores to attend MIT, or the like.

"You graduated from Washington State University."

"It was close to home. I didn't want to move away."

Pity. It might have done both Chanel and her mother a world of good. "You were still looking for a relationship with your mother."

He understood that, though he'd never told another soul. His parents had given him up in everything but name, but he'd never cut ties completely with them.

He'd spent his angst-ridden teen years waiting for them to wake up and realize he was still their son. It hadn't happened and by the time he left to attend university in the States, he'd come to accept it never would.

"I think I still am," Chanel answered with a melancholy he did not like.

"You are very different people."

"I'm the odd one."

"You are not odd." Unique, but not in a bad way.

"I wasn't the daughter she wanted. My younger sister is the much-improved model."

"That's ridiculous. You are exactly as you should be."

"Sometimes even I think you're being sincere."

Once again, she'd startled him. Because she was right. In that moment, he'd been speaking nothing but the truth with no thought of his final agenda.

Chanel wasn't sure of the proper way to go about inviting a man up to her apartment for sex.

Demyan wasn't making it easy, either. She wasn't entirely sure, despite the kiss earlier, that he would accept. He'd been attentive over dinner, made sure she enjoyed herself to the fullest. She'd even caught him giving her that look, the one that said he wanted her.

Only, she got this strange sense that he was holding back.

And not for the same reason she was so uncertain about this whole sex thing. No way was Demyan a virgin.

She couldn't help it—no matter how much her body was clamoring for sexual congress with this man, there was still a part of her that insisted that *act* was supposed to be a special one. Not very scientific of her, she knew.

Everyone from her mother, who had given up on Chanel's nonexistent love life, to friends who could not comprehend her "romanticized view of sex," agreed on one thing. Chanel's virginity was just another sign of how she did not fit into the world around her.

But making love was supposed to be something more than two bodies finding physical release, she was sure of it.

Chanel had never wanted just sex. Wasn't sure what effect it would have on her sense of self if she indulged in it now.

Things looked different at twenty-nine than they had at nineteen, though.

She should be more relaxed about the prospect of casually sharing her body with another person. She wasn't.

If anything, the older she got the more important she realized each human connection she made was. Sex was *supposed* to be the ultimate act of intimacy.

She had to admit she'd never felt the bone-deep connection with the few men in her past that she'd felt in that single kiss with Demyan.

She wasn't stupid. She knew losing the two people in her life who had loved her unconditionally at the tender age of eight had made her reticent about opening up to others, particularly men.

Her father and grandfather.

Chanel's stepfather hadn't loved her at all, never mind without limits. As for her mother, Chanel was twenty-nine and the jury was still out on that one.

Which, as an adult woman, had nothing to do with the question of if and how Chanel should offer her invitation to Demyan.

His car slid to a halt by the curb outside her apartment building. He cut the engine, reaching to unclip his belt in one smooth move.

Maybe she wouldn't have to figure it out, after all.

"You're coming up?"

"I will see you to your door."

"It's not necessary." She could have smacked herself. "I mean, only if you want to."

Oh, that was so much better.

One dark brow lifted as he pushed his door open. "Have I ever left you to see yourself inside?"

"It's only our third date." Hardly enough time to set a precedent in stone.

Her own words hit her with the force of a solid particle mass traveling beyond the speed of light. What was she thinking? *Sex with him when they'd barely spent more than a minute in each other's company?*

Still remembering the pleasure of his kiss earlier, her body screamed *yes* while her mind sounded a warning Klaxon of *nos*.

No closer to a verdict about how to handle the rest of the night, she stalled in frozen indecision.

Her door was opened and Demyan bent toward her in his too-darn-sexy dinner suit, his hand reaching toward her. "Are you coming?"

She fumbled with her seat belt, getting it unbuckled after the second try.

The knowing look in his dark eyes said he knew why she was so uncoordinated.

"Don't," she ordered.

The knowing glance turned into a smirk. "Don't?"

"You're smug," Chanel accused as she climbed from the car, eschewing the help of his hand.

Ignoring her attempt to keep her distance, he put his hand around her waist, tucking her body close to his as they approached her building. "I am delighted by your company."

Heat arced between them and, that quickly, she remembered why after only three dates she was ready to break a lifetime habit of virginity.

"I'm still not sure why we're here."

"You live here?" Amusement laced his voice as he led her into the unsecured building.

The lack of a doorman was a bone of contention between Chanel and her mother. If the older woman had been concerned for her safety, Chanel might have considered moving, but the issue was in how it *looked* for her to live in an unpretentious, entirely suburbanite apartment complex.

"I do not like the fact that the entrance to your home is so accessible. This dark cove outside your door is not entirely secure, either," Demyan complained as he took her keys and unlocked the door.

She hadn't quite decided if the action was some throwback to old-world charm or simply indicative of his dominating nature when he ushered her inside.

They moved into the living room and he shut the door behind them. There was meaning in that, right? The shut door. If he'd wanted only to see her inside, he could have left her on the landing.

"Would you like a drink or something?" Like her?

Was she really going to do this? Chanel thought maybe she was.

"Not tonight." The words implied he planned to leave, but the way he stepped closer to her gave an entirely different meaning.

She didn't reply, his proximity stealing her breath just that fast. For the first time in her life, she began to understand *how* her mother, Beatrice, had ended up pregnant by a man so very different from herself.

Sex *was* a powerful force. "Body chemistry is so much more potent than I ever believed." She sounded every bit as bewildered as she felt.

"Because you have never felt it so strongly with someone else." There was no question mark at the end of *that* sentence.

Chanel would take umbrage at the certainty in his tone if Demyan didn't speak the absolute truth.

"I'm sure *you* have."

Something strange moved across his features. Surprise? Maybe confusion. "No."

"You stopped earlier, not me."

"It was not easy."

Was that supposed to make her feel better about the fact he'd been more determined to go to the lecture than *she'd* been? Sarcasm infused her voice as she said, "I'm glad to hear that."

His eyes narrowed, a spark of irritation showing before it disappeared. She wasn't surprised. Demyan might not be the corporate shark her stepfather was, but he was not a man who liked to lose control, either.

Not that he had. Now, *or* earlier.

He had stopped after all, and right now, as much as she could read desire in his dark gaze, he wasn't acting on it.

She, on the other hand, was seconds away from kissing him silly. She, who had never initiated a kiss in her life.

"Do you want to stay?" she asked baldly.

Subtlety was all well and good for a woman who found the role of flirt comfortable, but that woman wasn't Chanel.

He smiled down at her. "Do you want me to?"

"I don't know."

Shock held his face immobile for the count of three seconds. *"You don't know?"*

She shook her head.

"You didn't seem unsure about what you wanted earlier tonight." Disbelief laced his voice.

She nodded, making no attempt to deny it. Subterfuge was not her thing. "I barely know you."

"Is that how it feels to you?"

She experienced that strange sense of disparity she'd had with him before. The words were right, the expression concurrent and yet, she felt the lack of sincerity.

Only, unlike at the dinner, there was a vein of honesty in his words that confused her.

"You already know you could take me to bed with very little effort."

"I assure you, the effort will not be minimal." Sensual promise vibrated in every word.

Chanel felt his promise to her very core and her thighs

squeezed together in involuntary response, not because she feared what he wanted but because it made her ache with a need she'd never known.

"That's not what I meant." Her voice cracked on the last word, but she pretended not to notice.

The slight flaring of his nostrils and the way his eyes went just that much darker said he had, though. "What did you mean then, *little one?*"

"I'm hardly little." At five foot seven, she was above average in height for a woman.

"Do not avoid the question."

"I wasn't trying to." She'd just been trying to clarify, because that was familiar territory.

The rest of this? Was not.

Only he knew how tall she was, so if he wanted to call her *little one,* maybe that was okay. "I suppose I do seem kind of short to you. You're not exactly average height for a man in North America, though maybe I should be comparing you to Ukrainians, as that's your country's formative gene pool."

In fact, he was well above average height, certainly taller than most of the men in her life, and that gave her a peculiar kind of pleasure. Which, like many things she'd discovered since meeting him, surprised her about herself.

She'd never thought she would enjoy feeling *protected* when she was with a man, or that the difference in their height would even succeed in making her feel that way. Maybe it wasn't just that difference but something else about Demyan entirely.

Something intangible that didn't quite match his casual designer sweaters and dark-rimmed glasses.

"You do not seem *short.*" He tugged at one of her red curls, a soft smile playing about his lips as if he could read her thoughts and was amused by them. "You are just right."

This time there was no conflict between the words and sincerity in his manner.

But it put the times there was in stark relief in her mind. "I can't make you out."

"What do you mean?" He looked surprised again and she got the definite impression that didn't happen a lot with him.

"Sometimes I think you mean everything you say, but then there are times, like at dinner tonight, when it seems like you're saying what you think I want to hear."

"I have not lied to you." Affront echoed through his tone.

"Haven't you?"

"No." Dead certainty, and then almost as if it was drawn from him without his permission, "I have not told you everything about myself."

"I didn't expect you to bring along an information dossier on our first date." Of course she didn't know everything about him; that was part of the dating process, wasn't it? "You don't know everything about me, either."

His gaze turned cold, almost ruthless. Then he adjusted his glasses and the look disappeared. "I know what I need to."

Sometimes there was a glimmer of another man there— a man that even a shark like Perry would swim from in a frantic effort to escape. Then Demyan would smile and the impression of that other man would dissipate.

CHAPTER THREE

DEMYAN DIDN'T SMILE now, but she knew the man in front of her wasn't a shark.

Not like the overcritical Perry, and definitely not like someone even more ruthless than her stepfather. There was too much kindness in Demyan, even if he was wholly unaware of it, as Chanel suspected he was.

"What did you mean earlier?" he asked, pulling her back to the original question.

Oh, yes…right.

"It's just…you must realize I'm a sure thing. Even if I'm not sure I *want* to be."

"Why aren't you sure?" he asked, deflecting himself this time.

Or maybe he just really wanted to know. Being the center of someone else's undivided attention when she wasn't discussing her work wasn't something Chanel was used to.

When she was with Demyan, he focused solely on her, though, as if nothing was more important to him. He wanted to know things others reacted to with impatience, not interest. It was a heady feeling.

Even so, peeling away the layers to reveal her full self to him wasn't easy. "You'll laugh."

"Is it funny?"

"Not to me." Not even a little.

"Then I will not laugh."

"How can you be so perfect?"

"So long as I am perfect for you, that is all that matters."

"Do you mean that?"

"Yes." There could be no doubting the conviction in his tone or handsome features.

"Why?"

"Are you saying you feel differently?" he asked in a tone that implied he knew the answer.

"Love at first sight doesn't happen."

"Maybe for some people it does."

All the breath seemed to leave the room at his words. "Are you saying…" She had to clear her throat, suck in air and try again. "Are you saying you feel the same?"

"I want to be your perfect man."

"You mean that." And maybe it was past time she stopped doubting his sincerity.

How much of her feeling he was saying what she wanted to hear stemmed from her own insecurities? Why was it so hard for her to accept that this man didn't need her to be something or someone different to want to be with her?

The answer was the years spent in a family she simply didn't fit, the daughter of a mother and stepfather who found constant fault with a child too much like her own father for their comfort.

"I do."

She nodded, accepting. Believing. "I've never had sex."

Once again she'd managed to shock him. And this time she didn't have to look for subtle signs.

His whisker-shadowed jaw dropped and dark eyes widened comically. "You are twenty-nine."

"I'm not staring retirement in the face, or something." She had eleven more years of relatively safe childbearing, even.

Not that she thought she was going to marry and have children. She'd given up on that idea when she realized that even in the academic world, Chanel was a social misfit.

"No, I didn't mean that." But his voice was still laced with surprise and his superior brain was clearly *not* firing on all cylinders. "You're educated. *American.*"

"So?" What in the world did her PhD in chemistry have to do with her virginity?

"Are you completely innocent?"

Man, did he even realize how that sounded?

And people thought she was old-fashioned. "Even if I'd had sex, I would still be innocent. Sex isn't a crime."

"You know that is not what I was referring to."

"No, I know, but *innocent?* Come on."

The look he was giving her was way too familiar.

"I'm awkward," she excused with a barely stifled sigh. "I told you." Had he forgotten?

"You are refreshingly direct." That wasn't disappointment in his tone and the look she thought she recognized.

Well, it wasn't. He almost looked admiring. If she believed it, and hadn't she diced to do just that? "Mother calls it ridiculously blunt."

"Your mother does not see you as I do."

"I should hope not."

They both smiled at her small joke that did nothing to dissipate the emotional tension between them.

He put his big hands on her shoulders, his thumbs brushing along her collarbone, the hold possessive like before. And just like earlier, she found a new unexpected part of her that liked that. A lot.

"Demyan." His name just sighed out of her.

She didn't know what she meant by it. What she wanted from him.

He didn't appear similarly lost, his gaze direct and commanding. "You say you've never had sex. I want to know what that means."

It took two tries to get words past her suddenly constricted throat. "Why does it matter?"

"You can ask that?"

"Um, yes." Hadn't she just done?

"You are mine."

"Three dates," she reminded him.

"Love at first sight," he countered.

"You... I..."

"We are going to make love. What I want to know is what you have done to this point." His thumbs continued the sensual caress along her collarbone. "You are going to tell me."

"Bossy much?"

"Only in bed."

She wasn't sure she believed him, was even less sure if it mattered. She wasn't worried about standing up for herself. She'd never conformed when it counted, no matter how much easier it would have made her life—especially with her family.

Right now she found she wanted to answer his question, needed to. Still, she kept it general. "Heavy petting, I guess you'd say."

"Be more specific."

"No." Heat crawled up her neck.

He shouldn't care, should he? Virginity wasn't an issue for modern men. *Or modern women,* her inner voice mocked her, *and yet you are a virgin.*

He bent so close their lips almost touched. "Oh, yes."

Thoughts came and went, no words making it past her lips until she made a sound she'd never heard from her own vocal cords before. It was something like surrender, but more.

It was sexual.

The air between them grew heavy with the most primal kind of desire, pushing against her, demanding her acquiescence.

In a last-ditch desperate bid for space, she shut her eyes, but it did no good. She could feel his stare. Could feel his determination to get an answer.

She was super sensitive to his nearness, too, her body aching to press against his, her lips going soft in preparation for his kiss.

The kiss didn't come.

"Tell me," puffed across her lips.

The sound of his voice whispered through her, increasing the sensual fire burning through her veins.

"It wasn't anything."

"Were you naked?"

"Once."

"Good." He kissed her, his lips barely there and gone before she could lose herself in the caress she wanted more than air or research funding. "When?"

"In college."

He just waited.

"He told me he loved me." She'd wanted to be loved so badly, she realized later.

"You didn't let him into your body."

"No."

"Why?"

"It didn't feel right." Old pain twisted through her heart.

She turned her head away, stepping back when a few seconds before she would have said she wasn't capable of moving at all, much less away from him.

"He hurt you." The growl in Demyan's voice made Chanel's eyes snap open, her gaze searching for him, for visual proof of what had been in his tone.

The anger in his eyes wasn't directed at her, but it still made Chanel shiver. "He broke up with me."

Her ex had called her a dried-up relic, a throwback woman who belonged in a medieval nunnery, not a modern university. Chanel had a lot of experience with disappointing her family, so her ex-boyfriend's words should not have had the power to wound.

She should have been inured.

But they'd cut her deeply, traumatically so.

She'd never shared with another person the experience that had left her convinced her mother and stepfather were right, had never admitted her ultimate failure.

"I'm hopeless with men." What was she doing here, wanting to give her body to a man destined to eviscerate her heart?

He wasn't ever going to stay with her. He said they were going to make love, but they couldn't. He didn't love her, no matter what his words had implied. He couldn't.

She wasn't that woman.

Chanel wasn't a bubbly blonde beauty like her sister, Laura. She wasn't a cool sophisticate like her mother. Chanel was the awkward one who could make perfect marks in chemistry courses but utterly fail at the human kind.

She shook her head, her hands cold and shaking. "You should leave."

Another primal sound of anger came out of him before he crossed the small distance between them and yanked her body into his with tender ruthlessness. "I'm not going anywhere. Not tonight. Not ever."

"You can't make promises like that." His breaking them was going to destroy something inside her that her parents and ex had been unable to touch.

The belief that she was worth *something*.

"I can."

"What? You're going to marry me?" she demanded with pain-filled sarcasm.

"Yes."

She couldn't breathe, her vision going black around the edges. Words were torn from her, but they came out in barely a whisper. "You don't mean that."

He cupped the back of her head, forcing her gaze to meet his. "I do."

"You can't."

"I am a man of my word."

"Always?" she mocked, not believing.

No one kept all their promises. Especially not to her. Hadn't her father told her he'd always be there for her? But then he'd died. Her mother had promised, in the aftermath of Jacob Tanner's death, that she and Chanel would always be a team, that she wouldn't leave her daughter, wouldn't die like her husband.

Beatrice *hadn't* died, but she'd abandoned Chanel emotionally within a year of her marriage to Perry, making it clear from that point on that the only team was the Saltzmans'. Chanel Tanner had no place on it.

"Try me," Demyan demanded, no insecurity about the future in *his* words.

"You'll destroy me."

"No."

"Men like you…" Her words ran out as her heart twisted at the thought of never seeing him again.

"Know our own minds." There was that look in his eyes again.

As if he was a man who always got what he set out to, no matter what he had to do to get it. As if she might as well give in because he *never* would.

"I wanted to wait until I got married. I didn't want to trap someone into a lifetime they would only resent."

"There are such things as birth control."

"My mom was on the Pill when she got pregnant with me. I was not part of her future plans. Neither was my father."

"She didn't have to marry him."

"She loved him. At first." Chanel didn't know when that had changed.

She'd been only eight when her dad died, but she'd believed her parents loved each other deeply and forever. It was her mother's constant criticism and unfavorable comparisons later that made Chanel realize Beatrice had not approved of her husband any more than she did their daughter.

"They were not compatible." Demyan said it like he really knew—not that he could.

"I thought they were, when I was little. I was wrong," she admitted.

"We aren't them. We are compatible."

"You don't know that."

"I know more than you think I do. We belong together." There was a message in his words she couldn't quite decipher, but his dark gaze wasn't giving any hints.

"I told you I was a sure thing." Though she wasn't sure that was true. Part of her was still fighting the idea of total intimacy, especially at the cost of opening herself up like this. "You don't have to say these things."

"I am not a man who makes a habit of saying things I do not mean."

"You never lie." He'd as good as said so earlier.

Something passed across his handsome features. "I have not lied to you."

His implication was unbelievable. "You really plan to marry me. After three dates?"

"Yes." There was so much certainty, such deep conviction in that single word.

She could not doubt him, but it didn't make sense. Her scientific brain could not identify the components of the formula of their interaction that had led to this reaction.

In her lab she knew mixing one substance with another and adding heat, or cold, or simply agitation resulted in identifiable and documented results.

Love wasn't like that. There was nothing predictable about the male-female interaction, especially for her.

But one thing she knew—a man could not hide his true reaction to a woman in bed. It was why she'd refused her ex back at university. He hadn't been completely into it.

Oh, he'd wanted to get off, but she could tell that it didn't matter it was *her* he was getting off with.

"Show me," she challenged Demyan now. "Make me believe."

His eyes narrowed, but he didn't pretend not to understand what she wanted.

Demyan could not let Chanel's challenge go unmet.

Whatever the cretin who had turned her off sex had done to her, at least part of her thought Demyan would do the same thing. He could see it in the wary depths of her gray eyes.

"You will see, *sérdeńko*. I am not that guy."

"You keep calling me little." She didn't sound as if she was complaining, just observing.

He noticed she did that when the emotions got too intense. She retreated behind the barrier of her analytical mind.

When this night was over there would be no barriers between them.

"You speak Ukrainian." Her dossier had mentioned she studied the language, but not how proficient she was.

To translate the endearment, which was a diminutive form of heart, implied a far deeper knowledge of his native tongue than the investigative report had revealed.

"I studied it so I could read scientific texts by notable scientists in their native tongue."

"And *sérdeńko* came up in a scientific text?" he asked with disbelief.

"No." She sighed as if admitting a dark secret. "I like languages. I'm fluent in Ukrainian, Portuguese and German."

"So you could read scientific texts."

"Among other things." She blushed intriguingly.

"What things?" he asked, his mouth temptingly close to hers.

He wanted to kiss her. She wanted the kiss, too—there could be no doubt.

"Erotic romance."

"In Ukrainian?" he asked, utterly surprised for the third time that night.

This woman would never be a boring companion.

"Yes."

"I am amazed."

"Why?"

"If you like reading about sex so much, how are you still a virgin?"

"I like reading murder mysteries, too, but I haven't gone out and killed anybody."

He laughed, unable to remember the last time he'd been so entertained by a female companion.

This marriage he had to bring about would not be a hardship. Chanel Tanner would make a very amiable wife.

With that thought in mind, he took the first step in convincing her that they belonged together.

He kissed her, taking command of her mouth more gently than he might have before her revelation.

She couldn't know it, but her virginity was a gift to him in more ways than one.

First, that he was the only man who would ever share her body in this way was not something to take lightly. Not even in this modern age.

But second, and more important to his efforts on behalf of Volyarus, once Demyan had awakened her passions for the first time, Chanel would be more likely to accept his proposal of marriage.

It meant adjusting his schedule up for her seduction, but he wasn't leaving her tonight. Doing so might cause irreparable harm to the building of trust between them. She needed to know he wanted her, and he did.

Unlikely as he would have considered it, he desired this shy, bookish scientist above all other women.

She didn't want to believe in forever with him, but she would learn. He had spoken the truth earlier. Prince Demyan of Volyarus did not break his promises.

And he had promised King Fedir that Demyan would marry Chanel Tanner.

She whimpered against his lips, her sexual desire so close to the surface he thought she needed her first climax to come early so she could enjoy the lead-up to the next one.

With careful precision, he built the kiss until the small sounds of need were falling from her lips to his in a steady cascade. Control starting to slip, he deepened the kiss, wanting more of her taste, more of her response…more of everything Chanel had to give.

A small voice in the back of his mind prompted that the time had come to pull back and lead her into the bedroom.

Only, his lips didn't want to obey, and for the first time in memory Demyan found himself lost in a kiss, his plans for a suave seduction cracking under the weight of his more primitive need.

He had just the presence of mind to move her backward toward the sofa. Unbelievably, *neither* of them was going to be able to stay vertical much longer.

Demyan maneuvered them both so Chanel sat sprawled across his lap, her dress hiked up, her naked thighs pressing against his cloth-covered ones.

He never let her lips slide so much as a centimeter away from his.

Demyan liked sex. According to Maks, he'd had more than his fair share of partners. Some of them were very experienced in the art of seduction, women who knew exactly how to use their bodies for maximum effect. None of them had turned him on as much as the uncalculated and wholly honest way Chanel responded to his kiss.

She moved with innocent need against him, her body undulating in unconscious sensuality that drove him insane with the need to show her what those types of movements led to.

He brought his hand down and cupped her backside, guiding those untutored rolls of her hips into something that would give them both more pleasure and fan the flames of desire between them into an all-out inferno.

She jolted and moaned as her panty-clad apex rubbed over his trapped hard-on. He couldn't hold back his own sounds of raw sexual desire and keep from arching his hips to increase the friction.

The kiss went nuclear and he did nothing to stop it, demanding entrance into her mouth with his tongue and getting it without even a token resistance.

This woman did not play the coquette. Her honest passion was more exciting than any practiced seduction could be. She couldn't know, though; she was too unused to physical intimacy. For that ignorance, at least, he could be glad.

She could not take advantage of a weakness she did not recognize in him, and damned if he would point it out. He might not be able to control himself completely this first time with her, but no doubt that was a big part of the reason why.

It *was* her first time and he found that highly erotic.

The one benefit was that it was clear Chanel was completely out of control and definitely imprinting on him sexually.

Equally important, after what she'd revealed, was for her to realize *he* wanted *her*.

As she'd demanded, he would show her.

She would never again doubt her feminine appeal to him, not after tonight. And perhaps that, even more than her virginity, would lead her to accept his speed-record-breaking proposal when it came.

That it might no longer be completely about his duty to country was a thought he dismissed as unimportant.

He would have her. She would have him and whether she knew it or not, she needed him. He was good for her.

It started with now, giving her what she hadn't realized she was missing.

After insuring she kept the rhythm that made her body shake, he mapped her body with his hands through the soft green silk of her dress, caressing her in ways reserved for a lover.

He enjoyed this part of sex, touching a woman in ways no one else was allowed and, in Chanel's case, never had been.

Knowing a woman had put her body in his very-capable-to-dole-out-pleasure hands turned him on. Demyan liked *that* control, too. For reasons he didn't feel the need to dwell on, that knowledge was even more satisfying with Chanel than it had been with other women.

She might not realize it, but the kind of response she gave meant she would let him do *anything*. That acknowledgment came with a heady kind of enjoyment destined to undermine his self-control further if he wasn't very careful.

It was important for her pleasure, particularly this first time, that he not let that happen. He had to maintain some level of premeditation, or he could hurt her.

That reminder sobered him enough to think—at least a little—again.

Touching her was good, though. Too damn good.

He cupped her breasts, reveling in the catch of her breath as his thumbs brushed over turgid nipples. He wanted to feel them naked, but even this was incredible.

His sex pressed against the placket of his trousers in response to the feel of her in his hands.

He pinched, knowing the layers of silk and her bra would be no true barrier between those buds and the sensation he gave her.

She tore her mouth from his, her eyes opening, pupils blown with bliss almost swallowing the stormy irises. "I... That..."

"Is good." He did it again, increasing the pressure just enough to give maximum pleasure that might border on pain but would never go over. "Say it."

CHAPTER FOUR

CONFUSION FLITTED ACROSS the sweet oval of Chanel's face. "What?"

"Say it feels good."

She didn't have to speak her refusal—it was there in the way her body stiffened and she averted her gaze.

"Look at me," he demanded, his fingers poised to give more pleasure but not offering it. "Look at me and say it."

Her storm-cloud gaze came back to his, her mouth working, no words coming out.

"You are a woman. You can acknowledge your own pleasure, Chanel. I believe in you."

"It's not that." The word cut off as if her air had run out. She took a deep breath and let it out, her tongue coming out to wet her lips. "I know sex is supposed to feel good."

"Do you?"

"I've read books."

"Erotic books."

"Yes."

"So, say it."

"You want to strip me bare," she accused.

He saw no point in denying it. "Yes."

"Why?"

"You have to let go."

"You never let go."

"I am the experienced one here. If I let go of my control, we'd both be in trouble."

"That doesn't make sense."

"Only because you haven't done this before."

She didn't deny his words. "I like it."

"I know." He pressed just slightly, giving her a taste of what was to come.

She moaned, her head falling back, her eyelids sliding down to cover the vulnerability in her gaze. "So, why do I have to say it?"

"For me. Say it for me."

"It feels good." The words came out in a low, throaty whisper infused with sincerity.

Oh, yes, this woman would learn to hold nothing back.

He rewarded her with more pleasure until she was rocking against him with gasping breaths. "Demyan!"

"What, *sérdeńko?*"

"You know! You have to know."

"This?" he asked as he pushed up to rub his hardness against her, pinching her nipples at the same time.

"Yes."

He did it again, making sure to continue the friction against that bundle of nerves through the damp silk of her panties. "Let go, Chanel."

"I…"

He didn't want arguments. He wanted her surrender. "Come for me, Chanel. You are mine."

And unused to this level of pleasure, she came apart, her body arching into a stiff contortion of delight while a keening wail sounded from her throat.

Oh, yes, this woman belonged to him. Her body knew it, even if her mind was still in some doubt.

He let the shivers of aftershock finish, concentrating on gaining his own breath and a measure of mental for-

titude. When he was sure he could do it without his own
limbs giving way, he tucked one arm under her bottom
and the other against her back and stood with her secure
in his hold.

Her head rose from where it had come to rest against
his shoulder, her face still flushed with pleasure, her gray
gaze meeting his. "What... Where?"

"Your first time will not happen on a sofa, no matter
how comfortable."

"It already did."

He shook his head. "That was not sex."

"But it was my first orgasm with another person."

Perhaps that small fact helped to explain why she was
still a virgin, too.

He didn't repeat his shock at her age, or his disgust
with her previous partners. "It will be the first of many,
I promise you."

She swallowed audibly, but nodded with appreciative
enthusiasm.

He felt his mouth curve into a very rare and equally
genuine smile.

How had she remained untouched so long?

This woman was sweetly sensual and engagingly honest. Far from socially inept. Demyan found her fascinating.

It did not bother him at all, though, that she would be
giving her body to him and only him. He would honor the
gift and she would find no reason to regret it.

He made the vow to himself, and Demyan never broke
his word. Chanel was still trying to catch her breath when
Demyan laid her oh so carefully on the bed after yanking
back the covers.

Sexual demand radiated off him like heat from a nuclear reactor. Yet there was no impatience in the way he
handled her.

The bedding? Yes. It lay in disarray on the floor, his powerful jerks pulling the sheet and blanket that had been tucked between the mattress and box spring completely away.

But her?

He settled with a gentle touch that belied his obvious masculine need.

"I was going to wait." He shrugged out of his suit jacket, letting the designer garment drop to the floor without any outward concern about what that might do to it.

"Why?"

"It seemed the thing to do."

"Because things are moving so fast between us," she said rather than asked.

He only loosened his tie and undid the top buttons on his shirt before pulling the whole thing over his head in one swift movement. "We will not be waiting."

His torso was chiseled in that way really fit men with natural strength were. Dark curls covered his chest, narrowing into a V that disappeared into the waistband of his trousers. She wanted to see where that trail of sexy hair led.

She might be a virgin, but she was pretty sure she wasn't a shy one.

"You are beautiful," she breathed.

"Men are not beautiful." But his eyes smiled at the compliment.

"The statue of David is beautiful."

"That is art."

"So are you."

He shook his head, his hands going to his trouser button. "I am a flesh-and-blood man, never doubt it."

How could she, with all that flesh staring her in the face?

His trousers slid down his legs, revealing CK black knit

boxers that conformed to every ridge of muscle and the biggest ridge of all. His erection.

Her mouth went dry, the moisture going straight to her palms. "You're big, aren't you?"

"I've never compared myself to other men." With that he shucked out of his boxers, leaving his very swollen, very rigid length on display.

"According to scientific studies, the average penile length is five to five-point-seven inches in length when erect." And Demyan was definitely longer, unless her eyes were deceiving her.

But Chanel was a scientist who had conducted enough measurements she could usually guess within a centimeter's accuracy.

He frowned and stopped at the side of the bed, his erection bobbing with the movement even as it curved upward toward his belly. That wasn't usual, either, she'd read. Most men erected perpendicularly with a slight leaning toward one side. Some even had a small downward angle.

For Demyan's hardness to be curving upward, it had to be *extremely* ready for intercourse.

"How do you know that?" he demanded with amusement in his voice.

"I read. A lot."

"You cannot believe everything you read in your Ukrainian erotica."

"Of course not."

His brow rose, the mockery there.

"I read that particular fact in a scientific journal."

His dark gaze pinned her to the bed, though he had yet to join her with his incredibly gorgeous naked body. "We have better things to do than discuss frivolous scientific research."

"It isn't frivolous to the tens of thousands of men who

have been feeling inadequate because of the supposed average lengths gleaned from self-measurement."

"What you are telling me is that men measure themselves as larger than they are?" He definitely sounded amused now.

"I don't think *you* would."

"I would not measure myself at all." From his tone, he found the idea of doing so absolutely ridiculous.

"I think I'd like to measure you."

"No."

"With my hand."

The erection in question jumped at her words and it was her turn to smile.

"Do not tease," he warned.

"I'm not teasing."

"You are smiling."

"I'm just really happy that you react to me so strongly." So strongly in fact that despite the fact she'd led them down one of the conversational byways that always annoyed others, his visible response to her had not dimmed in the least.

"You are a very sexy woman."

She couldn't help laughing at that assertion, but she didn't accuse him of lying. Honest desire burned in the brown depths of his eyes.

"It is time I did something about your lack of focus." He didn't sound mad about it, though.

She just nodded, wanting more of what they'd done in the living room, more kisses, more touching, more of that amazingly intimate connection.

"First we need to get you naked, too."

She'd already kicked her heels off in the living room and she wasn't wearing panty hose. That didn't leave much to get rid of.

She started tugging her skirt up, only to have his hands

join her in the effort. Only somehow he made the slide of silk up her body into a series of sensual caresses, so she was shivering with renewed passion by the time he pulled the green fabric over her head.

He tossed it away.

"My mother would be very annoyed if she saw you treating clothes the way you do." Especially high-end designer ones.

"Your mother has no place in our bedroom."

"It's not *our* bedroom."

"You belong to me. This room belongs to you. Therefore, it is ours."

She couldn't push a denial of his claim through her lips. There was too much truth to it.

It was almost scary, but she wasn't afraid.

In fact, that part of her that had felt alone in the world since her mother's marriage to Perry Saltzman warmed with an inexplicable sense of belonging.

"She's still my mother," was all Chanel could think to say.

"And she always will be, but her views and opinions about you are skewed by grief and a lack of understanding. Therefore, they have no place in our life together."

"We don't have a life together," she said with more vehemence than she felt.

But it was insane, this instant connection, his claim he planned a future with her. It just wasn't real. Couldn't be.

"We do. It starts with this." His hands reached behind her to unhook her bra clasp, sight unseen.

Her nipples, already tightened into hard points from his earlier manipulations, contracted further from the cooled air brushing across them.

There was no stifling the shiver that went through her in response to the extra stimulation.

His smile was predatory. "You have very sensitive breasts."

"Nipples," she couldn't help correcting. It wasn't her entire boob responding, was it?

He brushed his fingertips along the side of her breast, sliding forward, but not touching the nipple.

Desire coiled low in her belly, her body arching toward his.

He did it again. "Very responsive."

"You don't like to be wrong, do you?" she asked in a voice that hitched every other syllable with her gasping breaths.

"It is a rare occurrence."

"Arrogant."

"Certain."

"Same thing."

"It is not." Then he kissed her, preventing any more words.

It was a sneaky way to end an argument, but she couldn't make herself mind. Not when it felt so wonderful. It might be only their lips that were connected, but she felt as if he was touching her to the very depths of her soul.

He pulled back, their breath coming in harsh gasps between them. "One thing left."

"What?" she asked, nothing but his lips making any sense in that moment.

"Your panties."

Were surplus to requirements. She got the picture but found she was hopeless in the face of doing something about it.

It was okay, though. His long masculine fingers were sliding between her hips and the silk and then it was being tugged down, baring the last bit of her to him.

"There will be nothing between us," he growled, as if he could read her mind.

She looked up at him, their gazes locking, and what she saw in his left her in no doubt he *wasn't* just talking about clothing.

He'd pushed her in the living room, demanding she acknowledge her own pleasure, her own desires, this crazy thing happening between them.

He was going to push her further now.

"It's just sex," she claimed with a desperate attempt to believe her own words.

"We are making love, locking our lives together."

"This isn't real."

"It is very real."

"Please…"

He cupped her face, the move one she was becoming quite familiar with and incidentally learning to love. "Please, what?"

"Just tonight? Can it just be about tonight?"

He lowered his head until their lips almost brushed. "No."

This time, she kissed him. Couldn't help herself and was glad she hadn't when he took control and drew forth a response from her body that shouldn't have been possible. Not after she'd just climaxed.

Only it was.

It was as if they were connected by live electric current, energizing, transforming every synapse in its wake, so that her body was uniquely tuned to him. The way that big body blanketed hers, his hardness rubbing against the sensitive curls at the apex of her thighs indicated he was being tuned to the same frequency.

A frequency she thought would rule her body's responses for the rest of her life.

And if she could believe his words, it would.

The kiss pulled her out of time, suspending them in an intimacy that had no limits, not in hours and minutes, or in emotional connection.

It was beyond anything she thought two people could feel together.

His hands were everywhere, bringing pleasure, teaching her body his touch, making that indescribable pleasure spiral tighter and tighter inside her again.

She touched him, too, letting her fingertips learn his body, and just doing that gave her a level of delight she'd never known. She could caress this man, touch his naked skin and he wanted it, wanted *her* touch. Not just any woman's. *Hers.*

An empty ache started, making her body restless for what it had never known.

As if he knew exactly what she needed, he nudged her thighs apart and adjusted his body so the head of his erection pressed against the opening to her body. However, he made no move to enter her.

The moment felt so momentous that tears washed into her eyes and trickled down her temples. He broke the kiss, lifting his head, his expression knowing.

He touched the wetness, wiping at the tears with one finger. "It is not just about tonight."

"It's not supposed to be this big."

"You have waited twenty-nine years, *krýxitka*."

She wasn't a baby, not by any stretch, but having him call her one didn't feel wrong. "But women don't, anymore."

"You had your reasons."

"I want this."

"I know."

"You do, too."

"Yes."

"With *me*," she confirmed, maybe needing a little more reassurance than she'd realized.

"Only *you* from this point forward."

"You do not believe in infidelity?" A lot of businessmen thought it was their right when they flew out of town to leave their wedding ring in the bedside drawer of their hotel rooms.

Or so she'd read. Honestly, as awful as Perry might be toward Chanel, she couldn't imagine him cheating on her mother. It was one of the reasons she respected him, even if she didn't like the business shark.

She could never respect a man who didn't understand and adhere to the true meaning of loyalty and faithfulness.

"It is too damaging to everyone involved." There was something about Demyan's tone that said he knew exactly what he was talking about.

She would have asked about it, but right now all she could really focus on was how much she needed him inside her. "It's time."

"Not yet."

Unexpected anger welled up. "You're not going to get bossy about this. I'm not begging."

"I don't want you begging. Tonight."

"But—"

He smiled down at her, indulgence and tenderness she wasn't even sure he was aware of glowing in his dark gaze. "You are a virgin. A certain amount of preparation will make the difference between a beautiful experience and one you never want to have to remember."

"You make it sound so dire."

"It can be."

"Much experience deflowering virgins?" she asked with sarcasm and maybe just a hint of jealousy.

"Tonight is not the time for discussing past sexual encounters."

"That isn't what you said earlier."

His jaw hardened but he said, "Fine. She was young. I was young. It was a disaster."

"Did you love her?"

"Not even a little."

"Did she love you?"

"No." No doubt there.

"You decided to figure out how to fix the problem." She could so see him doing that.

She might not know everything there was to about this man, but some of his basic characteristics she understood very well.

He nodded even as he shifted again so there was room for his hand to get between them. A single finger gently rubbed along her wet folds.

"That feels good," she whispered.

"It is supposed to."

The touch moved up, circling her clitoris. It felt so delicious she gasped with the pleasure of it.

He kissed her and then lifted his head. "Touching you is such a pleasure. You hide none of your responses from me."

"Am I supposed to?"

"No." Very definite. Unquestionably vehement.

"You're kind of a control freak in bed, aren't you?"

"Giving you pleasure takes a lot of concentration. Why would you try to hinder my efforts by lying to me?"

"I never..." She gasped as his fingers moved a certain way. "Didn't say I would."

"Never?" he asked.

She could have accused him of taking unfair advantage, but really? It wouldn't have mattered if he'd asked her in the middle of the street standing ten feet away.

Her answer to that question would always be the same. "Never."

"Thank you." Demyan continued to touch her until she was moving restlessly beneath him.

"Please…" She wasn't even sure what she was asking for.

Intercourse? Maybe, but what she really wanted was resolution to the storm building inside her and Chanel didn't really care how she got it.

Even so, she was shocked when he shifted down her body, his intention clear. She'd read about this. Of course she had. Her ex-boyfriend had even wanted to do it to her, but he'd told her she'd have to shave her hair off first.

She'd refused.

Demyan didn't seem in the least put off by the damp curls between her legs, his tongue going with unerring accuracy right to where his finger had been.

She cried out, her hips coming off the bed. His mouth followed, his ministrations with lips and tongue never pausing.

This was oral sex? This intimate kiss that led to feeling so close to someone else that there was nothing embarrassing about it?

She always thought it would bother her to have a man's mouth *there*. She hadn't refused to shave her nether region just because she was a prude back then.

Only it didn't bother her. Not at all.

It felt so good, so perfect.

Demyan's fingers came back to play, this time with one of them sliding just inside her as his tongue swirled over her most sensitive spot. He moved the finger in and out, going a little deeper each time until he pressed gently against her body's barrier.

It didn't hurt; it was not too much pressure, but it would be different when he was inside her. Wouldn't it?

He would have to break through the barrier then. With his longer-than-average erection. That's what had to happen next.

Only, he didn't seem to have the script, because he kept licking, sucking and nibbling at her clitoris until she was on the verge of climax. His finger inside her continued sliding in and out of her channel, pressing just a little bit harder against the thin barrier every few times.

His other hand came up to play with her breasts and tease at her nipples, increasing the sensations below by a factor of ten. It was incredible. Amazing.

And she felt that precipice draw closer and closer. She didn't think she was supposed to climax again before they were joined, but she didn't worry about it. He knew what he was doing and wouldn't let her.

Only, he didn't seem concerned when she warned him it was getting to be too much. He only renewed his efforts, sucking harder on her clitoris and nipping it ever so gently with his teeth.

Without warning, her body splintered apart in glorious pleasure again, this time so intense she couldn't even get enough air to scream. He didn't stop the intimate kiss, but he gentled it, bringing her prolonged ecstasy that went on and on even as his finger pressed more insistently against that thin membrane of flesh inside.

Until, as she floated on a cloud of sensual bliss, she felt the sharp sting of pain and realized he'd broken through the barrier of her body. With his finger.

"What? Why?" she asked, the hazy peace cracking a little.

"It hurts less." He gently withdrew his finger before placing a single soft kiss against her nether lips.

It felt like a benediction.

He moved off her and she saw him grab a corner of the sheet from the floor to wipe his face and hand before he rejoined her on the bed.

Demyan pulled her body into his still-very-aroused one, his expression very satisfied. "You are beautiful in your passion, Chanel."

"We… Aren't you going to…"

"Oh, yes. But only when you are ready to begin building toward climax again."

She didn't know what he meant, but he showed her, after cuddling her and telling her how amazing and lovely she was. After his touch and nearness once again began to draw forth need to be joined with him.

When he finally pressed inside her, she cried for the second time that night. He didn't look in the least worried he'd hurt her, though. In fact, his expression was one of understanding overlaying utter male satisfaction.

She didn't begrudge him one iota of it, either.

He might have had a debacle with his first virgin, but he'd made this one's initiation into intimacy unbelievably good.

Once she started to move against him, his control slipped its leash and his passion turned harsh and exciting. She screamed her pleasure this time even as his body pounded into hers, and his shout was loud enough to make her ears ring.

Afterward he was quiet, his expression impossible to read. "You'll want a shower."

"Couldn't we shower together?" she asked.

"Your bathroom isn't meant for shared intimacies."

She hadn't been propositioning him, couldn't believe he thought she had any energy left for *that,* but she didn't say so.

While she was in the shower she tried to go over what had happened, but couldn't figure out why he'd withdrawn and wondered if he'd even still be there when she came out.

CHAPTER FIVE

HE WAS, THOUGH, and he'd remade the bed with fresh sheets.

"Thank you," she said, feeling unsure.

"We will be more comfortable sleeping on clean bedding."

That one small word washed through her like life-giving oxygen. *We.* He'd said *we.*

Before she could remark on it, or say anything at all, he started toward the bathroom. "I'll have my shower now. Get in bed."

"You said you were only bossy in the bedroom."

He stopped at the doorway to the bath and looked at her over his shoulder. "We are in the bedroom."

"Why don't you just admit you have oldest-child syndrome?"

His expression turned somber, though she didn't understand why. "Noted."

She would have teased that wasn't an admission, but Demyan disappeared into the bathroom.

Chanel didn't understand what was going on with him, but he wasn't leaving. She'd take that as a good sign.

Did he regret the implications toward the future he'd made before they had sex? Was he realizing now that he'd gotten his rocks off how ludicrous they'd been?

Maybe he thought she'd try to hold him to his words as if he'd made promises. She wouldn't.

Perhaps she needed to tell him that.

She crossed the room, but when she tried the door to the bath, it was locked.

She let her hand drop away. Okay, then.

Maybe she just needed to go to bed. Any talking could happen in the morning.

After only a few moments' deliberation, she opted to wear pajamas to bed. The mint-green jersey knit wasn't exactly sexy, but it was comfortable.

She was still awake when he joined her some indeterminate time later.

He didn't pause before pulling her into his arms, though he made a sound of surprise when his hands encountered fabric. "Why are you wearing this?"

Because she'd needed a barrier between them, a level of armor, even if it was just her favorite pair of pj's. "Why not?" she answered rather than admit that, though.

"Because I prefer naked skin and I think you do, too."

"I wouldn't know. I've never slept with another person," she replied a tad acerbically.

"Perhaps it is for the best tonight. You will be too sore tomorrow if we make love again in the night."

"Oh." He still wanted her?

That was good, right?

"Do not sound so disappointed. We will make love again. Many times."

As promises for the future went, that was one she could live with. "I'm glad."

They were silent for several seconds before she offered, "Thank you for making my first time so special."

"I lost control." And there it was.

What was bothering him. She *knew* it.

"I liked it."

"I could have hurt you."

"But you didn't and I think it *would* have hurt me if you hadn't lost yourself just as badly as I did."

"Yes?" he asked, as if the concept was foreign to him.

"Absolutely."

"I am very glad to hear it." He'd turned out the light, but she could still hear the smile in his voice.

"Go to sleep."

"Your wish is my command."

She would have said something sarcastic about that blatant fabrication, but her mouth didn't want to work and she slipped into sleep, comforted by their banter.

Chanel was astonished by how easily she grew used to sleeping with someone else.

Not to the sex, though. She wasn't sure she'd ever grow *used to* the level of pleasure she and Demyan found in one another's bodies.

He *was* bossy in bed, just like he'd told her, but it was all targeted toward her enjoyment. Every directive, every withholding of one instant gratification for something more was so that her final satisfaction was so incredibly overwhelming, she lost her mind with it.

But the sleeping together, that was different. That was all-night-long intimacy of another sort.

She, who had never even cuddled a bear in bed, found it difficult to sleep now when Demyan's arms weren't wrapped around her, his heartbeat a steady, comforting sound against her ear.

Hence her yawning this morning as she crunched the new data, despite three cups of coffee made in the new Keurig machine Demyan had gotten her.

He liked to buy her things, she'd noticed. Things *she* would like.

Her entire life, gifts had come with a subtle message to her to become something different. Designer clothes in a style unlike the one she favored, athletic shoes that were supposed to encourage her to take up running when she was perfectly happy with her tae kwon do training. Golfing gear, though she hated the game, a tennis racket despite the fact she'd never played.

But Demyan's pressies were different. They were all targeted to the woman she was now, with no eye to making her into someone else. He showed an uncanny ability to tap in to her preferences, even when she'd never shared certain things with him.

Like her addiction to flavored coffees in direct opposition to her frustration over the complicated business of making a good cup of the beverage. So Demyan had found a way to feed the one while minimizing the other.

And the coffee? Delicious. And so darn easy.

She couldn't mess it up even when she got sidetracked by a new algorithm she wanted to try.

Even when she was sleepy from waking every couple of hours, reaching for him in the bed only to find empty space.

Demyan had left Seattle in the wee hours of the previous morning for what Chanel assumed was a business trip. She hadn't asked what it was about and he hadn't offered the information.

What she did know was that he wouldn't be back for two more days and an equal number of nights. Forty-eight more hours without him.

In the time line of life, it was hardly a blip.

So why did it feel longer than a particularly depraved man's purgatory to her?

Chanel already missed him with an ache that made absolutely no sense to her scientific brain. Okay, so they'd been dating a month now, not just three days. Making love and sleeping together every single night of the past three weeks of that month.

Still. How could she have become more addicted to his company than caffeine?

Because Chanel knew without any doubts she could go without coffee a heck of a lot more easily than she was finding it to be without her daily dose of Demyan.

She didn't know if she'd fallen in love at first sight like he'd hinted at three weeks ago, but she was in love with him now.

And that scared her more than a weekend at the spa with her mother.

"How close are you to closing the deal?" Fedir asked without preamble once he and Demyan were alone in the king's study.

Demyan's cousin and Gillian had returned from their honeymoon, and Queen Oxana wanted *family time*. That meant everyone in their small inner circle had come to the palace for a few days of "bonding."

Since his own parents would cheerfully go the rest of their lives without seeing Demyan, he never took Oxana's desire to spend time as a *family* for granted.

Though on this particular occasion, his mother and father and siblings were also staying at the palace in order to get to know their future queen, Gillian, better.

His father wouldn't make any effort to spend one-on-one time with Demyan, though. For all intents and purposes, Demyan's younger brother was his acknowledged oldest son.

Pushing aside old wounds Demyan no longer gave the

power to hurt him, he answered his uncle's question. "She's emotionally engaged."

"When will you propose?"

"When I return."

Fedir nodded. "Smart. The time apart will leave her feeling vulnerable. She'll want to cement your bond. Women are like that."

Demyan didn't reply. His uncle was the last man, bar none, he would ask for advice on women.

"She'll sign the prenuptial agreement?"

"Yes." The more Demyan had gotten to know Chanel, the more apparent it had become that money was not a motivating factor for her.

She'd sign even the all-contingency prenuptial agreement Fedir's lawyers had drawn up simply because the financial terms would not matter to her.

"Good, good."

"I'll want changes made to some of the provisions before I present her with it, though."

Fedir frowned. "What? I thought the lawyers did a good job of covering all the bases."

"I want more generous monetary allowances for Chanel in the event our marriage ends in divorce or my death."

"What? Why?" Fedir's shock was almost comical. "Has a woman finally gotten under the skin of my untouchable nephew?"

Of course his uncle would immediately assume an emotional reason behind Demyan's actions. His sense of justice was a little warped by his all-consuming dedication to the welfare of Volyarus.

"I will do whatever I need to in order to protect this country, but I will do it with honor," Demyan replied.

"Of course, but your integrity is in no way compromised by your actions to insure the healthy future of our country."

Demyan wasn't sure he believed that. Regardless, he would minimize how much tarnish it took. "The terms will be changed to my requirements, or I won't offer the document to Chanel to sign."

As threats went, it wasn't very powerful. Baron Tanner's will had been clear and airtight. Chanel lost all claim to the baron's shares in Yurkovich Tanner upon marriage to any direct relation to the king.

"And without a prenup, there will be no wedding," Demyan added after several seconds of silence by his uncle.

"You don't mean that."

"When have you ever known me to bluff?" Demyan asked.

Fedir frowned. "She really does mean something to you."

"My integrity certainly does."

He was a ruthless man. Demyan knew that about himself. He could make the hard choices, but he was an honest man, too. And he didn't make those choices without counting the cost.

"A man has to make sacrifices, even in that area for the greater good."

Demyan shrugged. "I'll contact the lawyers with the changes I want made to the agreement."

He wasn't going to debate his uncle's choices. The other man had to live with them and their consequences. It might be argued that everyone in the palace did, too, but Demyan wasn't a whiny child, moaning how his uncle's decisions had cost him his family.

The truth was, his own parents and their ambition were every bit as culpable.

"I'll trust you to be reasonable in your demands."

"I appreciate that."

"Demyan, you will never be king, but you are no less a

son to me than Maksim." Fedir laid one hand on Demyan's shoulder and squeezed.

The words rocked through Demyan. His uncle was not an emotionally demonstrative man, in word or deed. Nor was he known for saying things he did not mean, at least not to family.

However, Demyan's cynicism in the face of life's lessons drove his speech. "A son you call nephew."

"A son I and all of Volyarus call prince."

"You never adopted me." According to Volyarussian law, which the king could change should he so desire, doing so would have made Demyan heir to the throne, not the spare.

He understood that, but it was also a fact that if he were truly every bit as much a son to Fedir, his place in the right of succession wouldn't have been a deterrent.

"Your parents refused."

Was Fedir trying to imply he'd asked? "I find that difficult to believe. They gave me up completely."

"But so long as you were legally their son, your father had leverage for his interests. He and your mother categorically refused to give that up."

His uncle's words rang true, particularly when weighed against how few of Demyan's father's efforts had met with support of the king since he'd become an adult. "I get my ruthlessness from him."

"But your honor is all your own. You are a better man than either of your fathers, the one by birth and the one by choice."

Fedir was not a man who gave empty compliments. So, Demyan couldn't help that the older man's words sparked emotion deep inside, but he wasn't about to admit that out loud.

"Oxana feels the same. She is very proud of both of her sons."

He thought of the excitement the queen had shown when Demyan had warned her that he'd found the one. "She wouldn't be proud of me if she knew why I'm pursuing Chanel."

"You're wrong. I am very proud of you." Oxana came into the room from the secret passageway entrance. "You have put the welfare of our people and your family ahead of your own happiness. How can I be anything but proud of that?"

Fedir started, clearly shocked his wife had been listening in.

"She's a special woman. She deserves a real marriage." It wasn't a sentiment Demyan would have expressed to Fedir without prompting, but this was Oxana.

She'd sacrificed her entire life for their country and her family. Yet she was not a bitter woman. She loved them all deeply, if not overtly. She deserved to know that Demyan wasn't going to play Chanel for the sake of her inheritance.

"So, give her one." Oxana smiled with the same guarded approval she'd given him since he was a boy, though as he'd grown older he'd learned to look deeper for the true emotion. It was there. "She is a very lucky woman to have you."

Since he wasn't about to comment on the latter and the former was Demyan's plan, he merely nodded.

"That's not a reasonable request," Fedir said forcefully.

"For you, we all know that is true. But Demyan is a different man. A *better* man, by your own admission."

Fedir scowled at his wife of more than three decades. "He is our son. How can you demand he sacrifice the rest of his life for the sake of this girl's feelings?"

"How can you ask him to sacrifice his personal integrity to save our country?" Oxana countered, deigning to look at Fedir.

"He is not being dishonest."

"Oh, so you've told Chanel about her inheritance?" Oxana asked Demyan.

But he knew she wasn't talking to him, not really, so he didn't answer with so much as a shake of his head.

"How do you know about it?" Fedir asked Oxana, with shock lacing his usually forceful tones.

"It is in the historical archives for anyone to read."

"Anyone with access to the private files."

"I am queen. I get access."

Fedir opened his mouth and then shut it again without a word being uttered, his face settling into a frown.

Oxana turned to face Demyan, effectively cutting Fedir out of the conversation. "Promise me one thing."

"Yes." He didn't have to ask what it was. He trusted Oxana in a way he didn't trust anyone besides Maks.

If she wanted a promise, he would give it to her.

"Don't tell this woman, Chanel Tanner, that you love her unless you mean it. Love isn't a bartering tool."

"She loves me." Chanel hadn't said so, but he was sure of it.

It's what he'd been working toward since he'd first walked into her office.

"No doubt. You are an eminently lovable man, but you owe it to her and to your own sense of honor not to lie about something so important."

"I never lied to you," Fedir inserted.

"Nothing has ever hurt as much as realizing Fedir had only said the words to convince me to give him the heir he needed for the throne."

"I did love you. I do love you."

Oxana spun to face her husband, but *not* her lover. "Like

a sister. The few times you shared my bed, you called out *her* name at the critical moment."

This was so much more than Demyan wanted to know, but he saw no way of extricating himself from the situation. He could walk out easily enough, but he wouldn't leave Oxana to face the aftereffects of the emotional bloodletting that had been decades in the making.

"You knew about Bhodana from the beginning."

"You told me you loved me. I thought that meant you were going to let her go."

"I never promised you that."

"No, you were very careful not to."

"Oxana."

She waved her hand, dismissing him and his words as she turned back to Demyan. "You promise me, be the better man. Do not make declarations you don't mean."

"You have my word."

"I look forward to meeting her."

"I didn't plan to bring her here before the wedding."

"You don't want to scare her away."

"No." Unlike many women, Chanel was less likely to marry a prince than a normal man. "I've taken great care not to frighten her off."

"Does she know the real you?" Oxana asked.

He thought about their time in bed, intimacy during which his plans flew straight to heaven in the face of his body's response to Chanel. He'd try to convince himself that it would only be the first time, but subsequent sessions of lovemaking had proven otherwise.

"Yes," Demyan said. "She may not realize it, but definitely."

"Then all will be well. She is marrying the man you are at your core, Demyan, my son, not your title or the corporate shark who runs our company's operations so efficiently."

He hoped once Chanel saw his true persona and position, she would agree with her future mother-in-law. It was the one element to his plan that he could not be absolutely sure about.

With another woman, maybe, but with Chanel…learning he was a de facto prince could turn her right off him.

Excited anticipation buzzed through Chanel as the limousine taking her to meet Demyan rolled through the wet streets of Seattle.

His flight had arrived that morning, but he'd had a full day of meetings. Thankfully he'd told her about them before she offered to take a vacation day to spend with him.

Needy much?

She cringed at how much she'd missed him and was fairly certain allowing him to see the extent of it might not be the best thing to do. Even someone as socially inept as Chanel realized that.

Still, it had been hard to play it cool and agree to let him send a driver for her without gushing over the idea of seeing him tonight and not having to wait until tomorrow.

They were attending an avant-garde live theater production downtown. No dinner. Demyan's schedule had not permitted.

Chanel was just glad he hadn't put off seeing her, but he'd seemed almost as eager to be with her as she felt about seeing him again. Considering the number of times their short phone call had been interrupted, she knew he'd had to force a slot into his schedule for her.

Knowing she was going to see him had made focusing on her work nearly impossible. Chanel had ended up taking the afternoon off and calling her sister for a last-minute shopping trip. Laura had helped Chanel pick out an outfit that was guaranteed to *drive the guy crazy*.

The sapphire-blue three-quarter-length-sleeve top was deceptively simple. With a scoop neckline outlined by a double line of black stitching and mock tuxedo tucking in the front, it was tailored in along her torso to emphasize her curves. The semi-transparent silk was worn over a bra in the same color. Not overtly slutty with the pleats in front, it still did a lovely job of highlighting Chanel's femininity.

The black silk trousers appeared conservative enough. Until she sat down, bent over or walked. Then the slit from midthigh to ankle hidden by the tuxedo stripe when she was standing gave intriguing glimpses of naked skin.

She'd never worn anything so revealing, but Laura insisted the peek-a-boo slit was interesting and not cheap. At the prices Chanel had paid for each piece of the outfit, she supposed *cheap* would not be a term that would ever apply to the clothing.

It had looked sophisticated in the boutique's full-length mirror, a little more scandalous in her own.

Laura had insisted on styling Chanel's ensemble as well, adding a demure rope of pearls knotted right below her breasts in an interesting juxtaposition that drew attention to the curves as effectively as the blue silk.

Her heels were strappy black sandals with what Laura called a *do-me-baby* heel. Chanel hadn't bothered to admonish her sister about the description.

She'd decided years ago that Laura was light-years ahead of Chanel in the girl-boy department. She didn't know if her baby sister was still a virgin like Chanel had been when she met Demyan, and honestly she had absolutely no desire to know.

The limousine slid to a halt and Chanel took a calming breath that did exactly no good.

She resisted the urge to pull at the carefully styled curls her sister had worked so hard to effect and waited for the driver to open the door.

It wasn't the chauffeur's hand reaching in to help her out of the limousine, though.

It was Demyan's, and his dark eyes glittered with lust as he took in her exposed thigh before meeting her gaze. "Hello, *sérdeńko*. I am very happy to see you."

She made no effort to stifle the smile that took over her features as she surged forward to exit the limo. If he hadn't been there with a steadying hand and then his arm around her waist, she would have fallen flat on her face.

But he *was* there and part of her heart was beginning to believe maybe he always would be.

He tucked her into his body protectively before leaning down to kiss her hello, right there in front of the crowd making their way into the theater.

She responded with more enthusiasm than probably was warranted, but he didn't seem to mind.

The kiss ended and he smiled down at her. "You look beautiful tonight. Very sexy."

"Laura played stylist."

"Your younger sister?"

"Yes. She's got even more acute fashion sense than Mom."

"Tell her I approve."

"She said you would."

His gaze skimmed her body. "Though I am not sure how I feel about everyone else seeing your body."

"They're just legs."

"Nice ones."

"It's the tae kwon do." Chanel's mother had heard somewhere that taking martial arts could improve Chanel's grace.

It hadn't done much for her poise and composure, but Chanel had discovered she *enjoyed* the classes. She'd insisted on continuing when her mother would have preferred she take a dance class.

Just one of many arguments between her and Beatrice during Chanel's formative years marked with parent-child acrimony.

"Then I am very grateful for your interest in Korean martial arts."

"You've never asked what color belt I am," she observed as he led her into the theater.

His thumb brushed up and down against her waist as if he couldn't help touching her. "What color?"

"Third-level black belt."

"Sixth-level black in judo," he said by way of reply.

"Want to spar?" she teased breathlessly.

The silk of her shirt transmitted the heat from his skin to hers and she wondered if she was the one who was going to end up teased to distraction by her outfit tonight.

"I spar with my cousin. I prefer less competitive physical pursuits with you."

She looked up into the side of his face, loving the line of his jaw, the way he held himself with such confidence. "Me, too."

He groaned.

"What?"

He stopped in the lobby and pulled her around so their gazes locked.

His was heated. "How can you ask what? You are dressed in a way guaranteed to keep my thoughts off the play and on what I plan to do to you once we get back to my condo."

CHAPTER SIX

HE SHOOK HIS HEAD as if trying to clear it. "What do you think has me groaning? It has been three nights."

She tried not to look as pleased as she felt, but was afraid she wasn't doing a very good job.

So she averted her head and met the envious gaze of another woman. Chanel ignored it, the envy having no power to pierce the bubble of happiness around her.

Demyan was with her and showed zero interest in being with, or even looking at, another woman.

She looked up at the sound of his laughter. He was watching her.

"I'm funny?" she asked.

"You are very pleased with yourself."

"I am happy with life, and you most of all," she offered.

She wasn't one to share her feelings easily, but Laura hadn't spent the afternoon just coaching Chanel on fashion choices. Her little sister had told Chanel that if she really liked this man, she needed to open up to him.

"You can't do that thing you do with Mom and Dad and everyone else besides me and Andrew," Laura had said.

Even though Chanel thought she knew, she'd asked, "What thing?"

"The way you hold the real you back so no one can hurt her."

"You're pretty insightful."

"For a teenager, you mean."

"For anyone." Their mother was nearly fifty and Beatrice had less understanding of her oldest daughter's nature.

Demyan's hand slid down her hip, his fingertips playing across her exposed flesh through the slit.

Chanel gasped and jerked away from the touch.

His look was predatory. "I don't like to be ignored."

"I wasn't ignoring you."

"You weren't thinking about me."

"How can you tell?"

"I know."

"You're arrogant."

"So you have said, but you know I do not agree."

And the more she knew of him, the less she believed the accusation herself. There was a very hard-to-detect strain of vulnerability running through the man at her side. You had to look very closely to see it, but she watched him with every bit of her formidable scientist's brain focused entirely on one thing. Deciphering the data that made up Demyan Zaretsky.

"I'm thinking about you now," she promised.

"I know."

She laughed, feeling a light airiness that buoyed her through the crowd.

"Demyan!" a feminine voice called.

There was no mistaking the way his body tensed at the sound, not with him so close to Chanel as they walked.

He was coiled tightly, even as he turned them toward the woman who had called his name, with one of those fake smiles Chanel hadn't seen since their very first dates on his face. "Madeleine."

Madeleine's fashion sense and poise was everything Chanel's mother wished for her daughter.

Unfortunately, Chanel refused to make it a mission in life to live up to such hopes. She'd learned too young that nothing she did would ever be enough; therefore, what would be the point in trying to be someone she was not?

Madeleine's blond hair probably wasn't natural, but there were no telltale indicators. She wore her Givenchy dress with supreme confidence, her accessories in perfect proportion to the designer ensemble.

Chanel couldn't tell the other woman's age by looking at her but guessed it was somewhere between thirty and a well-preserved forty-five.

The look she gave Demyan said *he* knew her age, intimately.

If this had happened a month ago, Chanel would have withdrawn into herself and given up the playing field.

But what she'd denied on their third date was a certainty now. She was head over heels in love with Demyan Zaretsky, though she hadn't had a chance to tell him yet. Wasn't sure exactly when she wanted to.

While he'd never said the words, either, he hinted at a future together almost every time she saw him.

That love and his commitment to their future gave her strength.

Drawing on a bit of her mother's aplomb, Chanel stepped forward and extended her hand. "Chanel Tanner. Are you an *old* friend of Demyan's?"

Madeleine didn't miss Chanel's slight emphasis on the word *old*, her eyes narrowing just slightly with anger but no righteous indignation. So, she was older than she looked.

"You could say that." Madeleine put her hand on Demyan's sleeve. "We know each other quite well, though I admit I *didn't* know he wore glasses."

Demyan adroitly stepped away from the touch while keeping a proprietary arm around Chanel. "Is your husband here tonight, Madeleine?"

Stress made Chanel's body rigid. Had Demyan and this woman had an affair? He'd said he didn't believe in infidelity.

Had he been lying?

"He couldn't get away from the Microsoft people. I'm quite on my own tonight." Madeleine smiled up at Demyan, her expression expectant.

It was clear she was angling for an invitation to join them, though Chanel wasn't sure how that was supposed to happen.

Their tickets had assigned seats.

Demyan ignored the hint completely. "The cost of being married to a man with his responsibilities."

The older woman frowned again, this time genuine anger lying right below the surface. "Does your little friend here know that? Or is she still in the honeymoon phase of believing you'll make her a priority in your life?"

"She is a priority." He pulled Chanel closer.

She didn't know if the move was a conscious one, but Madeleine noticed it, too.

That made Madeleine flinch and Chanel felt unexpected compassion well up inside her. "I'm sure you're a priority to your husband. He works to make a good life for you both."

That's what she remembered her father saying to her mother.

"I knew what I was getting when I married him." Madeleine gave a significant look to Demyan. "And what I was giving up. I liked my chances with Franklin better."

"He married you. You read the situation right." There was a message in Demyan's voice for the other woman.

He was telling her *he* wouldn't have married her, and her words had put Chanel's mind at rest about the affair. Oh, it was clear the two had shared a bed at one time, but it was equally obvious that circumstance had ended before Madeleine married Franklin.

"How long were you two together?" Chanel asked with her infamous lack of tact but no desire to pull the question back once it was uttered.

It might be awkward, but it struck her how very little she really knew about Demyan.

"Didn't he tell you about me?" Madeleine asked, her tone just this side of snide.

And still Chanel couldn't feel anything but pity for her. She didn't look happy with her choices in life.

"No."

The other woman didn't seem happy with the answer. Maybe Madeleine had thought she'd made a bigger impact on Demyan's life than she had. "You're a blunt one, aren't you? Did your mother teach you no tact?"

"To her eternal disappointment, no."

That brought an unexpected but small smile to Madeleine's lips.

Demyan leaned down and kissed Chanel's temple, no annoyance with her in his manner at all. "She is refreshingly direct," he said to Madeleine while looking at Chanel. "There is no artifice in her."

"So, she does not see the artifice in you," Madeleine opined, sounding sad rather than bitter.

"He holds things back," Chanel answered before Demyan could, but she did the older woman the courtesy of meeting her gaze to do so. "But if I know that, he's not hiding anything. I understand how hard it can be to share your true self with someone else."

"Heavens, don't you have *any* filters?" Madeleine demanded.

"No."

It was Demyan's turn to laugh, the sound genuine and apparently shocking to the other woman. Madeleine stared at him for a count of five full seconds, her mouth agape, her eyes widened comically.

Finally, she said, "I've never heard you make that sound."

"He's just laughing." Okay, so he didn't do it often, but the man had an undeniable sense of humor.

"*Just,* she says. This young thing really doesn't know you at all, does she?" Madeleine was the one looking with pity on Chanel now.

"It was a pleasure to run into you, but we need to find our seats. If you will excuse us," Demyan said, his tone brooking no obstacles and implying the exact opposite to his words.

Madeleine said nothing as they walked away.

When they reached their seats Chanel understood how the other woman had thought she might be included in their evening. Demyan had a box.

Although there was room for at least eight seats in it, there were only two burgundy-velvet-covered Queen Anne-style chairs. A small table with a bottle of champagne and two-person hors d'oeuvres tray stood between them.

Demyan led her to one of the seats, making sure she was comfortable before taking his own.

He looked out over the auditorium, stretching his long legs in front of him. "She's wrong, you know."

"Madeleine?"

"Yes."

"About what?"

He turned his head, looking at her in that way only he

had ever done. As if she was a woman worthy of intense desire, of inciting his lust. "You know the man at the base of my nature."

"I hardly know anything about you." The words came from the scientist's nature even as her heart knew he spoke the truth.

That man who lost his control when he tried so hard not to, that man was the real Demyan.

Demyan shook his head, his dark eyes glowing with sensual lights she now recognized very well. "You know the most personal things about me."

"So does she."

"No."

"You had sex with her." And even though she now knew that Madeleine hadn't been married at the time, Chanel realized it still bothered her a little.

She knew he'd been with other lovers. Probably lots of them, but she really didn't want to keep running into them.

"She never saw the more primal side of my nature. No other woman has seen it."

"You think I know you better than anyone else because you don't show absolute control in the bedroom?" It's what she'd thought only seconds before, but saying it aloud made the very concept seem unreal.

"Yes."

"I want to know about your past. Not names of every woman you've been with. I hope I never meet another one, but I don't know *anything* about you." Except that to him, she was special.

She kept that to herself. She wanted more.

"It's the future that counts between us."

"But without a connection to the past, there is no basis for understanding the future." Historians made that claim all the time and scientists knew it to be true as well, for different reasons.

"I thought scientists were all about progress."

"Building on the discoveries of the past."

"Not making something entirely new?"

"Nothing is new, just newly discovered."

"Like your sexy fashion sense?" he teased.

"That's all Laura."

"I don't see Laura here now."

"I'd like you to meet her." If they had a future, they had to share their present lives.

Even the less-than-pleasant bits, which meant he'd have to meet her mother and Perry, as well.

"I would enjoy that very much."

"You would?"

"Naturally. She is your sister."

"A part of my past."

"And your present and your future."

"Yes, so?" she prompted.

He gave her a wary look she didn't understand. "You want to meet my family?"

"Very much. Unless… Do you not get on?" Maybe his relationship with his parents was worse than hers with Beatrice and Perry.

"I get on very well with the aunt and uncle who raised me."

"What happened to your parents?"

"Ambition."

"I don't understand."

"They gave me to be raised by my aunt and uncle to feed their own ambition."

There had to be more to the story than that, but she understood this was something Demyan didn't share with everyone. "Do you ever see them?"

"My aunt and uncle? Often. In fact, that's where I spent the last three days."

"I thought it was business."

"I did not say that."

"You didn't say anything at all."

"You did not ask."

"Do I have the right to ask?"

"Absolutely."

That was definitive and welcome. "Okay."

"My parents come to family social occasions," he offered without making her ask again, proving he'd known what she meant the first time around.

"And?"

"They do not consider me their son."

"Or their beloved nephew."

"Not beloved anything." His expression relayed none of the hurt that must cause him.

"I am sorry."

"You don't have it much better with your mother and Perry."

"I'm not sure I have it better at all," she admitted.

"Your parents do not understand you."

"They don't approve of me. That's worse, believe me." It would have been so much easier for her if her mother and Perry simply found her an enigma.

Instead, they considered her a defective model that needed constant attempts at fixing.

"I approve of you completely."

"Thank you." She grinned at him, letting her love shine in her eyes. She had a feeling the words weren't far from her lips, either. "I approve of you, too."

"I am very glad to hear that." He picked up the champagne bottle and poured them each a glass.

"Why champagne?" she asked.

If it was his favored wine of choice, she wouldn't ask, but he'd shared with her he drank champagne on only very special occasions.

He handed her a glass. "I'm hoping to have something to celebrate in very short order."

Goose bumps broke out over Chanel's skin, her heart going into her throat. "Oh?"

He reached into his pocket and brandished a small box that was unmistakable in size and intent.

"Isn't this supposed to happen after a five-course dinner and roses, and..." Her breath ran out and so did Chanel's words.

"I am not a man who follows other people's dictated scripts."

She had no trouble believing that. "Just your own."

Something passed through his eyes, almost like guilt, but that didn't make any sense. He might be bossy outside the bedroom a bit, too, but it was nothing to feel guilty about.

Chanel was no shrinking violet that she couldn't stand up to him if need be.

He moved, and suddenly he was on one knee in front of her, the ring box open and in his palm. "Marry me, Chanel."

"You... I... This... How can you want... It's only been a month..."

"Is longer than three dates. I knew I wanted to marry you from the beginning." There could be no questioning the truth of that statement.

It was there in his eyes and voice. Nothing but honesty. He'd known he wanted her, had never wavered in that belief.

"What about love?"

"Do you love me?" he countered.

She nodded.

"Say it."

She glared. "You first."

"I may never say the words. You will have to accept that."

"If I want to marry you."

"Oh, you want to."

She did, but she didn't understand. "Why can't you say the words?"

"I can promise you fidelity and as good a life together as it is within my power to make for us. Is that not enough?"

The syntax change was odd and then she realized that as a native Ukrainian speaker, he was using the sentence structure of his first language. Did that mean he was nervous despite how calm and assured he appeared?

She looked at him closely and saw it, that small strain of vulnerability she knew he'd rather she never witnessed. "I do love you."

"And I will always honor that."

"I don't know."

He flinched, uncertainty showing in his expression for a brief moment before his face closed. "You need time to consider it. I understand."

He stood up, pocketing the ring. "Lights will be going down momentarily for the play."

The gulf between them was huge, but she didn't know what to do to bridge it. She couldn't say *yes* right then. She didn't know if it was enough to never hear the words. Did not saying them mean he didn't feel the sentiment?

Maybe if he'd tell her *why* he couldn't say them, but clearly he didn't want to.

Still. He wanted to marry her. "Tell me why."

"Why, what?"

Was he playing dense, or did he really not know? "Why you won't say the words."

"I made a promise."

"To who?"

"The mother of my heart."

Chanel tried to understand. "She doesn't want you to get married?"

"Of course she does. She's very eager to meet you."

"But she doesn't want you to love me?" That didn't sound promising.

"She does not want me to use the words to convince you to marry me. It must be your decision entirely."

"Is this a Ukrainian thing?"

"We are not Ukrainian. We are Volyarussian."

Unlike their Ukrainian brothers, the Volyarussians had not been subject to Russian rule and loss of identity. Their ties to the old ways of doing and thinking from their original homeland were probably stronger than in the current Ukraine, but she understood what he was saying.

"Okay, a Volyarussian thing."

"It is a Yurkovich family thing."

"Your last name is Zaretsky."

"My parents never gave up legal rights."

"You could change your name now." He was an adult. There was nothing stopping him.

He jolted as if the idea had never occurred to him. Then he smiled. "Yes, I could."

"Maybe you should."

"Maybe if you agree to share it, I will change my last name to the one of my heart."

Those words played through Chanel's mind as the lights dimmed and the play began. She couldn't follow what was happening on the stage; she was too busy trying to figure out what was going on in Demyan's mind.

He'd asked her to marry him. He'd as good as told her he planned to, but she hadn't let herself believe.

She cast one of many glances in his direction, but his attention seemed riveted by the performance. He'd backed off so quickly, given up so easily.

That wasn't in character for him. Her certainty on that matter pulled her thoughts short. She'd claimed not to know him. He'd said she knew the man he was at his most basic nature. And she'd taken that to mean sexually.

But the truth was she knew him well in a lot of areas. He was a man driven by his own agenda, even ruthless in achieving it. The way he brought her pleasure, withholding both hers and his own until they'd reached *the* place indicated as much.

Demyan didn't give up easily, either. He pushed for what he wanted. Like convincing her to try making love while her hands were tied with silk scarves. She'd been leery and unwilling to do it, but he'd convinced her.

And it had been amazing.

Which begged the question: Did he not want her badly enough to fight, or was he sitting in that chair right now plotting how to get her while pretending to watch the actors on the stage?

She was pretty sure she knew the answer and it wasn't a disheartening one, though it was kind of alarming.

He was plotting, but she *wasn't* ready to give him an answer. Which meant she had to orchestrate a preemptive strike to prevent whatever it was he was planning. Probably to make love to her until she was an amenable pile of happy goo who would say *yes* to anything.

Not letting herself think about it too long and lose her nerve, Chanel scooted off her chair and onto the floor. Demyan's head snapped sideways so he could see her, proving he was highly attuned to what she was doing.

Definitely plotting.

"What are you doing?" he whisper-demanded.

She knee-walked the couple of feet between her chair and his. "You know, you could have opted for a more romantic setting. This would be easier if you'd had a settee brought in."

He stared at her, shock showing with flattering lack of artifice on every line of his handsome face. "What?"

"This." She reached for his belt.

He grabbed her wrist. "What are you doing?"

"You're repeating yourself and I would have thought it was obvious."

"Here?" he demanded, not sounding like himself at all. She liked that. Very much.

In answer, she tugged her wrist free so she could undo the buckle on his belt. Once it was apart, she unbuttoned the waistband and then slowly and, as quietly as she could, she began to lower the zipper on his trousers in the darkened theater box.

No one could see her, though there were literally hundreds of people mere feet away.

The backs of her fingers brushed over an already erect shaft and a small laugh huffed out of her.

"What is funny?"

"I was wrong."

"About?"

"I thought you were over here plotting, but the truth is, you were thinking about sex, weren't you?"

"Yes."

"Or were they one and the same?" she asked, realizing belatedly the one did not necessarily preclude the other.

He didn't answer, which was answer enough.

"We've done a lot of things."

His head nodded in a jerky motion.

"But not this."

"No."

"Why?"

"I did not know if you wanted to."

"You decided I wanted a lot of other things I wasn't sure about."

"This is different."

Maybe it was. Maybe this had to come at her instigation. "This is me, instigating."

"I do not understand."

She smiled at the confusion in his tone. "Here I thought you could read my mind."

"Not even I can do that."

Not *even* him. She almost laughed. "But you're not arrogant."

CHAPTER SEVEN

"CONFIDENT. NOT THE SAME." His words came out gritty and chopped, not at all like him.

Understandable and welcome in the circumstances.

"No, maybe it's not." She worked his hot shaft out through the slit in his boxers, thankful they were made from stretchy fabric. "I've never done this before."

"Do whatever you want. I promise to enjoy it."

She smiled. She believed him. There was one area of their relationship she was absolutely certain about and that was the amount of pleasure he took from their physical intimacy.

The man could not get enough of her.

So she didn't let herself worry if she was doing it right when she bent forward and licked around the head of his erection. It was wide and she knew she'd have to stretch her lips to get him inside. No way was much of him going to fit into her mouth, though.

She didn't worry about that right now, but concentrated on enjoying the taste of him. It was salty and kind of bitter, but sort of sweet, too. His skin was warm and clean and hot against her lips and tongue.

She liked it. A lot.

He didn't try to rush her, though a steady stream of pre-ejaculate was now weeping from his slit and his thighs were rock-rigid with tension. She jacked the bulk of his shaft with her hands while sucking on the end.

He made small, nearly nonexistent noises, letting her know he was enjoying this as much, or more, than she was.

Suddenly he grabbed her head and pulled it back, messing up the curls Laura had taken such effort to tame. "You have to stop."

"No."

"I'm going to come," he said fiercely.

"That's the point," she whispered back.

He shook his head. "You're not swallowing your first time. You don't know if you'll like it."

"You're being bossy again and this is not the bedroom."

Ignoring her less-than-stern admonition, he pulled her into his lap, maneuvering her so she could continue to touch him. Then he handed her a napkin from the table.

She grinned and almost asked what it was for to tease him, but the light in his eyes had gone feral. And really, she wasn't looking to get arrested for public indecency, which might well happen if his control slipped his leash completely.

So she finished him with her hand, catching his ejaculate with the napkin and his shout with a passionate kiss.

When he was done, he slumped in the chair, though his hold on her remained tight. "You did that on purpose."

"To give you pleasure?"

"That, too."

She snuggled into him. "I'm not giving you an answer tonight."

"Okay."

"Really?" She kissed under his chin, a little startled by the reality of his suit and tie still pristinely in place.

"Yes, but that will not stop me taking you back to my condo and showing you what our married life will be like."

"I've got no doubts about the great sex."

"We will make sure of that by morning."

"Should I call in at work tomorrow?" She didn't want to try to do the complicated calculations for their current phase on no sleep.

And the look in his dark eyes said while she might get to know his bed very well, she wasn't going to be doing a lot of resting there.

"I think perhaps you should."

She did. In the early hours of the morning after he made love to her through the night in his condo that turned out to be a penthouse taking up the entire top floor of one of the more historic Seattle buildings.

Demyan woke her with kisses and caresses a few hours later.

Their lovemaking was slow and almost torturous in its intensity. He seemed set on proving something to her, but Chanel wasn't convinced it was what she needed to know to agree to marry him.

When she was once again sated and relaxed, he informed her he'd called her sister and arranged to invite Chanel's entire family, including Andrew, whom he was flying up for the weekend in his private jet, for dinner the following evening.

"My parents are coming here?" Postcoital bliss evaporated like water pooled on a rock in the desert as she jumped out of his king-size bed and started pacing the darkly masculine bedroom. *"Tomorrow?"*

"Yes."

"Didn't you think you should ask me first?" she demanded.

Looking smug and certain of his answer, he said, "You were asleep."

"You could have waited until I woke up."

"I was bored."

"Right. And you had nothing else to occupy your time but calling my sister. How did you even get her number?" Had he gone snooping through her phone?

He averted his gaze without answering.

She sighed. "You got sneaky and underhanded, didn't you?"

It wasn't exactly a challenging conclusion to draw. As if there was any other way to get her sister's private cell number without waking and asking Chanel.

"The prospect does not make you angry?" he asked with a cautious look.

Nonplussed, she stared at him. "You aren't worried about how annoyed I am that you made plans with my family, just how irritated I am about your method for getting my sister's number?"

He shrugged.

"News flash—I find it a lot less upsetting that you scrolled through my phone's contacts while I was sleeping than the fact you used said contacts to set up a dinner with my family." She shook her head. "Well, this ought to be interesting."

With that, she went into the bathroom for a shower. It was her turn to lock the door.

Being the sneaky, underhanded guy he was, Demyan found his way inside regardless. Chanel hadn't expected anything else.

So she didn't jump when his hand landed on her hip and his big body added to the heat behind her from the shower. "You told me you wanted me to meet your family."

"I said my sister," Chanel gritted out.

The man was far too intelligent not to have made the distinction.

He turned her in his arms, his expression more amused than concerned. "You know I will have to meet all of them eventually. Why not now?"

"Because I'm not ready!" She made no effort to control her volume, but she wasn't a yeller by nature, so the words came out sounding only about half as vehement as they did in her head.

The argument might have escalated, but he had the kissing-to-end-conflict technique down to a fine art.

They made love, moving together under the cascading water, his body behind hers, his arms wrapped around her so his hands could reach her most sensitive places.

As he brought her the ultimate in pleasure, he promised, "It will be all right, *sérdeńko.*"

She desperately wanted to believe him, but a lifetime of experience had taught her otherwise. "You'll see me through their eyes."

"Or I will teach them to see you through mine."

Maybe, just maybe, his supreme self-confidence would guide his interactions with her family down that path.

She could hope.

The following night, her entire family showed up at Demyan's condo right on time.

Chanel was so happy to see Andrew and Laura that her stress at seeing her mother and stepfather didn't reach its usual critical levels instantly. That might also be attributed to the way Demyan kept one comforting arm around her throughout introductions and the launch into the usual small talk.

He'd brought in catering with servers so Chanel didn't have to cook or play hostess getting drinks. Somehow he'd known that those domestic social niceties had always been a source of criticism and failure with her family in the past.

She hadn't invited her parents to her apartment since moving out as a fresh-faced nineteen-year-old. Chanel had thought that having her own place would make a difference in how Beatrice and Perry responded to her efforts at cooking.

She'd learned differently quickly enough when they'd made it clear she fell short in every hosting department. The meal was too simple, the drinks offered too narrow in choice and even her bright stoneware dishes from a chain department store were considered inferior.

As could be inferred by her mother's gift of appropriate understated chinaware on Chanel's next birthday. She'd donated it to Goodwill and continued using her much less expensive, bright and cheerful dishes.

Since then, Chanel had assiduously avoided her mother's inferences and even direct suggestions that Chanel might like to host one of the smaller family get-togethers over the years. In the ten years since that first debacle, Chanel had made sure there were no situations in which she'd have to invite her mother or stepfather into her home for so much as a drink of water.

Perry was clearly impressed by Demyan as a host, though, the older man's expression shining with approval over the high-end penthouse and being offered his highball by a black-clad server.

Demyan kept them occupied with small talk, redirecting the conversation any time it looked like it would go into the familiar *let's-criticize-Chanel* direction. He was also overtly approving, verbalizing his appreciation for Chanel in ways that could not be mistaken or overlooked by her parents.

His protective behavior touched her deeply and Chanel found herself relaxing with her family in a way she could not remember doing in years.

"So, you work for Yurkovich Tanner?" Perry asked Demyan over dinner.

"I do."

Chanel added, "In the corporate offices."

A vague answer never satisfied her stepfather and she wasn't sure her addition would, either, but she could hope. She didn't want to spend the rest of the evening listening to Perry grill Demyan about his connections and job prospects.

She realized moments later that she needn't have worried.

Demyan adroitly evaded each sally until Perry gave up with a rather confused-sounding "Well, maybe you can put a good word in for Andrew. I tried contacting them on his behalf, you know, because of Andrew's connection to one of the original founders."

Andrew wasn't the one connected to Bartholomew Tanner. That was Chanel and her connection was tenuous at best, but trust Perry to dismiss her blood relationship to the founder and receipt of a Tanner Yurkovich university scholarship as unimportant altogether.

"I haven't heard back." Perry shrugged. "It was a long shot, but business is all about contacts."

Demyan nodded and then looked away from Perry to smile at Chanel. "I'm always happy to put a good word in for family."

Oh, the fiend. Chanel kicked Demyan's ankle under the table, but he didn't even have the courtesy to flinch.

So, that's why the dinner tonight. He'd said he was okay with waiting for her answer on his proposal, but really he had every intention of getting her family on his side. He had to realize it wouldn't take much.

Beatrice Saltzman had given up hope her oldest daughter would ever marry, and had never had any that it would be advantageously. She would be Demyan's biggest supporter once she realized the plans he wanted to make.

Chanel was going to kill him later, but right now she had to deal with the fallout of his implication.

It wasn't her mother or Perry who picked up on it, either. They wouldn't

"You're getting married?" Laura gasped, her eyes shining. She grinned at Chanel. "I told you that outfit was going to hook him."

"I wasn't looking to *hook* anybody. We're not engaged."

"But I have asked Chanel to marry me."

Chanel's mother stared at her agape. "And you haven't said *yes?* No, of course you haven't." She shook her head like she couldn't expect anything else from her socially awkward eldest.

"I'm thinking about it." Chanel glared daggers at Demyan, but he smiled back with a shark's smile she was now convinced was *not* her imagination.

"Don't think too long. He's likely to withdraw the offer," Perry advised in serious, almost concerned tones. "You're not likely to do better."

"It's not a business deal." Chanel ground out the words, refusing to be hurt by her stepfather's observation.

Because it was true. She couldn't imagine anyone *better* than Demyan ever coming into her life, but that wasn't what was holding her back, was it?

"No, it's not," Andrew chimed in, giving his dad a fierce scowl. "Leave her alone about it. Demyan would be damn lucky to have Chanel for a wife and he's obviously smart enough to realize it."

Their mom tut-tutted about swearing, but Andrew ignored her and Chanel just gave her little brother a grateful smile. He and Laura had never taken after their parents' dim view of Chanel. Their extended family, other friends and colleagues of the Saltzmans might, but not her siblings.

For that, Chanel had always been extremely thankful. Because she loved Andrew and Laura to bits.

Instead of looking annoyed by Andrew taking Chanel's part, Demyan gave him an approving glance before turning a truly chilling one on Perry. "Neither of us is likely to do better, hence my proposal."

"Well, of course," Perry blustered, but no question—he realized he'd erred with his words.

Chanel wanted to agree to marry Demyan right then, but she couldn't. There was too much at stake.

Chanel was sitting down to watch an old-movie marathon on A&E when her doorbell rang the next evening.

She'd turned down Demyan's offer of dinner and a night in at the penthouse, telling him she wanted some time alone to think.

He hadn't been happy, insisting she could think as easily in his company as out of it. Knowing that for the fallacy it was, she'd refused to budge. No matter how many different arguments he brought to bear.

Chanel had taken the fact she'd gotten her way as proof she could withstand even the more forceful side of his personality. *And* that he respected her enough to accede to her wishes when he knew she was serious about them.

If he was the one ringing the bell, both suppositions would be faulty and that might be the answer she needed.

As painful as it might be to utter.

It wasn't Demyan through the peephole, though. It was Chanel's mom.

Stunned, Chanel opened the door. "Mother. What are you doing here?"

"I wanted to talk to you. May I come in?"

Chanel stepped back and watched with some bemusement as her mother entered her apartment for the first time since she'd moved in years ago.

Beatrice sat down on the sofa, carefully adjusting the skirt of her Vera Wang suit as she did so. "Close the door, Chanel. The temperature has dropped outside."

"Would you like something to drink?" Chanel asked as she obeyed her mother's directive and then hovered by the door, unsure what to do with herself.

"No, thank you." With a slight wave of her hand toward the other end of the sofa she indicated Chanel should sit down. "I... You seemed uncertain about your relationship with Demyan last night. I thought you might want to talk about it."

"To you?" Chanel asked with disbelief as she settled into her seat.

Her mother grimaced, but nodded. "Yes. I may not have been the best one these past years, but I am your mom."

"And he's rich." His penthouse showed that even to someone as oblivious as Chanel could be. Beatrice would have noticed and probably done a fair guesstimate of Demyan's yearly income off it.

"That's not why I'm here."

"He has corporate connections Perry and Andrew might find useful, too. I suppose that might carry even more weight with you." After all, scientists could be rich, but Beatrice had never made any bones about not wanting another one in the family.

Her mom sighed. "I am not here on behalf of your brother or my husband, either."

"You're here for my sake," Chanel supplied with full-on sarcasm.

But her mother nodded, her expression oddly vulnerable and sincere. "Yes, I am. The way you two are together. It's special, Chanel, and I don't want you to miss that."

"We've only been dating a month," Chanel said, shocking herself and voicing her biggest concern.

Beatrice nodded, as if she understood completely. "That's the way it was for me and your dad. We knew the first time we met that we would be together for the rest of our lives."

"You stopped loving him." What would Chanel do if Demyan stopped wanting her?

Her mother's eyes blazed with more emotion than Chanel could ever remember seeing in them. "I never did."

"But you said…" Pain lanced through Chanel as her voice trailed off.

There were too many examples to pick only one.

"He was *it* for me."

"You married Perry."

"I needed someone after Jacob died."

"You had me. You promised we would always be a team." That broken promise had hurt worst of all.

"It was too hard. You were too much like him. I tried to make you different, but you refused to change." Her mother sighed, looking almost defeated. "You are so stubborn. Just like him."

For the first time, Chanel heard the pain in those words her mother had never expressed.

Some truths were just as hurtful to her. "Perry hates me."

"He's a very jealous man."

"He wasn't jealous of me. You weren't affectionate enough to me to make him jealous."

Sadness filled Beatrice's eyes. "No, I haven't been. He was jealous of Jacob."

"Because you never stopped loving him." Despite all evidence to the contrary.

"How do you stop loving the other half of your soul?"

Finally Chanel understood a part of her childhood she'd always been mystified by. She'd tried with Perry at first. Really tried. "Perry blamed me. He took his jealousy out on me."

"Your father wasn't around to punish."

"You let him."

Beatrice looked away and shrugged. As if it didn't matter. As if all that pain was okay to visit on a child.

"You let him," Chanel said again. "You knew and you let him hate me in effigy of my father."

Her mom's head snapped back around, her expression dismissive. "He doesn't hate you. He wanted you to be the best and all you wanted was your books and science."

"It's what I love. Didn't that ever matter to you?"

"Of course it mattered!" Beatrice jumped up, showing an unfamiliar agitation. "Science stole your father from me. Do you for one second believe I wanted it to take you, too?"

"So, you pushed me away instead."

"That wasn't my intention."

"I don't fit with the Saltzmans."

Beatrice didn't deny it, but she didn't agree either. Should Chanel be thankful for small mercies?

"I did fit with the Tanners."

"Too well, but they're all gone, Chanel. Can't you see that?"

"And you think I'll die young like Dad did because of my love for science?"

"You're too much a Tanner. You take risks."

"I don't!" She'd been impacted by the way her father and grandfather had died, too. "I'm very careful."

"If you are, then I've succeeded a little, anyway."

"You succeeded, all right. You succeeded in picking away at our relationship until there wasn't one anymore." Chanel nearly choked on the words, but she wouldn't hold them back anymore. "You couldn't handle how much having me around reminded you of Dad, so you pushed me away with both hands."

"And now you can barely bring yourself to see me even once a month."

"Visits with you are too demoralizing."

"Your sister and brother see you more often."

Even Andrew. He was away at university, but Chanel went to visit her brother at least once a term. She always made sure she got time with him when he was home. While she'd done her best to nurture her relationships with her siblings, Chanel had avoided her mother with the skill of a trained stunt driver.

"You have your sister date with Laura every week, but somehow you manage to avoid seeing me or Perry."

"Can you blame me?" Chanel demanded and then shook her head. "It doesn't matter if you do, or don't. I know whose fault it is we don't have a relationship and it's *not* mine."

Finally, she truly understood that. It wasn't that Chanel wasn't lovable. Unless she'd been willing to become a completely different person, with none of her father's passions, mannerisms or even affections, Chanel had been destined to be the brunt of both her mother's grief and Perry's jealousy.

There was no way she could be smart enough, well behaved enough or even pretty enough to earn their approval.

Not with hair the same color as her dad's and eyes so like his, too. Not with a jaw every Tanner seemed to be born with and her bone-deep desire to grow up and be a scientist.

Beatrice's eyes filled with grief that slowly morphed into resolution. "No, it's not. You deserved better than either Perry or I have given you. You deserve to be loved for yourself and by someone who isn't wishing every minute in your company you would move just a little differently, speak with less scientific jargon..."

"Just be someone other than who I am."

"Yes. You deserve that." Her mom's voice rang with a loving sincerity Chanel hadn't heard in it since she was eight years old and a broken vulnerability she *never* had. "That's why I'm urging you with everything in me not to push Demyan away because how you feel about him scares you. I wouldn't trade the years I had with your father for anything in the world, not even a life without the constant pain of grief that never leaves."

"You think Demyan loves me like Dad loved you?"

"He must." In a completely uncharacteristic gesture, Beatrice reached out and took both Chanel's hands in her own. "Sweetheart, a man like that, he doesn't offer you marriage when he could have you in his bed without it, not unless he wants all of you, but especially the life you can have together."

Her mother hadn't called her sweetheart in so long that Chanel had to take a couple of deep breaths to push back the emotion the endearment caused. "He's really possessive."

And bossy in bed, but she wasn't going to share that tidbit with her mom.

"He needs you. For a man to need that deeply, it's frightening for him. It makes him hold on tighter."

"Did Dad hold on tight?"

"Oh, yes."

Chanel had a hard time picturing it. "Like Perry?"

"Nothing like Perry. Jacob wasn't petty. Ever. He wasn't jealous. He trusted me and my love completely, but he held on tight. He wanted every minute with me he could get."

"He still followed his passion for science."

"Yes. I used to love him for it."

"You grew to hate him, though, didn't you?" That made so much sense.

Chanel hadn't just spent her childhood as scapegoat to Perry for a man who couldn't be reached in death. Her mom had punished her for being too like her father, too.

"I did." Tears welled and spilled over in Beatrice's eyes. "I betrayed our love by learning to hate him for leaving me."

Chanel didn't know what to do. Not only had she not seen her mother cry since the funeral, but they didn't have the kind of relationship that allowed her to offer comfort.

"He doesn't blame you." Chanel knew that with every fiber of her being. Her dad's love for her mom had had no limits.

"For hating him? I'm sure you're right. He loved so purely. But if he were here now to see the damage I've done to you, to our bond as a family, he'd be furious. He *would* hate me, too."

CHAPTER EIGHT

CHANEL COULDN'T RESPOND.

Her throat was too tight with tears she didn't want to shed, but her mom was probably right.

Jacob Tanner had loved his daughter with the same deep, abiding emotion he'd given his wife. He'd expected a different kind of best from both of them than Perry ever had.

The good kind. The human kindness kind.

Beatrice sighed and swiped at the tears on her cheek, not even looking around for a tissue to do it properly. "I wish I could say I would do it all differently if I could."

"You can't?" Chanel asked, surprised at how much that hurt.

"As I have grown older and watched your brother and sister mature, had the opportunity to observe the way you are with them, it's opened my eyes to many things. I have come to realize just how weak a person I am."

"If you see a problem you have the power to fix and do nothing to change it, then yes, I think that does make you weak."

"So pragmatic. Your father would have said the same thing, but you both would have assumed I had the power to change myself. If I did, do you think I would have worked so hard at changing you?"

"So, that's it? Things go on like always?"

"No," Beatrice uttered with vehement urgency. "If you'll give me another chance, I will do better now."

"So, you *have* changed." Could Chanel believe her?

"I've acknowledged the true cost of my weakness. The love and respect of my daughter. It's too much."

"I don't know if I can ever trust you to love me."

"I understand that and I don't expect weekly mother-daughter dates."

"I don't have time." Chanel realized how harsh that sounded after she said the words, and she winced.

Her mom gave her a wry smile. "Your time is spoken for, but maybe we could try for more often than once every couple of months."

"Let's see if we can make those visits more pleasant before we start making plans for more." Words were all well and good, but Chanel had two decades of her mother's criticisms and rejections echoing in her memories.

Beatrice nodded and then she did yet another out-of-character gesture, opening her arms for a hug. When Chanel didn't immediately move forward to accept, her mother took the initiative.

Chanel responded with their normal barely touching embrace, but her mom pulled her close in a cloud of her favorite Chanel No. 5 perfume and hugged her tight. "I love you, Chanel, and I'm very proud of the woman you've become. I'm so very, very sorry I wasn't a better mother."

Chanel sat in stunned silence for several seconds before returning the embrace.

"You don't think I'm too awkward and geeky for Demyan?" she asked against her mother's neck.

Still not ready to see the older woman's expression in case it wasn't kind.

But Beatrice moved back, forcing Chanel to meet her

eyes. "You listen to me, daughter. You are more than enough for that man. You are *all* that he needs. Now *you* need to believe that if you're going to be happy with him."

"It's only been a month, Mom."

"Your dad proposed on our third date."

The synergy of that took Chanel's breath away. Demyan hadn't proposed on their third date, but he'd told her then that they were starting something lifelong, not temporary. "I thought you got married because you were pregnant with me."

"I was pregnant, yes, but we'd already planned to get married. Only, our original plan was to do it after he finished his degree."

"You said…"

"A lot of stupid things."

Chanel's mouth dropped open in shock at her mother's blunt admission.

Beatrice gave a watery laugh. "Close your mouth. You'll catch flies."

"I love you, too, Mom."

"Thank you. That means more than you'll ever know. I know I don't deserve it."

"I didn't say I liked you," Chanel offered with her usual frankness and for once didn't regret it.

Their relationship was going to work only if they moved through the pain, not try to bury it.

"You will, sweetheart. You loved your daddy, but I was your favorite person the first eight years of your life."

"I don't remember." She didn't say it to belabor the point. She just didn't.

"You will. I'm stubborn, too. You didn't get it all from Jacob."

"What about Perry?"

"I'll talk to him. I guess I never realized how bad it was

in your mind between you. He really doesn't hate you. He's even told me he admires you."

Chanel made a disbelieving sound.

"It's true. You're brilliant in your field. I think it intimidates him. He's a strong businessman, but if he had your brains he'd be in Demyan's position."

With a penthouse with a view of the harbor? Her parents lived in the suburbs and she couldn't imagine them wanting anything different.

Her mother left soon thereafter, once she'd promised again to change and make sure Perry knew he had to alter the way he interacted with Chanel, too.

No one could have been more shocked than Chanel when she got a call from the man himself later that night. He apologized and admitted he'd thought she had always compared him unfavorably to her dad, just like her mom did.

Chanel didn't try to make him feel better. Perry did compare unfavorably with Jacob Tanner. Her dad had been a much kinder and loving father, but Chanel agreed to try to let the past go if the future was different.

How had Demyan affected such change in her life in so little time? She wasn't going to kid herself and try to say it was anything else, either.

Somehow Demyan had blown into her life and set it on a different path, one in which she didn't have to be lonely or rejected anymore.

If she could let herself trust him and the love she felt for him, the rest of her life could and would be different, too.

She picked up the phone and called him.

"Missing me, little one?" he asked without a greeting.

"Yes." There was a wealth of meaning in that one word, if he wanted to hear it.

"*Yes* as in yes, you miss me, or *yes* as in you will marry me?" he asked, sounding hopeful but cautious.

"Both."

"I will be there in ten minutes."

It was a half-hour drive from his penthouse, but she didn't argue.

Demyan knocked on Chanel's door with a minute to spare in the ten he'd promised her.

What he hadn't told her when she called was that he was already in the area.

The door swung open, and Chanel's eyes widened with disbelief. "How did you get here so fast?"

"I was already on the road." Had been for the better part of an hour, driving aimlessly, with each random turn taking him closer and closer to her apartment complex.

She frowned. "On your way here?"

"Not consciously." He'd argued with himself about the wisdom of calling or stopping by after she'd told him she wanted the night to think.

So far, respecting her wishes had been winning his internal debate.

"Then what were you doing over here?"

He gently pushed past her, not interested in having this discussion, or any other, on the stoop outside her door. "I was out for a drive."

"On this side of town?" she asked skeptically.

"Yes."

"But you weren't planning to come by."

"No." And that choice had clearly been the right one, though more difficult to follow through on than he wanted to admit.

"Do you go out for drives with no purpose often?" she asked, still sounding disbelieving.

"Not as such, no." He went through to the kitchen, where he poured himself two fingers of Volyarussian vodka before drinking half of it in two swallows.

He'd brought the bottle with him one night, telling her that sometimes he enjoyed a shot to unwind. She'd told him he could keep it in the freezer if he liked.

He did, though he rarely drank from it.

"Are you okay, Demyan?" she asked from the open archway between her living room and kitchen. "I thought you'd be happy."

"I didn't like the emptiness of my condo tonight." He should have found the lack of company peaceful.

A respite.

He hadn't. He'd become too accustomed to her presence in the evenings. Even when she only sat curled up with one of her never-ending scientific journals while he answered email, having her there was *pleasant*.

Had almost become necessary.

"I missed you, too."

"You wanted your space. To think," he reminded her, the planning side of his facile brain yelling at him that his reaction wasn't doing his agenda any favors.

"It was fruitful. Or have you forgotten what I told you on the phone?"

He slammed the drink onto the counter, clear liquid splashing over the sides, the smell of vodka wafting up. "I have not forgotten."

Her gray eyes flared at his action, but she didn't look worried. "And you're happy?"

"Ecstatic."

"You look it." The words were sarcastic, but an understanding light glowed in her lovely eyes.

"You are a *permanent fixture* in my life. It is only natural I would come to rely on your companionship to a certain extent." He tried to explain away his inability to remain in his empty apartment and work, as he'd planned to.

A small smile played around her mobile lips. "So, you considered me a permanent fixture before I agreed to marry you?"

"Yes." He was not in the habit of losing what he went after.

"I see. I wasn't nearly so confident, but I missed you like crazy when you were in Volyarus."

"And yet you refused my proposal at first."

"I didn't. I told you I had to think."

"That is not agreement."

"Life is not that black-and-white."

"Isn't it?"

"No." She moved right into his personal space. "I think you're even more freaked out by how fast everything has gone between us than I am."

"I am not." It had all been part of his plan, everything except this inexplicable reaction to her request for time away from him.

"You're acting freaked. Slamming back vodka and driving around like a teenager with his first car."

"I assure you, I did not peel rubber at any stoplights."

"Do teens still do that?"

"Some." He never had.

It would have not been fitting for a prince.

"I said yes, Demyan." She laid her hands on his chest, her eyes soft with emotion.

His arms automatically went around her, locking her into his embrace. "Why?"

Her agreement should have been enough, but he needed to know.

"My mom came by to talk. She told me not to give up on something this powerful just because it scares me."

"Your mother?" he asked, finding that one hard to take in.

"Yes. She wants to try again, on our relationship."

"She does realize you are twenty-nine, not nineteen?"

Chanel smiled, sadness and hope both lurking in the storm-cloud depths of her eyes. "We both do. It's not happy families all of a sudden, but I'm willing to meet her partway."

"You're a more forgiving person than I am."

"I'm not so sure about that, but one thing I do know. Holding bitterness and anger inside hurts me more than anyone who has ever hurt me."

A cold wind blew across his soul. Demyan hoped she remembered that if she ever found out the truth about her great-great-grandfather's will.

She frowned up at him. "You were driving without your glasses?"

"I don't need them to drive." He didn't need them at all but wasn't sure when he was going to break that news to her.

"You always wear them, except in bed."

"They're not that corrective." Were in fact just clear plastic.

"They're a crutch for you," she said with that analytical look she got sometimes.

"You could say that."

"Do you need them at all?"

He didn't even consider lying in answer to the direct question. "No."

He expected anger, or at least the question, *why did he wear them?* But instead he got a measured glance that implied understanding, which confused him. "If I can step off the precipice and agree to marry you, you can stop wearing the glasses."

The tumblers clicked into place. She saw the glasses

as the crutch she'd named them for him. Being who she was, it never occurred to her that they were more a prop.

"Fine." More than. Remembering them was a pain.

She grinned up at him and he found himself returning the expression with interest, a strange, tight but not unpleasant feeling in his chest.

"Want to celebrate getting engaged?" she asked with an exaggerated flutter of her eyelashes.

The urge to tease came out of nowhere, but he went with it. "You want a shot of my vodka?"

He liked the man he became in this woman's presence.

"I was thinking something more *mind-blowing* and less about imbibing and more about experiencing." She drew out the last word as she ran her fingertip across his lips, down his face and neck and on downward over his chest, until she stopped with it hovering right over his nipple.

He tugged her closer, his body reacting as it always did to her nearness. "I'm all about the experience."

"Are you?" she asked.

He sighed and admitted, "Not usually, no. My position consumes my life."

"Not anymore."

"No, not anymore." He hadn't planned it this way, but marrying Chanel Tanner was going to change everything.

He could feel it with the same sense of inevitability he'd had the first time he'd seen her picture in his uncle's study. Only now he knew marrying her wasn't going to be a temporary action to effect a permanent fix for his country.

And he was glad. The sex *was* mind-blowing, but that didn't shock him as much as it did her. What *he* hadn't anticipated was that her company would be just as satisfying to him, even when it came without the cataclysm of climax.

Right now, though? He planned to have both.

* * *

Chanel adjusted her seat belt, the physical restraint doing nothing to dispel the sense of unreality infusing her being.

Once she'd agreed to marry Demyan, he'd lost no time setting the date, a mere six weeks from the night of their engagement. He'd told her that his aunt wanted to plan the wedding.

Chanel, who was one of the few little girls in her class at school who had not spent her childhood dreaming of the perfect wedding, was eminently happy to have someone else liaise and plan with her mother. Beatrice was determined to turn the rushed wedding into a major social event.

And the less Chanel had to participate in that, the better. If she could have convinced Demyan to elope, she would have, but he had this weird idea that she *deserved* a real wedding.

Since she'd made it clear how very much she *didn't* want to be the center of attention in a big production like the type of wedding her mother would insist on, Chanel had drawn the conclusion the wedding was important to Demyan.

So, she gave in, both shocked and delighted to learn that her mom had agreed to have the wedding take place in Volyarus with no argument.

Beatrice had been vague when Chanel had asked why, something about Demyan's family being large and it only being right to have the wedding in his homeland. Chanel hadn't expected that kind of understanding from her mom and had been glad for it.

She'd even expressed genuine gratitude to Beatrice for taking over the planning role with Demyan's aunt. Chanel had spent the past weeks working extra hours so she could leave her research in a good place to take a four-week honeymoon in Volyarus.

She hadn't been disappointed at all when Demyan had

asked her if she'd be willing to get to know his homeland for their honeymoon.

She loved the idea of spending a month in his company learning all she could about the small island country and its people, not to mention seeing him surrounded by family and the ones who had known him his whole life.

There was still a part of Chanel that felt like Demyan was a stranger to her. Or rather a part of Demyan that she did not know.

Her mother had flown out to Volyarus two weeks before to finalize plans for the wedding with Demyan's aunt. Perry, Andrew and Laura were on the plane with Chanel and Demyan now.

Perry *had* made a determined effort not to criticize her, but Chanel couldn't tell if that was because of her mother's talk with him or out of deference for Demyan. She'd never seen her stepfather treat someone the way he did Demyan, almost like business royalty, or something.

It made Chanel wonder.

"What is it you do at Yurkovich Tanner?" she asked as the plane's engines warmed up.

Demyan turned to look at her, that possessive, content expression he'd worn since the morning after she agreed to marry him very much in evidence.

"Why do you ask?"

"Because I realized I don't know."

"I am the Head of Operations."

"In Seattle?" she asked, a little startled his job was such a high-level one, but then annoyed with herself for not realizing it had to be.

Only, wasn't it odd for the corporate big fish to personally check out the recipients of their charitable donations?

"Worldwide," he said almost dismissively. "My office is in Seattle."

"I knew that, at least." Worldwide, as in he was Head of Operations over all of Yurkovich Tanner?

She'd done a little research into the company after they gifted her with a university education. It wasn't small by any stretch. They held interests on almost every continent of the world and the CEO was the heir apparent to the Volyarussian throne.

That Demyan was Head of Operations meant he swam with some really exalted fish in his tank.

"You are looking at me oddly," Demyan accused.

"I didn't realize."

He brushed back a bouncy curl that had fallen into her eye, his own expression intent. "Does my job title matter so much?"

"I know your favorite writer, the way you like your steak and how many children your ideal family would have, but I don't know anything about your job."

"On the contrary, you know a great deal. You have sat beside me while I took conference calls with our operations in Africa and Asia."

"I tuned you out." Corporate speak wasn't nearly as interesting as science…or her erotic readings.

Now that she had practical experience, they were even more fascinating.

He smiled with a warm sincerity she loved, the expression almost common now. At least when directed at her. "You did not miss anything that would interest you."

"I figured." She sighed. "I just feel like I should understand this side of your life better. You work really long hours."

So did she, but it occurred to her that maybe his long hours weren't going to go away like hers now that she'd caught up on work for her extended honeymoon.

"It is a demanding job."

"Do you enjoy it?"

"Very much."

"Will you continue working twelve- to sixteen-hour days after we get back from Volyarus?"

"I will do my best to cut my hours back, but twelve-hour days are not uncommon."

"I see. Okay, then."

"Okay, what? You have that look you get."

"What look?"

"The stubborn one." His brows drew together. "The same one you got when you insisted on buying your wedding dress without your mother's or my aunt's input."

Demyan's aunt, Oxana, had offered a Givenchy gown. Chanel had turned her down. Demyan hadn't been happy, wanting to save Chanel the stress and expense of searching for the perfect dress. He knew clothes were not usually her thing, but Chanel refused to compromise on this issue.

While she couldn't really care less about the colors for the linens, what food would be served or even the order of events at the reception, there were two things Chanel did care about.

What she wore and who officiated.

On the officiate, she'd agreed to have Demyan's family Orthodox priest perform the service so long as the pastor from the church she'd attended since childhood, a man who had known and respected both her father and grandfather, led them in their personally written vows and spoke the final prayer.

Her dress she wasn't compromising on at all. Chanel and Laura had spent three weeks haunting eBay, vintage and resale shops, but they'd finally found the perfect one.

An original Chanel gown designed by Coco herself.

Because while her mother had named Chanel after her favorite designer, she'd also named her after the designer she'd been wearing when Chanel's dad proposed. Chanel had wanted a link to her dad on her wedding day and wearing the vintage dress was it.

The rayon lace overlay of magnolia blossoms draped to a demure fichu collar. However, the signature Coco Chanel angel sleeves with daring cutouts gave the dress an understated air of sexiness she liked.

The dress was designed to enhance a figure like Chanel's. Clinging to her breasts, waist and hips only to flare slightly from below the knee, the gown made her look and feel feminine without being flouncy and constrictively uncomfortable.

Buying it had nearly drained Chanel's savings account and she really didn't care. Her job paid well and Demyan wasn't exactly hurting for cash.

Demyan's mouth covered Chanel's and she was kissing him before she was even conscious he'd played his usual *get-Chanel's-attention-when-her-mind-is-wandering* card. She had to admit she liked it a lot more than the sharp rebukes she got from others because of her habit of getting lost in thought.

After several pleasurable seconds, he lifted his head.

Dazed, she smiled up at him even as she was aware of her brother making fake gagging gestures in his seat across the aisle.

Perry shushed him, but Chanel paid neither male any heed.

She was too focused on the look in Demyan's eyes. It was so warm.

"That's better," he said.

"Than?"

"You thinking about something else. You're only thinking about me, now."

She laughed softly. "Yes, I am."

CHAPTER NINE

"WHAT PUT THAT stubborn look on your face before?"

She had to think and then she remembered. "You said you worked twelve-hour days, usually."

"I did and you said that was okay."

"No, I said *okay* in acknowledgment."

"You do not approve of twelve-hour days."

She shrugged. "That's not really the issue."

"It's not?"

"No."

"What is the issue?"

"Children."

His brows drew together like he was confused about something. "We agreed we wanted at least two."

He'd figure it out. He was a smart man.

"We also agreed that because of health considerations and family history, I wouldn't get pregnant after thirty-five."

"So?"

"So, we may have to adjust for an only child, or no children at all."

"Why?" he asked, sounding dangerous, the expression on his gorgeous face equally forbidding.

"Children need both parents' attention."

"Not all children have two parents."

"But if they do, they deserve both of those parents to make them a priority."

"I will not shirk my responsibility to my children."

"A dad does more than live up to responsibilities. He takes his kids to the beach in sunny weather and attends their soccer games. You can't do that if you're working twelve-hour days five days a week."

Something ticked in his expression.

Her heart sank. "You work weekends."

"Thus far, yes."

Was this a deal breaker? No.

But she didn't like figuring it out now, either. "I'll volunteer with after-school programs," she decided. "I don't have to have children to have a complete life."

"You are threatening not to have children if I do not cut my hours?"

"I'm not threatening. I'm telling you I'm not bringing any children into this world who are going to spend their childhoods wondering how important they are to their dad, if at all."

"And you accuse me of seeing the world in only two colors."

"I see lots of shades and shadows. That doesn't mean my children are going to live under one or more of them."

"Have you never considered the art of compromise?"

"I suck at it." Hadn't he realized that already?

She gave in on what didn't matter, and on what did? Well, she could be a bit intransigent.

"This may be a problem. I am not known for giving in on what matters to me." He said it like she might not know.

"It's a good thing we agree on this issue, then."

Demyan didn't look comforted. "How is that?"

"You said you wanted to be the best father possible,

that you never wanted your children to doubt their place in your life."

"Yes."

"Then you agree it is better not to have them if your work schedule isn't going to change."

He looked tired suddenly, and frustrated. "It is not that simple."

"It can be."

"What do you suggest? That I let Yurkovich Tanner run into the ground?"

"I suggest you hire three assistants, one for each major market, men and women who know the company, who care about it and that you trust to make minor decisions. They're the first line for policy and decision making, leaving you open to spend your time on only the most high-level stuff."

"And if that's all I work on already?"

"It's not."

"You told me you tuned out my calls."

"That doesn't mean I can't access the memories."

"You're scary smart, aren't you?"

She shrugged, but they hadn't even bothered finishing her IQ test in high school after she completed the first three exercises before the tester even got the timer going. The teacher hadn't wanted her to feel like a freak.

If only he'd been able to coach her parents.

"You just found out what my job is and you're already giving advice on it." Far from annoyed, Demyan sounded admiring.

"I'm a quick thinker."

"You'd be brilliant in business."

"No interest." Much to both her mother's and Perry's distress.

"I'll talk it over with my uncle."

"Is he your business mentor?"

"He's my boss."

"He works for Yurkovich Tanner?"

"He's the King of Volyarus."

She waited for the rest of the joke, only it didn't come, and the look Demyan was giving her said it wasn't going to.

She knew that ultimately the ownership of Yurkovich Tanner resided with the monarchy of that country. However, the thought that Demyan's uncle and the king were one and the same person had never entered her mind.

"Your uncle is a king."

"Yes."

"Oxana?"

"Queen."

"She told me to call her Oxana."

"That is her privilege."

Chanel felt like she was going to be sick. "You never said."

"I didn't want to scare you off."

"Holding back important information is like lying."

"I'm called Prince Demyan, but I'm no knight in shining armor. At heart I am a Cossack, Chanel. You must realize that. Any armor I have is tarnished. I am a human man with human failings." He said it as if admitting a darkly held secret.

Another time, she would have teased him about his melodrama and the arrogance behind it. Right now? She needed to think.

"I wasn't expecting this. You're this corporate guy who wears sweaters." Only, he hadn't been wearing them, or the jeans, so much lately.

She hadn't really noticed, until now. Clothing didn't matter much to her. She wasn't her mother, or even Laura in that regard. But looking back, she realized there had been a lot of subtle changes over the past six weeks.

He dressed in suits so sharp they could have come out of the knife drawer. She hardly ever saw the more casual attire he'd been wearing when they first met. Sometimes in the evenings, but he never left the house in the morning wearing a sweater.

She never noticed him reaching to adjust glasses that weren't there anymore, either.

Which meant what? That he was a lot more confident than she'd thought.

Okay, anyone who thought Demyan Zaretsky lacked confidence needed to take a reality check. Her included.

She didn't know why he'd worn the glasses, but they weren't a crutch for some deep-seated insecurity.

And honestly, did that matter right now?

"Chanel," he prompted.

She stared at him, trying to make the difference between *who* he was and *what* he was make sense through the shock of his revelation. "You're a prince."

"It's a nominal title only."

"What does that even mean?" What she knew about royalty wouldn't fill a page, much less a book.

"Officially, I am a duke, but I am called prince at the pleasure of my uncle, the king."

"The one who raised you?" Still not making sense, and getting cloudier rather than clearer.

"He and Oxana raised me as a brother to Maksim, the Crown Prince. I was spare to the throne."

"Was?"

"My cousin's wife is expecting their first child."

"Next in line to the throne now?"

"Yes."

"It's just all so strange."

She looked around the plane, which had taken off at

some point but she couldn't have said when. Her family were all staring, making no effort to hide their interest.

Perry didn't look surprised at all, but Andrew's and Laura's eyes were both saucer wide.

"Mom and Perry knew," she guessed.

"Yes."

"They never said."

"They agreed my position might scare you off me. I wanted time to show you *I* am the man you promised to marry."

"But *you* are a prince."

"Does that change how you feel about me?" he demanded, no give for prevarication in his voice.

There were a lot of conflicting things going on inside Chanel, but this wasn't something she was in any question about. "No. I love you, not what you are."

"I am glad to hear it." The relief in his tone couldn't be faked.

"This is so cool," Andrew said, reminding Chanel of their audience.

She frowned at her little brother. "You might think so."

"I do, too," Laura said.

"The only thing that matters is what you think," Demyan said from beside her.

"The jury is still out on that one."

"Don't be flip."

She glared up at him. "I'm not. I mean it. Give me some time to process."

"Chanel—"

"No. I don't want to talk about it right now."

She didn't want to talk at all, and shut down every attempt either he or her family made on the rest of the flight, going so far as to feign sleep to get them all to just leave her alone for a bit.

Life had changed so fast and she'd thought she'd come to terms with that, but Demyan was still throwing her curve-balls and Chanel had never been good at sports.

Their arrival in Volyarus was less overwhelming than she might have expected given Demyan's position.

Thankfully, there was no fanfare, no line of reporters with oversize cameras. Of course if there had been, she would have shown them all just how she'd gotten her black belt in tae kwon do, with Demyan as her unwitting assistant in the endeavor.

However, other than some official-looking men who looked like they were straight off the set of *Men in Black,* there were only two other people—Chanel's mother and a beautiful woman with an unmistakable regal bearing. Queen Oxana.

Demyan guided Chanel toward the two women with his hand on the small of her back. He stopped when they were facing his aunt and he introduced them all.

The queen put her hand out to Chanel. "It's a pleasure to meet you. Demyan speaks very highly of you, as does your mother."

Chanel did her best not to show her surprise.

She knew Beatrice was trying, but the idea she had actually *complimented* Chanel to the other woman was still too new to be anything but startling. Oxana had spent the past two weeks in Beatrice's company. In the past, Chanel would have been sure the results would be catastrophic for any hopes she might have of gaining the queen's regard.

From the look of both women, that wasn't something she had to worry about anymore.

Unexpected and warm pleasure poured through Chanel's heart, filling it to the brim, and she smiled at her mother before squeezing the queen's hand. "Thank you for making Demyan a part of *your* family. Someone taught him how to protect the people he cares about and I think that was you."

The lovely dark eyes widened, Oxana's mouth parting in shock and then curving into an open smile. "I believe he will be in very good hands with you, Chanel."

The king was waiting at the palace when they arrived, his manner more reserved and less welcoming to Chanel. She didn't mind.

She thought she understood.

Everyone else was acting as if it was perfectly normal for a prince to get engaged after a month and married six weeks later.

Obviously, King Fedir had his qualms about it.

Since Chanel still had her own fears, she had no problem with the fact he might have some, as well.

Wedding plans made it impossible for Chanel and Demyan to have any time alone for the rest of the day. She was not surprised to find him in her room late that night after she left her mother and the indefatigable Oxana still discussing seating charts.

Demyan pulled Chanel into his arms and kissed her for several long seconds before stepping back. "That is better."

"You missed me."

"I spend all day without you at work."

"But it was different here."

"Yes."

"Worried the mom of your heart would let slip too many of your secrets?" she teased, unprepared for the clearly guilty look that crossed his features. "What?"

He shook his gorgeous head. "Nothing."

"Demyan?"

"She is the mother of my heart."

"Have you told her and the king you filed for an official name change?"

"They will hear when the priest names me during the ceremony."

"You're a closet romantic, aren't you?"

"I am no romantic, Chanel."

"You just go on thinking that." Then a truly horrific thought assailed her. "Are people going to call me Princess after we are married?"

"Are you going to refuse to marry me if I say yes?" he asked, sounding way too serious.

"I'm not going to refuse to marry you, but Demyan, it's not easy, this finding-out-you're-royalty thing."

He nodded, as if he understood, but how could he? He'd grown up knowing what he was.

"So, about the princess thing…" She wasn't willing to let this go. Chanel wanted an answer.

He'd left enough out up to this point.

"That depends on my uncle."

"If he calls me princess…"

"Then others will."

"Oh." Considering the cool reception she'd received from King Fedir, she didn't think he was going to call her princess anytime soon.

"You look relieved."

"I'm not a princess in his eyes." As she said the words, she knew them to be absolute truth. And she didn't blame King Fedir for feeling that way. "I'm not nobility."

"You are. You inherited the title from your great-great-grandfather—you are a dame. Marrying me will make you a duchess."

"So?"

"So, even if you are not called princess, most will call you by your title." His expression and tone said he was perfectly aware she wasn't going to see that truth as a benefit to marriage.

"That's medieval."

"No. Trust me, the nobility system is alive and well in many modern countries."

"But…" She didn't want to be called duchess.

"The correct term is Your Grace."

"That makes me sound like, like… What do they call them, a cardinal or something in the Catholic church."

He laughed, like she'd been joking.

She wasn't. "I'm… This is…"

He didn't let her keep floundering. Showing he knew exactly what Chanel needed—him—Demyan pulled her into his arms and kissed her.

All thoughts of unwanted titles and unexpected ties to royalty went flying from her head in favor of one consuming emotion. Love for the man so intent on making her his wife.

Over the next few days, Chanel hardly saw Demyan—except when he came to her room at night and made passionate, almost desperate love to her.

She didn't understand, but it felt like he was avoiding her. Not sure that wasn't her old insecurities talking, she refused to voice her concerns aloud.

He didn't seem inclined to anything serious for pillow talk either, but she understood that. Chanel certainly didn't want to talk about the wedding and its never-ending preparations and plans. Nor was she interested in discussing her fledgling closer relationship with her mother and stepfather.

Beatrice was in her element planning a wedding for her daughter to a prince. A cynical part of Chanel couldn't help wondering how much of her mother's newfound approval stemmed from this unexpected turn of events.

Perry wasn't nearly as overtly critical as he had been in the past, but he didn't go out of his way to extend even pseudo fatherly warmth, either.

As they had been for the majority of her life, Laura and Andrew were two bright beacons of sincere love and affection for Chanel. Their steady presence reminded her that no matter how her life might change by marrying royalty, some things—the truly important things—remained.

Though she saw little of him during the day, Demyan arrived in her room every night—sometimes very late and clearly exhausted. Apparently when he was in Volyarus, his duties extended beyond the company business into the family business: the politics of royalty.

Sometimes they didn't make love before falling into exhausted slumber, but those nights he woke her in the wee hours in order to bring amazing pleasure to her body.

He'd found time to sit with her today, though, while she and her stepfather's lawyer went over the prenuptial agreement. Perry had offered his expertise as well, but honestly?

Chanel trusted Demyan to watch out for her best interests more than her stepfather.

Once she'd read it through, though, she didn't think she needed anyone else's interpretation. For a legal document, the language was straightforward and to the point.

There was some serious overkill in her opinion, but nothing that bothered Chanel to sign.

Upon her marriage, she and her heirs gave up any and all rights they might have in Volyarus, its financial and political endeavors and anything specifically related to the business enterprises of the Yurkovich family.

The fact that particular paragraph was followed by one giving any children she had with Demyan full interest as *his* heirs, she felt was particular overkill.

Clearly, the royal family was very protective of their interests, though. King Fedir's influence, no doubt.

The man had not warmed up to her at all, but he'd never been unkind, either. After her years with Beatrice and Perry, Chanel was practically inured to anything less than overt hostility.

Even with what she was sure were the king's stipulations, the terms of the agreement were very generous toward Chanel, considering the fact she wasn't bringing any significant accumulated wealth to the marriage. The agreement guaranteed an annual sum for living expenses that Chanel couldn't imagine spending in five years, never mind one.

Unless it was on research, but she didn't see Demyan approving using their personal finances to fund her scientific obsessions. Yurkovich Tanner had been generous in that regard already.

One thing the prenup spelled out in black and white, oversize and bolded print to her heart was that Demyan wanted their relationship to be permanent. If she'd been in any doubt.

Which she wasn't.

The financial provision did not decrease in the event of his death. The annual income was Chanel's and her children's for her lifetime and theirs.

There were some other pretty stringent requirements that would insure she didn't divorce Demyan or be unfaithful to him, though. Not that she would ever do either.

But the agreement spelled out quite clearly that any children born of a different father had absolutely no financial interest through her or any other source in the Yurkovich, Zaretsky or Volyarussian wealth.

Oddly, if she divorced Demyan, or he divorced her for anything other than *her* infidelity, she would still be well taken care of. Until she remarried. If she were ever to marry someone else, or have irrefutable evidence of infidelity brought against her, she lost all financial benefits from her marriage to Demyan.

It wasn't anything less than she expected, but having it spelled out in black and white sent a shiver along her spine that was not exactly pleasant.

Demyan laid his hand over hers before she signed. "You are okay with all the terms?"

"They are more than generous."

"I will always make sure you have what you need, no matter what the agreement says."

"I believe you." And she did. With everything in her.

CHAPTER TEN

THE MORNING OF Chanel's wedding was every bit as te-
diously focused on beauty, fashion and making an impact
as she'd feared it might be with Beatrice in charge.

Strangely, for the first time in her life, Chanel found
she didn't mind her mother's fussing over her appearance.

For once, going through the paces of having her legs
waxed, her hair done and makeup applied resonated with
an almost welcome familiarity in this strange new situation that had become her life.

It had been years since Chanel had sat through one of
her mother's preparation routines for a social function,
but the sound of Beatrice's voice giving instruction to the
stylists resonated with old memories.

Memories were so much easier to deal with than the reality of the present. She was marrying a prince.

It was beyond surreal.

"Your fingers are like ice." The manicurist frowned
as she took Chanel's hand out of the moisturizing soak.
"Why did you say nothing? The water must be too cold."

Beatrice was there in a second, testing the water with
her own finger and giving Chanel a look filled with concern. "Are you all right, sweetheart?"

Chanel nodded.

Her mom did not look comforted. "The argan oil solution is warm enough, but the manicurist is right. Your hands feel like they've been wrapped around an icicle."

Chanel shrugged.

"Mom, she's marrying a prince. That's not exactly Chanel's dream job," Laura said in that tone only a teenager could get just right. "She's stressed out."

"But he's perfect for you."

"You've barely seen us together. How would you know?" Chanel asked, with little inflection.

"You love him."

Chanel nodded again. There was no point in denying the one thing that would prompt her to marry a man related to royalty.

"He adores you."

Laura grinned at Chanel, her eyes filled with understanding. "I agree with Mom on that one, at least."

"I think he does," Chanel admitted. Demyan acted like a man very happy with his future.

Beatrice reached out and put her hand against Chanel's temple, frowning at whatever she felt there. "You're in shock."

"Sheesh, Mom, way to state the obvious." Laura didn't roll her eyes, but it was close.

Beatrice frowned. "I do not appreciate your tone, young lady."

"Well, you're acting like Chanel should be all excited and happy when it's probably taking everything in her not to run away. She's a scientist, Mom, not a socialite."

"I am well aware of my daughter's chosen profession." Beatrice was careful not to frown—that caused wrinkles— but her tone conveyed displeasure.

The interaction fascinated Chanel, who hadn't realized her mother and Laura had anything less than the ideal mother-daughter relationship.

Beatrice looked at Chanel. "Do you need some orange juice to bring up your blood sugar?"

Chanel shook her head. "It just doesn't feel real."

"Believe it or not, I threw up twice before walking down the aisle to your father," Beatrice offered with too much embarrassment for it not to be sincere.

Laura snorted. "You were preggers, Mom. It was probably morning sickness."

"I was not morning sick. I was terrified. I nearly fainted when I was getting ready for my wedding to *your* father."

Chanel couldn't imagine her mother agitated to that level. "Really?"

"It's a huge step, marriage. No matter how much you love the man you're marrying."

"I don't know what the big deal is. If it doesn't work out, they can get divorced," Laura said with the blasé confidence of youth.

Their mother glared at her youngest daughter. "That is not the attitude women of this family take into marriage."

"You and Chanel can get all stressed about it, but I'm not going to. If I get married at all. It all seems like a lot of bother over something that ends in divorce about fifty percent of the time. I think living together makes a lot more sense."

Chanel almost laughed at the look of absolute horror crossing their mother's features. She would have, if she could feel anything that deeply.

Right now the entire world around her was one level removed.

"Stop looking like that, Mom. You and Chanel take everything so seriously. I'm not like you."

It was a total revelation to Chanel that Laura considered her like their mother.

"You're more like us than you realize, young lady. Regardless, there will be no more talk of divorce on your sister's wedding day."

Chanel had never heard her mother use that particular tone with her golden-child sister.

And Laura listened, but her less-than-subdued expression implied she *had* heard it before and didn't find it all that intimidating.

How much had Chanel missed about the world around her? She hadn't realized Demyan was a corporate king, much less a real-life prince. She'd had no idea her mother still loved her father and she'd been sure Beatrice no longer loved *her*.

Chanel had been wrong on all counts.

It was a sobering and hopeful realization at the same time.

Nevertheless, she continued through the rest of her personal preparations for the wedding in the fog of shock that had plagued her since waking without Demyan in her bed.

As the makeup artist finished the final application of lip color, a knock sounded at the door.

"The driver is here. Are you both ready?" Beatrice asked, managing to the look the part of the mother of the bride for a prince, anyway.

Laura looked like a blond angel in her ice-blue Vera Wang maid-of-honor dress that was a perfect complement to Chanel's vintage designer gown.

Chanel hoped her mother had worked some kind of magic and she looked her part, as well. She hadn't looked in the mirror since the hair stylist had shown up.

"It's not the driver," Laura announced after opening the door. Then she dropped into a curtsy and Chanel's throat constricted.

Had the king come to tell her he didn't want Chanel

marrying his quasi-adopted son? No, that was an irrational thought.

But…her thoughts stopped their spin out of control in the face of the majesty that was Queen Oxana in full regalia. The Queen of Volyarus swept into the room, making the huge chamber feel very small all of a sudden.

"Good morning, Chanel. Beatrice." The queen gave Chanel's mother a small incline of her head and then a smile to Laura. "Laura, you look lovely."

"Thank you, Your Majesty," Laura replied with her irrepressible smile.

"And you, my dear," the queen said as she focused her considerable attention on Chanel. "You look absolutely perfect. That's an original by Coco Chanel herself, is it not?"

"Yes."

"She was a brilliant and innovative designer who changed the face of female haute couture almost single-handedly. I find your choice to dress in one of her gowns singularly appropriate as I am sure you will be equally as impacting in your field."

It was the first time anyone who mattered to Chanel emotionally had made such a claim. Bittersweet joy squeezed at her heart, even through the layer of numbness surrounding that organ. "Thank you."

Oxana smiled. "You are very welcome." She offered Chanel a medium-sized dark blue velvet box meant for jewelry. "I would be honored if you would wear this."

Expecting pearls, or something of that nature, Chanel felt her heart beat in a rapid tattoo of shock at the sight of the diamond-encrusted tiara. It wasn't anything as imposing as the crown presently resting on the queen's perfectly coiffed hair, but it *was* worthy of a princess.

"I'm not… This is…" Chanel didn't know what to say, so she closed her mouth on more empty words.

"Part of my own wedding outfit," the queen finished for her. "It would please me to see it worn again."

"Didn't Prince Maksim's wife wear it?" Laura asked, managing to verbalize at least one of the questions swirling through Chanel's brain.

"King Fedir gave her his mother's princess tiara. It was decided between us that mine would be reserved for the wife of our eldest."

Chanel's heart warmed to hear Demyan referred to as the eldest child of the king and queen.

Somehow, though the stylist had been unaware that a tiara would be added later, the updo she had designed for Chanel lent itself perfectly to the diamond-encrusted accessory.

Or so her mother told Chanel.

"Here, see for yourself," Oxana insisted.

Both Laura and Beatrice gave her a concerned look. So, they had noticed she hadn't looked in the mirror since that morning.

But Chanel didn't want visual proof that she didn't look like a princess.

"I trust your judgment," Chanel hedged.

"Then you will trust my instruction to look at yourself, my soon-to-be daughter." Oxana's expression did not invite argument.

Oh, gosh…she'd never even considered this woman would truly consider herself Chanel's mother-in-law.

"You look like a princess," Beatrice said with far more sincerity than such a trite statement deserved.

"You're going to knock Demyan on his butt," Laura added with a little less finesse, but no less certainty.

Far from offended, the queen laughed and agreed. "Yes, I do believe you will."

Taking a breath for courage, Chanel turned to face the impartial judge that could not be gainsaid. The mirror reflected only what was—it made no judgments about that image.

The woman staring back at Chanel with wide gray eyes did not look like a queen. No layers and layers of organza to look like any princess bride Chanel had ever seen in the tabloids, either, but in this moment she *was* beautiful.

The vintage Coco Chanel design fit her like it had been tailored to her figure, the antique lace clinging in all the right places. The single-layer floor-length veil and tiara added elegance Chanel was not used to seeing when she looked in a mirror.

The makeup artist had managed to bring out the shape and pink tint of Chanel's lips while making her eyes glow. Her curls had been tamed into perfect corkscrews and then pinned up so that the length of her neck looked almost swanlike.

This woman would not embarrass Demyan walking up the aisle.

Chanel turned to her mother and hugged Beatrice with more emotion than she'd allowed herself to show in years with the older woman. "Thank you."

"It was my pleasure. It has been a very long time since you allowed me to fuss over you. I enjoyed it." Beatrice returned the embrace and then stepped back, blinking at the moisture in her eyes.

Chanel and her mother would probably never agree on what it meant to *fuss* over someone else, but she began to see that, in her own way, her mother hadn't abandoned Chanel completely as a child.

* * *

Wearing the gold-and-dark-blue official uniform of the Volyarussian Cossack Hetman, Demyan waited at the bottom of the palace steps, as it was his country's royal tradition that he ride with Chanel in the horse-drawn carriage to the cathedral.

His dark eyes met hers, his handsome face stern and unemotional. Yet despite wearing what she'd come to think of as his "corporate king" face, there was an unmistakable soul-deep satisfaction glimmering in his gaze.

He put his hand out toward her. The white-glove-covered appendage hung there, an unexpected beacon. He wasn't supposed to take her hand yet; he wasn't supposed to touch her at all. They had been instructed to enter the carriage separately. She was to sit with her back toward the driver and he was to face the people on the slow procession to the Orthodox cathedral.

According to the wedding coordinator and royal tradition, she and Demyan were not supposed to touch so much as fingertips until the priest proclaimed them man and wife.

So this one gesture spoke volumes of her prince's willingness to put Chanel ahead of protocol.

Without warning, the mental and emotional fog surrounding Chanel fell away, the world coming into stark relief for the first time that day. Though it was early fall, the sun shone bright in the sky, the air around them crisp with autumn chill and filled with a cacophony of voices from the crowds lining the palace drive that were suddenly loud.

Love for Demyan swelled inside Chanel, pushing aside worry and doubt to fill her with a certainty that drove her forward toward the hand held out to her.

Their fingers touched, his curling possessively and decisively around her cold ones. He tugged her forward even as electric current arced between them despite the barrier of his glove.

Devastating emotion shuddered through her, completely dispelling the last of the strange, surreal sensations that had plagued her since waking.

His eyes flared and then he was pulling off the cape from his uniform and wrapping it around her. Several gasps sounded around them and the king said something that Chanel had no doubt was a protest.

She couldn't hear him, though, not over the blood rushing in her ears. The long military cloak settled around her shoulders. She didn't argue that she wasn't really cold, because it carried the fragrance of Demyan's cologne and skin, making her feel embraced by him.

He helped her into the open landau carriage, further eschewing protocol to sit beside her.

Cameras flashed, people cheered and while all of it registered, none of it really impacted Chanel. She was too focused on the man holding her hand and looking at her with quietly banked joy.

"It's just you and me," she said softly, understanding at last.

"Yes."

He didn't relate to her as a prince, though he was undeniably that. Demyan related to her as the man who wanted to share his life with her.

That life might be more complicated because of his title, but at the core, it was the life she wanted. Just as at the core, she knew this man and connected to him soul to soul.

The deep happiness reflecting in his gaze darkened to something more serious. "Always believe that, no matter what else might come up, our marriage is about you and me. Full stop."

"Period," she finished, her heart filled to bursting with such love for this man.

It didn't have to make sense, or be rational, she realized. She had fallen for him immediately and she was wholly and completely *in love* with him now.

They could have waited another year to marry and she wouldn't be any surer of him than she was right now.

As her mom had said, this man was *it* for Chanel, the love of her life, and he felt the same. Even if he hadn't said the words.

Even if he never did.

"I love you," she said to him, needing to in that moment as much as she needed to breathe.

"I will treasure that gift for the rest of my life, I promise you."

He made the vow official less than an hour later when he said it in front of the filled-to-capacity cathedral as part of the personal vows they'd agreed to speak. He also promised to care for her, respect her and support her efforts to make the world a better place through science.

Chanel, who never cried, felt hot tears tracking down her cheeks—thank goodness for her mother's insistence on waterproof makeup—as she spoke her own personal promises, including one to love Demyan for the rest of her life.

It wasn't hard to promise something she didn't think she had a choice about anyway.

His name change was also acknowledged for the first time publicly during the wedding ceremony, when the Orthodox priest led them in their formalized vows before pronouncing them married.

A murmur rippled through the crowd, but Demyan seemed oblivious, his attention wholly on Chanel.

The king's expression was filled with more emotion than Chanel thought the rather standoffish King of

Volyarus capable of as he made his official acknowledgment of his *son's* new married state.

Crown Prince Maksim and his wife were both gracious and clearly happy about the name change when Chanel finally met them for the reception line after the ceremony.

She'd thought it odd she hadn't yet met Demyan's *brother* and was relieved when Princess Gillian remarked on it, as well.

It had been clear from several remarks Demyan made that the two men were close. The fact Chanel hadn't been introduced before had had her wondering if maybe the Crown Prince had disapproved of the wedding.

Only now it was obvious he hadn't even known about the upcoming nuptials until he'd been summoned back to Volyarus by his parents. Chanel didn't understand it, but she was the first person to admit that most politics of social interaction and even family relationships went right over her head.

Prince Maksim seemed nice enough and quite willing to accept Chanel into the family. His own wife wasn't royalty or even nobility, so he had to have a fully modern view of marriage within his family.

Though a comment, or two, made by his wife implied otherwise.

Once they'd finished greeting those allowed into the formal reception line, the entire Yurkovich family addressed the people of Volyarus from the main balcony at the front of the palace. The king gave a speech. They all waved and smiled for what felt like hours before everyone but she and Demyan retreated inside.

He addressed the crowd, telling them how honored he was that Dame Chanel Tanner had agreed to be his wife, that he knew her ancestor Baron Tanner would have been very happy, as well.

Then he kissed Chanel.

And it wasn't a chaste, for-the-masses kiss. Demyan took her mouth with gentle implacability, showing her and everyone watching how very pleased he was she was now officially *his*.

Chanel found herself separated from Demyan during the reception, but she wasn't surprised.

He'd prepared her for the way the formal event would unfold, during which they would have very little time together. He had promised to make up for that on their wedding night and the extended honeymoon that was to follow.

What did surprise Chanel was to find herself completely without any of the people who had seemed intent on making sure she was never on her own in the highly political gathering.

Queen Oxana was occupied talking to Princess Gillian. Chanel's mother had been waylaid by an elderly duke, while Andrew flirted with the man's granddaughter under the watchful and not-very-happy gaze of the teen's eagle-eyed mother. Perry was talking business in a corner somewhere—not that he was one of Chanel's self-appointed minders.

Even Laura had lost herself in the crowd.

Chanel thought now would be the ideal time to find a quiet place to regroup a little. The crush of people was overwhelming for a scientist who spent most of her days in the lab, the mixture of so many voices sounding like a roar in her ears.

Seeing a likely hallway, she ducked out of the huge ballroom. The farther she walked along the hallway, the more muted the cacophony of voices from the ballroom became and the more tension drained from her until even her hands, which had been fisted unconsciously at her sides, uncurled.

Only as her fingers straightened did she realize how very hard she'd been holding them.

She could hear voices ahead, one whose tones she recognized with a smile. Demyan.

Delighted by the opportunity to see him amidst the chaos of her wedding day, she quickened her steps, only slowing down when she realized who he was with.

King Fedir.

The one person who intimidated Chanel and brought out her barely resolved and all-too-recent insecurities. There were two other voices as well, a woman and a man.

They were all speaking Ukrainian, thinly veiled anger resonating in at least two of the speakers' tones.

As Chanel slowed her progress, their conversation resolved itself into actual words she could understand.

The unknown woman demanded, "How dare you humiliate us this way?"

"My actions were not intended as an insult toward you." Demyan did not sound particularly worried the woman had taken whatever he'd done as such, though.

"How could they be taken any other way?" a man who was not the king said. "You have repudiated us before all of Volyarus."

"I didn't repudiate you. I aligned myself with my true family."

"I gave you birth," the woman said in fury.

And the identity of the other two people became clear to Chanel: Demyan's birth parents.

"You also *gave* me to your brother, abdicating any responsibilities and all emotional connections to me. I am no longer your son."

"You are not a child." The man speaking had to be Demyan's biological father. "You know why that was necessary."

"I know that you traded your son for the chance at leverage over your brother-in-law, the king. I know that Fedir and Oxana needed a secondary heir to the throne, but they have always treated me as more than an expedience."

"I'm very pleased you took our house's name, Demyan," the king said with sincerity. "Your parents could have avoided this surprise today by allowing Oxana and me to adopt you as a child. It was their choice not to, as you said...for their own expedience. I, for one, was joyfully surprised and I know your mother feels the same."

Chanel smiled, pleased the outwardly cold man so obviously cared about his adopted son. Demyan said something she did not catch.

"You think you are more than an expedience to the king and queen?" Duke Zaretsky sneered. "He has just ensured you sacrificed the rest of your life for the sake of his family's wealth. You are far more his tool than you were ever mine."

Chanel didn't understand what the duke meant by his words, but there was no question they were intended to wound. And she wasn't about to stand by while anyone tried to hurt Demyan.

She pushed open the door to what turned out to be a very impressive masculine study and crossed to Demyan's side quickly.

His dark gaze flared with something that looked like worry before pleasure at her presence sparked to life, as well. "Hello, *sérdeńko*."

"What are you doing here?" the king asked with his usual less-than-warm attitude toward her.

"The reception was getting too loud."

"You cannot abandon your responsibilities as a hostess on a whim."

"Really? Then what are you doing back here?" she asked with enough sarcasm to be mistaken for her sister. "Correct me if I'm wrong, but wasn't it *your* name on the invitation listed as host of this party?"

Demyan laughed, taking her hand and pulling her to his side. "You make an excellent case, little one."

Everyone in the room except Chanel showed differing levels of surprise at his humor. The king recovered first, giving her a grudging look of respect when she'd expected a frown and polite dressing-down.

She had a lot of experience with both and a lifetime realizing she was no good at taking the path of least resistance, even if it meant avoiding them.

"Point taken," King Fedir said. "We should *all* be getting back."

"Does she know yet?" the duke asked, his expression calculating, his tone undeniably malicious.

CHAPTER ELEVEN

CHANEL DIDN'T ASK what he meant, or even acknowledge the man had spoken.

He'd done it in Ukrainian. Somehow she doubted Demyan had been into sharing confidences with the older man, which meant the duke had no idea she understood the language. That made his choice to converse in it pointedly without courtesy.

"You will be silent," the king replied in the same language to his brother-in-law, his tone harsh.

Ignoring both posturing men, Chanel smiled up at Demyan. "I missed you."

"Oh, how sweet," Princess Svitlana said in a tone that made it clear she thought it was anything but.

Demyan's expression was an odd mixture of tenderness and a strange underlying anxiety as he looked down at Chanel. "I am very proud of you. Not many science geeks would do so well at an affair of state with so little training."

"You assigned a very potent group of babysitters."

His nostrils flared as if her words surprised him.

"You didn't think I realized you'd asked them to watch over me?" Once she had, she'd felt very well cared for.

Demyan would never leave Chanel to sink or swim in the shark-infested waters of his life.

"I could not be with you the entire time," he said by way of an explanation.

Not that she'd needed one. "Because you're a prince."

"It's a nominative title only," his birth mother said with more venom, in English this time. "He's no more a prince than you are a well-bred princess."

Chanel gave the older woman a measure of her attention, but kept her body and clear allegiance toward Demyan. "I am not a horse and I wasn't born in a breeding program. While I won't claim to be a princess, Demyan is definitely a prince."

"He won't inherit. Not now that Princess Gillian is carrying the next heir to the throne."

"But he is the king and queen's son. That makes him a prince."

"I gave birth to him," the duchess said.

Chanel found it odd that the duke never verbalized his claim at fatherhood. "Congratulations."

"Are you mocking me?"

"No. I don't know what your other children are like. Hopefully more like their older brother than their parents, but I do know you gave birth to an amazing man in Demyan. I'm sure you are very proud of that accomplishment, but you aren't his mother any more than I am a princess."

"Oxana is my mother," Demyan asserted with absolute assurance.

"And you would do anything for her and the man you consider your father, even marry some socially backward American *scientist* to protect the Yurkovich financial interests." She said scientist as if it was a dirty word.

Chanel almost smiled. She'd never considered her vocation as beyond the pale before.

"That is enough, Svitlana." The king's tone was again harsh, his expression forbidding.

"Oh, so you *haven't* told her?" Duke Zaretsky asked snidely, clearly ignoring his king's evident wrath and this time taking evident pleasure in speaking English. "I could almost feel sorry for her. She gave up hundreds of millions of dollars by marrying you and she doesn't even know it."

There could be no doubt the duke was talking about Chanel, but the words made absolutely no sense.

"I didn't give up anything and gained everything marrying Demyan," she fiercely asserted.

The duchess looked at her pityingly. "You have no idea, but no matter what kind of prenuptial agreement these two convinced you to sign, until you spoke your vows three hours ago, you were a twenty-percent owner in Yurkovich Tanner."

"I wasn't. My great-great-grandfather left his shares to the Volyarussian people." He'd told her great-grandmother so in a letter still in Chanel's possession, along with the family Bible.

"And they have been used to finance infrastructure, schools and hospitals since then," the king assured her.

She smiled at him, holding no grudge for his unwelcoming demeanor. "I know. I did some research when I got the scholarship. Your country is kind of amazing for its progressive stance on the environment and energy conservation."

"I am glad you think so."

"That money was yours," the king's sister insisted. "Until you married my son."

The claims were starting to make an awful kind of sense, but Chanel had no intention of allowing the two emotional vultures in front of her to know about the splinters of pain slicing their way through Chanel's heart.

She simply said, "He's not your son."

"Would you like to see your grandfather's will?" the duke asked, clearly unwilling to give up.

Two things were obvious in that moment. The first was that there had to be some truth to what the duke and his wife were saying. If there wasn't, Demyan and the king would have categorically denied it.

Also, they were both way too tense now for the claims to be entirely false.

Second, whatever the duke and Princess Svitlana's motives for telling Chanel, it had nothing to do with helping or protecting *anyone*. Her least of all.

In fact, she was fairly certain their intention was to hurt the son who had finally made a public alliance with the family who had raised him.

She turned away from the duke and duchess to face Demyan. "Tell me your siblings don't take after your egg and sperm donors."

Duplicate sounds of outrage indicated the Zaretskys had heard her just fine.

Demyan didn't respond, an expression she'd never seen in his eyes. Fear.

She wasn't sure what he was afraid of. Whether he was afraid she would mess up whatever plan he'd made with King Fedir, or worried she would go ballistic at their very politically attended reception, or something else really didn't matter.

Whatever Demyan felt for her, Chanel loved him and she wasn't going to let the two people whose rejection had already caused him a lifetime of pain hurt him anymore.

"I think it's time we all returned to the reception." She couldn't quite dredge up a smile, but she did her best to mask her own hurt.

He spoke then, the words coming out in a strange tone. "We need to talk."

She didn't want him showing vulnerability in front of the Zaretskys. Chanel wasn't giving them the satisfaction of believing they'd succeeded in their petty and vindictive efforts.

She reached up and cupped his face, like he did so often with her, hoping it gave him the same sense of comfort and being cared for it had always done her, no matter how much of a lie it might have been at the time. "Later."

"You promise?"

"Yes."

"She is a fool," the duke said in disgusted Ukrainian.

Chanel looked at him over her shoulder, her expression a perfect reflection of her mother's favorite one for disdain. "The only fool here is you if you think for one second you have the power to influence my prince's life for good or ill today, or any time in the future. You simply don't matter."

She had also spoken in his native language and enjoyed the shock that produced in the overweening nobleman.

The duchess gasped. "You're American."

"Which does not equate to uninformed, stupid or uneducated." Chanel met eyes so similar in color but different in expression from Demyan's. "My heritage in this country may not be royal, or as long-standing, but when it comes to the welfare of Volyarus, it is equally as important as yours."

Her grandfather had helped this nation stay afloat financially three decades ago and his efforts were still benefitting the Volyarussians.

"You already knew," the duchess said, almost as if she admired Chanel's acumen. "But then why did you marry him?"

"Because she loves me," Demyan said, his voice gravelly.

Chanel turned back to him without agreeing or giving his parents another single solitary moment of her time. She hadn't known about the will being different than what her great-grandmother had believed, or what that had to do with Chanel's marriage to Demyan, though she could make a pretty educated guess based on the prenuptial agreement.

She wasn't about to admit that to the Zaretskys, though.

Demyan was searching her face as if trying to read Chanel's thoughts. So far in their relationship, she'd been an open book. She had little hope of hiding what was going on in her head right now.

But she didn't have to talk about it. Especially in front of the older generation of the royal family.

"Leave," the king said to his sister and brother-in-law.

The Zaretskys started for the door of the study.

"No," the king instructed. "Out through the secret passage. You will not return to the reception and you will be out of the palace within the hour."

"What? You cannot be serious. How would that look?" his sister demanded.

"Like you threw a temper tantrum when your son chose to change his name to reflect his true parentage," the king replied, his tone arctic.

Princess Svitlana crossed her arms, but stopped just shy of stomping her feet. "I won't do it."

"You will. Do not presume to forget that this is not a nominal King of Volyarus. I hold the power to revoke your citizenship and deport you. Do not tempt me to use it."

The duke and his wife both paled at the king's words, Princess Svitlana doing a fair imitation of a gasping fish, though no words passed her lips.

The expression in her brother's eyes suggested she keep it that way.

Showing she was marginally more intelligent than evidence might suggest, the princess left without another word. Through the secret passageway. Her husband followed close behind her.

Chanel stepped back from Demyan, intending to return to the reception. The crowds of people and litany of voices that fifteen minutes ago had seemed so overwhelming now called like a beacon for escape from the thoughts that were multiplying by the second in her head.

And with every new thought came a shard of pain Chanel had no idea how long she could contain.

The king blocked her exit, his gaze searching hers as much as his adopted son's had done. However, the level of ruthlessness behind his perusal chilled her; she'd felt only confusion mixed with hurt at Demyan's look.

She said nothing, simply waited for the King of Volyarus to move.

He frowned. "You will not return to the reception only to cause a scene."

She was doing her best to hold back an emotional devastation she hadn't experienced since her father's death. Did he really think his display of bossiness was helping the situation?

"Let me give you a small piece of advice, Your Majesty."

His brows rose in obvious shock at her tone.

She went on, "Right this second, all I see when I look at you is a man who would use whatever underhanded means are necessary to rob a woman and her family of a legacy they knew nothing about."

"There was nothing underhanded about your marriage to my son. It is legal in every sense. You cannot undo it."

She said a word that rarely passed her lips, but called the lie for what it was. Oh, he might be correct in that she could not undo whatever legality the wedding had wrought, but as for nothing about it being devious?

That was an ugly bit of nonsense. "All I've done so far is tell you my opinion, not offered my advice. If you're smart, you will take it."

"Chanel, you cannot speak to him like that," Demyan said, sounding tired rather than corrective. "He is your king."

"Not *my* king." Any more than Demyan was *her* prince.

King Fedir asked before Demyan could reply to that claim, "What is your advice?"

"Do not attempt to tell me what to do. Because though my intention is *not* to embarrass my family, or Queen Oxana who has been nothing but kind to me, your very instruction not to cause a scene is nearly overwhelming impetus to do so."

"You love my son."

She didn't deny it. What would be the point? Everyone in that room knew the truth about her emotions. And his now, no matter how misled she'd been that morning.

"But I don't even like you," she told Demyan's adopted father very succinctly.

The king flinched, his face slackening in shock as if he'd never had anyone speak to him in such a way before. Maybe he hadn't.

"Chanel…" That was Demyan, the tone in his voice not one she wanted to hear or could even begin to trust right then.

Definitely not admonishment for her rudeness to his father, but what it was, she refused to name.

She spun to face him, her heart in a vise that brought pain with each indrawn breath. "Don't. Just *don't,* Demyan. However horrible their intentions, the duke and duchess were more honest with me than you've been."

"No." He lurched forward, as if he'd been yanked by a string attached to his chest.

She stepped back quickly, sure of one thing. She could not allow him to touch her right now. "Stop. I said later. I meant *later.*"

"Perhaps you two should speak *now,*" the king said, sounding less certain than he had to this point.

Chanel made no attempt to hide the utter dislike she felt when she faced him. "You're doing it again. You say maybe we should talk and all I can think is how much more certain I am that there isn't going to be any more talking."

"You are a contrary woman."

"You have no idea how contrary I can be, but spend a few minutes talking with my stepfather and he'll fill you in."

"I have spent some time in his company already."

And heard an earful, Chanel was sure. For the first time in her life, she simply didn't care if Perry had managed to turn someone right off her. "I'm sure he enjoyed that."

"He's an opportunistic man."

"He is." Something clicked in her mind, two memories coming together to form a single conclusion. "He's the one, isn't he, the reason you had to act now?"

The king's face smoothed over into an emotionless mask, but not before she saw the flare of surprise at her guess.

Because she was right.

"My great-great-grandfather Tanner died, apparently with a very different will to the one my great-grandmother believed to have been in existence. Yet no one from your family has approached mine in four generations to secure Baron Tanner's shares in your precious company."

"It is not just a company—it is the financial cornerstone of an entire country."

"Your country."

"Yours now, too."

"That remains to be seen."

"Chanel—" Demyan tried to say something.

She put her hand up. "No. Not you. Not now. Trust me when I tell you it is better for everyone if you show that ruthless patience you are so well-known for in business."

"How do you know about that?"

"I've spent six weeks learning you." Too bad he hadn't done the same.

He would have realized there was no worse way she could have learned of his subterfuge than to be told by an outside party. But then maybe he had realized and it simply didn't matter.

He wouldn't risk upsetting whatever scheme he and his father had set in motion to protect their precious wealth and thereby their country.

She focused on the king again. "My stepfather approached your company trying to trade on connections he didn't really have, but it got you all worried."

"He is a resourceful man."

"He's a shark, though I think maybe Demyan is a bigger, and much meaner, one."

"Without doubt." The king sounded proud.

But then he would be, wouldn't he? His son's ruthless resourcefulness had netted him full interest in Yurkovich Tanner for the first time in four generations.

She didn't know how, or what the details were, but that much she had gleaned from what had and had not been said in this room tonight.

"There are half-a-dozen moderately accessible chemical compounds that would eat the flesh from a shark's body in less than a minute, did you know that?"

The king shook his head, his expression almost bemused.

"I did. I know every single one of them."

"Are you threatening him?"

"I am reminding you that even sharks get eaten if they aren't careful and it doesn't always take a bigger shark to do it."

"I believe there is a strand of ruthlessness in you, too."

"Would you like to find out?"

The king opened his mouth and then closed it, giving Demyan a look of concern before his expression turned thoughtful. "No."

"Good."

"What do you plan to do?"

"Throw the bouquet."

"You know that is not what I meant."

"I care?"

The king's mouth tightened, but he stepped aside, having seemingly finally gotten the message that his admonitions were more effective goads to bad behavior than preventers of it.

Chanel threw the bouquet.

She even managed to dredge up a photo-op-worthy smile when Laura caught it and tossed it away again immediately. Her sister's attitude toward the institution of marriage couldn't have been more obvious.

Chanel had to wonder if the teenager had caught the bouquet just so she could throw it away again. The entire ballroom erupted into laughter and even Beatrice was smiling.

She should be.

Her disappointment of a daughter had managed to land a prince. No wonder she'd come to Chanel's apartment with stories of undying first love.

Chanel couldn't believe she'd thought her mom was

finally showing a vested interest in her oldest daughter's happiness.

But then she'd let herself be convinced that Demyan *wanted* to marry *her*. Not Bartholomew Tanner's only surviving heir.

Smile still fixed firmly in place, Chanel looked out over the ballroom full of people. Her gaze settled on Queen Oxana. The older woman looked pleased, her normally controlled expression filled with unmistakable happiness.

Was that because she knew the Yurkovich fortune was secure, or was she happy at what she thought was her son's marriage to someone she believed was his one true love?

Another memory clicked into place and the smile fell away from Chanel's face. Oxana was the one who had made Demyan promise not to use protestations of love to convince Chanel to marry him.

The queen knew about the will. She must, but she had scruples where her husband and son did not. She might be the only person Chanel could trust to tell her the truth.

She was tempted to leave the reception early, but every time she let her gaze find Demyan, he was watching her. He would only follow her, but she wanted a chance to talk to his mother, to get some answers on her own first.

She got her chance unexpectedly when Oxana came up to her and laid a hand on her arm. "Are you all right, Chanel?"

Chanel looked toward Demyan. He returned her regard, his dark-eyed expression unreadable, but something in the way he watched Chanel and his mother told Chanel he had sent the older woman to her.

"You know," Chanel said instead of answering.

"That you and my husband had something of an altercation earlier? Yes."

Interesting that the queen considered the argument to

be between Chanel and the king, not Chanel and Demyan. "Did he tell you?"

"Demyan did."

Even the sound of his name on Oxana's lips hurt Chanel in some indefinable way. "You were aware of their plans because of my great-great-grandfather's will."

Oxana nodded.

"You made him promise not to lie about loving me. Thank you." She wasn't sure how much worse the pain inside her would be if she'd believed false words of love. "I want to read the will."

"If you ask Demyan, he will tell you everything."

"I don't want to hear from him. He had his chance to tell me. He chose not to."

"He was trying to protect our nation."

Chanel couldn't help mocking. "Because I'm such a huge security risk."

Oxana looked around them, obviously concerned someone might overhear. No one was in range of their subdued tones, but that could change any second.

"I don't want to be here," Chanel admitted hopelessly.

There was nowhere else she could be without someone she didn't want to talk to following her, which included pretty much everyone but Oxana at the moment.

The queen sighed, looking at her sadly. "He cares for you."

Maybe Oxana wouldn't be the best company either. Chanel just shook her head, moving to turn away.

But Oxana's hand on her arm stopped her from putting distance between them. "Come, I will take you someplace away from the scrutiny and company of others."

Chanel thought it a bit obvious when the queen led her to the retiring room for the ladies, but they didn't stop in the outer room as she expected. The queen led her into one of the three small chambers with toilets, closing the door behind them.

While the room was larger than the usual commode stall, it wasn't exactly meant for two people and Chanel didn't think talking about sensitive subjects with only a door between them and anyone who walked into the lounge was a good idea.

But Oxana did not ask any questions, or make any attempts at comfort. She simply pushed up on a section of wainscoting and then the wall behind the commode swung backward.

Oxana put her hand out to Chanel. "Come, I'll take you to the private papers library for the House of Yurkovich. Your great-great-grandfather's will has been stored there."

CHAPTER TWELVE

DARKNESS SURROUNDED CHANEL as she stood on the balcony overlooking the now-silent grounds of the palace. The reception was long over, the last guest's car having left the drive thirty minutes before.

Temperatures had dropped since that morning and she shivered in the cold air, but she did not go back inside.

Before leaving her to read over the will and relevant places in Bartholomew Tanner's diaries the queen had marked for Chanel, Oxana had told her that her favorite place for solitude was this balcony.

"The bedrooms do not have security cameras in them, but they do have infrared monitoring. The public rooms and hallways are all covered with video feed, though. The only two places in the palace where you can relax unmonitored in any way are the public address balcony and the one outside Fedir's rooms."

"Isn't that a security risk?" Chanel had asked.

But Oxana had shaken her head. "The walls and every approach are covered."

Which meant that Demyan would eventually find her because Chanel's path to the balcony would have been tracked by video monitoring once she left the secret passageway.

She could have left the palace completely. Chanel was

a resourceful woman and there had been dozens of cars departing the grounds over the past few hours.

But she wasn't a coward and she'd never hidden from the truth, no matter how much it might hurt to face.

What that truth was, however, wasn't entirely clear. Not after reading the will. Not after remembering Demyan's words in the carriage that morning.

Not after having Oxana tell Chanel exactly what promise she'd extracted from her son over the *love* thing.

Not until Chanel asked Demyan the only question that really mattered.

"Chanel."

She turned at the sound of her name on Demyan's lips.

He stood framed by the light from the hall. He reached and flipped a switch. More golden light flooded the balcony.

"Turn it off," she said, angling her head away so he could not see the damage tears had done on even the indelible makeup job her mother's professional artist had applied.

"No. We do not need more shadows in our relationship."

She swung back to face him head-on, anger making her muscles rigid with tension. "The shadows are all you."

He nodded, his expression as tortured as she felt, if she could believe the evidence of her eyes.

She wasn't sure she trusted her own perceptions at all, though, not after how easily he'd taken her in. However, she didn't think he could fake the parchment-pale of his complexion, the way his black pupils nearly swallowed the espresso irises or the way he breathed in what she would consider panicked gasps in anyone else.

"That day in my lab. It was planned."

"I needed to meet you. You are not a social person."

"So Yurkovich Tanner donated five million dollars to my department for research. That's an expensive introduction." Though nothing in comparison to what the Yurkovich fortune stood to lose if she had made her claim on the Tanner shares in the company.

"It also ensured you were predisposed to look on me favorably."

"Your idea, or the king's?"

"Does it matter?"

"No."

"You've read the will."

"Oxana told you."

"I saw you go into the personal archives library on the video monitor feedback."

"Oh."

"I spent two hours watching the tapes, trying to find you."

"We used the secret passages."

"Yes. You only showed up for brief periods on the video monitors and there were too many extra people in the palace to track you with the infrared body counter and placement."

"Poor you."

"Cha…" Her name choked off and he stepped forward, stumbling, though she knew the stone floor was smooth with no hindrances.

"You never needed your glasses." For anything.

He stopped a couple of feet from her. "I told you that."

"But I thought you needed them as an emotional crutch."

"I do not use crutches."

"No. A man without emotions doesn't need crutches for them, does he?"

"I am human, damn it, not a puppet. I have emotions."

"I bet it was the king's idea to approach me looking like a corporate geek to match my science-nerd personality."

"He believed I would be too intimidating in my usual way."

"That man, the corporate shark, he's part of you."

"Yes."

"But he's not all of you."

"I thought he was."

"Until when?" she pushed.

"Until I met you."

"You don't mean that."

"I've never meant anything more."

"You lied to me."

"I am ruthless when it comes to protecting my country and those I love."

"I noticed."

"There is little hope that will change."

"No. It's part of your nature. You would have made a very good Cossack."

"We still have the elite in our army. As tradition dictates, I spent two years training with them before going to university."

"Wasn't that Prince Maksim's job?"

"He wasn't the oldest son to the king."

"But he is heir to the throne."

"Yes."

"Does that bother you?"

"No. I hate politics."

"I hate being deceived."

"I will not do it again."

"Can you really promise that, with your ruthless nature?"

"Yes."

"Why?"

"I don't understand."

"I think you do."

If anything, his face paled further. "Don't, Chanel."

"Don't what? Make you admit your vulnerabilities. If you have any, that is."

"I do."

"I'm not stupid by any stretch, you know. Legalese may not be science speak, but I understand it well enough."

"Yes?"

"Yes. Bartholomew Tanner's will is unambiguous. My marriage to you negated all claim I, or any of my children, had to Yurkovich Tanner."

Demyan nodded.

"The prenuptial didn't need to spell that out at all."

"No."

"You had that paragraph added as a kind of warning to me, didn't you?"

He shrugged.

"You also made sure I would be taken care of financially despite the fact that legally I would have no way of pursuing any monetary interests in the future."

"You are my wife. I wanted you provided for."

"I bet the king just loved the terms of the prenup."

"He agreed to them."

She was sure there was a story there, but right now she wasn't interested in hearing it. "You came after me with the intention of securing Volyarussian economic stability, no matter the cost."

"Yes." The word sounded torn out of him.

"You could have just asked me to sign the shares over and I would have done it. Especially after reading my grandfather's diaries."

"His diaries?"

"He spelled out his intention of leaving the shares to the people of Volyarus, but at first he was still holding out hope your great-uncle would marry my great-grandmother, then he got his hopes set on the next generation. He died before he could try to make that alliance happen."

"I am aware."

"What you didn't know was that he'd written my great-grandmother and told her that he planned to leave his interest in Yurkovich Tanner to the Volyarussian people. I never would have tried to undermine his clear wishes."

"Your stepfather would not be so sanguine. He might well have convinced your mother to bring suit on her deceased husband's behalf."

"A suit that wouldn't have gone anywhere without my cooperation, and I wouldn't have given it."

"We did not know that."

"You had to have realized, as you got to know me."

"Once I commit to a purpose, I do not change my direction on a whim or the hope of a different outcome."

"Maybe you decided you *wanted* to marry me." It was hard to say the words, to put it out there like that, but this man was about as in touch with his emotions as the puppet he was so adamant he was not.

"I did want to marry you."

"Why?"

He stared at her, his expression so open she wanted to cry. Because it showed so much that he so clearly didn't know how to express verbally. One thing was really obvious. This man did not know what to do with his emotions.

"We are very compatible."

"Are we?"

"You know we are."

"You're a prince. I'm a scientist."

"Those are our titles, not who we are at the core."

"Okay, then you're ruthless and I'm insecure. We're both emotionally repressed."

"But you are more secure about yourself with me."

"And you are less ruthless with me?" she asked, already knowing the answer.

Looking back on it, she saw that the prenuptial agreement was practically a love letter from Demyan.

The uncertainty in his expression was heartbreaking. "Yes?"

She couldn't hold back from touching him any longer. She stepped right into his personal space and he wrapped his arms around her like it was the most natural thing in the world to do.

"Yes, Demyan. *Yes*." His ruthlessness wasn't always a bad thing, but she brought out the best in him, too.

Now, if she could just get him to realize what that meant.

"You turn me on like no other woman ever has." He spoke as if that fact confused him. "I don't like being without you. Not even for a couple of days. It makes it hard to focus."

"I'm glad to hear that. I feel the same way."

"I miss you," he stressed. "Every hour we are apart. Even when I am working."

No matter how this thing between them had started, it had caught Demyan in the whirlwind of emotion right along with her. Which was the conclusion she'd finally come to after a lot of pain-filled soul-searching and examination of every memory from the moment they'd met.

"It hurt finding out about the will and your reason for marrying me from your sperm donor."

Pain twisted Demyan's features. "I am sorry." He reached up to wipe along the tear streaks on one cheek. "You cried."

"At first, all I could think was that you'd tricked me into loving you when you felt nothing for me at all. That you probably planned on getting rid of me as soon as the ink was dry on the marriage certificate."

"No!" He kissed her, the connection between their mouths infused with a desperation stronger than anything she'd ever felt from him.

It was a magnified version of the feelings that emanated off him at night when making love since their arrival in Volyarus.

She did nothing to stop the kiss for a long time, needing this connection as badly as he so clearly did.

But eventually, she broke her mouth away. "Were you going to tell me?"

"Maybe someday. I do not know. I did not want to."

"You were afraid."

"I am never afraid."

"Not usually, but the idea of losing me scared you."

"Have I lost you?" His arms tightened around her even as he asked the question.

"No."

"No?" he asked, his voice breaking so the word sounded as if it had two syllables.

"Definitely not. Yet."

His big body went absolutely rigid. "Yet?"

"It all depends on your answer to a question."

He stared down at her.

"You never break your promises, right?" She let her body mold completely to his, trying to give him strength.

That's what people who loved each other did—they lent their strength when it was needed.

"Right."

"Tell me you love me."

The tension emanating off him increased exponentially.

"Your mom told me what she made you promise her."

Demyan's expression was haunted.

"You promised not to say you love me unless you really mean it," Chanel reminded him. "You can say it now, Demyan. I will treasure your love forever, too."

"But…"

"You love me."

"I do?"

"That stuff you were saying earlier, about missing me, being afraid to lose me, even the way you changed the prenuptial agreement, it all means one thing."

"It does?" Comprehension and acceptance dawned over his features, making him smile with heartbreaking happiness. "It does. I love you, Chanel, more than my life as a prince. More than anything."

More tears filled her eyes, but these didn't burn or hurt her heart. "I love you, too."

"I mean it."

"I know."

"No, I mean…we don't have to live with the whole royalty thing. I know it's not the life you want. I can abdicate my role."

It wasn't an empty promise and it would not come without significant cost to this amazing man. Especially after finally acknowledging his true role as son of Oxana and Fedir, but Demyan was entirely sincere in his offer.

"No. I love you, Demyan. Ruthless prince. Corporate king and shark. All of you."

"I love you for all that you are, too, Chanel, and that includes the woman who has never aspired to be a socialite."

"I'm not going to be one now, either."

"My uncle…father is not going to know what to do with you."

"He'll probably call me princess just to annoy me."

Demyan laughed, the sound freer and filled with more joy than she'd ever heard from him. "You may well be right."

"So long as you call me love."

"*Koxána moja,*" he said, calling her his love in Ukrainian. "Always and forever. You are the very heart that beats inside my chest."

And then he took her back to the rooms they would share whenever staying at the palace for the years to come and made tender, night-long love to her, using those words and so many others to tell Chanel that this man truly loved her and always would.

Later she snuggled into his body and yawned as she said, "I guess it's a good thing you've got a sneaky, underhanded side."

"Is it?"

"Yep."

"Why?"

"We never would have gotten together otherwise. You snuck past all my barriers."

"It is only fair, since you destroyed mine."

Two broken people who had not even realized they were broken had been made whole by love.

Yes, Chanel thought, that was exactly right and fair.

"Love you, Demyan."

"I love you."

"Always."

"For the rest of our lives."

"And beyond." Eternity would not end a love so strong.

"And beyond."

EPILOGUE

OXANA CUDDLED HER latest grandchild. The tiny infant was only three days old, but he was so alert that the queen could not help smiling into soft gray eyes so like his mother's.

Little Damon was her fourth grandchild and she had no doubts he would bring her every bit as much joy as the other three she'd been gifted by her sons and their wives.

The oldest, Mikael, was five and the only child Gillian and Maksim had conceived. Their youngest was adopted, a beautiful little girl who had both her besotted parents wrapped around her dainty little fingers.

Demyan and Chanel's oldest had turned two, four months before the birth of her little brother. Both children were cosseted and adored by parents who showed a decided ruthlessness when it came to putting their family first.

Oxana could not be more pleased. She'd given up a lifetime of love and found little personal happiness in order to give her sons the best chance at a better life. One would be king, the other would continue to oversee their business interests, but both were blissfully happy.

And Oxana thought that a more-than-fair compensation for the sacrifices she'd made. After all, she had her grandchildren around her now. They called her Nana, not Your Majesty, and didn't hesitate to muss her designer couture with messy fingers.

How incredibly blessed she was, but her sons had received the true gift beyond measure.

A lifetime love with women who not only knew but accepted both men for who and what they were.

Fedir often didn't know what to make of his independent-minded daughters by marriage, but he loved being a grandfather and already had grand plans for the children.

Oxana didn't tell him, but she had plans, too, and she knew exactly what each grandchild needed for the future. Love.

Just as she had done her best to make sure both her sons realized their loves, she would do whatever it took to ensure each of her grandchildren knew true love, as well.

Fedir could plan all the machinations he wanted, but in the end? Love would triumph.

Just as it had for her children.

* * * * *

Join Britain's BIGGEST Romance Book Club

50% OFF your first parcel

- **EXCLUSIVE offers every month**
- **FREE delivery direct to your door**
- **NEVER MISS a title**
- **EARN Bonus Book points**

Call Customer Services
0844 844 1358*

or visit
millsandboon.co.uk/subscriptions

* This call will cost you 7 pence per minute plus your phone company's price per minute access charge.

BKCB3

MILLS & BOON®

Why shop at millsandboon.co.uk?

Each year, thousands of romance readers
find their perfect read at millsandboon.co.uk.
That's because we're passionate about
bringing you the very best romantic fiction.
Here are some of the advantages of
shopping at www.millsandboon.co.uk:

* **Get new books first**—you'll be able to buy
  your favourite books one month before they
  hit the shops

* **Get exclusive discounts**—you'll also be
  able to buy our specially created monthly
  collections, with up to 50% off the RRP

* **Find your favourite authors**—latest news,
  interviews and new releases for all your
  favourite authors and series on our website,
  plus ideas for what to try next

* **Join in**—once you've bought your favourite
  books, don't forget to register with us to rate,
  review and join in the discussions

Visit **www.millsandboon.co.uk**
for all this and more today!